THE COMING OF
THE WORM

All too soon the Worm arrived. It was indeed a dragon—a vicious worm grown monstrous. The Worm exhaled a puff of steam and slid forward. Its legs were puny compared to its bulk, but the horrendous claws seemed fully adequate to the task of gutting a human efficiently. The Worm's tube-mouth opened to show a ring of six-inch teeth, pointing inward.

The metallic scales were drab and dirty, but Stile had no doubt they were invulnerable to ordinary attack. Theoretically, the point of a sword could be slid up under a layer of scales—but that could lead to a shallow, slanting wound that would only aggravate the monster. And what would the Worm be doing while the swordsman was making such an insertion?

All this, Stile realized abruptly, was academic. He did not have a sword. He had forgotten to conjure one!

Blue
Adept

Piers Anthony

A Del Rey Book

BALLANTINE BOOKS • NEW YORK

A Del Rey Book
Published by Ballantine Books

Copyright © 1981 by Piers Anthony

Library of Congress Catalog Card Number: 80-21754

ISBN 0-345-28214-0

Manufactured in the United States of America

First Edition: May 1981

Paperback format
First Edition: April 1982

Cover art by Rowena Morrill

TABLE OF CONTENTS

Map of Phaze		vi
1.	Unicorn (F)	1
2.	Lady (F)	19
3.	Proton (SF)	44
4.	Little People (F)	77
5.	Riddles (SF)	128
6.	Unolympic (F)	164
7.	Hulk (SF)	187
8.	Quest (F)	207
9.	Music (SF)	225
10.	Red (F)	244
11.	Trap (SF)	277
12.	Dance (SF)	309

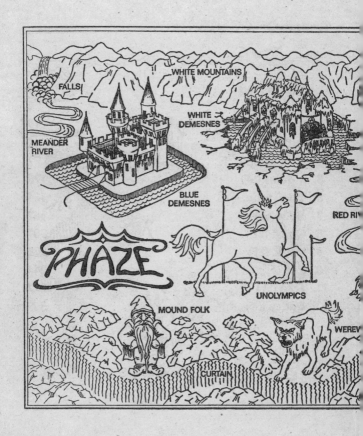

SNOW
DEMONS

GOBLINS

DEAD VILLAGE

VAMPIRES

VER

BROWN
RIVER

TROLLS

RED
DEMESNES

OLVES

BROWN
DEMESNES

PURPLE MOUNTAINS

CHAPTER 1

Unicorn

A lone unicorn galloped across the field toward the Blue Castle. It was a male, with a glossy dark blue coat and red socks on his hind feet and a handsomely spiraled horn. As he moved he played a melody through that hollow horn, sounding like a mellow saxophone. The notes floated across the field ahead of him.

Stile walked to a parapet and looked down. He was an extremely small but fit man, a former jockey who remained in shape. He was dressed in a blue shirt and blue jeans, though there were those who felt that neither became his station. His station was such, however, that he could ignore it with impunity—to a degree.

"Clip!" he exclaimed, recognizing the visitor. "Hey, Neysa—your brother's here!"

But Neysa already knew it. Her hearing was better than his. She trotted out of the castle and met Clip at the front gate, crossing horns briefly in greeting. Then the two went into their more extended ritual of reunion, prancing out side by side in unison as they played a duet. Neysa's horn had the sound of a harmonica, and it blended beautifully with the music of the saxophone.

Stile watched and listened, entranced, and not by magic. He had always been fond of horses, and he liked unicorns even better. He was of course biased; Neysa was his best friend in this frame. Still—

The two equines intensified the beat, their hooves striking the turf precisely. Now they went into the syncopation of the five-beat gait, the Unicorn Strut, their music matching it. Stile, unable to resist, brought out his good harmonica and matched the tune, tapping the beat with his heel as well as he could. He had a natural flair for music, and had sharpened his skill recently because it related so intimately to his magic. When he played, intangible magic formed around him. But he refused to let that inhibit him; the magic only became tangible when he invoked it in his special fashion.

When the unicorns finished their dance of delight, they trotted back to the castle. As they approached the gate they shifted to human-form, becoming a handsome young man and an elfishly small but also quite pretty woman. Stile hurried down to meet them in the courtyard.

"A greeting, Adept, and a message from the Herd Stallion," Clip said. He was holding hands with his sister, somewhat to her mute embarrassment; he was more expressive than she. Both wore the garb of archaic Earth as interpreted by nonhuman viewpoint, more or less matching their natural equine colors.

"Thy greeting is welcome, Clip," Stile said. "And thy message too, be it in peace."

"It is, Adept. The Stallion is pleased to summon Neysa the Mare this season to be bred." He paused, then appended his own remark: "At long last."

"That's great!" Stile exclaimed. "After three seasons denied, she will finally get her foal!"

Then he saw that Neysa was not reacting with the delight expected. Stile looked at her with concern. "Dost this not please thee, oath-friend? I thought it was thy fondest ambition to—"

Clip, too, was glancing at her with perplexity. "Sibling, methought I bore great tidings."

Neysa averted her gaze. She was a well-formed girl an inch or so shorter than Stile—a stature that appealed to him though he knew this was foolish. She was the smallest of mares, barely fourteen hands; any shorter and she would have been classified as a pony: a member of the equine Little Folk. Her human-form merely reflected this, with only the tiny button-horn in her forehead signifying her true nature.

Stile had long since learned to live with the fact that most women and all men were taller than he, and of course

Neysa was not human at all. That did not prevent her from being his closest companion in ways both human and equine. Though she could speak, she was not much on verbal communication. Vivacity was not her way, though she had a certain filly humor that manifested subtly on occasion.

Clip and Stile exchanged glances. What did this mean? "Would a female know?" Clip asked.

Stile nodded. "One would." He raised his voice only slightly. "Lady."

In a moment the Lady Blue appeared. She was, as always, garbed in variants of blue: blue corduroy skirt, pale blue blouse, dark blue slippers and star-blue tiara. And, as always, her beauty struck Stile with special force. "Master," she murmured.

Stile wished she wouldn't do that. In no way was he her master, and she knew that well. But he was unable to take effective issue with the conventions of this frame—or with the half-subtle reminders she gave him. She considered him to be an imposter in the Blue Demesnes, a necessary evil. She had cause.

"Lady," he said, maintaining the formality she required of him. "Our friend Neysa is summoned to be bred by the Herd Stallion, and have her foal at last—yet she seems not pleased. Canst thou fathom this, and wilt thou enlighten us males?"

The Lady Blue went to Neysa and embraced her. No aloofness in this acquaintance! "Friend of mine oath, grant me leave to explain to my lord," the Lady said to Neysa, and the unicorn-girl nodded.

The Lady faced Stile. "It be a private matter," she said, and walked sedately from the court.

She hadn't even asked; she had known intuitively! "I'll be back," Stile said, and quickly followed.

When they were alone, they dropped the pretenses. "What's the mystery?" Stile snapped. "She's my best friend —a better friend than thou. Why won't she tell me?"

"Thy magic is strong," the Lady replied. "Thy comprehension weak. Left to thine own devices, thou wilt surely come to grief."

"Agreed," Stile said easily, though he was not pleased.

"Fortunately I have Hulk and Neysa and thee to look after me. Soon will I eliminate the major threat to my tenure as Adept, and will stand no longer in need of such supervision."

What irony there was rolled off her without visible effect. The fairness and softness of her appearance concealed the implacable skill with which she fought to preserve the works of her late husband. There was nothing soft about her dedication to his memory. "Be that as it may—the mare feels un-free to leave thee at this time. Hulk may depart and I am not committed to thee as Neysa is. Therefore she prefers to postpone breeding until thou'rt secure."

"But this is senseless!" he protested. "She must not sacrifice her own welfare for mine! I can offer her only hardship and danger."

"Aye," the Lady agreed.

"Then thou must talk to her. Make her go to the Stallion."

"Who is as masculinely logical as thee," the Lady said. "With every bit as much comprehension of her concern. Nay, I shall not betray her thus."

Stile grimaced. "Didst thou treat thy husband likewise?"

Now she colored. "Aye."

Stile was immediately sorry. "Lady, I apologize. Well I know thou didst love him alone."

"Not enough, it seems, to save his life. Perhaps had he had a unicorn to guard him—"

There it was, that needle-sharp acuity. "I yield the point. There is no guardian like Neysa. What must I do to oblige her?"

"Thou must arrange postponement of the breeding, until she feels free to leave thee."

Stile nodded. "That should be feasible. I thank thee, Lady, for thine insight."

"What thou askest for, thou hast," she said coolly. "Thou art now the Blue Adept, the leading magician of the realm. Only have the human wit not to offend the mare in the presentation of thy decision."

"And how do I find the wit not to offend *thee*, bride of my defunct self? Thou knowest his tastes are mine."

She left him, not deigning to answer. Stile shrugged and returned to the courtyard. He wanted the Lady Blue more than anything he could imagine, and she was aware of this. But he had to win her the right way. He had the power to convert her by magic, but he would not use it; she knew this too. She understood him in certain ways better than he understood himself, for she had experienced the love of his other self. She could handle him, and she did so.

Clip and Neysa had reverted to unicorn-form and were grazing on the patch of rich bluegrass maintained beside the fountain for that purpose. The two were a beautifully matched set, his blue against her black, his red socks complementing her white ones. Clip was a true unicorn in coloration; Neysa had been excluded from the herd for some years because her color resembled that of a horse. Stile still got angry when he thought about that.

Neysa looked up as he approached, black ears perking forward, a stem of grass dangling from her mouth. As with most equines, her chewing stopped when her attention was distracted.

"I regret the necessity," Stile said briskly. "But I must after all interfere with Neysa's opportunity. The Blue Adept has, as we know, an anonymous enemy, probably another Adept, who has murdered him once and seeks to do so again. I have no second life to spare. Until I deal with this enemy, I do not feel secure without completely competent protection and guidance. No one can do that as well as the mare. Therefore I must seek a postponement of the Stallion's imperative until this crisis abates. I realize this works a hardship on Neysa, and is selfish of me—"

Neysa snorted musically, pleased, and not for a moment deceived. She resumed chewing her mouthful. Clip angled his horn at her in askance, but saw that she was satisfied, so kept silent.

One problem had been exchanged for another, however. It was not any mare's prerogative to gainsay the Herd Stallion. Stile would have to do that himself, as the Blue Adept. In the informal but rigorous hierarchy of this world, herd-leaders, pack-leaders, tribe-leaders and Adepts were roughly equivalent, though the ultimate power lay with the Adepts. Stile would deal with the Herd Stallion as an equal.

First he had to settle things at the Blue Demesnes. Stile talked with his human bodyguard from the other frame, Hulk. Hulk was as big as Stile was small: a towering mass of muscle, expert in all manner of physical combat but not, despite the assumption of strangers, stupid.

"It is necessary that I leave this castle for a day or so," Stile told him. "I must negotiate with the unicorn Herd Stallion, and I cannot summon him here."

"That's for sure," Hulk agreed. "He never did have much of a liking for you. Uh, for thee. I'd better go with thee. That unicorn is one tough character."

"Nay, friend. I am in no danger from the unicorns. It is the Lady Blue I worry about. I wish thee to guard her in mine absence, lest my nameless enemy strike at me through her. Thou hast not magic—at least, thou hast not practiced it; but if no others know I am gone there should be no hostile spells. Against else, thy skills suffice as well as mine."

Hulk made a gesture of acquiescence. "She is surely worth guarding."

"Yes. She maintained the Blue Demesnes after her lord, mine alternate self, was murdered. Without her help I could not fill this office of Adept. I have the power of magic, but lack experience. I am reminded daily of this." Stile smiled wryly, remembering how the Lady Blue had just set him straight about Neysa. "And—"

"And she is an extraordinarily attractive woman," Hulk finished. "A magnet for mischief."

"Mine alternate self had excellent taste."

"That's one thing I don't quite understand yet. If only a person whose double in the other frame is dead can cross the curtain that separates one frame from the other, what about me? Do I have an alternate self here who died?"

Stile considered. "Thy tenure in the other frame of Proton was for twenty years. Was thy family there before thee?"

"No. I came at age fifteen for my enlistment. My time would have been up in a few more months. My family never set foot on Planet Proton. They live fifteen light years away."

"So thy existence on this planet stems only from thy tenure as a serf," Stile concluded. "Thou hast no natural existence in this other frame of Phaze. There is no alternate self to fill thy place in the alternate scheme. So thou art free to cross the curtain."

"So I was not murdered," Hulk concluded. "That's a relief."

Stile smiled. "Who could murder thee? Thou couldst pulp any normal man with the grip of one hand."

"Except thee, when we played the Game."

"The fortunes of chance," Stile said. "How could I match thee, in fair combat?"

Hulk laughed good-naturedly. "Tease me not, little giant. Thy stature is as mine, in martial arts."

"In mine own weight-class," Stile qualified. It was good to talk with someone who understood Stile's home-world and the Game.

They started off within the hour. Stile played his harmonica, accumulating his magic, then sang one of the spells he had worked out: "By the power of magic vested in me, make me blank so none can see." He was unable to heal himself or cure himself of illness, but he could change his aspect before other people. He held up his hand, then waved it before his face: nothing. He was invisible.

Neysa, of course, knew him by smell and sound. She was not spooked. "This way," he explained, "it will not be obvious that I am departing."

"A watcher could see that the mare carries a burden," the Lady pointed out.

"That's right," Stile agreed, surprised. He considered a moment, then sang: "By the power of magic vested in me, make me as light as I can be." He felt the weight of his body dissipate. "Excellent."

Both Hulk and the Lady looked perplexed. Stile laughed. "I shall answer thy questions in turn. Lady, thou knowest by my voice that I remain standing on the floor; how is it that I do not float to the ceiling? Because my spell is very similar to the last, and since no spell may be used twice in succession, much of its force was abated. I am not as light as I can be; my weight is perhaps a fifth normal. About twenty pounds, or a trifle more. Hulk, how is it that I do not glow like the sun, since that is also a meaning of the term I used, 'light'? Because my words only vocalize what is in my mind, and my mind provided the definition of my terms. Had I wished to light brightly, despite already being invisible, I could have used the same spell, shifting only my mental intent, and it would have worked that way."

"Methinks Stile likes magic," Hulk muttered. "Personally, I do not believe in it."

"Else mightest thou be Adept too," Stile said, laughing to show the humor, though he suspected there was some truth in it. Every person could do some magic, but few could do strong magic. Stile's own magic talent was reflected in the science frame of Proton as considerable ability in other things, such as the Game, and Hulk was almost as capable there. Hulk might be able to learn to be a magician, if he ever cared to try. Perhaps there were many others who could be similarly competent at magic, if they only believed they could and worked to perfect their techniques. But only one person in perhaps a thousand believed, so there were very few Adepts. Of course, the established Adepts ruthlessly eliminated any developing rivals, so it was safer to opt out of that arena entirely. The enmity of an Adept was a terrible thing.

Stile bid his final farewells, mounted Neysa, needing no saddle or bridle, and they joined Clip. The two unicorns trotted briskly out the gate. To an observer it would seem Clip was conducting his sibling to the breeding site, as required. The little bit of weight Neysa carried hardly made a difference.

It was good to travel with his unicorn again. Stile was not sure whether he could transport himself magically from place to place. If that came under the heading of changing his aspect before others, then probably he could; if instead it came under the heading of healing or changing himself, then he probably could not. So far he had deemed it expedient not to experiment; magic gone wrong could be fatal. So he needed transportation, and Neysa was the best he could ask for. She had been his first steed in this magic frame, and his first true friend. His love of horses had translated instantly to unicorns, for these creatures were horse-*plus*: plus a musical horn that was also a devastating weapon; plus special gaits and acrobatic abilities beyond the imagination of any horse; plus human intelligence; plus the ability to change shape. Yes, the unicorn was the creature Stile had been searching for all his life without realizing it until he met one.

Neysa, in girl-form, had become his lover, before he had met the Lady Blue and realized that his ultimate destiny had to lie with his own kind. There had been some trouble between Neysa and the Lady Blue at first; but now as oathfriend to the Blue Adept, the unicorn needed no further reassurance. In this magic frame, friendship transcended mere male-female relations, and an oath of friendship was the most binding commitment of all.

It was ironic that now that Neysa could achieve her fondest wish—to have her own foal—that oath of friendship interfered. Neysa's logic was probably correct; Stile did need her to protect him from the pitfalls of this barely familiar world until he could deal with his secret enemy. Unicorns were immune to most magic; only Adept-class spells could pass their threshold. Stile had reason to believe his enemy was an Adept; his own Adept magic, buttressed by the protective ambience of the unicorn, should safeguard him against even that level. As the Lady Blue had pointed out, the original Blue Adept had not had a unicorn to guard him, and that might have made the difference. He really did need Neysa.

They moved into a canter, then a full gallop as the two unicorns warmed up. Clip and Neysa ran in perfect step, playing their horns. She took the soprano theme on her harmonica, he the alto on his saxophone. It was another lovely duet, in counterpoint, augmented by the strong cadence of their hooves. Stile wished he could join in, but he had to preserve his anonymity, just in case they were being observed. There were baleful things lurking in these peaceful forests and glades; the unicorns' familiarity with

the terrain and reputation as fighters made the landscape
become as peaceful as it seemed. But there was no sense
setting up the Blue Adept as a lure for trouble.

Clip knew the way. The unicorn herd grazed wherever
the Herd Stallion decreed, moving from pasture to pasture
within broad territorial limits. Other herds grazed other
territories; none of them intruded on these local demesnes.
Human beings might think of this as the region of the Blue
Adept, but animals thought of it as the region of this
particular herd. Werewolves and goblins and other creatures also occupied their niches, each species believing itself to be the dominant force. Stile made it a point to get
along as well as he could with all creatures; such détente
was much more important here in the frame of Phaze than
it was in any nonmagical frame. And he genuinely respected those other creatures. The werewolves, for example, had helped him to discover his own place here, and the
entire local pack was oath-friends with Neysa.

They galloped west across the terrain where Stile had
first encountered Neysa; it was a spot of special significance for them both. He reached around her neck to give
her an invisible hug, and she responded by twitching ear
back and rippling her skin under his hands as though shaking off a fly. Secret communication, inexpressibly precious.

To the south was the great Purple Mountain range; to
the north the White Mountain range. There was surely a
great deal more to Phaze than this broad valley, but Stile
had not yet had occasion to see it. Once he had dealt with
his enemy and secured his position, he intended to do some
wider explorations. Who could guess what wonders might
lie beyond these horizons?

They moved west for two hours, covering twenty miles.
This frame used the archaic, magic-ridden units of mea-
surement, and Stile was still schooling himself in them.
Twenty miles was roughly thirty-two kilometers in his
more familiar terms. Stile could have covered a similar
distance in similar time himself, for he was among other
things a runner of marathons. But for him it would have
meant a great effort, depleting his resources for days; for
these animals it was merely pleasant light exercise. Uni-

corns could travel twice this speed, sustained, when they had to, and faster yet for shorter distances.

Now the sun was descending, getting in their eyes. It was time to graze. Unicorns, like horses, were not simple running machines; they had to spend a good deal of their time eating. Stile could have conjured grain for them, but actually they preferred to find their own, being stubbornly independent beasts, and they rested while grazing. Neysa slowed, found a patch of bare rock, and relieved herself in the equine manner at its fringe. This covered any sound Stile might make as he dismounted. Then she wandered on, grazing the rich grass, ignoring him though she knew exactly where he was. She was very good at this sort of thing; no observer would realize that an invisible man was with her, and the rock concealed any footprints he made.

Stile had brought his own supplies, of course; the Lady Blue had efficiently seen to that. No sense requiring him to make himself obvious by performing unnecessary magic to fetch food, apart from the general caution against wasting one-shot spells. He would sit on the rock and eat, quietly.

Stile levered himself down, careful not to put strain on his knees. Knees, as he had learned the hard way, did not readily heal. Magic might repair them, but he could not operate on himself and did not as yet trust the task to any other Adept. Suppose the Adept he asked happened to be the one who wanted to kill him? He could get along; his knees only hurt when flexed almost double. He could still walk, run and ride comfortably. His former abilities as an acrobat had suffered, but there was still a great deal he could do without flexing his knees that far.

After grazing, Neysa came to the edge of the rock and stood snoozing. Stile mounted her, as she had intended, and slept on her back. She was warm and safe and smelled pleasantly equine, and there was hardly a place he would have preferred to sleep—unless it were in the arms of the Lady Blue. That, however, was a privilege he had not yet earned, and might never earn. The Lady was true to her real husband, Stile's double, though he was dead, and in no way did she ever mistake Stile for that other man.

Next morning they were off again. They cantered gently until noon, when they spied the herd. It was grazing on a broad slope leading down to an extensive swamp. Beyond that swamp, Stile remembered, lay the palace of the Oracle, who answered one and only one question for any person, in that person's life. The Oracle had advised Stile to "Know thyself"—and despite the seeming unhelpfulness of it, that had indeed been the key to his future. For that self he had come to know was the Blue Adept.

A lookout unicorn blew a trumpet blast, and the members of the herd lifted their heads, then trotted together to form a large semicircle open toward the two approaching unicorns. Perceiving that formidable array of horns, Stile was glad he was not approaching as an enemy. Neysa had drilled him in the use of his rapier by fencing with her horn, and he had come to appreciate what a deadly weapon it could be. This was another respect in which unicorns were fundamentally different from horses: they were armed—more properly, horned—and were as likely to attack as to flee. No sensible tiger, for example, would attempt to pounce on a unicorn.

They trotted into the open cup of the semicircle. The Herd Stallion stood in the center, a magnificent specimen of equine evolution. His body was pearly gray deepening into black legs, his mane and tail were silver, and his head golden. He stood some eighteen hands tall, and was splendidly muscled. His horn was a glinting, spiral marvel: truly a shaft to be reckoned with. He played a melodic accordion chord on it, and the circle closed in behind the new arrivals.

Stile felt his weight increasing. He saw his arms before him. His spells of lightness and invisibility were abating, though he had not terminated them.

The Stallion snorted. Clip and Neysa hastily spun about and retreated to the rim. Stile sprang to the ground before the Stallion. Stile was now fully solid and visible.

The Stallion shifted to man-form. He was huge and muscular, though not to Hulk's extent. He had a short horn in his forehead. "Welcome to the Herd Demesnes, O Blue Adept," he said. "To what do I owe the dubious pleasure of this encounter?"

So the closing of the unicorn circle nullified even the spells of an Adept! Stile's magic could prevail over a single unicorn, but not over the full herd—except in special cases. Of course his two spells were now a day old and must have weakened with time and use, since no spell was eternal. Still, the effect was worth noting. Stile was not in danger from hostile magic here, because the unicorn ring would also nullify the spells of any enemy Adept. He retained the basic privacy of his mission. "A greeting, Stallion. I come to negotiate."

The man-Stallion put three fingers to his mouth and blew another chord that still sounded like an accordion. Two unicorns trotted in, supporting a structure on their horns. They set it down and retreated. It was a table fashioned of old unicorn horns, with attached seats. It was surely far more valuable than ivory, for much of the magic of unicorns was associated with their horns.

The Stallion sat, gesturing Stile to do the same. "What has an Adept to negotiate with a simple animal like me?"

Stile realized this was not going to be easy. The Herd Stallion was not partial to him, since Stile had embarrassed the creature in the course of their first encounter. He would have to explain carefully. "Thou knowest I was murdered not long ago."

"Thou hast no need to negotiate for recognition of thy status or right to thy Demesnes," the Stallion said, surprised. "We honor the way that is. Only this herd and Kurrelgyre's werewolf pack know thou art not the original Adept. We accept thee in lieu, since thy magic is equivalent and thou'rt a being of integrity, as are we. No news of thy condition has escaped the herd."

Stile smiled. "It is not that, Sire. I have not made a secret of my status. It is that I must secure my position and avenge my murder."

"Indubitably."

"I believe it is an enemy Adept I seek. Therefore I must approach the matter cautiously, and trust myself only to my most reliable companion. That, of course, is mine oath-friend Neysa. Therefore—"

"Now I chew on thy gist. A gravid mare would not be fit for such excursion."

"Exactly. I therefore seek a postponement of her breeding, until my mission is done."

The Stallion frowned. "She has missed two seasons—"

"Because she was excluded from the herd—because of her color," Stile said grimly. "Her color has not changed."

"Ah, but her status has! She has connections she lacked before. The animals of my herd have taken a fancy to her, and the wolves of the pack we oft have fought no longer attack, because of her. In all the herds of all the valleys of Phaze, none save her is steed to an Adept."

"Steed and friend," Stile said. "A friendship well earned."

"Perhaps. In any event, that makes up for her deficiency of—"

"Deficiency?" Stile demanded ominously, reaching for his harmonica. He had intended to keep this civil, but this was a sore point.

The Stallion considered. They were within the unicorn circle, but it had not been proven whether that would stop a newly fashioned spell performed in the heat of the Blue Adept's ire. No creature insulted an Adept, or anything dear to an Adept, carelessly. The Stallion retreated half a step, figuratively. "Shall we say, her color pleases me now, and what pleases me shall not be cause for comment by any other unicorn."

"An excellent statement," Stile agreed, putting away his instrument. He had discovered that one unicorn seldom objected to praise or defense of another. It would be beneath the Herd Stallion's dignity to stud an inferior mare. "Her presence at my side pleases me now," Stile continued. "Who in thy herd can travel the flying league faster than she?"

The Stallion raised his human eyebrow in an elegant gold arch. "Who besides me, thou meanest?"

Now Stile had to back off diplomatically. "Of course. I meant among mares—"

"I concede that for her size—"

"Is aught amiss with her size?" This was another power-ploy, for Neysa was no smaller among unicorns than Stile was among men.

"It is a serviceable size. I am certain she will bear a fine foal."

They were sparring, getting nowhere. The Stallion still intended to breed Neysa.

"I think thou didst not entirely withstand the oath of friendship," Stile remarked. "The mare is more attractive to thee than she was before."

The Stallion shrugged. It had been Stile's potent spell that caused the other unicorns and the werewolves to swear friendship with Neysa, and the Stallion did not like to admit to being similarly affected. Yet he was proof against such gibes. "Perhaps. But here thy power may yield to mine, even as mine paled before thine in thy Demesnes."

Stile had set the unicorn back, during that prior encounter. Now the Stallion was having his satisfaction. One offended a creature of power at one's own risk, even if one had the power of an Adept. "I need Neysa, this season. How may I obtain postponement of the breeding?"

"This is a matter of honor and pride. Thou must contest with me in mine own manner, weapon to weapon. An thou dost best me in fair combat, thou winnest thy plea. An thou dost fail—"

Stile had a notion how savage such an encounter could be. "If?" he prompted.

The Stallion smiled. "An thou dost fail, I win mine. We contest not for life here, but only for the proper priority of our claims. I claim the right to breed my mares as I see fit and in mine own time; thou claimest the bond of friendship to this mare. It ill behooves us two to strive against each other on any except a civil basis."

"Agreed." Stile certainly had no need of a life and death combat here! He had hoped a simple request would suffice, but evidently he had been naive. "Shall we proceed to it now?"

The Stallion affected amazement. "By no means, Adept! I would not have it bruited about that I forced my suit against one who was ill-prepared. Protocol requires that a suitable interval elapse. Shall we say a fortnight hence, at the Unolympics?"

"The Unolympics?"

"The annual sportive event of our kind, parallel to the Canolympics of the werewolves, the Vampolympics of the batmen, the Gnomolympics of—"

"Ah, I see. Is Neysa to compete therein?"

The Stallion evidently hadn't considered that. "She has not before, for reasons we need not discuss. This year I believe she would be welcome."

"And no apology to be made for any nuance of color or size that any less discriminating creatures might note?"

"None, of course."

Stile did not like the delay, but also knew he had no serious chance against the Stallion, who looked to weigh a full ton, was in vibrant health, and had quite a number of victory notches on his horn. The creature was in fact providing him time to reconsider, so that Stile could change his mind and yield the issue without suffering humiliation in the field. It was a decent gesture, especially when coupled with the agreement to let Neysa enter the general competition if she wanted to. Stile knew she could perform the typical unicorn maneuvers as well as any in the herd, and this would give her the chance to prove it at last. She had suffered years of shame; now she could publicly vindicate herself. "A fortnight," he agreed.

The Stallion extended his hand, and Stile took it. His own hand was engulfed by the huge and calloused extremity with hooflike nails. Stile fought off his automatic resentment and feeling of inadequacy. He was *not* inadequate, and the Stallion was being honorable. It was a fair compromise.

The Stallion shifted back to his natural form. He blew another chord on his horn. The unicorn circle opened. Stile began to feel lighter. His body faded. His spells were returning, as the anti-magic power of the unicorns diffused. That also was worth noting: his spells had never ceased operating, they had merely been damped out temporarily.

Neysa stepped forward hesitantly. "The Stallion invites thee to participate in the Unolympics in two weeks," Stile told her as he mounted.

She was so surprised she almost shifted into girl-form, which would have been awkward for him at the moment.

She blew a querying note, hardly daring to believe the news. But the Stallion made a chord of affirmation.

"And I will go there too, to meet the Stallion on the field of honor," Stile added, as though this were an afterthought.

This time she did change shape. Stile found himself riding the girl-form piggy-back, his legs around her tiny waist. Hastily he dismounted. "Nay—" she said.

"Neigh indeed! If I weren't invisible and featherlight, thou wouldst have been borne to the ground by my weight in most indelicate fashion. Get back to thy proper form, mare!"

Hastily she complied. He remounted, and she galloped away from the herd. It seemed that none of the unicorns had noticed anything—until one mocking saxophone peal of music sounded. Clip had been unable to hold back his mirth any longer.

Neysa fired back an angry concatenation of notes, then galloped harder. They fairly flew across the slope. Soon they were well away. "Just for that, thou shouldst make him participate in the Unolympics too," Stile suggested, and she snorted affirmatively.

But now his own problem came to the fore. "Maybe I can ask the Oracle how to handle the Stallion," Stile mused aloud. But that was no good; he had used up his single Oracular query before, in the process of discovering his Phaze identity.

"One other thing bothers me," Stile remarked after a bit, as they galloped across the lovely plain. "Why is the Herd Stallion being so polite about it? He could easily have insisted that I fight him today, and he surely would have won. He has no special brief for me, yet he treated me with extraordinary fairness."

Neysa veered to approach an island copse of oat trees. Safely inside the tangle of growth, she made a shrug that hinted he should dismount. When he did, she shifted to girl-form again. "It is thy spell," she said. "All the herd is oath-friend to me, and if he took me unfairly, humiliating thee, they would turn against him."

Stile struck his head with the heel of his unseen hand.

"Of course! Even a king must consider how far his subjects can be pushed." So his magic had indeed affected the Stallion, albeit circuitously, by affecting those the Stallion had to deal with.

Neysa stood, not yet shifting back, looking at him expectantly though of course her eyes could not focus on him. Stile took her in his arms. "I believe these are more words than thou has spoken to me in thy life before," he said, and kissed her.

He turned her loose, but still she waited. He knew why, yet could not act. They had been lovers, and she remained, in girl-form, the nicest and prettiest girl he knew, and he was not turned off by the knowledge that she was in fact a unicorn. But their relationship had changed when he met the Lady Blue. He found himself not constitutionally geared to have more than one lover at a time in a given frame. The irony was that he did not have the Lady Blue as lover or anything else, though he wanted everything else. If companionship, loyalty, and yes, sex sufficed, Neysa was his resource.

And there it was. His aspirations had made a dimensional expansion. He was not certain that he could ever have all of what he wanted, yet he had to proceed as if it were possible. And he had to explain this to Neysa without hurting her feelings.

"What we had before was good," he said. "But now I must look forward to a female of mine own kind, just as thou must look forward to the breeding and foal that only a male of thine own kind can give thee. Our friendship endures, for it is greater than this; it has merely changed its nature. Had we any continuing sexual claim on each other, it would complicate my friendship to thy foal, when it comes, or thine to my baby, if ever it comes."

Neysa looked startled. It was almost as if her human ears perked forward. She had not thought of this aspect. To her, friendship had been merely a complete trusting and giving, uncomplicated by interacting relationships of others. Stile hoped she was able to understand and accept the new reality.

Then she leaned forward to kiss him again, locating him with uncanny accuracy—or was his spell weakening?—and

as their lips touched, she shifted back to equine form. Stile
found himself kissing the unicorn. He threw his arms
about her neck and yanked at her lustrous black mane,
laughing.

Then he mounted, hugged her again, and rode on. It was
all right.

CHAPTER 2

Lady

Back at the Blue Demesnes, Stile uninvoked the spells,
became visible and full-weight, and turned Neysa out to
graze. Then he talked to Hulk and the Lady Blue.

"I must meet the Stallion in ritual battle a fortnight
hence," Stile said. "At their Unolympic celebration. This is
for honor, and for the use of Neysa this season—yet I
know not how I can match him, and am bound to suffer
humiliation."

"Which is what he wants," Hulk said wisely. "Not thy
blood, but thy pride. He wants to take a thing of value
from the Blue Adept, in public, not by theft or by techni-
cality but by right."

The Lady's blue eyes flashed. In this frame, it was literal: a momentary glare of light came from them. She was
no Adept, but she did have some magic of her own. Stile
remained new enough to Phaze to be intrigued by such
little effects. "No creature humiliates the Blue Adept!" she
cried.

"I am not really he, as the Stallion knows," Stile reminded her unnecessarily.

"Thou hast the image and the power and the office," she
said firmly. "It is not thy fault that thou'rt not truly he.
For the sake of the Demesnes, thou canst not let the unicorn prevail in this manner."

The preservation of the Blue Demesnes was of course what this was all about, to her mind. Stile was merely the figurehead. "I am open to suggestions," he said mildly. "I would ask the Oracle how I might prevail, had I not expended my question in the course of achieving my present status."

"The Oracle," Hulk said. "It answers one question for any person?"

"Only one," Stile agreed.

"Then I could ask it!"

"Thou shouldst not waste thine only question on a concern not thine," Stile said. "Ask instead about thine own future here in Phaze. There may be an ideal situation awaiting thee, if thou dost but inquire as to its whereabouts."

"Nay, I want to do it," Hulk insisted. "Neysa is my friend too, and it was thou who showed me how to cross the curtain into this marvelous and not-to-be-believed world. The least I can do is help thee in this matter."

"Let him go," the Lady murmured.

Stile spread his hands. "If thou truly dost feel this way, go with my blessing, Hulk. I shall be in thy debt. I will arrange for thee a magic conveyance—"

"Nay, I can walk."

"Not that far, and return in time to be of much help. I need to know how to prepare as soon as possible. If I must master a special skill—"

"Okay," Hulk agreed. "But I'm not good at riding unicorns."

The Lady smiled, and there seemed to be a momentary glow in the room. "Only two I know of have ever ridden a unicorn, except at the unicorn's behest: my lord Stile and I. The Adept will summon for thee a traveling carpet—"

"Oh, no! Not one of those flying things! I'd be constantly afraid its magic would poop out right over a chasm or near a nest of dragons. I'm not the lightest of creatures, thou knowest. Can't we find a motorcycle or something?"

"A motorcycle?" the Lady asked blankly.

"A device of the other frame," Stile explained. "A kind of traveling wheel, rather like a low-flying carpet. It is an idea. Science is inoperative here, yet I might fashion a magic wagon."

They went about it, and in the end Hulk had his motor-cycle: two wooden wheels, a steering stick, a seat, a windshield. No motor, no fuel, no controls, for it was motivated by magic. Hulk had only to give it key verbal commands and steer it. Both men were clinically interested in the construction, determining how far magic would go, and where the line between functional magic and nonfunctional science was drawn.

Hulk boarded the magic machine and rode away in a silent cloud of dust. A flock of grouse took off, startled by the apparition. "I just hope he follows the map and doesn't drive into a chasm or meet a monster," Stile said. "He might hurt the monster."

"Nay, Hulk is kind to creatures," the Lady said, over-looking the humor. "He is a gentle man, under all that muscle. A clever and honorable man."

"True. That is one reason I brought him here."

The Lady rose and turned about, her blue gown flinging out sedately. Every motion she made was elegant! "Now we are alone, I would talk to thee, Adept."

Stile tried to still his suddenly racing pulse. She could not mean she had had a change of heart about him; he remained an imposter in her eyes. Her loyalty to her true love was a thing he envied and longed for. Should such loyalty ever be oriented on him ... "Any time," he agreed.

They went to her apartment, where she bade him be seated in a comfortable blue chair. She maintained the blue insignia of these Demesnes with loving determination. It was a wonder, he thought with fond irritation, that she did not dye her fair hair blue. "Thy friend Hulk told me of thy life in Proton-frame," she said. "I bade him do it during thine absence, as it behooves me to know of thee."

Pumping Hulk for information: a natural pastime. "I would have told thee, hadst thou asked." But of course she had wanted to obtain a reasonably objective view. What was she leading up to?

"Now I know, from that third party, that thou art much the way my husband was. A man of great honor and skill, yet one who has suffered abuse because of size. Neysa, too, has told me of thy qualities."

"Neysa talks too much," Stile muttered. It was a joke; the unicorn was a marvel of brevity.

"Thou art a good man, and I wrong thee by mine aloofness. Yet must I am the way I am. I feel it only fair to acquaint thee with the way I was."

"I do not seek to force information from thee, Lady," Stile said quickly. But he really wanted to hear anything she wanted to tell him.

"Then it comes to thee unforced," she said, with a fleeting smile that melted his heart. Could she, could she really be starting to soften toward him? No, she was not; she was merely doing what she felt was right, giving him necessary background.

Stile listened to her narration, closing his eyes, absorbing her dulcet tones, picturing her story in full living color and feeling as it unfolded.

Long and long has our realm of Phaze endured apart from other worlds, from that time when first it separated from the science frame of mythology. Three hundred years, while our kind slowly spread across the continent and discovered the powers that existed. The animal kingdoms too expanded and warred with each other and found their niches, the dragons to the south, the snow demons to the north, the giants to the far west and so on. Soon the most talented among the Human Folk became adept at magic, restricting others from its practice except in specialized ways, so that no more than ten full magicians existed at any one time. Only talent distinguished them, not honor or personal merit, and any who aspired to Adept status but was less apt at sorcery than the masters were destroyed by the established magicians. Today the common folk eschew all save elementary enchantments, and associate not with Adepts; likewise the animals keep largely to themselves.

I grew up in a village of fifteen families to the east, near the coast, far removed from strong magic except the natural spells of the deepwoods. I thought I might marry a local boy, but my folks wanted me to wait, to meet a wider range before deciding. I realized not their reason, then;

they knew me to be fair, and thought I might waste myself on some farmer's boy or fisherman if I chose quickly. Had they known whom I was destined to marry, they would have thrown me at the nearest pigherder! But they knew not that an Adept sought me, and we were well off, with good fields and animals, so that there seemed no need to go early into matrimony. My father is something of a healer, whether by nature or effort I know not, and I am too. We helped the ill or injured animals of the village, never making show of our talent, and never did the dire attention of a hostile Adept focus on us for that.

When I was nineteen the lads and lasses of mine age had already mostly been taken. But I loved the animals, and felt no loss. It has been said that the women most attractive to men are the ones who need them least, and so it seemed to be in my case. Then my horse's foal wandered too far afield, returning not to our stable. I called her Snowflake, for her color was white as snow though her spirit was hot as peppercorn. Ever was she wont to take that extra step, and this time she was lost. I rode out on my good mare Starshine, Snowflake's dam, searching, searching, but the prints we followed led into the deepwoods. Then I knew in my heart that Snowflake was truly in trouble, but I was nineteen and I loved that foal, and I went into that jungle though I knew it was folly.

And in that wood I came upon moss that shrouded whole trees and reached out for me, all green and hissing, and sand that sucked at my horse's feet, and there were shapes and shadows looming ever-near and nearer, and I was afraid.

Then did I know I must turn back, that Snowflake was doomed, and I would be in dire strait too an I not give over this hopeless task presently. But still I adored my foal, as I adore all horses, and the thought of Snowflake alone and in straits in that wilderness tormented me, and I made pretexts one after another to quest beyond yet another tree or yet another looming rock. I thought I heard a tremulous neigh; gladly I dismounted and ran, but there was nothing, only a branch creaking in the rising wind.

A storm was coming, and that meant mischief, for in our region the trolls come out in foul weather, yet I dallied foolishly afoot. This time I was sure I heard a plaintive neigh. I pursued it, but again found naught; it was a will-o'-the-wisp.

Then the brooding sky let down and in a moment I was drenched with the chill spillage of the heavens. A crack of thunder spooked Starshine, and she bolted for home, forgetting me, nor could I blame her. I fled for home myself, shivering with more than cold, but the reaching brambles tore at my skirts and the gusts buffeted me so harshly I could not see. I cried out, hoping to be heard at home, but this was futile in the fury of this storm.

It was the trolls who harkened, and when I saw the grim apparitions I screamed with much-heightened force. But the gross monsters caught hold of me, all gape and callus, and I knew I was done for. I had not saved the life of my pet; I had sacrificed mine own.

A troll clutched me by the hair, dangling me above the ground. I was now too terrified to scream. I feared for death, assuredly; more I feared for that which would surely precede it, for the troll folk ever lust after human folk.

Then came the beat of hooves, approaching. Now did I manage to cry out again, faintly, hoping Starshine was returning, perhaps ridden by my father. And the beat came nigh, and it was no horse I knew, but a great blue stallion with mane of purple and hooves like blue steel, and on it a manchild in blue—

("The Blue Adept!" Stile exclaimed, interrupting her. The Lady nodded soberly, and resumed her narrative.)

I knew not who he was, then. I thought him a lad, or perhaps one of the Little Folk. I cried out to him, and he brandished a blue sword, and the trolls gibbered back into the shadows. The small youth came for me, and when the trolls saw what he sought, they let me go. I dropped to the ground, unhurt in body, and scrambled toward him.

The lad put down a hand to help me mount behind him, and I did, and then the blue stallion leapt with such power the trolls scattered in fear and I near slid off his rear, but that I clung desperately to my rescuer.

It seemed but a moment we were out of the wood, pounding toward our village homestead. The rain still fell;

I shivered with chill and my dress clung chafingly to me, but the boy seemed not affected. He brought me to mine own yard and halted the stallion without ever inquiring the way. I slid down, all wet and relieved and girlishly grateful. "Young man," I addressed him, in my generosity granting him the benefit of a greater age than I perceived in him. "Thou'rt soaked. Pray come in to our warm hearth—"

But he shook his head politely in negation, speaking no word. He raised a little hand in parting, and suddenly was off into the storm. He had saved my honor and my life, yet dallied not for thanks.

I told my family of mine experience as I dried and warmed within our home before the merry fire. Of my foolish venture into the wood, the storm, the trolls, and of the boy on the great blue stallion who rescued me. I thought they would be pleased that I had been thus spared the consequence of my folly, but they were horrified. "That is a creature of magic!" my father cried, turning pale.

"Nay, he is but a boy, inches shorter than I," I protested. "Riding his father's charger, hearing my cry—"

"Did he speak thus?"

I admitted reluctantly that the blue lad had spoken naught, and that was no good sign. Yet in no way had the stranger hurt me or even threatened me; he had rescued me from certain horror. My parents quelled their doubts, glad now to have me safe.

But the foal was still missing. Next day I went out again to search—but this time my father went with me, carrying a stout cudgel. I called for Snowflake, but found her not. It was instead the blue lad who answered, riding across the field. I saw by sunlight that the horse was not truly blue; it was his harness that had provided the cast. Except perhaps for the mane, that shone iridescently. "What spook of evening goes abroad in the bright day?" I murmured gladly, teasing my father, for apparitions fear the sunlight.

My father hailed the youth. "Art thou the lad who rescued my daughter yesterday?"

"I am," the lad replied. And thereby dispelled another doubt, for few monsters are able to converse in the tongues of man.

"For that my deepest thanks," my father quoth, relieved.

"Who art thou, and where is thy residence, that thou comest so conveniently at our need?"

"I was of the village of Bront, beyond the low midvalley hills," the lad replied.

"That village was overrun by trolls a decade past!" my father cried.

"Aye. I alone escaped, for that the monsters overlooked me when they ravaged. Now I ride alone, my good horse my home."

"But thou must have been but a baby then!" my father protested. "Trolls eat babies first—"

"I hid," the lad said, frowning. "I saw my family eaten, yet I lacked the courage to go out from my hiding place and battle the trolls. I was a coward. The memory is harsh, and best forgotten."

"Of course," my father said, embarrassed. "Yet no one would term it cowardice for a child to hide from ravaging trolls! Good it is to remember that nature herself had vengeance on that particular band of trolls, for that lightning struck the village and destroyed them all in fire."

"Aye," the lad murmured, his small face grim. "All save one troll cub." At that my father looked startled, but the lad continued: "Thou searchest for the lost foal? May I assist?"

My father thought to demur, but knew it would draw blame upon himself if he declined any available help, even in a hopeless quest. "If thou hast a notion. We know not where to begin."

"I am on tolerable terms with the wild equines," the lad said. "If the Lady were to ride with me to the herds and question those who may know . . ."

I was startled to hear myself defined as "Lady," for I was but a grown girl, and I saw my father was similarly surprised. But we realized that to a lad as small as this I might indeed seem mature.

"This is a kind offer," my father said dubiously. "Yet I would not send two young people on such a quest alone, and I lack the time myself—"

"Oh, please!" I pleaded, wheedling. "How could harm come on horseback?" I did not find it expedient to remind my father that I had gotten into trouble on horseback very recently, when I dismounted in the wood near the trolls. "We could range carefully—" Also, I wanted very much to see the wild horse herds, a thing seldom privileged to villagers.

"Thy mare is in mourning for her foal," my father said, finding another convenient objection. "Starshine is in no condition for such far riding. She knows not thy mission."

I clouded up in my most appealing manner. But before I spoke, the lad did. "I know the steed for her, sir. It is the Hinny. The mare of lightest foot and keenest perception in the wilds. She could sniff out the foal, if any could."

I clapped my hands in that girlish way I had. "Oh, yes!" I knew nothing about that horse except that a hinny was the sterile issue of stallion and jenny, most like a mule but prettier, yet already I was eager to ride her.

My father, more sensible than I, brooded. "A hinny, and wild. I trust this not. Such crossbreeds bear little good will to men."

"True," the blue lad said. He never contradicted my father directly. "But this is not any hinny. She is *the* Hinny. She can be bred, but only by my blue stallion. For that price she will be the best mount anyone could ask. She is fit and wise in the ways of the wilderness; no creature durst cross her, not even a troll or dragon. Like unto a unicorn she is, almost."

My father wavered, for he had a deep respect for good horses. To encourage his acquiescence, I threatened to cloud again. I had a certain talent at that, and my father had a certain weakness for it; oft had we played this little game. "Canst thou summon this hinny here?" he inquired, temporizing. "I would examine this animal."

The lad put fingers to his mouth and whistled piercingly. Immediately, it seemed, there was the sound of galloping, and an animal came. What a creature it was! She was shades of gray, lighter on the flanks and withers, darker at the extremities with a mane of both shades a good yard long that rippled languorously in the breeze. Her tail, too, was variegated gray, like carven onyx, and flowed like the waves of an ocean.

My father, prepared to be skeptical, gaped. "The speed of that horse!" he breathed. "The lines of her!"

"Thy daughter will be safe on her," the blue lad assured him. "What the Hinny cannot defeat she can outrun, except for the unicorns, who leave her alone. Once she accepts the commission, she will guard her rider with her life."

But my father was already lost. He stared at the Hinny, the most beautifully structured mare ever to be seen in our village. I knew he would have given his left hand to own such a mount. "And she hearkens to thy summons," he said, awed.

"Nay," the lad demurred quickly. "Only to my stallion." Then he approached the Hinny and extended his hand, slowly, as one must do for a strange horse, allowing her to sniff it. Her ears were angled halfway back, silken gray. When they tilted forward, reassured, he addressed her directly. "Hinny, I require a service of thee, for the price thou knowest."

The mare switched her nacreous tail and lifted her head. She was by no means large, standing about fifteen hands tall, but she had a slender elegance that made her classic. She glanced sidelong at the blue stallion, and it was as if magic electricity lifted her mane. She was interested.

"A service for a service," my father murmured, intrigued. He contemplated the lines of the blue stallion, recognizing in this creature the very finest of the breed. The foal of such a union would be special.

"Thou must bear this Lady," the blue lad said, indicating me. "Thou must carry her on her search for her lost foal, and bring her back safely to her father. I will travel with thee, assisting. An we find the foal not, but the Lady is safe, payment will be honored. Agreed?"

"How can a horse comprehend all that?" my father muttered skeptically. But the Hinny surveyed him with such uncanny certainty that he could not protest further.

The Hinny now oriented on me. I held out my hand and she smelled it, then sniffed along the length of my arm, across my shoulder and up to my face. Her muzzle was gray velvet, her breath warm mist with the sweetness of cured hay. I loved her that moment.

The Hinny turned back to the blue lad, one ear moving forward with agreement. My father found himself unable to protest; he too was enthralled by the mare. And it seemed but a moment until arrangements were complete and we were riding out, the Hinny's canter so gentle I could close my eyes and hardly know we were moving, yet so swift that the wind was like that of a storm. I had never before ridden a steed like her!

It seemed but another moment, but when I opened mine eyes we were miles from my village, proceeding west toward the interior of the continent where the greatest magic lay. The groves and dales were passing like the wind. No horse could maintain such a pace, so smoothly—yet the Hinny ranged beside the blue stallion, now and then covertly turning a sleek ear on him: she desired the service only he could serve. I wondered fleetingly whether it could be like that for me as well, with only one man destined to be my husband. Little did I know how close to the truth that was, and that he was as close to me then as the stallion to the Hinny.

"Whither do we go?" I asked the lad.

"The wild horses should know where thy foal has strayed," he replied. "They range widely, but my steed is searching them out."

"Aye," I said. "But will they not flee at the approach of our kind?"

He only smiled. Soon we spied a herd, and its stallion lifted his head toward us, and stomped the ground in warning. But the blue lad put his two hands to his mouth, forming a conch, and blew a whistle-note, and at that signal all the horses relaxed, and remained for our approach.

"They respond to thy whistle?" I asked, perplexed.

"They know my stallion," he said easily.

So it seemed. The wild stallion was a great buckskin with dark legs, not as large as the blue stallion. The two sniffed noses and thereafter politely ignored each other. The Hinny was ignored from the start; she was not quite their kind, being half-breed.

The lad dismounted, and I followed. It had been a long, fast ride, but both of us were excellent riders, and both our steeds were easy to use. They grazed, for horses are ever hungry. We passed among the small herd—and strange it was to be around these wild horses, who never ordinarily tolerated the nearness of man. I was in young delight. They were mostly fine, healthy mares, with a few foals, but one among them ailed. The blue lad went to this one, a spindly colt, and ran his hands over the animal's body, and the dam watched without interference while I stood amazed.

"What's wrong with him?" I asked, for I could not determine the malady. I, who thought I knew horses.

"Spirit worms," the lad responded absently. "A magical infestation, common in this region." Then he said to the colt in a singsong lilt: "Comest thou to me, the worms will flee." It was nonsense verse, a joke—yet suddenly the colt perked up, took a step toward the lad, and there was a ripple in the air as invisible yet ugly somethings wriggled away. Instantly the colt seemed healthier, and his dam nickered gratefully. I realized that a little encouragement was all the colt had needed; he was not really sick, merely undernourished.

The blue lad approached the herd stallion and said: "We search for a lost foal, that went astray yesterday. Hast thou seen it, or dost thou know aught of it?"

The stallion glanced at me as though requiring news from me, and I said: "It is a filly, only a month old, pure white and lovely and helpless. I call her Snowflake."

The stallion snorted.

"He says he has not seen the foal," the blue lad said. "But he knows of one who collects white foals, and found one in this area, and that is the Snow Horse."

"Where is this Snow Horse?" I asked.

"He knows not, for the Snow Horse ranges far and associates not with ordinary equines. Only Peg can tell where he might be now."

"Peg?" I asked, perplexed.

"I will take thee to her."

We remounted our steeds and were off again like the wind. We ranged south across plains and woods, fording streams and surmounting hills as if they were nothing. We passed a young unicorn stallion grazing; he had pretty green and orange stripes, and his hooves were ebony, and his horn spiraled pearl. He started up, approaching us, and I grew nervous, for that the unicorn is to the horse as the tiger is to the housecat. But he merely ran beside us, and then drew ahead, racing us. He wanted to play.

The blue lad smiled, and leaned forward, and the blue stallion leaped ahead as though he had been merely idling before, and the Hinny set back her ears and launched herself after him. Oh, these fine animals loved a race! Now the ground shot behind in a green blur, and trees passed like arrows, and I clung to the Hinny's quicksilver mane for fear I would fall, though her gait remained wonderfully smooth. We passed the unicorn.

Now the unicorn lengthened his stride and made great leaps, passing right over bushes and rocks while we had to go around them. He recovered the lead, flinging his tail up in a mirthful salute. But again the blue stallion bore down, and the Hinny's body became like a hawk flying through a gale, and we pounded out a pace that passed the horned stallion again. Never had I traveled at such velocity!

A third time the unicorn accelerated, and now his body was shimmering with heat, and fire blasted from his nostrils, and sparks cast up from his hooves, and slowly he moved ahead of us once more. This time we could not match him, for that our steeds carried burdens and were merely physical equines, not magical. Yet had we given that unicorn a good race, and made him heat before he bested us. Very few natural horses could do that.

We eased off, cooling, and I patted the Hinny's shoulder. "Thou'rt the finest mare I ever met," I murmured. "I could ride with thee forever and never be bored." And so I believed.

Then we came to the purple slope of the great southern range of mountains, ascending until the air was rare and the growing things were stunted. There on a crag was a huge nest, and in it lay what at first I took to be a monstrous bird, for that I saw the feathers on it. Then the creature stood, perceiving our approach, and spread its wings—and lo, it was a horse!

"Peg," the blue lad called. "We crave the favor of information. Wilst thou trade for it?"

Peg launched into the air, circled briefly, spiraled to the ground and folded her pinions. The white feathers covered her whole body so that only her legs and tail and head projected, and the tail also had feathers that could spread for aid in navigation in air. I had not before imagined how large such wings would be! She neighed, her nose flicking toward the nest.

"Mayst thou have what's best for thy new nest," the lad said appreciatively, again in that lilt.

Then I noticed what I had not seen before: a pile of vines, perchance the refuse of some farmer's harvest, too long and tough to be ground for fodder. Peg went to them as though she too had only now become aware, tugging one out with her teeth, delighted. This was ideal fiber for her nest. She neighed again.

"She says the Snow Horse is moving toward its fastness in the White Mountains, and will be there by dawn tomorrow," the lad said. "For us it will be a ride of more than a day; we shall have to camp the night."

"Thou dost understand the language of horses?" I asked, remembering how he had seemingly conversed with the stallion of the herd, too. There was so much I knew not, then!

He nodded. "How could I love them as I do, and not converse with them? Who is better company than a horse?" And of course I could not gainsay that.

We mounted and rode north. It was noon, and we had far to go; we slanted north and west, wending toward the white range. We halted for an hour when we came across a grove of apple trees; we fed ourselves and our steeds on delicious apples. The Hinny ate from my hand, and how I wished she could be mine for life, but I knew she was only on loan. I was not sorry this quest was stretching out; I wanted to save Snowflake, but I wanted also to be a little longer with the Hinny, and to experience more of the magic of the interior wilds of Phaze.

In the early afternoon we halted again, for our steeds had to graze and rest. The blue lad found raspberries growing on a slope, and a streamlet with freshest water, and some ripe grain. He gathered dry wood and made a small fire; from his saddlebag he brought a pot. We boiled the grain until it was tender. I did not realize then that he had used magic to facilitate things; the farthest thing from my mind was that he could be Adept. He was only, after all, a boy!

He brought next from his saddlebag—he had a bag without a saddle, oddly—some material that he formed into a canopy for me beside the fire. I lay down to sleep feeling quite safe, for few wild creatures brave the fire, and the two horses were grazing near.

But at dusk, as I was nodding off, glare-eyed little monsters erupted from a trapdoor in the ground and swarmed toward me. They were goblins, huge of head and foot, vicious, out for human flesh. They feared not the fire, for they used it in their subterranean demesnes. I screamed.

The Hinny was nearest me, for I had been placed in her care. Now I discovered what that meant. She squealed and charged, her hooves striking like clubs, each strike crushing a goblin's head, while I huddled beside the fire in terror. The goblins fought her, for they liked equine flesh almost as well as human; they scrambled up her tail, clung to her mane, and tried to grab at her feet. There were so many! I saw one get on her head, and open its big frog mouth to clamp its sharp alligator teeth on her sweet soft gray ear—and suddenly I was on my feet and there, my hands on its grotesque rat body, hurling it off her and away.

Then the blue stallion arrived, his hooves making the very ground shudder, and he bellowed a battle-challenge that nearly blasted the hair from my head and I cowered in terror though I knew it was not me he fought. The goblins panicked and fled, the stallion pursuing; where his foot struck, the broken body of a goblin flew twenty feet across the flickering night and dropped like a clod of dirt. The stallion's eyes flashed like blue fire and the snort from his flaring nostrils was like tempest-wind and the sheen of his great muscles danced about his body as he plunged and reared and kicked. In a moment the last living goblin had vanished down the hole, and the trapdoor clanged shut. The stallion stomped it again and again until naught save rubble remained. It would be long before the goblins used that exit again!

I collapsed in reaction. Never in my life had I been so horrified, except perhaps during the episode of the trolls, for goblins come not into the villages of the man-folk. The

Hinny came and nuzzled me, and I was ashamed for that I had let her fight while I did naught. But the blue lad told me: "She thanks thee for casting the goblin from off her ear; she knows what courage it required of thee for that goblins terrify young ladies." Then I felt better, though by no means proud, and resolved to be less squeamish in future. I stroked my hands over the bruises and scratches and bites on the Hinny's body, helping to heal them and abate the discomfort, and she nudged me with that so-soft nose and everything was nice.

The goblins came not again—and who would have, after tasting the wrath of the blue stallion? I slept safely until dawn. The blue lad was up before me, and had found ripe pears from whence I knew not, and we ate and mounted and were off again. I thought I might be sore from the prior day's riding, but the Hinny's gait was so gentle I suffered not at all. I wondered what the winged horse's gait was like; what was the cadence of footfalls in air?

In due course we came to the White Mountains that bound our land in the north, and ascended their foothills. The way grew steep, and there was hardly any easing as we crested ridges and drove on up. For the first time the Hinny's gait became rough, as she labored to carry me on swiftly, and even the blue stallion was sweating, his nostrils flaring and pulsing with the effort. We climbed slopes I would not have cared to navigate on foot, rising into the mountain range proper. The air grew chill, and wind came up, and I gathered my cape about me, shivering.

The blue lad glanced at me. "May I speak bold?" he inquired melodiously. "Thou art not cold."

"Not cold," I agreed bravely, for I knew that if we desisted this quest now, never would I find Snowflake, and evermore would I curse myself for my neglect. And, strangely, I no longer felt the chill; it was as if my clothing had become doubly insulative. It was of course his magic, that I did not recognize. I was so young then, and so innocent!

We climbed on into the snows, and there in a cave half-hid in the white we found the lair of the Snow Horse. He stood there awaiting us expectantly, a fine albino stallion whose mane and tail resembled glistening icicles and whose hooves were so pure white I could hardly tell where they left off and the packed snow beneath them began.

The lad dismounted and walked to the Snow Horse. I made to dismount too, but the Hinny swung back her head, warning me "no" with a backward glance, so I obeyed her and stayed put. I was learning already that here in the wilderness the final word was not mine.

In a moment the lad returned. "The Snow Horse did lure thy foal," he said to me. "He thought her of his kind, for her color, but when they reached the snow she was cold, and he knew she was no snow filly and he let her go, never intending harm to her. But the snow demons came and took her ere she could return to thee."

"The snow demons!" I exclaimed, appalled. Never had I heard good tidings of that ilk.

"Pray we are in time," he said.

"In time?" I asked blankly. "Snowflake is lost forever! We can not brace snow demons, even if they have not yet eaten her." I felt the hot tears burning mine eyes. "Yet if there is a chance—"

"A white foal they will save—for a while." He mounted and led the way along the slope.

We made our way deeper into the snowy region, and the breath plumed out from the nostrils of our steeds, but still I was not cold. Then the blue stallion halted, sniffing the snow, and pawed the slope. I knew we were near the lair of the demons, and I shivered with fear, not with cold. Almost, I preferred to let the foal go—but then I thought of the demons devouring her shivering flesh, and horror restored my faint courage.

A snow demon appeared on a ledge above us. "Whooo?" it demanded, with sound like winter cutting past a frozen crag.

The blue lad did not answer in speech. He stood upon the back of his stallion and spread his arms, as if to say "Here am I!" I was both impressed and concerned. It was clever of him to keep his balance like that, but he could so readily fall and hurt himself. Though he acted as if the demon should recognize him and be awed, in fact it was a foolish posturing. An ogre or a giant might awe a demon; the lad was pitiful in his insignificance.

To my astonishment, the demon drew back as if confronted by a giant. "Whiiiy?" it demanded.

The lad pointed to the Hinny, then moved his hands together to indicate small size. He had come for the foal.

The demon scratched its icicle-haired head in seeming confusion: no foal here! The blue lad then did something strange indeed. He brought out a large harmonica—I had not known he carried such an instrument—and brought it to his mouth. He played one note—and the demon reacted as if struck. Sleet fell from it like droplets of perspiration, and it pointed down the slope. I looked—and there, in a patch of green in a narrow valley, stood my beloved Snowflake. The poor little filly was huddled and shivering, for nowhere in the White Mountains is it warm.

The demon faded back into its crevice, and we made our way down the steep slope to the valley. The way was tortuous, but the blue stallion picked out footholds where I thought none existed, and slowly we descended. It was like being lowered into a tremendous bowl, whose sides were so steep our every motion threatened to start a snowslide that could bury the foal. Oh, yes, we moved cautiously!

At last we reached the patch of green. I dismounted and ran to Snowflake, and she recognized me with a whinny. The warmth that encompassed me seemed to enclose her too, and she became stronger. "Oh," I cried, hugging her. "I'm so glad thou art safe! I feared—" But my prior worries were of no account now. The blue lad had enabled me to rescue Snowflake, even as he had promised.

Then I heard a rumble. Alarmed, I looked up—and saw the snow demons on high, pushing great balls of snow off ledges. They were starting an avalanche—and we were at the base of it! It was a trap, and no way could we escape.

For the first time I saw the blue lad angry. Yet he neither swore nor cowered. Instead he brought out his harmonica again and played a few bars of music. It was a rough, aggressive melody—but what good it could do in the face of the onrushing doom I knew not. Soon the sound was drowned out by the converging avalanche.

The snows came down on us like the lashing of a waterfall. I screamed and hugged Snowflake, knowing our end

had come. But as I braced myself for the inevitable, something strange happened.

There was a blinding flash of light and wash of heat, like
as an explosion. Then warm water swirled around my feet.

Warm water? I forced open mine eyes and looked,
unbelieving. The snows had vanished. All the valley, high
to the tallest surrounding peaks, was bare of snow, with
only water coursing down, and steam rising in places. We
had been saved by some massive invasion of spring thaw.

"It must be magic!" I cried, bewildered. "Unless this is a
volcanic region. But what a coincidence!"

The lad only nodded. Still I recognized not his power!

We walked up the slope, escaping the valley and the
deepening lake that was forming at its nadir. I rode the
Hinny, and Snowflake walked beside. It was a long climb,
but a happy one.

At the high pass leading to the outside the cold intensified. From out of a crevice a snow demon came. "Yyoooo!"
it cried windily, and with a violent gesture hurled a spell
like a jag of ice at the blue lad.

But the Hinny leaped forward, intercepting that scintil-
lating bolt with her own body. It coalesced about her front
legs, and ice formed on her knees, and she stumbled,
wheezing in pain. I leaped off, alarmed.

The blue lad cried out in a singsong voice, and the foul
demon puffed into vapor and floated away. Then the boy
came to minister to the Hinny, who was on the ground, her
knees frozen.

"That bolt was meant for me," he said. "Hinny, I can
cure thee not completely, for knees are the most difficult
joints to touch and thou canst not rest them now, but I will
do what I can." And he played his harmonica again, a few
bold bars, then sang: "Hinny's knees—now unfreeze."

The ice vanished from her legs. The Hinny hauled herself to her feet. She tested her knees, and they were sturdy.
But I could see some discoloration, and knew they had
been weakened somewhat. It seemed she could walk or run
on them, but special maneuvers might now be beyond her.

Then I realized what I should have known before. I
turned to the lad. "Thou didst that!" I accused him. "Thou
canst do magic!"

He nodded soberly. "I concealed it not from thee," he said, like as a child caught with hand in cookie-jar. He was so shamefaced and penitent I had to laugh.

I put mine arm about his small shoulders and squeezed him as a big sister might. "I forgive thee," I said. "But do not play with magic unduly, lest thou dost attract the notice of an Adept."

He made no comment. Shamed am I to recall now the way I patronized him then, in mine ignorance! We remounted and went on out of the mountains, slowly, in deference to the Hinny's almost-restored knees and the weakness of the foal. At last we reached the warmth of the lowlands, and there we camped for the night. Snowflake grazed beside the Hinny, who watched out for her in the manner of a dam, and I knew the foal would not come to harm. We foraged for berries and nuts, which fortunately were plentiful and delicious. Such fortune was ever in the presence of the blue lad, for he preferred to use his magic subtly.

At dusk the sunset spread its splendor across the western sky, and in the east a blue moon rose. The lad brought out his harmonica again, faced the moon, and played. Before, he had produced only single notes and brief strident passages. This time he started gentle, as it were tuning his instrument, warming it in his hands, playing a scale. His little hands were hardly large enough to enfold it properly, yet they were marvelously dextrous. Then, as the moon waxed and the sun waned, he essayed a melody.

I was tired, not paying real attention, so was caught by surprise. From that instrument emerged music of such beauty, such rare rapture as I had never imagined. The tune surrounded me, encompassed me, drew me into itself and transported my spirit up, high, into the ambience of the blue moon. I sailed up, as it were, into the lovely blue-tinged clouds, riding on a steed made of music, wafting through blue billows toward the magic land that was the face of the moon. Larger it grew, and clearer, its landscape ever-better defined. As I came near it I saw the little blue men on its surface, blacksmiths hammering out blue steel. Bluesmiths, I suppose. Then I saw a lady in blue, and her hair was fair like mine, and she wore a lovely blue gown and blue slippers set with blue gems for buttons, and on her head a blue tiara, and she was regal and beautiful beyond belief. She turned and fixed her gaze on me, and her eyes were blue like mine—and she was me.

Amazed, flattered and alarmed, I retreated. I flew back past the blue mists like a feather-shafted arrow, and suddenly I was on the ground again. The boy stopped playing, and the melody faded hauntingly.

I realized it not then, but he had shown me the first of the three foundations of my later love for him: his music. Never in all Phaze was there a man who could make such—

(The Lady Blue paused, resting her head against her hand, suffering. Stile started to speak, but she cut him off savagely. "And thou, thou image, thou false likeness! Thou comest to these Demesnes bearing *his* harmonica, using it—"

("His?" Stile asked, astonished.

("Has it not the word 'Blue' etched upon it?" she demanded. "He had it imported from the other frame, to his order."

(Stile brought out the harmonica, turning it over. There, in small neat letters, was the word. "I conjured his instrument," he murmured, awed and chagrined. "I must return it to his widow."

(She softened instantly. "Nay, it is thine. Thou art the Blue Adept, now. Use it well, as he did." Then she returned to her narrative.)

I shook my head. "Never have I heard the like, thou darling child!" I said. "How could a lad thine age master music so well?"

He thought a moment, pensive in his concentration, as though pondering some weighty ethical matter. Then he replied: "May I show thee my village on the morrow? It is not far out of our way."

"Was not that village destroyed?" I asked thoughtlessly.

"Aye, it was."

I was sorry for my question. "Of course we can go there, if it please thee. Unless the trolls remain—"

"No trolls remain," he assured me gravely, and I remembered that lightning had destroyed the trolls.

Next day we came to the site. It was nothing, only a glade of greenest grass and a few mounds. All had been destroyed and overgrown. I was vaguely disappointed, having anticipated something more dramatic—yet what is dramatic about long-past death?

"May I show thee how it was?" he inquired, his small face serious.

"Of course," I said graciously, not understanding what he meant.

"Go and graze," he said to our steeds. They moved out gladly, and little Snowflake with them.

Then the blue lad played his harmonica again. Once more the absolutely lovely music leaped out, encompassing us, and some intangible presence formed. I saw a cloud about the glade, and then it thinned to reveal a village, with people going about their business, washing clothing, eating, hammering horseshoes, playing. I realized that this was a vision of his home as it had been, years ago, before the disaster. A village very like mine own.

The village was perhaps a little better organized than mine, however, more compact, with the houses in a ring and a central court for socializing and supervision of the children. Mine was a sea-village, mainly, open to the water; this was an inland establishment, closed against the threats of the land. The sun was shining brightly—but then the shadows moved visibly, and I knew this was to show time passing. Night fell, and the village closed down.

Then in the stillness of dark the trolls came, huge, gaunt and awful. Somehow they had broken through the enchantment that protected the village, and they descended on it in a ravening horde. Faintly I heard the screams as the monsters pounced upon sleeping villagers. Men woke fighting, but each troll was large and strong, and there were many of them. I saw a woman torn apart by two trolls who were fighting over possession; they laughed with great grotesque guffaws as her left arm ripped out of its socket, and the troll holding that arm was angry because he had the smaller share, and clubbed the other troll with it while blood splattered everywhere. But then a screaming child ran by, a little girl, and the troll caught that child and

brought her to its face and opened its awful mouth and—
and bit off her screaming head.

Then the image faded, mercifully, for I was screaming
myself. Never had I seen such horror! The darkness covered all. After a pause, the dawn came. The trolls were
hidden in the houses, gorged; they would not go abroad by
light of day, and suffered no fires, for that they were the
opposite of goblins in this respect and the light was painful
to them. They had buried themselves under piled blankets,
shutting out all signs of the day. They were safe; no villager
remained alive.

No—one remained. A child, a boy—he emerged from
the trunk of a hollow tree. It seemed he had been playing
in it when the trolls descended, or doing something he
wasn't supposed to, like practicing spells, then had hidden
frozen in fright until dawn made it safe to emerge. Now he
stood, surveying the ruin—and it was the blue lad.

"Thou!" I exclaimed. "Thou didst witness it all! Thy
village, thy family, most brutally destroyed!"

"Have no sympathy for me," he replied grimly. "I was
transformed that hideous night from youth to enchanter. I
realized that no force but magic could restore the balance,
and so—" He spread his hands. "Look what I did."

I looked—and saw the figure in the image raise his
hands, and I heard him faintly singing, though I could not
make out the words. Then, suddenly, a ring of fire appeared, encircling the village, blazing ferociously. Magic
fire, I knew, but still fierce and hot. It burned inward, not
outward, while the blue lad watched. He must have spent
his sleepless hours in hiding devising that terrible spell,
perfecting it. It ignited the outer thatch cottages. Now the
trolls woke, and ran about in the fire, burning, terrified—
but they could escape only inward toward the center of the
village. And there the fire pursued them, itself a ravening
demon.

Now it was the trolls who gibbered in horror, and were
granted no reprieve, as they huddled in the center of the
village, heads covered, backs to the fire. Inevitably it closed
on them, torturing them before it consumed them, and
then fain would I have felt sorry for the trolls, but that I

remembered the woman torn apart and the decapitated child. No mercy for the merciless! The trolls fought each other, trying to keep place in the closing circle, showing not the faintest compassion for their fellows, only selfishness.

At last the dread fire burned itself out, its magic consuming flesh as readily as wood. Only mounds and ashes remained. All of the trolls had been destroyed. Except—except there was a stirring in a mound, and from it came a little troll, that must have been deeply buried by its mother, so that it alone survived. Now it looked about and wailed, afraid of the coming day.

The blue lad spied it, and knew that this one could not have killed any people, and he cast a spell of darkness that clothed it, and let the little troll go. "Thou'rt like me," the blue lad quoth. Then he turned his back on what had been his home, and walked away.

The music stopped and the vision dissipated. I looked across at the blue lad. He had shown me his second major component: his power. Yet I did not realize, or perhaps refused to let myself know, the significance of this deadly ability.

"Thou—thou wast as thou art now!" I exclaimed. "Thou hast not changed, not grown. But the destruction of thy village occurred ten years ago! How could—"

"I was seventeen," he replied.

"And now thou'rt—twenty-seven?" I asked, realizing it was true. "I thought thee twelve!"

"I am small for my size," he said, smiling.

He was as much older than I, than I had thought him younger. No child of twelve, but a full-grown man. "I—" I began, nonplussed.

"Thou didst ask how a person my age could play the harmonica so well," he reminded me.

"Aye, that I did," I agreed ruefully. Now that the joke was turned on me, I felt at ease.

The blue lad—blue *man*—summoned our steeds, and we proceeded on. We made good progress, and arrived the next day at mine own village. Almost, I had been afraid I would find it a smoking ruin, but of course this was a foolish fantasy born of the horror I had viewed. My folks rushed out to greet me in sheer gladness, and Snowflake was reunited with her dam Starshine, and all was gladness and relief.

Then the blue man said to his blue stallion: "Go service the Hinny; she has completed her pact with me." And the stallion went off into the privacy of the forest with the Hinny, who must have been in heat—aye, in heat from the first time she spied that stallion!—and I was glad for her. She would have her foal, and well had she earned it.

My father's gaze followed them. "What a stallion! What a mare!" he murmured. "Surely that foal shall be like none known among us."

The blue man shrugged, and said to me: "Lady, an thou ever needest me, sing these words: 'Blue to me—I summon thee.'" Then he turned to my father, thinking me distracted by my tearful mother, for that my days-long absence had worried them much. "Sir, may I marry thy daughter?" he asked, as if this were a question about the weather.

My mouth dropped open in sheerest surprise, and I could not speak.

"Art thou the Blue Adept?" my father asked in return.

I was stunned again, knowing suddenly the answer. How could I have missed it, I who had seen his power!

Then the Blue Adept shook hands with my father and walked in the direction the horses had gone. No answers had been given, for none were needed. Normal people associated not with Adepts, and married them never.

The Lady Blue finished her narrative and looked up at Stile. "Now canst thou go about thy business, Adept," she said.

"I thank thee, Lady," Stile said, and departed her presence.

CHAPTER 3

Proton

Neysa carried Stile across the fields to the forest where the nearest usable fold of the curtain passed. "While Hulk remains away, and I am in the other frame, do thou protect the Lady Blue from harm," Stile murmured as she galloped. "I have no better friend than thee to do this bidding."

The unicorn snorted musically. He hardly needed to tell her! Were they not oath-friends?

They reached the curtain, where it scintillated faintly in the shadowed glade. "I will try to return in a day," Stile said. "If I do not—"

Neysa blew a word-note: "Hulk."

"That's right. Send Hulk after me. He knows the frame, he knows the Game. Should anything untoward happen to me in Proton-frame—"

She blasted vehement negation. Her horn could sound quite emphatic on occasion.

"Oh, I'll look out for myself," he assured her. "And Sheen is my bodyguard there. She has saved me often enough. But in the remote chance that—well, thou canst go and get bred immediately, and raise thy foal—"

Neysa cut him off with a noise-note, and Stile let the subject drop. It had been difficult enough getting her to accept the fact of his Adept status; she was not about to accept the prospect of his demise. He hoped he would not disappoint her.

Stile faced the curtain. Through it he made out the faint outline of a lighted hall, and piles of crates. A person was walking down the hall, so Stile waited until it was clear. Most people had no awareness of the curtain, and there was a tacit agreement among curtain-crossers that the ignorance of such people be allowed to remain pristine. Then he hummed an impromptu tune as he undressed and folded his clothing carefully and hid it away in the crotch of a branch.

As he stood naked, Neysa shifted into naked girl-form, embraced him, kissed him, and laughed. "I am like Proton!"

"Takes more than nakedness to be part of Proton-frame," Stile said gruffly. "Thou'rt full of mischief, unicorn." He disengaged from her and resumed his humming before the curtain.

"Send me all into that hall," he singsonged, stepping forward.

He felt the tingle as he passed through. He was in the hall, naked, alone. He turned around and faced Neysa, who was faintly visible beyond the curtain. She had shifted back to her natural form. "Bye, friend," he called, and waved to her.

Then he went resolutely back and walked rapidly down the hall. It was strange being bare again, after getting accustomed to the mores of the other frame.

Soon the hall intersected a main travel route, where many naked serfs walked swiftly toward their places of employment. He merged with them, becoming largely anonymous. He was smaller than all the men and most of the women and some of the children, but he was used to this. He still resented the disparaging glances some serfs cast at him, but reminded himself that a person who made a value judgment of another person solely in consideration of size was in fact advertising his own incompetence to judge. Still, Stile was glad to get out of the public hall and into his private apartment.

His handprint keyed open the door. Stile stepped inside.

A naked man looked up, frowning. For a moment they stared at each other. Then the other stood. "Sheen did not tell me you would return this hour. I shall retire."

"One moment," Stile said. He recognized the man as his double: the robot who filled in for him while he was in the magic frame of Phaze. Without this machine, Stile's absences would become too obvious, and that could make mischief. "I have not encountered you before. Does Sheen treat you well?"

"Sheen ignores me," the robot said. "Except when others are present. This is proper in the circumstance."

"Yet you are programmed to resemble me in all things. Don't you get bored?"

"A machine of my type does not get bored unless so directed."

"Not even when you are put away in the closet?"

"I am deactivated at such times."

This bothered Stile, who felt sympathy for all oppressed creatures. "If you ever do feel dissatisfied, please let me know. I'll put in a word for you with the mistress."

"Thank you for your courtesy," the robot said without emotion. "It does not fit my present need. I am a machine. Should I retire now?"

"When is Sheen due back?"

"In four minutes, fifteen seconds from . . . mark."

"Yes, retire now. I'll cover for you."

The robot, of course, did not assimilate the humor. Robots came in many types and levels, and this one was relatively unsophisticated. It had no consciousness feedback circuits. It walked to the wall, looking completely human; it bothered Stile to realize that this was exactly the way he looked to others, so small and nondescript. The robot opened a panel and stepped into the closet-aperture behind. In a moment it was out of sight and deactivated.

Stile was reminded of the golem that had impersonated him, or rather, impersonated his alternate self the Blue Adept until he, Stile, arrived on the scene to destroy it. What was the difference, really, between a golem and a humanoid robot? One was activated by magic, the other by science. There were more parallels between these two frames than geographical!

Stile sat down at the table the robot had left. A game of cards—solitaire—was laid out. If the robot did not experience boredom, why was it playing cards? Answer: because Stile himself would have done this, if bored, sharpening obscure Game-skills. The robot probably followed Stile's program of acrobatic exercises, too, though it could hardly benefit from these. It was emulating him, so as to improve verisimilitude—the appearance of authenticity.

He analyzed the situation of the cards, then resumed

play. He was deep in it when the door opened and Sheen appeared.

She was beautiful. She was only slightly taller than he, with over-perfect proportions—breasts slightly larger and firmer and more erect than the computer-standard ideal for her size and age; waist a trifle smaller, abdomen flatter, hips and buttocks fuller—and luxuriantly flowing fair hair. The average man wanted a better-than-average woman; in fact he wanted a better-than-ideal woman, his tastes distorted by centuries of commercialized propaganda that claimed that a woman in perfect health and fitness was somehow less than lovely. Stile's tastes were average— therefore Sheen was far from average.

She reminded him moderately of another girl he had known, years ago: a woman smaller than himself, a female jockey he had thought he loved. Tune had been her name, and from that encounter on he had been addicted to music. Yet Sheen, he knew objectively, was actually a prettier and better woman. She had only one flaw—and he was not inclined to dwell on that at the moment.

Stile rose and went to her, taking her in his arms. "Oh— is someone here?" she asked, surprised.

"No one," he said, bringing her in for a kiss. "Let's make love."

"With a robot? Don't be silly." She tried to break free of his embrace, but he only held her more tightly.

"It is best with a robot," he assured her.

"Oh." She considered momentarily. "All right."

Oops. She was going along with it! "All right?" he demanded. "Just how far do you go with robots?"

"My best friends are robots," she assured him. "Come to the bed."

Angry now, Stile let her go. But she was laughing. "You amorous idiot!" she exclaimed. "Did you think I didn't know you?" And she flung her arms about him and kissed him with considerably more passion than before.

"What gave me away?" Stile asked.

"Aside from the differences between man and robot that I, of all people, know?" she inquired mischievously. "Things like body radiation, perspiration, heartbeat, respiration and the nuances of living reactions?"

"Aside from those," Stile said, feeling foolish. He should have known he couldn't fool her even a moment.

"Your hands are tanned," she said.

He looked at them. Sure enough, there was a distinct demarcation where his Phaze-clothing terminated, leaving his hands exposed to the strong rays of the outdoor sun. All living-areas on Proton were domed, with the sunlight filtered to nondestructive intensity, so that only moderate tanning occurred. And of course there were no demarcations on the bodies of people who wore no clothing. Not only did this uneven tanning distinguish him from the robot, it distinguished him from the other serfs of Proton! "I'll have to start wearing gloves in Phaze!"

"No such heroic measures are necessary," she assured him. She brought out some tinted hand lotion and worked it into his hands, converting them to untanned color.

"I don't know what I'd do without you," Stile said gratefully.

"You'd stay in Phaze the whole time, with that blue lady."

"No doubt."

"Well, this is another world," she informed him. "I had a piece of you before you ever knew she existed. You have a good six hours before the first Game of the Tourney, and I know exactly how to spend it."

She did, too. She was as amorous as she was lovely, and she existed only to guard and to please him. It was easy to yield to her. More than easy.

Afterward, as they lay on the bed, she inquired: "And how exactly are things in Phaze?"

"I killed the golem who was impersonating me, and gave my friend Kurrelgyre the werewolf advice on how to regain his standing in his pack—"

"I know about that. You returned here for the final pre-Tourney qualifying Game, remember? What did you do on your last trip there?"

"The werewolves and the unicorns helped me to establish my identity as the Blue Adept," Stile said, grossly simplifying the matter. "I do magic now. But I have to fight the unicorn Herd Stallion to preserve Neysa from breeding for a season."

"I like Neysa," Sheen said. "But doesn't she get jealous of the Lady Blue?"

"No, they are oath-friends now. Neysa knows my destiny lies with my own kind."

"With the Lady Blue," Sheen said.

Stile realized he had carelessly hurt Sheen. "She is not of this world, as you pointed out."

"That's what you think. It's a different world, but she's here too. She can't cross the curtain, can she? So she must have a double on this side."

Stile suffered a shock of amazement. "That's right! There must be another self of her living here. My ideal woman, all the time right here in Proton." Then he caught himself. "An ideal—"

"Oh, never mind," Sheen said. "We both know I'm not your kind, however much I might wish to be."

"But why did you tell me—"

"Neysa helped you reach the Lady, didn't she? Can I do less?"

There was that. Sheen identified with Neysa, and tried to emulate her reactions. "Actually, I can't afford to go looking for her now—and what would I do if I found her?"

"I'm sure you'd think of something," Sheen said wryly. "Men usually do."

Stile smiled. "Contrary to appearances, there is more than one concern on this male mind. I am fated to love the Lady Blue, though she may not be fated to love me—but how can I love two of her? I really have no business with her Proton-alternate."

"You don't want to see her?"

"I don't *dare* see her."

"My friends can readily locate her for you."

"Forget it. It would only complicate my life, and it is already somewhat too complicated for equanimity. How long can I continue functioning in two frames? I feel a bit like a bigamist already, and I'm not even married."

"You really ought to settle this."

He turned on her. "Why are you doing this?" But he knew why. He had hurt her, and she was expiating the hurt by exploring it to the limit. There was a certain logic in this; there was always logic in what Sheen did. They both knew he could never truly love Sheen or marry her, any more than he could have loved or married Neysa. Sheen would always love him, but could never be more to him than a temporary mistress and guardian.

"You're right," she said, her pursuit abated by his pointed question. "It is best forgotten. I shall store it in the appropriate memory bank."

"You don't forget something by remembering it!"

"We have a Tourney to win," she reminded him, aptly changing the subject in the manner of her sex.

"You understand," he cautioned her. "I can not reasonably expect to win the Tourney. I'm not at my peak Game capacity, and in a large-scale double-elimination competition like this I can get lost in the crush."

"And if you lose early, your tenure as a Proton serf ends, and you'll have to stay in Phaze, and I'll never see you again," Sheen said. "You have reason to try. We need to find out who has been trying to kill you here, and you can only pursue an effective investigation if you become a Citizen."

"There is that," he agreed. He thought of the anonymous Citizen who had had his knees lasered and gotten him washed out as a jockey. The series of events that action had precipitated had paradoxically enriched his life immeasurably, introducing him to the entire frame of Phaze—yet still an abiding anger smouldered. He had a score to settle with someone—and Sheen was right, it was an incentive to win the Tourney if he possibly could. For the winner would be granted the ultimate prize of Proton: Citizenship. Runners-up would receive extensions of their tenure and the chance to compete again in a subsequent Tourney. So he did have a chance, a good chance because of his Game abilities—but the odds of final victory remained substantially against him.

He wondered, coincidentally, whether the history the Lady Blue had recently related had any bearing. A snow demon had fired a freeze-spell at the Blue Adept, and it had caught the Hinny and damaged her knees. Stile had been lasered in the knees while riding a horse. Was this an example of the parallelism of the two frames? Things did tend to align, one way or another, but sometimes the route was devious.

"One Game at a time," Sheen said. "If and when you lose, I'll just have to abide by that. I know you'll try."

"I'll try," he agreed.

They reported on schedule to the Game Annex. Sheen could not accompany him inside; only Tourney entrants were permitted now. She would go to a Spectator Annex and tune in his game on holo, unless it happened to be one in which a live audience was permitted. She would lend her applause and opinion when feedback opportunity occurred.

There was a line at the entrance. There was hardly ever such a crowd—but the Tourney came just once a year. Six hundred serfs had to report at once, and though the Game facilities were extensive, this was a glut.

When he stepped inside, the Game Computer interviewed him efficiently. "Identity?" a voice inquired from a holographic image of the capital letters GC suspended a meter before him at head height. The computer could make any image and any sound emanate from anywhere, but kept it token. Proton was governed by Citizens, not by machines, and the smart machine maintained that in memory constantly.

"Stile, serf, ladder 35M, Rung 5." That gave his name, status, age, sex and the fact that he had qualified for the Tourney by holding the fifth rung of the competitive ladder for his bracket: the minimum entry requirement. He could have been first on his ladder had he gone for it earlier; he was actually one of the best players extant. But all that really counted was qualification. All had equal Tourney status.

"Stile 35M-5, assigned number 281 for Round One only," the voice of the Game Computer said. A decal emerged from a slot. Stile took it and set it against his forehead. Now he was marked, for the purpose of this Round, with the number and name: 281 STILE. "Proceed to the 276-300 sub-annex and encounter your opposite number. Your Game will be announced in due course. Respond immediately or forfeit."

"Acknowledged," Stile said. The floating GC faded out

and he proceeded to the designated annex. For this Round, a number of waiting rooms and hall alcoves had been converted to rendezvous points. After the first few Rounds many of these would revert to their normal uses, as the number of entrants decreased.

Already the annex was filling. Each person wore the decal on his or her forehead, all numbers in the 276-300 range. Most were naked men and women, some familiar to him. But before Stile could fully orient, a clothed man stepped forward. "Salutation, opposite number," the man said.

Stile was taken aback. This was a Citizen, fully garbed in tan trousers, white shirt, jacket and shoes. But he did bear the number on his forehead: 281, with no name. Citizens were generally anonymous to serfs. Anonymity was a privilege of status that showed most obviously in the clothing that concealed bodily contours. Serfs had no secrets.

"Sir," Stile said.

"We are all equal, ad hoc," the Citizen said. He was handsome and tall, a good decade older than Stile, and as self-assured as all Citizens were. "Come converse in a nook." He put his hand on Stile's elbow, guiding him.

"Yes, sir," Stile agreed numbly. His first match was against a Citizen! Of course he had known that Citizens participated in the Tourney; he just had not thought in terms of playing against one himself. On Proton there were two classes: the Citizens and the serfs. The Haves and the Have-nots. Stile himself was employed by a Citizen, as every serf was; no unemployed serf was permitted on the planet beyond a brief grace period, and no employed serf could remain beyond his twenty-year tenure—with certain very limited exceptions. This was part of what the Tourney was about.

The Citizen guided him to a bench, then sat down beside him. This alleviated his third-of-a-meter advantage in height, but not his immeasurable advantage in status. "I am popularly known as the Rifleman. Possibly you have heard of me."

Stile suffered a second shock. "The Tourney winner—fifteen years ago! I watched that Game . . . sir."

The Rifleman smiled. "Yes, I was a serf like you. I won my Citizenship the hard way. Now the perennial lure of the Game brings me back. You never do get it out of your system! Who are you?"

"Sir, I am—"

"Ah, now I connect! Stile is the designation of one of the top current Gamesmen! I had not realized your tenure was expiring."

"It had three years to go, sir. But I had a problem with my employer."

"Ah, I see. So you had to go for double or nothing. Well, this is a pleasure! I've entered other Tourneys since my ascent, but the moment I matched with a serf he would throw it into CHANCE, and two or three of those in succession washed me out early. It is hard to beat a person unless he thinks he can beat you. I'm sure you will give me an excellent game."

"Yes, sir," Stile agreed. "I don't like CHANCE." He didn't like having to play a Citizen either, but that could not be said here. Of all the people to encounter this early! A former Tourney winner! No wonder the Rifleman's opponents in other Tourneys—a Citizen could enter anything he wanted, of course, being immune to the rules governing serfs—had avoided honest contests. CHANCE was at least a 50-50 proposition, instead of a virtually guaranteed loss. It was axiomatic that the poorer players preferred CHANCE, while the better ones disliked it, and the top players wished it would be abolished as a category.

Stile had been twenty years old, already an avid follower of Tourneys, when the Rifleman fought his way up to ultimate victory by shooting six target ducks against his opponent's three. A highly skilled player, who had of course taken a name reflective of that victory.

But that had been a long time back. The man could be out of practice and out of shape. Unless he had been practicing privately. Yet why should a Citizen bother? He had nothing to win in the Tourney. A Citizen, almost by definition, had everything. Fabulous wealth, power, and prestige. If a Citizen saw an attractive serf-girl, he could hire her and use her and fire her, all within the hour. It would not even occur to her to protest. A Citizen could

have a household of humanoid robots, virtually indistin-
guishable from living people (until one got to know them,
which did not take long) to serve his every need. The finest
creature comforts of the galaxy were his, and the most
exotic entertainments. Small wonder that many Citizens
grew indolent and fat!

"I can virtually read your thoughts," the Citizen said.
"And I will answer them. I am not in the shape I was when
I won, but I have practiced somewhat and remain reasonably formidable. Of course I lack motive, now; victory will
not benefit me, and defeat will not harm me. Yet it would
be satisfying to win it again."

Stile was spared the awkwardness of answering by the
Game Computer's introductory announcement. "Attention
all entrants. The Tourney roster is now complete: four
hundred Citizens, six hundred serfs, and twenty-four aliens.
Pairing for individual matches is random each Round.
The Tourney is double-elimination; only entrants with two
losses are barred from further competition. Serfs among
the final sixty-four survivors will receive one year extension
of tenure. Those proceeding beyond that level will receive
commensurately greater rewards. The Tourney winner will
be granted Proton Citizenship. Judging of all matches in
the objective sphere is by computer; subjective judging is
by tabulated audience-response; special cases by panels of
experts. Bonus awards will be granted for exceptional
Games. Malingerers will forfeit." There was a momentary
pause as the computer shifted from general to specific. Now
it would be addressing the annexes individually. "Game-
pair 276 report to grid."

Hastily two serfs rose, a man and a woman, and walked
to the grid set up in the center of the room. They began the
routine of Game-selection.

"Ah, this is like old times," the Rifleman said appreciatively.

"Yes, sir," Stile agreed. He would have liked to follow
the first couple's progress, but of course he could not ignore the Citizen. "Not old to me, sir."

"Contemporary times for you, of course," the Citizen
said. "I have followed your progress intermittently. You

have played some excellent Games. Perhaps I misremember; don't you happen also to be an excellent equestrian?"

"I was a winning jockey, yes, sir," Stile agreed.

"Ah, now it comes back! You were lasered. Anonymously."

"Through the knees, yes, sir."

"That had to have been the action of a Citizen."

"Yes, sir."

"Citizens are a law unto themselves." The Rifleman smiled. "Don't forget, I was a serf for nineteen years, and a Citizen only fifteen. My fundamental values are those of the serf. However, I doubt that even most birthright Citizens would approve such vandalism. There are licit and illicit ways to do business, and no Citizen should need to resort to the illicit. A rogue Citizen would be a menace to other Citizens, and therefore should be dealt with firmly for a practical as well as legal reason."

"Yes, sir."

"As you know, I am in this Tourney merely for titillation. I now perceive a way to increase that interest. Allow me to proffer this wager: if you overmatch me in this Round, I shall as consequence make an investigation into the matter of the lasering and report to you before you depart the planet. Agreed?"

No serf could lightly say no to any Citizen, and Stile had no reason to demur. He wanted very much to know the identity of his enemy! Yet he hesitated. "Sir, what would be my consequence if you defeat me?"

The Rifleman stroked his angular beardless chin. "Ah, there is that. The stakes must equate. Yet what can a serf offer a Citizen? Have you any personal assets?"

"Sir, no serf has—"

The Citizen waggled a finger at him admonishingly, smiling, and Stile suddenly found himself liking this expressive man. No serf could afford to like a Citizen, of course; they were virtually in different worlds. Still, Stile was moved.

"Of course a serf has no material assets," the Rifleman said. "But serfs often do have information, that Citizens are not necessarily aware of. Since what I offer you is information, perhaps you could offer me information too."

Stile considered. As it happened, he did have news that should interest a Citizen—but he was honor-bound not to impart it. He happened to know that a number of the most sophisticated service robots were self-willed, acting on their own initiative, possessing self-awareness and ambition. Theoretically there could eventually be a machine revolt. But he had sworn not to betray the interests of these machines, so long as they did not betray the welfare of Planet Proton, and his word was absolute. He could not put that information on the line. "I regret I can not, sir."

The Citizen shrugged. "Too bad. The wager would have added luster to the competition."

As though the future of a serf's life were not luster enough? But of course the Citizen was thinking only of himself. "Yes, sir. I'm sorry, sir. I would have liked to make that wager, had I a stake to post."

"Are you not aware you could make the wager, and renege if you lose? You really don't have much to lose."

Stile, under tension of the Tourney, was suddenly angry. "That's reprehensible!" Then, belatedly, "Sir."

"Ah, you are an honest man. I thought as much. I like that. Most top Gamesmen do value integrity."

Stile was spared further conversation by the interjection of the computer. "Game-pair 281 report to grid."

The Rifleman stood. "That's us. Good luck, Stile." He proffered his hand.

Stile, amazed, accepted it. He had never heard of a Citizen shaking hands with a serf! This was an extension of courtesy that paralleled that of the Herd Stallion in Phaze: the disciplined encounter of respected opponents.

Phaze! Suddenly Stile realized what he had to offer. The knowledge of the existence of the alternate frame! The information might do the Citizen no good, since most people could not perceive the curtain between frames, let alone cross it, but it would surely be of interest to the man. There was no absolute prohibition about spreading the word, though Stile preferred not to. But if he won the Game, he wouldn't have to. This seemed to be an acceptable risk.

"Sir," Stile said quickly. "I do have information. I just remembered. I believe it would interest—"

"Then it is a bargain," the Citizen said, squeezing Stile's hand.

"Yes, sir. Only I hope you will not share the information with others, if—"

"Agreed. This is a private wager and a private matter between us—either way."

"Yes, sir."

"Second call for Game-pair 281," the computer announced. "Appear at the grid within ten seconds or both forfeit."

"You bucket of bolts!" the Rifleman snapped. "Whom do you suppose you are addressing?"

A lens swung about to fix on the Citizen. The response was instant. "Abject apologies, sir. Time limit is waived."

The Rifleman's glance swept across the silent room. "You may laugh now."

The remaining serfs burst into laughter.

"Rank hath its privileges," the Rifleman said. He put his hand on Stile's elbow, guiding him to the grid. This was a public mark of favor that awed the serfs present, Stile included. This Citizen had been friendly and reasonably solicitous throughout, but now he was being so when all eyes were upon him.

"You lout," another Citizen said, laughing. "Now we'll all have to show favor to our serfs!"

"What is Proton coming to?" a third Citizen inquired. This one was a woman, elaborately gowned and coiffed, with sparkling sapphires on her wrists and ankles and a nugget of Protonite on her forehead, reminding Stile of Neysa's snub-horn in her girl-form. Parallelism again, perhaps. This Citizen, too, was smiling, seeming almost like a person.

It occurred to Stile that even Citizens might get bored with their routine existences, and appreciate comic relief on rare occasions. The Tourney was a great equalizer!

Now he faced the Rifleman, the grid unit between them. This was a column inset with panels on opposite sides. The weight of the two men beside it caused the panels to illuminate. Stile's showed four categories across the top: 1. PHYSICAL 2. MENTAL 3. CHANCE 4. ARTS. Four more were down the side: A. NAKED B. TOOL C.

MACHINE D. ANIMAL. The latter facet was highlighted:
Stile had to select from the letters.

He experienced the usual pre-Game tension, made worse
by the fact that this was no routine Game, but a Round for
the Tourney. And made worse yet by the fact that his
opponent was a Citizen. What column would the Rifleman
choose? PHYSICAL or MENTAL, surely; he was neither
a gambler nor an artist, and he wanted a good game. He
would want to get into 1B or 1C, tool- or machine-assisted
physical games like tennis or shooting, where his major
expertise lay, or into 2B where he might get into chess. He
had won a Tourney Game dramatically in chess, Stile remembered now, on his way up; in fifteen years he had
probably improved his game. It was necessary to stay clear
of this: Stile could play chess well himself, but he had not
had fifteen idle years to practice.

He was up against someone who really could play the
Game. This could be the toughest opponent he would face
in the entire Tourney. A good Game that he lost in a contest was no good; he needed a likely winner. His only real
course seemed to be ANIMAL. Then he could get into
horseracing or liontaming. His knees were weak, but this
only became acute when he flexed them completely; he
could do ordinary riding better than anyone he knew, and
remained pretty good at trick-riding. His smaller weight
would give him an advantage, for the Tourney made no
allowances for size or sex. All games were unhandicapped.
And he liked animals, while the Rifleman, an expert
hunter, probably did not have as close rapport. Yes.

Stile touched D. Immediately a new grid showed: 1D,
PHYSICAL/ANIMAL. The Rifleman had chosen as expected.

Now the top line was 1. SEPARATE 2. INTERACTIVE
3. COMBAT 4. COOPERATIVE, and the sideline was A.
FLAT B. VARIABLE C. DISCONTINUITY D. LIQUID.
Stile had the letters again, which was fine. Horseracing was
on a flat surface, and he had control of the surfaces. He
did not want to get involved with trained sharks or squid
wrestling in the LIQUID medium, and feared the Rifleman
might be experienced in falconing in DISCONTINUITY,
i.e., air. Mountain Rodeo would be all right, in the VARI-

ABLE surface; Stile had bulldogged mountain goats before. But that category also included python tug-of-war in trees, and Stile did not care for that. So he stuck with A. FLAT.

The Rifleman selected 2. INTERACTIVE. So they were in box 2A. No horseracing, but there could be two-horse polo or—

The new grid was upon them, nine squares to be filled in by turns. Lists of games and animals appeared.

The Rifleman met Stile's gaze over the column. "Take it," he said, smiling. He was giving Stile the advantage of first selection, rather than requiring the Game Computer to designate the turn randomly. Such minor courtesies were permitted; they facilitated the selection process.

"Thank you, sir." Stile designated POLO/HORSE in the center box.

The Citizen put BASEBALL/ANDROID in the right upper box.

Oh, no! Stile had not considered that androids counted as animals for Game purposes. Baseball was played by modified twentieth-century rules: nine players per team. It was a ballgame, but there was some overlap in categories; ballgames could appear in several sections of the master grid. This was an animal-assisted ballgame, as was polo. The difference was, there were a number of animals here, not used as steeds but as actual players. Obviously the Rifleman was expert at this sort of game, while Stile was only fair. He had walked into a trap.

Sure enough, while Stile filled in other individual animal contests, the Rifleman filled in android team games: Soccer, Basketball, Football. And when they played the grid, the Citizen won: FOOTBALL/ANDROID.

Disaster! Stile had not played team football in a long time. He could pass, kick and catch a football, but an hour-long session with twenty bruisingly huge androids? What a horror!

There was no chance now to brush up on the antique Earth-planet Americana the Rifleman evidently liked. Stile had to play immediately, or forfeit. The Citizen did not bother to ask him to concede, knowing he would not. For better or worse, this had to be fought out on the field.

They adjourned to the bowl-stadium. It was sparsely attended by spectators, since there were several hundred Games in progress and serf interest was divided. However, a number began to file in as the news of a Citizen-serf-android match spread. It was not that serfs were interested in Stile, at this point; they merely hoped to see a Citizen get knocked about a little with impunity.

"In the interest of economy of time and efficient use of facilities, this Game will be abbreviated to thirty minutes playing time without interruption," the Game Computer announced. "Each party will select twenty animal players, from which a continuous playing roster of ten will be maintained. Substitutions are limited to one per team per play, performed between plays. Proceed."

The computer was certainly moving it along! And no wonder, for a second playing field was already being utilized, and the remaining two would surely be in use before Stile's game finished.

They reviewed the androids. The artificial men stood in a line, each hulking and sexless and stupid but well muscled. Each carried a placard labeling its specialty: FULLBACK, HALFBACK, QUARTERBACK, and an array of offensive and defensive linemen. The capability of each was set within a standard tolerance; an android could perform exactly what it was supposed to do, no more and no less. Thus the outcome of the Game would be determined by the management and strategy and participation of the two human players, not the skill of the androids.

The largest imponderable was that of human skill. For this was not a remote-control game; the androids were there merely to assist the real players, who could occupy any position on their teams, but had to participate continuously. A good contestant would enable his team to prevail; a bad one would drag his team down to defeat. Stile feared that the Rifleman would prove to be good, while Stile himself, partly because of his size, would be less-than-good.

The Rifleman selected four pass receivers and a solid offensive line. He was going for an aerial offense, without doubt! Stile chose pass receivers too, and a passing quarterback, then concentrated on his defensive line. He had to hope for a stalled game and errors; as he saw it, defense was the refuge of incompetence, and that was apt to be him. He dreaded this Game!

It began. Chance gave Stile's team first possession of the ball. His animals were in white, the Rifleman's in black. The opposing team lined up like faceless demons from the frame of Phaze, darkly formidable. They swept forward, kicking the ball ahead, converging on its locale as it landed. Stile's receiver-android had no chance; he was down on the ten-yard line.

Yards, Stile thought. This was one of the few places where the old system of measurements prevailed on Planet Proton, because of the vintage and origin of this particular game. It was easiest to think of them as scant meters.

Now the onus was on him to devise a strategy of play that would bring the football down the field and across the opposing goal line. Stile had a hunch this would not be easy. He assigned himself to be a pass receiver, and scheduled the play for his runner. That should keep Stile himself from getting crushed under a pile of android meat. Of course he knew the androids were programmed to be very careful of human beings. Still, a tackle was a tackle, and that could be bruising. He was thoroughly padded in his white playing suit, of course, but he knew accidents could happen.

The play proceeded. The pass receivers dodged the opposing linemen and moved out on their patterns. Stile got downfield and cut back as if to receive the ball—and found himself thoroughly blocked off by the android pass defender. Catch the ball? He could not even see it! The only way he could hope to get it, had it been thrown to him, was if it passed between the animal's legs.

Fortunately he knew no pass was coming. Stile's runner bulled into the line, making one yard before disappearing into the pileup. That, obviously, was not the way to go.

Still, this first drive was mainly to feel his way. The nuances were already coming back to him, and he was getting a feel for the performance tolerances of the androids. He should be able to devise good strategy in due course.

Next play he tried a reverse end run. He lost a yard. But he was watching the Black team's responses. The androids, of course, lacked imagination; a really novel play would fool them, and perhaps enable his team to make a big gain or even score.

On the third play he tried a screen pass to one of his receivers. The pass was complete, but the receiver advanced only to the line of scrimmage before getting dumped. No breakthrough here!

Fourth down and time to kick the ball downfield. Stile signaled his kicker to come in—and realized belatedly that he had selected no kicker. None of his animals specialized in any kind of kick, and therefore could not do it. If he had his quarterback make the attempt, the job would surely be bungled, and the other team would recover the ball quite near the goal line. Yet if he did not—

A whistle blew. The referee, penalizing his team for delay of game. Five yards. He *had* to kick it away!

No help for it; Stile would have to kick it himself. He would not have the booming power of an android, and he dreaded the thought of getting buried under a mound of tackling animals, but at least he could accomplish something. If he got the kick off promptly, he might get away without being bashed.

No time to debate with himself! He called the play, assigning the kick to himself. The teams lined up, the ball was snapped, and the enormous Black line converged on Stile like a smashing storm wave.

Stile stepped forward quickly and punted. Distracted by the looming linemen, he dropped the ball almost to the ground before his toe caught it. The ball shot forward, barely clearing the animals, and made a low arch downfield, angling out of bounds just shy of the fifty-yard line. Not bad, all things considered; he had gained about forty yards. He had been lucky; had the Black androids had the wit to expect an incompetent punt, they might have blocked it or caught it before it went out, and had an excellent runback.

Luck, however, seldom played consistent favorites. Stile had to do better, or the first bad break would put him behind.

Now it was the Rifleman's turn on offense. The Citizen had stayed back during the prior plays, keeping himself out of mischief. Now he made his first substitution, bringing in one of his pass receivers. Stile exchanged one of his receivers for a pass defender. The first plays would probably be awkward, since most of Stile's players were offensive and most of the Rifleman's players defensive—but the longer the drive continued, the more qualified players could be brought in, at the rate of one per play. Of course the offensive and defensive lines were fairly similar, for Game purposes, so the exchange of as few as three backfield players could transform a team. All the same, Stile hoped the drive did not continue long.

The Rifleman assumed the position of quarterback. His animals lined up. The play commenced. Stile's line charged in, but the Rifleman reacted with poise, making a neat, short bulletlike pass to his receiver on the sideline. It was complete; the pass had been too accurately thrown for the receiver to miss, too swift for the defender to interfere with. The Citizen had a net gain of eight yards.

The Rifleman—now Stile appreciated how this applied to football, too. The Citizen was a superior player of this arcane game, better than an android passer. Therefore he had a superior team—while Stile had an indifferent team.

Stile substituted in another pass defender—but the Citizen brought in another receiver. Stile could not double-cover. Those passes were going to be trouble!

They were. The Rifleman marched his team relentlessly downfield. Not every pass connected, and not every play was a pass, but with four tries to earn each first down, the offensive team had no trouble. All too soon the Rifleman scored. Then the Rifleman substituted in his own place-kicker and let him make the extra point. The score was 7-0, the Rifleman's advantage.

Complete team substitutions were permitted after a touchdown. It was a new game, with Stile receiving again, except that he was now in the hole. Five playing minutes had elapsed.

Stile's team received the ball and attempted a runback. His animal got nowhere. Stile had his first down on the twelve-yard line.

It was time to get clever. If he could fool the defenders and break an android free, he might score on a single play. But this could be risky.

He set up the play: a fake run to the right, and a massive surge to the left, with every android lineman moving across to protect the runner.

The result was a monstrous tangle as stupid animals got in each other's way. His runner crashed into his own pileup, getting nowhere, and the referee imposed a fifteen-yard penalty for unnecessary roughness, holding, and offensive interference. Half the distance to Stile's goal line.

Second down, long yardage, from the six-yard line. So much for innovation! Stile tried to complete another pass, this time to himself; maybe the Rifleman wouldn't expect him to expose himself that way, and the surprise would work. A long bomb, trying for the moons, double or nothing.

The play commenced. Stile ducked through the line and charged straight downfield. The Rifleman cut across to guard him. Together they turned at the fifty-yard line, and Stile cut back to the appointed spot to receive the pass, and the Rifleman cut in front of him and intercepted it while it remained too high in the air for Stile to reach.

"Sorry about that, friend," the Citizen said as Stile hastily tackled him and the whistle blew to end the play. "Height has its advantage."

It certainly did. Stile had lost the ball again without scoring. He heard the roar of reaction and applause from the filling audience section of the stadium; the Rifleman had clearly made a good play. Now Stile would have to defend again against the devastating passing attack of his opponent.

He was not disappointed. Methodically the Rifleman moved the ball down the field until he scored again. This time he passed for the extra points, and made them. The score was fifteen to nothing.

The first half of the game was finished: fifteen minutes of playing time. Stile had tried every device he could think of to stop his opponent from scoring, and had only managed to slow the rate of advance and use up time. The Rifleman had averaged a point per minute, even so. Stile had to move, and move well, in the second half, or rapidly see the game put out of reach. He needed a dramatic, original system of defense and offense. But what could he do?

Surprise, first. What could he do that really would surprise his opponent, while staying within the clumsy rules of this game? He couldn't run or pass or kick the ball away—

The kick. It was possible to score on the kick. Field goals, they were called, worth three points each. Except that he had no kicker other than himself. That was only slightly better than nothing, considering his near bungle of his first attempt to punt. The moment he set up for a placekick instead of a punt, those Black armored animals would be upon him. Even if he got the kick off, even if he somehow scored, he would wind up crushed at the bottom of the pile of meat. There was not any great future in that. If by some fluke he scored several field goals, enough to win, he would still be so battered he would be at a serious disadvantage in other Games of the Tourney. It would really be better to forfeit this one; it took two losses to eliminate an entrant, so he could afford that gesture.

No! He was not about to forfeit anything! If he lost, it would only be because he had been fairly beaten.

Still, the kick seemed to be his best chance. A surprise punt on first or second down, catching the Rifleman with his guard down. Then an attempt to force an error, an interception, or a fumble. Playing for the breaks. It would take nerve and luck and determination, but it was a chance.

Stile's team received the kickoff. This time the ball bounced into the end zone, and was brought out to his twenty-yard line for play.

Stile called for the punt, after a fake pass. His quarterback would simply fade back and hand the ball to Stile, then serve as interference to the tacklers while Stile got the kick off.

It worked. Stile got a beautiful—for him—punt off, escaping unscathed himself. The ball was low and fast, skimming over the heads of the animals, bouncing, and rolling rapidly onward. No one was near it.

The Rifleman, playing the backfield, was first to reach the ball. But the thing was still hopping crazily about, the way an unround and pointed ball was apt to do, as if it were a faithful representative of its crazy period of history, and it bounced off the Citizen's knee. Now, according to the peculiarities of this sport, it was a "live" ball, and Stile's onrushing animals had the limited wit to pounce on it. There was a monstrous pileup—and Stile's team recovered the football on the thirty-yard line of Black. A fifty-yard gain!

"Nicely played," the Rifleman said, smiling. "I was beginning to fear the game would be unconscionably dull."

"No Tourney Game is dull," Stile said. "Sir."

Now he had the ball in good field position—but could he seize the opportunity to score? Stile doubted it. He simply did not have the ability to advance the ball consistently.

So he would have to attempt to score from this range. That meant a forty-yard field goal. No, Stile doubted he had the power or accuracy for that. He would merely be throwing the ball away, unless he could get closer to the goal. His androids evidently couldn't do that, and Stile himself was too small to carry it; the pass interception had shown that. This was one game where no advantage could be achieved from small size.

Or could it? These android brutes were accustomed to dealing with creatures their own size, and were slow to adjust. An agile, acrobatic man *his* size—why not show them some of the tricks he could do? Stile was small, but no weakling, and the androids were programmed not to hurt real people. He just might turn that into an advantage.

In the huddle he had specific instructions for his center. "You will hike the ball to me—make sure you get it to me, for I am smaller than your regular quarterback—then charge forward straddle-legged. I clarify: hike the ball, then block forward and up, your feet spread wide. Do you understand?"

Dully, the android nodded. Stile hoped the creature would follow orders literally. These androids were the match of real people physically, but science had not developed their brains to work as well as the human kind. Androids cast in petite female forms were said to be quite popular with some men, who considered their lack of wit to be an asset. Specialized androids were excellent for other purposes such as sewer cleaning. It just happened that in this Game, Stile had to push to the intellectual limit of the type. In a real game of football, as played on Earth centuries ago, such an android would have been fully competent: this was not that situation.

The creature did as ordered. Stile took the ball, ducked down—and charged forward between the animal's spread legs. The slow-witted opposing androids did not realize what had happened; they continued to charge forward, looking for a ball carrier to tackle. Stile scooted ahead five, ten, and finally fifteen yards before the Rifleman himself brought him down. "Beautiful play!" the Citizen said as they bounced together on the turf, their light armor absorbing most of the shock of impact. With a fifteen-point lead, he could afford to be generous. But the growing stadium audience also cheered.

Stile had his first down on the fifteen-yard line, but he knew better than to try the same stunt again. At any rate, he was now in field goal range, for his kicking ability—except that he still did not relish getting crushed in the blitz that would converge on the placekicker.

Then he dredged from his memory an alternative: the dropkick. Instead of having the ball held in place by another player for the kick, the kicker simply dropped it to the ground and kicked it on the bounce. A dropkick, unlike a punt, was a scoring kick. Its disadvantage was that it was less reliable than a placekick, since the bounce could go wrong; its advantage was that it could be done on extremely short notice. Short enough, perhaps, to surprise the androids, and enable Stile to complete it before getting tackled and buried.

He decided to try it. He took the ball as quarterback, faded back a few yards, then dropped it for the kick. The ball bounded up, and the androids ceased their charge, realizing that this differed from a punt.

Stile watched with gratification as the football arced between the goal posts. It was wobbly and skewed but within tolerance. The referee signaled the score: three points.

"The drop kick!" The Rifleman exclaimed. "I haven't seen one of those in years! Magnificent!" He seemed more pleased about it than Stile was.

But now it was Stile's turn to kick off to the Rifleman. He decided to gamble again. "Do you know the onside kick?" he asked his teammates.

Blank stares were returned. Good—the animals had not been programmed for this nuance. Probably the other team's androids would not know it either, so could reasonably be expected to flub it. The Rifleman would know it—but Stile intended to kick the ball away from him.

He tried it and it worked. Stile's team had possession of the football at midfield. "Oh, marvelous!" the Rifleman exclaimed ecstatically.

Back in the huddle. "Number One will field the ball," Stile told the animals, referring to the Rifleman's shirt designation. "Charge him, box him in, but do not tackle him. I will tackle him."

Uncomprehending, the androids agreed.

Stile punted on first down. This time he had the feel of it, and hung the ball up high, giving his players time to get down to it before it landed. The Rifleman, alert to this play, caught the ball himself, calling his own players in around him. Thus the two groups formed in a rough circle, Stile's animals trying to get past the Rifleman's animals without actually contacting the Rifleman.

Perplexed by this seeming diffidence, the Citizen started to run with the ball. That was when Stile shot between two of his own players, took a tremendous leap, and tackled the Rifleman by the right arm where the football was tucked. He made no bruising body contact, for that would have brought a pénalty call, but yanked hard on that arm.

As the two twisted to the ground, the ball passed from the Citizen's grasp to Stile's. Stile was of course adept at wresting control of objects from others; he had specialized in this maneuver for other types of games. Once again, his team had possession of the ball.

"Lovely," the Rifleman said, with slightly less enthusiasm than before.

The ball was now just inside the twenty-yard line. Stile drop-kicked another field goal. Now he had six points. And eleven minutes remaining in the game.

He knew he would not get away with another onside kick. The Rifleman would already have alerted his team to that. This time Stile would have to play it straight, and hope to stop the Citizen's devastating drive.

Stile kicked it deep, and it went satisfyingly far before being fielded by a Black android. Stile's androids were alert to this routine situation, and they brought the carrier down on the twenty-yard line.

Now Stile had to stifle the passing attack. He decided to concentrate on rushing the passer and hoping for an interception. He himself would cover one of the Rifleman's receivers, while double-covering the other with androids.

This seemed to be effective. The Rifleman faded back for his pass, did not like the situation, but did not want to run or get tackled. So he overthrew the ball, voiding any chance for an interception. According to the quaint conventions for this sport, all parties knew exactly what he was doing, and it mandated a penalty for deliberate grounding, but none was called. Because if deliberate grounding of the ball was done with discretion, it was presumed to be a throwing error instead of what it obviously was. Presumably this sort of thing added luster to the game.

On the second down the Rifleman tried a pass to the double-covered receiver, but two androids were better than one and again it went incomplete. Good: one more such failure and he'd have to turn over the ball on a kick. Stile was at last managing to stifle the Citizen's passing attack.

On third down, the Rifleman rifled the ball directly to the receiver Stile was covering. He aimed it high, to be out of Stile's reach, but reckoned without Stile's acrobatic ability. Stile leaped high to intercept it—and was banged aside by the receiver, who had not realized what he was going to do. No android would have leaped like that. A referee's flag went down.

The penalty was offensive pass interference. Stile's team had the ball again. This time the Rifleman's congratulation was definitely perfunctory.

The ball was on the Black thirty-five-yard line. Time remaining was nine minutes. Those incomplete passes had expended very little time. Still, Stile was getting nervous; he really needed to break loose and score a touchdown.

"Number 81—can you receive a lateral?" he asked.

"Yuh," the animal agreed after a brief pause for thought.

"Then follow me and be ready." Stile turned to a lineman. "When the ball is hiked, you turn, pick me up, and heave me over the Black line." He seemed to remember an ancient penalty for such a trick, but it was not part of the Game rules.

"Duh?" the android asked. The concept was too novel for his intellectual capacity. Stile repeated his instructions, making sure the animal understood what to do, if not why.

When the ball was hiked, Stile tucked it into his elbow and stepped into his lineman's grasp. The android hurled him up and over. Stile had been given such a lift in the course of gymnastic stunts, and was pretty much at home in the air. He flipped, rolled off a lineman's back, landed neatly on his feet and charged forward toward the goal line.

This time, however, the Rifleman had a couple of guards in the backfield, and they intercepted Stile before he had gone more than ten yards.

Now Stile lateraled to Number 81, who was right where he was supposed to be. What these creatures did, they did well! The android caught the ball and bulled ahead for eight more yards before being stopped.

They were within kicking range again. Stile decided not to gamble on another running play; he drop-kicked another field goal. The score was now 15-9, with eight minutes remaining. At this rate, he could do it—provided he had no bad breaks. Unfortunately, he was overdue for one of those. He had been playing extremely chancy ball.

Should he try another onside kick? No, that would only cost him yardage at this stage. He had to make the Rifleman travel as far across the field as possible, so that he had the maximum opportunity to make an error. So Stile played it straight.

This time he managed to put the ball all the way into the end zone. The Rifleman put it into play on the twenty-yard line. This time, wary of passing into Stile's double coverage, he handed it off to his runner. But the android proceeded without imagination and was downed at the line of scrimmage. Any play left purely to the animals was basically wasted time; the capacities of the androids had evidently been crafted for that. The human players *had* to make their physical and/or mental skills count.

Now Stile was sure the Citizen was beginning to sweat. The Rifleman knew that if he failed to move the ball, he would have to turn it over—and then Stile would find some devious way to score. A touchdown and extra point would put Stile ahead in the closing minutes. But the Citizen was unable to advance the ball. What was he to do?

What *could* he do? He risked another pass to his double-covered android receiver. It was perfectly placed, threading between the defenders to reach its target. How that man could pass! But one defender managed to tip it, and the receiver did not catch it cleanly. The ball squirted out of his grasp, bounced on the ground, and one of Stile's animals, not realizing the ball was dead, fell on it.

It was obviously an incomplete pass. But the referee signaled a fumble. Now it was Stile's ball on the thirty-two-yard line.

"Now, wait," Stile protested. "That's a miscall. The receiver never had control of the ball."

"Aren't you aware that these referees are programmed to make at least one major miscall per game?" the Rifleman called to him. "That's to emulate the original style of play, back on crazy Earth. You happen to be the beneficiary of that error."

The referees were robots, of course; Stile hadn't noticed. They could be set at any level of competence. "But that's luck, not skill!"

"There's an element of luck in most games. That lends a special fascination. The human species loves to gamble. Play, before you draw another delay-of-game penalty." The Rifleman did not seem upset, perhaps because this change-of-possession was obviously no fault of his own.

Hastily, Stile played. He accepted the hiked ball, faded back for a pass, found his receivers covered, saw three huge animals bearing down on him, dodged them all, circled behind one and safely overthrew his covered receiver. The moment he released the ball, he hunched over as though still carrying it. The turning android saw that and grabbed him, not having seen the ball go.

The tackle was bruising despite the armor, but at least the padding protected him from more than superficial abrasion. A flag went down.

Roughing the passer. Fifteen-yard penalty. First down. Once again Stile was within field goal range.

He drop-kicked again, of course. The audience cheered. The stadium was almost full now; news of this game was evidently spreading. But he had to keep his attention on the field. Now he had twelve points, and six minutes to go. Maybe he could pull it out after all.

But the Rifleman had the ball again, and now he was determined. There were not going to be any more breaks or mistakes.

Stile's misgivings were well taken. The Rifleman shot his passes too high and fast for Stile to intercept, settling for swift, short gains. When Stile tried too hard he got tagged for interference. Slowly and erratically, but inevitably, the Citizen hammered out the yardage.

On Stile's thirty-yard line, the Rifleman's first pass attempt failed. On second down his run got nowhere. On third down Stile gambled on a blitz, sending eight of his animals in to overrun the quarterback before he could pass. It worked; the Rifleman was sacked. Loss of six yards.

Now it was fourth down, and the Rifleman had to kick out. He tried a placekick and field goal, but was too far out; the ball fell short, to Stile's immense relief.

Stile had the ball again, with four minutes remaining. Time enough—if he could move the ball.

He moved it. He had his animals open a hole in the center, and he slipped through for several yards. He had his passer send a screen pass to him, and he dodged and raced up the sideline for several more yards. He was wise to the ways of the androids, now; he knew their little individual foibles. Some were faster than others; some were less stupid. One android did not have the wit to out-maneuver another, but Stile did. He could get past them— so long as he did it himself, not delegating the job to an animal of his own. So long as he carried the ball himself, he could progress; that was the key. That was why the Rifleman had succeeded so well in moving the ball at the outset, while Stile floundered. The Rifleman had drawn on his own abilities, not limited by those of the androids. Now Stile was doing it too—and had been doing it, every time he kicked. Now, so late in the game, understanding came. It really was a game of two, not of twenty-two.

But this was bruising. The constant exertion and battering were taking it out of him, and Stile could not maintain the drive. It stalled out on the Rifleman's forty-yard line. Too far for another field goal. Stile had to punt, regretfully.

He went for the coffin corner, angling the ball out of bounds at the four-yard line. That forced the Rifleman to play in his own end zone.

The Citizen was showing overt nervousness now. He did not like being backed up this way. He tried a pass, but it was wobbly and off-target, incomplete.

Now it was time to strike. Stile caught the arm of his center as the lines reformed. "Make a hole to spring me through," he said, and the creature nodded. The androids were slow thinkers, but they did orient somewhat on the needs of their supervisors. This one now understood what Stile wanted.

When the ball was hiked, the android shouldered into his opposite number, lifting him entirely off the ground. Stile scooted through, so low that his flexing knees hurt, and emerged directly in front of the Rifleman.

"Oh, no!" the Citizen exclaimed. Losing his poise, he tried to run from Stile instead of throwing the ball away. It was a mistake; he moved right into a pocket of White linemen and was downed in his own end zone.

It was a safety: two points. The score was now 15-14, with two minutes left to play. And Stile's team would get the ball.

It was put into play by a free kick from the Rifleman's twenty-yard line. The kicker, under no pressure from the opposing line, got off a booming spiral that lofted high and far. One of Stile's receivers took it on his thirty-yard line and ran it all of two yards before getting buried.

Now Stile was highly conscious of the clock. He dared not give up the ball again, for the Rifleman would surely consume the remaining time in a slow drive and win by a single point. But how could Stile move it down to field goal range against the desperation defense he knew he would encounter?

Answer: he had to do it himself. He would get battered, but it was the only way.

"Run interference for me," he told his three most competent animals. "You two in front, you behind. Right end run. You two receivers go out for a fake pass. And you, you runner—you fake a run to the left." He was pulling out all the stops. If the Rifleman anticipated his strategy, he would swamp Stile with a blitz. It had to be risked.

But the Citizen, too, was tiring. He was in fit condition —but Stile was not merely fit, he was an excellent athlete in peak condition, strongly motivated. His toughness and endurance were counting more heavily now. The Citizen stayed well back, avoiding physical contact whenever possible. In effect, he had dropped off his team. That meant that not only did Stile have eleven effective players to ten, but he had the most animated team. Now he could put together a sustained drive—theoretically.

His animals blocked and Stile ran around the end. And —it worked. He made several yards before his escort fell in assorted tangles. Now a huge Black android pounced on him for the kill—and Stile cut in under the brute and threw him with a solid shoulder boost. It was partly the disparity of size that enabled Stile to come in low, and partly surprise that put him in close instead of where the android expected him. The creature went tumbling across Stile's back and rolled to the turf.

Suddenly Stile was in the relative clear, and still on his feet. He accelerated forward, drawing on his reserves of energy, determined to make the most of his opportunity. Dimly he heard the roar of the crowd, excited by the dramatic run. The stadium had been constantly filling, and now more than half the seats were filled—and it was a fair-sized chamber, sufficient for perhaps a thousand. Stile knew these spectators didn't care who won the Game; they merely responded to unfolding drama. Still, their applause encouraged him. His bruises and fatigue seemed to fade, and he shot ahead at full speed. Five yards, ten, fifteen, twenty—

In the end it was the Rifleman who caught him. The man was not to be tricked by a martial arts throw; after all, he was a former Tourney winner who had to be conversant with all forms of physical combat. He caught Stile by one arm and swung him around and down. He tried to wrest the ball away, but Stile was on guard against that, and plowed into the turf without giving it up.

He was now on the Rifleman's forty-five-yard line with a first down. His ploy had paid off handsomely.

On the next play Stile tried a short pass, from android to android. While he himself faked another run. This was not as spectacularly successful as his last play, but it was good for eight more yards. Most of the attention had been on Stile's fake, and the Rifleman's pass defense had loosened up.

Then a quarterback sneak, good for three more yards, and a first down on the thirty-four-yard line. He was getting near field goal range—but now he had only thirty seconds remaining. With no time-outs, he had no time to spare for fancy planning. "Give me the ball," he said. "Protect me."

But this time he got nowhere; his strategy had been too vague. Fifteen seconds remaining. Time for one final desperation measure. "Take a lateral," he told his primary pass receiver. "Step clear and lateral back to me."

Stile took the hiked ball, stepped back, lateraled to his receiver, and shrugged at the onrushing tacklers as they struggled to avoid him. The Rifleman didn't want any game penalties stopping the clock at this point!

The android lateraled back. Stile stood alone, having been forgotten by the tacklers. As the pileup formed about the pass receiver, Stile dodged forward, passing confused androids of both teams who somehow thought the play had ended, and were slow to reorient. He cut to the left, getting clear of the central glut, then forward again. He had made it to field goal range!

Then he heard the final gun. He had used up all his time in the course of his maneuvering, and now the game was over. There would be no more plays, no chance to dropkick the winning field goal.

Stile slowed to a walk, disconsolate. So close—only to

fail. To reach the fifteen-yard line in the clear, and have to quit, defeated by a single point.

Then, from the front tier of seats, he heard Sheen's voice. "Run, you idiot!" And he saw the animals of both teams converging on him.

Suddenly he realized that the game was not quite over. The play was still in session. Until he was tackled, it was not finished.

But the Rifleman, more alert to the situation than Stile had been, was now between him and the goal line. The Citizen was calling directions to his troops. Stile knew he could not make it all the way.

He began running across the field, toward the center, where more of his own animals were. "Protect me!" he bawled.

Dully, they responded. They started blocking off the pursuit. Stile cut back toward the goal, making it to the ten-yard line, the five—

A Black android crashed through the interference and caught Stile from behind. Stile whomped down in a forward fall, and the ball squirted from his grasp. A fumble at the worst possible time!

The androids knew what to do with a loose ball. Animals of both teams bellyflopped to cover it. In a moment the grandest pileup of the game developed. The whistle blew, ending the play and the game.

The delirious cheering of the crowd abruptly stilled. Obviously the ball had been recovered—but where, and by whom? It was impossible to tell.

Slowly, under the supervision of the referees, the androids were unpiled. The bottom one wore a White suit, and lay just within the end zone.

Stile had six more points.

Now the crowd went absolutely crazy. Serfs and Citizens alike charged onto the field. "Let's get out of here before we're both trampled to death!" the Rifleman exclaimed, heading for the exit tunnel.

"Yes, sir!" Stile agreed.

"By the way—congratulations. It was an excellent Game."

"Thank you, sir."

They drew up inside the tunnel. Here they were safe; the crowd was attacking the goal posts in some kind of insane tradition that went back before Planet Proton had been colonized. "I have not forgotten our private wager," the Rifleman said. "You played fair and tough and made a remarkable game of it, and you prevailed. I shall be in touch with you at another time."

"Thank you, sir," Stile said, unable to think of anything better.

"Now let's get out of these uniforms."

"Yes, sir."

Then Sheen was trotting toward them, her breasts bouncing handsomely. She was ready to assume control of Stile's remaining time in this frame. It would be several days before all of the Round One matches cleared, since there were 512 of them. But Stile would not be able to linger long in Proton-frame; he had to get back to Phaze and find out how to handle the Unicorn Herd Stallion in combat. Otherwise his tenure in Phaze could become even shorter than his tenure in Proton.

But Sheen was aware of all this. She took him in tow, stripping him of his armor in literal and figurative fashion. Stile was able to tune out the contemporaneous proceedings. How good it was to have a friend like Sheen here, and one like Neysa there!

CHAPTER 4

The Little People

Stile stepped through the curtain into the deep and pleasant forest of Phaze. He recovered his clothing, dressed, then hummed up an ambience of magic. He could signal Neysa with a spell, and she would come for him.

Then it occurred to him that this would consume time that would be better spent otherwise. Why not experiment, and discover whether he could indeed transport himself? He pondered a moment, finding himself quite nervous, then singsonged a spell: "Transport this man to the Blue Castle's span." It was not good verse, but that didn't matter; abruptly he stood in the castle court.

He felt dizzy and nauseous. Either he had done an inexpert job, or transporting himself was not good procedure. Certainly he would not try that again in a hurry; it had gotten him here, but at the expense of his feeling of equilibrium and well-being.

Neysa was in the court, nibbling on the magic patch of bluegrass. Every bite she took was immediately restored, so there was no danger of overgrazing, despite the smallness of the patch. She looked up the moment he appeared, her ears swiveling alertly. Then she bounded across to join him.

"Careful! Thou wilt spear me!" he protested, grabbing her about the neck and hanging on to steady himself.

She snorted. She had perfect control of her horn, and would never skewer something she didn't mean to, or miss something she aimed for. She blew a questioning note.

"Nice of thee to inquire," Stile said, ruffling her sleek black mane with his fingers. He was feeling better already; there was a healing ambience about unicorns. "But it's nothing. Next time I'll have thee carry me; thou dost a better job."

The unicorn made another note of query.

"Oh, that," he replied. "Sheen took care of me and got me to the Game on time. I had to match with a Citizen, a former Tourney winner. He nearly finished me."

She blew a sour note.

"No, he was a top Gamesman," Stile assured her. "A player of my caliber. It was like doing battle in this frame with another Adept! But I had a couple of lucky breaks, and managed to win in the last moment. Now he's going to help me find out who, there, is trying to wipe me out." He tapped his own knee, meaningfully. "And of course once we settle with the Herd Stallion, we'll set out to discover who killed me here in Phaze. I don't like having anonymous enemies." His expression hardened. "Nay, I like that not at all!"

The Lady Blue appeared. She wore a bathing suit, and was as always so lovely it hurt him. It was not that she was of full figure, for actually she was less so than Sheen, but that somehow she was exquisitely integrated, esthetically, in face and form and manner. The term "Lady" described her exactly, and she carried its ambience with her regardless what she wore. "Welcome back, my lord," she murmured.

"Thank thee, Lady." He had been absent only a day, but the shift of frame was so drastic that it seemed much longer.

"Thy friend Hulk has returned."

"Excellent," Stile said. He was somewhat stiff from the bruising football game, but glad to be back here and quite ready to receive the Oracle's advice.

"Thou'rt weary," the Lady said. "Let me lay my hands on thee."

"Not necessary," Stile demurred. But she stopped him and ran her soft hands across his arms and around his neck, and where they touched, his remaining discomfort faded. She kneaded the tight muscles of his shoulders, and they loosened; she pressed his chest, and his breathing eased; she stroked his hair and the subconscious headache became nonexistent. The Lady Blue was no Adept, but she did possess subtle and potent healing magic, and the contact of her fingers was bliss to him. He did not want to love her, yet, for that would be foolhardy; but only iron discipline kept him from sliding into that emotion at a time like this. Her touch was love.

"I would that my touch could bring the joy to thee that thy touch does to me," Stile murmured.

She stopped immediately. It was a silent rebuke that he felt keenly. She wanted no closeness with him. Not while she mourned her husband. Perhaps not ever. Stile could not blame her.

They moved on into the castle-proper. The Lady preceded him to the bath, where Hulk soaked in a huge tile tub set flush with the floor, like that of a Proton Hammam. The huge man saw the Lady, nodded, then in an afterthought sought ineffectively to cover himself. "I keep forgetting this is not Proton," he muttered sheepishly. "Men don't go naked in mixed company here."

"Thou'rt clothed in water," the Lady reassured him. "We be not overly concerned with dress, here. My present suit differs not much from nudity." She touched the blue material momentarily. "I have myself stood naked before a crowd and thought little of it. The animals wear no clothing in their natural forms, and oft not in their human shapes. Even so, I would not have intruded, but that my lord is here and needs must be informed immediately."

"That's right!" Hulk agreed. "Do thou step outside a moment, Lady, and I'll get right out of this."

"No need," Stile said. "I am here." He had been behind Hulk, whose attention had been distracted by the prior entry of the Lady.

"Oh. Okay. I have the Oracle's answer. But thou dost not have much time, Stile. May I talk to thee privately?"

"If the Lady is amenable," Stile agreed.

"And what is this, unfit for mine ears?" the Lady Blue demanded. "Well I know you two are not about to exchange male humor. Is there danger?"

Hulk looked guilty. He used his fingers to make a ripple in the bath water. "There may be, Lady."

The Lady looked at Stile, silently daring him to send her away. She called him "lord" and deferred to him in the presence of others, for the sake of appearances, but he had no private power over her.

"The Lady has suffered loss already," Stile said. "I am no fit replacement, yet if the Oracle indicates danger for me, she is rightfully concerned. She must not again be forced to run the Blue Demesnes without the powers of an Adept."

"If thou wishest," Hulk agreed dubiously. "The Oracle says that thou canst only defeat the Herd Stallion by obtaining the Platinum Flute."

"The Platinum Flute?" Stile repeated, perplexed.

"I never heard of it either," Hulk said, making further idle ripples with his hand. The ripples traveled to the edges of the tub, then bounced back to cross through the new ripples being generated. Stile wondered passingly whether the curtain that separated the frames of science and magic was in any way a similar phenomenon. "But there was another querist there, a vampire—"

"The likes of us have naught to do with the likes of them!" the Lady Blue protested.

"Or with the unicorns or werewolves?" Stile asked her, smiling wryly.

She was silent, unmollified. Certainly her husband had not had much association with such creatures. The free presence of unicorns and werewolves in the Blue Demesnes dated from Stile's ascendance. He felt this was an improvement, but the Lady was evidently more conservative.

"Actually, he was not a bad sort at all," Hulk said. "I lost my way, going in, and he flew by in bat-form, saw I was in trouble, and changed to man-form and offered to help. He hadn't realized I was human; he thought I was a small giant or an ogre, and those pseudomen sort of look out for each other. I think he was rather intrigued by my motorcycle, too; not many contraptions like that in Phaze! I was afraid I was in for the fight of my life, when I realized what kind of creature he was, but he told me they only take the blood of animals, which they normally raise for the purpose and treat well. In war, they suck the blood of enemies, but that's a special situation. They never bother friends. He laughed and said it wasn't true that people bitten by vampires become vampires themselves; that's a foul myth propagated by envious creatures. Maybe that story originated from a misinterpretation of their love-rites, when a male and a female vampire share each other's blood. The way he told it, it almost sounded good. A fundamental act of giving and accepting. I guess if I loved a vampire lady, I'd let her suck—" He broke off abruptly, embarrassed. "I didn't say that well. What I mean is—"

Stile laughed, and even the Lady smiled briefly. "There is no shame in love, any form," Stile said.

"Uh, sure," Hulk agreed. "I got to talking with him, and the more I knew him, the better I liked him. He drew me a map in the dirt so I could locate the Oracle's palace without getting in trouble. Then he changed back to a bat and flew off. And you know, that route he pointed out for me was a good one; I made it to the Oracle in a couple more hours, when it could've been days the way I had been going."

Hulk made another wave on the water, one that swamped the pattern of wavelets. "I'm finding it harder not to believe in magic. I saw that man change, I saw him fly. He was there when I arrived, and showed me that room where the Oracle was—just a tube sticking out of the wall. I felt sort of silly, but I went ahead and asked 'How can Stile defeat—' I forgot to use thy Phaze title, but it was too late, and it didn't seem to matter to the Oracle—'How can Stile defeat the unicorn Herd Stallion in fair combat at the Unolympics?' And it replied 'Borrow the Platinum Flute.' I couldn't understand that, and asked for a clarification, but the tube was dead."

"The Oracle has no patience with fools," the Lady said. "It answers only once, and considers all men fools; no offense to thee, ogre."

Hulk smiled. It seemed he had been nicknamed after the monster he most resembled, and he did not mind. "So I discovered. But I feared I had failed thee, Stile."

"I was as baffled when it told me to 'Know Thyself,'" Stile said. "My friend Kurrelgyre the werewolf was told to 'Cultivate Blue' and could not understand that either. We all have trouble with Oracular answers, but they always make sense in the end."

"Not always desired sense," the Lady Blue agreed. "When it told me 'None by One,' I thought it spouted nonsense. But now I know to my grief what—" She turned away, but Stile had glimpsed the agony that transfixed her face before she hid it. He had not realized that she had ever been to the Oracle. That answer must have related to the death of her husband.

Hulk filled in the awkward pause. "I talked again with Vodlevile Vampire—that's his name—and we compared notes. It seemed he had asked the Oracle how to help his son, who was allergic to blood—that's no joke to a vampire—"

"I should think not!" Stile exclaimed.

Hulk was quite serious. "They don't live on blood all the time. But they need it to be able to change to their bat-form and fly. The blood facilitates the magic. So his boy couldn't keep up with the family, if—well, I guess I'd be concerned too, in that situation."

"Of course," Stile agreed, sorry that he had even considered any humorous side to this.

"But all the Oracle told him was 'Finesse Yellow.' That made him furious, because he said Yellow is an Adept, and vampires don't deal with Adepts. They live near one, and they're afraid of her and leave her strictly alone. But if they did have truck with Adepts, they wouldn't try to cheat them or anyone else, and Yellow was the very worst one anyway. Several of their number have been trapped by her and sold to other Adepts, who spell them into blind loyalty and use them for spying and for terrorizing other captives. Gives the whole tribe a bad name. So he was going home without an answer he could use. I couldn't help him; I don't know anything about Adepts. It was too bad."

"He sounds like a creature of character," Stile said. "Why should the Oracle suggest to such a creature that he cheat? That's the same as no answer."

"Finesse is not the same as cheat," the Lady pointed out. "It implies some artifice or devious mechanism, not dishonesty."

"Vodlevile is a very forthright person," Hulk said. "No tricks in him. Still, he helped me. He told me that most of the metal tools and weapons and musical instruments of Phaze are made by the Little People, the tribes of Dark Elves, and that some worked with bone, and some with wood, and some with silver, or with gold, or with platinum. So probably if thou canst find the right tribe of elves—"

"The Little Folk are not easy to find," the Lady Blue said. "They dwell mainly in the Purple Mountains, and they dislike normal men and deal with them seldom. Most of all they detest Adepts. When my lord desired an excellent musical instrument, he could not go to them, but had to trade with a hawkman who had a connection across the curtain. He said he would like to be in touch with the Little Folk, but that they wanted naught he had to offer."

"So Vodlevile informed me," Hulk said. "That's what I meant about danger. It seems that the more precious the metal a tribe works with, the less use that tribe has for men, because men try to steal the artifacts. Especially they hate big men. I'd be dead the moment I set foot in their territory. And the Blue Adept—" He shook his head. "So my Oracle answer isn't much use either. But I report it to thee, for what it's worth, and hope this doesn't cause mischief."

Stile was already deep in thought. "The advice of the Oracle is always practical, if obscure. One has to work to understand it, usually. But it surely makes sense—for both me and the vampire. And him I may be able to help, in return for his help to thee."

"I had hoped thou wouldst see it that way," Hulk admitted. "It really is thy mission he tried to facilitate."

"I like this not," the Lady said. "Thou meanest to go among the Little Folk."

"Perhaps," Stile agreed. "That's the mischief Hulk feared, knowing mine inclination. But first I must tackle the matter nearer at hand. It will take me a moment to devise a suitable spell. Let's meet in the courtyard in ten minutes."

"No spell will take thee safely to the fastness of the Little Folk," she protested. "Like the unicorns, they resist magic. Better thou goest among trolls or goblins; there at least thou wouldst have a fair chance."

"I had in mind summoning the Yellow Adept."

"The Yellow Adept!" she cried, horrified. "In these Demesnes?"

"I swore never to return to her Demesnes, so must needs she visit mine. Thus do I finesse the restriction. Come on—we have to give Hulk a chance to get dressed." Stile led the way out. The Lady was spluttering, but offered no further resistance.

They met in due course in the courtyard. The Lady had evidently communicated the situation to the unicorn, for Neysa was moving her horn about angrily and snorting just beneath the level of meaning.

Stile played his harmonica to bring the magic ambience. Then he intoned: "Yellow Adept, I ask of thee, come to the Blue Demesnes, to me."

Abruptly the yellow hag was there before them. "Blue, methought we were at quits!" she snapped. "Seekest thou war between Adepts?"

"By no means, Yellow. I only wish to bargain with thee, to mutual advantage, and may not invade thy Demesnes again."

Her somewhat beady eyes peered about. "There is that, my handsome. Thou'rt a man of thy literal word. But I am not garbed for socializing. Give me leave to freshen up first." And she felt about her baggy old dress, searching for a potion.

"Allow me, since thou'rt my guest." Stile played a bar of music, then intoned: "While Yellow visits Castle Blue, grant her youth, image and hue."

In place of the old crone stood a ravishingly beautiful young woman with an hourglass configuration and long golden-yellow tresses, wearing a marvelously fetching evening gown. Hulk's jaw fell, and the Lady Blue's eyes widened. Neysa merely snorted disparagingly; she had seen it before.

Lovely Yellow brought out a vial, shook out a drop, and caught it as it formed into a mirror. "Oh, thou shouldst not, thou darling man! Yes, thou hast recaptured it perfectly, my delicious!"

"Yet she remains a witch," the Lady Blue said tightly. Neysa snorted agreement.

Yellow shot a glance at them. "Witch, thou sayst? And aren't we all, regardless of our shapes or magic? What chance does any man have, against a vamp of whatever color?"

"None," Hulk muttered. Neysa made as if to stab him with her horn, and he hopped out of the way.

"What I wish is this," Stile said briskly. "There is a vampire man, Vodlevile, whose son is allergic to blood. The Oracle told him to finesse Yellow. He refuses to deal—"

"Aye, I have a potion to cure that malady," Yellow agreed. "But what does he offer in return?"

"Nothing," Stile said. "The vampire folk are wary of thee, for what reason I do not pretend to comprehend."

She waggled a pretty finger at him warningly, in much the way the Rifleman had in Proton. "Play not the innocent with me, pretty man! I have back orders for bats galore. Though I daresay their fear of female Adepts derives somewhat from propinquity, since they reside near one the canines would term 'woman.' "

Hulk stifled a chuckle. Insults were very much a matter of viewpoint, here.

"Vodlevile will not deal with thee," Stile said evenly. "But I will. If thou wouldst trade favors with me, as one professional to another, this is the favor I crave."

"What has the bat done lately for thee?"

"He helped my friend Hulk, who was on a mission for me. Never did the bat ask for mine assistance, nor does he know it is coming."

She shook her head. "The machinations of honor and friendship are a fascination to the likes of me! Thy generosity to animals will cost thee yet, Blue." She glanced at Neysa, whose ears angled quickly back. "Yet 'tis a true finesse that does appeal to me. My livelihood is in dealing and wheeling, and I will deal with thee. The bat shall have his potion."

"I thank thee, witch. And what favor dost thou crave in return?"

She considered prettily. "I could wish that thou wouldst come to see me, as once I thought thou wouldst—" Her eyes traveled to the Lady Blue, who gazed disdainfully away, and back again to Neysa, whose nostrils were beginning to steam. "Yet thine oath forbids, and if it did not, I think others would say nay, or neigh."

Now a small jet of fire shot from Neysa's nostril, and the tip of her horn made a tiny motion suggestive of mayhem. "Even so," Stile agreed, straight-faced. He despised Yellow's business of trapping and selling live animals, but he rather respected her personally. A romantic alliance was certainly out of the question, as well she knew; Yellow was only teasing the competition. Such lighthearted malice was no doubt more of a pleasure for the men to note, than to the females against whom it was directed.

"Then methinks I will take it on the cuff," Yellow decided. "Some day, when I am in some minor way in need and call on thee for aid—"

"Agreed," Stile said. "Provided only that the service violates no ethic of mine, and I am then alive."

"There is that. Thou hast a veritable stormcloud of a

future." She pondered again. "Then let me protect mine
investment, and give thee a potion." She fished a tiny bottle
out of her bodice and presented it.

Stile accepted it, disregarding Neysa's fiery snort. "If I
may ask—"

"No secret, my scrumptious. This elixir renders the
wearer less noxious to the Elven folk."

"Thou vixen!" Stile exclaimed. "Thou conniving wench!
Thou wert aware of my mission all the time!"

"Even so, on all counts," she said. "Though I prefer the
term 'foxy' to 'vixen.'" She vanished.

"Some company thou keepest!" Hulk remarked appreciatively. "She *is* foxy!"

"Or bitchy," the Lady Blue muttered as she and Neysa
walked stiffly away.

Stile smiled. "She's not a bad sort, considering that she
really *is* a hag and a witch. She really did look like that, a
century 'or so ago when she was young." He considered
briefly. "Hulk, I don't have much time for the probable
magnitude of this mission, so I'll set off for the Purple
Mountains this afternoon, as soon as I do some spot research to pinpoint the platinum-working elves."

"I'll go with thee!"

"Nay, friend! Thy appearance would only antagonize
these folk, and I go not to quarrel but to borrow. I need
thee to guard the Lady Blue, as thou hast done so ably
before."

Hulk frowned. "I prefer not to do that, Stile."

Stile was perplexed. "Thou likest it not here? I would not
hold thee—"

"I like it well here. That is the problem."

"Something tells me I am being opaque about something."

"Aye."

"Thou dost not get along with the Lady Blue?"

"The Lady is a wonderful person."

"Then I don't see—"

"Thou needest an Oracle?"

Stile shook his head. "I must."

The big man paced the courtyard. "Thou and I strike
others as quite different. The giant and the dwarf. Yet we

are similar. The same age, the same culture, similar Game skills, similar honor." He paused. "Similar taste in women."

Stile began to get the drift. "Thou didst like Sheen at the first sight of her, and thou dost get along great with Neysa—"

"Yes. But for their special natures—" Hulk shrugged. "The Lady Blue is another matter. It befits me not to guard her any more."

Now Stile began pacing. "Thou knowest she is not mine."

"She sure as hell isn't mine!" Hulk exploded. "She may not be thine now, but she is destined for thee and no other. Thou'rt the Blue Adept, the keeper of these Demesnes, and she is the Lady Blue. She is the finest woman I have known. Were there another like her—"

"There *is* another like her," Stile said, remembering Sheen's comment. "And I owe thee for the manner in which thou hast given up thine only Oracle answer to my need."

The two men exchanged glances, a remarkable notion dawning. "Another—in Proton," Hulk said. "Of course. Her alternate self. But that one too should be—"

"Nay. Not mine. I can not love two."

"With all the qualities I have seen, but versed in Proton culture." Hulk smiled, liking the notion. "Then thou wouldst not oppose—?"

"That Proton-lady sure as hell is not mine," Stile said, smiling as he echoed Hulk's expression. "Go to Proton. It is a different frame. Thou knowest thou canst never bring her here."

"Yet even for brief visits—it is all I could ask."

"Cross the curtain, talk to Sheen. Her friends will locate the lady for thee."

Hulk nodded. He stopped before Stile and put forth his hand. Stile shook it gravely, knowing this was their parting. Hulk would not come to the Blue Demesnes again. Stile felt a certain smouldering resentment that the big man had taken an interest in this particular woman, and a certain relief that there was in this case a solution, and a certain guilt for both the resentment and the relief. Hulk was a good man; he deserved the best, and the best was the Lady

Blue. Her Proton alternate surely had similar qualities. So this was a triumph of fortune and common sense—yet it bothered him. He was simply not as generous in his private heart as he was externally. He had some growing to do, yet.

Now he had no guard for the Lady Blue. He could not leave her alone for any length of time; whatever enemy had struck down Stile's alternate self, the true Blue Adept, would surely strike again now that it was known the Blue Adept had been reconstituted. Stile had been constantly devising and rehearsing spells and strategies to deal with such an attack, and felt reasonably confident he could handle the situation. But suppose the enemy took the Lady Blue hostage and used her against Stile? He could not risk that.

While he pondered, the Lady reappeared. "The ogre prepares to depart. Know ye why?"

"I know," Stile said.

"I like this not."

How did she feel about this arrangement? "He is a good man, worthy of the likes of thee, as I am not."

If she grasped his hidden meaning, she gave no sign. "Worth is not the issue. I have a premonition of doom about him."

"I confess to being uneasy. I thought it was jealousy or guilt."

"Those, too," she agreed, and then he was sure she understood. But she did not elaborate.

He changed the subject. "Now I fear to leave thee here alone—yet must I seek the Flute, lest mine enemy move against me. Neysa will go with me."

"Is it security thou seekest—or vengeance?"

Stile grimaced, looking at her. "How is it thou knowest me so well?"

"Thou'rt very like my love."

"Would he not have sought vengeance?"

"For himself, nay. For those he held dear—" She halted, and he suspected she was remembering her vision of the fiery destruction of the trolls who had wiped out the Blue Adept's village. Then she met his gaze again. "Without

Hulk or Neysa, the Blue Demesnes be not safe for me now. I must go with thee to the Purple Mountains."

"Lady, it may be dangerous!"

"More dangerous with thee and thy magic than without thee?" she inquired archly. "Have I misjudged thee after all?"

Stile looked askance at her. "I had thought thou dost not crave my company. For the sake of the good work done by the Blue Adept thou callest me lord, but in private we know it is not so. I do not mean to impose my presence on thee more than necessary."

"And with that understanding, may not the Lady accompany the Lord?"

Stile sighed. He had made due protest against a prospect that in fact delighted him as much as it made him nervous and guilty. "Of course she may."

The Lady rode a pale blue mare, the offspring of the foal of the Hinny and the Blue Stallion. As she had described, this mare's color was mainly an echo of the blue harness, but the effect was there. The Blue Stallion had been alive but aging when the Blue Adept was killed; the horse, it was understood, had died of grief.

Stile rode Neysa. He had never ridden another steed since taming her. No horse could match her performance, but it was more than that. Much more.

They crossed the fields south of the Blue Castle and entered the forest adjacent to the Purple Mountain range. Soon they were in the foothills. According to Stile's references, the geographical tomes collected by his other self, the tribe of the Dark Elves who worked platinum lived on a mountain about fifty miles east of where the convenient curtain-access to Proton was. The animals knew the way, once it had been determined; Neysa had ranged these lands for years and knew the location by description, though she was not conversant with the actual Elven Demesnes.

Here the lay of the land was gentle, and the air balmy, with patchwork clouds making the sunshine intermittent. The ride became tedious despite the pleasure of the surroundings. Had Stile been riding alone, he would have slept, trusting Neysa to carry him safely, or have played his harmonica, or simply have talked to the unicorn. But the presence of the Lady Blue in her natural splendor inhibited him.

"It was across this country I rode the Hinny, so long it seems ago," she remarked.

Stile found no appropriate response. He rode on in silence, wishing that the tragedy of his other self did not lie between them.

"The Hinny," she repeated musingly. "How I miss that fine animal!"

This was safer ground. "How is she now? Ten years is a fair span in the life of a horse, about thirty of ours, but not interminable."

"Of course thou knowest not," the Lady said somberly. "The Hinny was bred by the Blue Stallion, and returned to her wilderness fastness alone. The blue lad went back to his business, about which we inquired not, but which I believe was the meticulous construction of the Blue Castle. I remained with my family and with Snowflake, the white foal we had rescued. Sometimes out in the fields we thought we glimpsed the Hinny, and our hearts yearned toward her, but never came she nigh. Yet I was ill at ease. The revealed identity of my erstwhile companion the blue lad astounded me, and I was shamed. Yet I was intrigued too, and potently flattered by his suit. I remembered the vision I had had while he played his music, the Lady in the blue moon, and the subtle appeal of that notion grew. Later I learned that he had gone to inquire the identity of his ideal wife, and the Oracle had named me. It had for once been not obscure or circuitous or capable of alternate interpretation; it had told him exactly where and when to find me. Hence he had come at the designated moment, extremely fortuitous for me as I hung dangling in the clutch of the troll, and preserved my life when else it would have ended there. He had done all that he had done only to win my favor, though I was his by right from the moment he rescued me. And I only an ignorant peasant-girl!"

"The Oracle knew better," Stile murmured. "Thy Lord's legacy lives on in thee, when else it would have perished."

She continued as if she had not heard him. "Ah, what a

foolish girl was I in that time. Long and long was it before ever I gave him the third Thee."

"I beg thy pardon, Lady. I don't follow—"

She gestured negligently with one hand. "Of course thou art from another culture, so I needs must inform thee. In Phaze, when a person loves another and wishes to have it known without obligation, she omits the statement and repeats only the object, Thee, three times. Then that other may do as he wishes, without reproach."

"I don't understand," Stile said. "Just to say to a person 'Thee, th—' "

Neysa nearly bucked him off as she drowned him out with a blast from her horn.

"Say it not carelessly nor in jest," the Lady reproached him. "It has the force of an oath."

Shaken, Stile apologized. "I have much to learn yet of this culture. I thank thee, Lady, for educating me, and thee, Neysa, for preventing me from compromising myself ignorantly." But it would not have been a lie if he had said it to the Lady; this was a battle all but lost at the outset. Still, it would have put her in an awkward situation.

"When next I saw the Hinny," the Lady continued blithely, "she was in sad state. Gravid, she had been beset by cowardly predators, jackals, and was nigh unto death. She limped to our gate, remembering me, and I screamed and roused my father. Never did I see him so angry, for the Hinny had been his admiration since the instant he saw her first. He took his cudgel and beat off all the curs that harried her, while I tried to help her. But all was for naught; she had lost much blood, and expended her last store of vitality reaching us, and the Hinny died at our door.

"Then did I remember the spell the blue lad had left me. 'Blue to me—I summon thee!' I cried. And he was there. When he saw the Hinny he gave a great cry of agony and fell upon her, taking her head in his arms, and the tears flowed down his face. But she was dead, her open eyes seeing naught, and all his magic availed not.

"The lad brought out his harmonica and played a tune, wondrously sad, and two moons clouded over and the sun faded, and a shimmer formed in the air between us. It made a picture, and it showed the Hinny, as she had been in life, great with foal, grazing near the wood. Then a pack of jackals charged, a foul horde, surly ill-kempt curs of scant individual courage, like to wolves as goblins be to men, seeking to overrun their quarry by sheer mass. She leaped away, but the weight of the foal within her made her ponderous and somehow her front feet stumbled, causing her to fall and roll, and the brutes were on her in a motley pile, ripping at her flesh, tearing at her ears and tail. She struggled to her feet, but they hung on her like despicable leeches, and her precious blood was flowing. Gashed and weakening, she struggled out of that wood, the jackals constantly at her feet, leaping at her, trying to drag her down again, so that she left a trail of blood. So at last she came to me, and I saw myself scream and throw my hands to my head, reacting hysterically instead of helping her, and then my father came with his cudgel, and the magic vision faded.

"My father stood beside me, watching the sorrow of Blue, and indeed we shared it. Then did I comprehend the third of the great qualities about the Blue Adept that were to be the foundation of my love for him. His music, his power—and his abiding love for—" She hesitated momentarily. "For equines."

Stile realized she had been about to say "horses" and had reconsidered, from deference to Neysa.

"At last the blue lad rose, and it was as if the blood had been drained from him as it had from the Hinny. 'Because her knees were weak, the jackals caught her,' he said. 'The knees she sacrificed for me.' And I could not say nay, for I had seen it happen.

" 'Yet can I do somewhat,' he continued, and there was that in him that frightened me, and I began to get a glimmer of the meaning of the sorrow and anger of an Adept. 'Turn you both about, lest you see what pleases you not.' And my father, wiser than I, took mine arm and made me turn with him. There was a pause, then sweet, bitter music as the lad played his harmonica. Then the muttering of an incantation, and an explosion of heat and odor. We turned again—and the corpse of the Hinny was gone, blasted by Blue's magic, and in the swirling smoke the lad stood, holding in his arms a newborn foal, light blue in hue.

" 'The Hinny be dead, but her foal lives,' he said. 'This is why she came to thee.' Then before we could properly react, he addressed my father. 'This foal is birthed before her time. Only constant, expert care can save her. I am no healer; she requires more than magic. I beg thee, sir, to take her off my hands, rendering that which only thou canst give, that she may survive and be what she can be.'

"My father stood bemused, not instantly comprehending the request. 'The Hinny came to thee,' the lad continued, 'knowing thou couldst help her. More than all else, she wanted her foal to live and to be happy and secure. No right have I to ask this favor of thee, knowing it will be years before thou art free of this onus. Yet for the sake of the Hinny's faith—' And he stepped forward, holding forth the foal. And I knew my father was thinking of the Hinny, the finest mare of any species he had ever beheld, and of the Blue Stallion, the finest stud, and seeing in this foal a horse like none in Phaze—worth a fortune no man could measure. And I realized that in the guise of a request, the lad was proffering a gift of what was most dear to my father's dreams. It was Blue's way.

"My father took the foal in silence and bore her to our stable, for she needed immediate care. I remained facing the lad. And something heaved within my breast, not love but a kind of gratitude, and I knew that though he looked to be a lad and was in fact a nefarious magician, he was also a worthy man. And he inclined his head to me, and then he walked away toward the forest where the jackals had attacked the Hinny. And in a little while there was a brilliant burst of light there, and that whole forest was aflame, and I heard the jackals screaming as they burned. And I remembered how he had destroyed the trolls, and was appalled at this act of vengeance. Yet did I understand it also, for I too loved the Hinny, and who among us withholds our power when that which is dear to us is ravaged? The power of an Adept is a terrible thing, yet the emotion was the same as mine. No creature aggravates an Adept but at the peril of his kind. Yet when later I rode

Starshine out to that region, I found the forest alive and green. Only the charred skeletons of the jackals remained; none other had been hurt. I marveled again at the power of the Adept, as awesome in its discretion as in its ferocity.

"After that my father made no objection to Blue's suit, for it was as if he had exchanged me for the precious foal, and duly the banns were published and I married the Blue Adept though I did not really love him. And he was ever kind to me, and made for me the fine domicile now called the Blue Demesnes, and encouraged me to develop and practice my healing art on any creatures who stood in need, even trolls and snow demons, and what I was unable to heal he restored by a spell of his own. Some we healed were human, and some of these took positions at the castle, willingly serving as sentries and as menials though no contract bound them. But mainly it was the animals who came to us, and no creature ever was turned away, not even those known as monsters, so long as they wreaked no havoc. It was a picturebook marriage."

She abated her narrative. "I thank thee for telling me how it was," Stile said carefully.

"I have not told thee the half of how it was," she said with surprising vehemence. "I loved him not, not enough, and there was a geas upon our union. He knew both these things, yet he treated me ever with consummate respect and kindness. How I wronged him!"

This was a surprise. "Surely thou dost overstate the case! I can not imagine thee—"

But confession was upon her. Neysa made a little shake of her horn, advising him to be silent, and Stile obeyed. "The geas was inherent in his choice of me to wed. He had asked the Oracle for his ideal wife, but had failed to include in that definition the ideal mother of his children. Thus I learned when I queried the Oracle about the number and nature of my children-to-be. 'None by One,' it told me in part, and in time I understood. There was to be no child by my marriage to him; no heir to the Blue Demesnes. In that way I wronged him. And my love—" She shrugged. "I was indeed a fool. Still I thought of him as a lad, a grown child though I knew him for a man, and a creature of incalculable power. Perhaps it was that power

that straitened my heart against him. How could I truly
love one who could so readily destroy all who stood against
him? What would happen if ever he became wroth with
me? And he, aware of this doubt, forced me not, and
therefore had I guilt. So it was for years—"

She broke off, overcome by emotion. Stile remained silent. This was an aspect of her history that instilled misgiving, yet he knew it was best that he know it.

"Those wasted years!" she cried. "And now too late!"

They had come to rougher territory, as if the land itself
responded to the Lady's anguish of conscience. These were
the mere foothills to the Purple Mountains, Stile knew, yet
the ridges and gullies became steep and the trees gro-
tesquely gnarled. The turf was thick and springy; the steeds
were not partial to the footing. Stile found the landscape
beautiful, original, and somehow ominous—like the Lady
Blue.

"Can we skirt this region?" Stile asked Neysa.

The unicorn blew a note of negation. It seemed that this
was the only feasible route. Stile knew better than to challenge this; the unicorn could have winded a dragon or
some other natural hazard, and be threading her way safely
past. So they picked their path carefully through the
rugged serrations of the land, making slow progress toward
the major range.

The Lady's horse balked. She frowned and gently urged
it forward, but the mare circled instead to the side—and
balked again.

"This is odd," the Lady commented, forgetting her recent emotion. "What is bothering thee, Hinblue?"

Then the Lady's fair tresses lifted of their own accord,
though there was no wind.

Neysa made a double musical snort. *Magic!*

Stile brought out his harmonica. "Nay, play not," the
Lady said hastily. She did not want him to show his power
in the vicinity of the land of the Little Folk.

But her hair danced about and flung itself across her
eyes like a separately living thing, and her horse fidgeted
with increasing nervousness. Neysa's horn began to lower
to fighting range.

"Just a melody," Stile told her. "Neysa and I will play a little tune, just to calm thy steed." And to summon his magic—just in case.

They played an impromptu duet. Neysa's music was lovely, of course—but Stile's carried the magic. It coalesced like a forming storm, charging the immediate atmosphere.

And in that charge, dim figures began to appear: small, slender humanoids, with flowing hair and shining white robes. They had been invisible; now they were translucent, the color slowly coming as the music thickened the magic ambience. Stile's power was revealing them. One of them was hovering near the Lady, playing with her hair.

"The Sidhe," the Lady breathed, pronouncing it "Shee." "The Faerie-folk. They were teasing us."

Stile squeezed Neysa's sides with his knees questioningly. She perked her ears forward: a signal that there was no immediate danger.

Stile continued playing, and the ethereal figures solidified. "O, Sidhe," the Lady said. "Why do you interfere with us? We seek no quarrel with your kind."

Then a Faerie-man responded. "We merely played with thee for fun, Lady of the Human Folk, as we do so often with those who are unaware of our nature. Innocent mischief is the joy of our kind." His voice was winningly soft, with the merry tinkle of a mountain streamlet highlighting it. Stile could appreciate how readily such a voice could be mistaken for completely natural effects—flowing water, blowing breezes, rustling leaves.

"And thou," a Sidhe maid said to Stile as he played. "What call hast thou, of Elven kind, to ride with a mundane woman?" Her voice was as soft as the distant cooing of forest doves, seductively sweet, and her face and form were similarly winsome.

Stile put aside his harmonica. The Sidhe remained tangible; now that they had been exposed, they had no further need of invisibility. "I am a man," he said.

"A man—on a unicorn?" she inquired derisively. "Nay, thou art more likely a giant kobold, serving in the house of the human lady. Thou canst not fool her long, sirrah!

Come, I will offer thee entertainment fit for thy kind." And
she did a little skip in air that caused her white skirt to sail
up, displaying her immortal legs to advantage.

"Thou'rt not my kind," Stile insisted, intrigued.

"Dost thou jilt me already?" she flashed, and evanescent
sparks radiated from her hair. "I will have thy fanny in a
hoist, ingrate!"

Neysa shifted her horn to bear on the Faerie-lass, who
skipped nimbly aside. These magical creatures might not
fear the weapons of human beings, but the unicorn's horn
was itself magical, and would take its toll of any creature.

Stile lifted his harmonica to his mouth again.

"Yea, play!" the Sidhe lady exclaimed. "I will forgive
thee thine indiscretion if thou playest while we dance."

It was a face-saving maneuver on her part, but Stile
decided to go along. He did not want to have to use overt
magic here. He played, and Neysa accompanied him, and
the music was marvelously light and pretty. Stile had been
a fair musician before he came to Phaze, but he had improved substantially since.

The Sidhe flocked in and formed their formation in midair. They danced, wheeling in pairs, singing and clapping
their little hands. The males stood about four and a half
feet tall, with calloused hands and curly short beards; the
females were closer to four feet, and all were delicate of
limb and torso. They whirled and pranced, the girls flinging
their skirts out with delightful abandon, the men doing
elaborate dance steps. It was beautiful, and looked like an
extraordinary amount of fun.

After a time, the Sidhe damsel floated back down to
Stile. She perched on Neysa's horn, somewhat to the unicorn's annoyance. She was breathing briskly, her full
bodice flexing rhythmically. "Give o'er, giant elf; thou'rt
forgiven!" she exclaimed. "Now come dance with me, before sunset, while thy steed plays her horn." And she
reached out a hand to him, the tiny fingers beckoning.

Stile glanced at the Lady Blue, who nodded affirmatively.
Neysa shrugged. Both evidently felt it was better to go
along with the Faerie-folk than to oppose them. They were
getting along well at the moment; better not to disrupt the
mood, for such creatures could be unpleasant when an-

gered, and their tempers were volatile. Stile had seen that in the mercurial reactions of this little lady.

Yet he demurred, more diplomatically this time. "Elven lass, I can not dance in air without magic." And he was not about to reveal his true nature now. Already he understood that Adepts were held in as poor regard by the Little Folk as by ordinary human people.

"Then shall I join thee below," she said, descending lightly to the turf. Then, abruptly shy: "I am Thistlepuff."

Stile dismounted. "I am Stile." He stood almost a foot taller than she, and really did feel like a giant now. Was this the way Hulk saw the world?

"The bridge between pastures?" Thistlepuff exclaimed, correctly interpreting his name. Then she did a pirouette, again causing her skirt to rise and expose her fine and slender legs. This was a characteristic gesture with her. In the frame of Proton, where all serfs were naked, no such effect was possible, and Stile found it almost embarrassingly appealing. The brief glimpse seemed better than the constant view, because of the surprise and mystery. Clothing, he realized, was also magic.

Stile had played the Game in Proton for most of his life. Part of the Game was the column of the Arts, and part of the Naked Arts was Dance. He was an athlete and a gymnast, and he had a good memory and sense of pace. Hence Stile could dance as well as any man, and a good deal better than most. He had watched and analyzed the patterns of the Faerie dance, and now understood it well enough. If this sprite thought to make a fool of him for the entertainment of her peers, she would be disappointed.

He went into a whirl of his own, matching Thistlepuff's effort. There was a faint "Oooh" of surprise, and the other Faerie-folk gathered about to watch. Yes, they had thought to have sport with him!

The lass stepped blithely into his arms, and he swung her in Sidhe fashion. Her head topped at the level of his shoulder, and she was light as a puff of smoke, but she was also lithe and sweet to hold. She spun out and kicked one leg high in the manner of a ballerina—oh, didn't she love to show those legs!—while he steadied her by the other hand. Then she spun back into his embrace, making a little leap so that her face met his in a fleeting kiss that struck and dissipated like a breath of cool fog.

They moved into a small promenade, and he tossed her into the air for a graceful flip and caught her neatly at the waist. Light as she was, it was easy to do the motions, and he enjoyed it. He felt more and more like the giant he never had been, and privately he reveled in it.

When the demonstration was through, the Sidhe spectators applauded gleefully. "Thou hast danced before!" Thistlepuff exclaimed, her bosom heaving with even more abandon. "Yet thou dost claim to be human!"

"Human beings can dance," Stile said. "The Lady I serve could do as well." He hoped that was the case; it occurred to him as he spoke that though he had seen the Lady Blue ride marvelously well, he had never seen her dance. Yet of course she could do it!

Neysa blew a note of caution. But it was too late. Stile, in his inexperience with the Faerie-folk had made another blunder. Thistlepuff was frowning mischievously at the Lady Blue.

"So thou sayest?" the Sidhe inquired, as sharply as the sound of the wood of a tree-limb snapping under too great a burden of snow. "Thou art of the Elven kind, surely; but she is as surely mundane. We shall see how she can dance." And the Sidhe recentered their ring on the lady.

He had gotten her into this; he would have to get her out. Stile crossed to the Lady as she dismounted. He could not even apologize; that would betray the situation to the Faerie-folk. He had to bluff it through—and he hoped that she could and would go along.

The Lady Blue smiled enigmatically and took his proffered hand. Good; at least she accepted him as a partner. It would have been disaster with a mischievous four-and-a-half-foot-tall Sidhe male for a dancing partner! At least Stile would keep his feet mainly on the ground.

It would have to be impromptu free-form, for they had had no rehearsal. Stile hoped the Lady had analyzed the dancing patterns as he had. But he let her lead, so that she could show him what she wanted.

Suddenly they were in it. The Lady was taller than he and as heavy—but also as lithe and light on her feet as a woman could be. When he swung her, she was solid, not at all like Thistlepuff, yet she moved precisely. He did not try to toss her in air, but she was so well balanced he could hold her up readily, and whirl her freely. When he moved, she matched him; when he stepped, she stepped; when he leaped, she was with him. In fact, she was the best dancer he had encountered.

It was a fragment of heaven, being with her like this. For the moment he could almost believe she was his. When they danced apart, she was a marvel of motion and symmetry; when they danced together, she was absolute delight. Now he wished this dance could go on forever, keeping his dream alive.

But then Neysa brought her harmonica melody to a close, and the dance ended. The Sidhe applauded. "Aye, she can dance!" Thistlepuff agreed ruefully. "Mayhap she has some inkling of Faerie blood in her ancestry after all. Thou hast shamed us, and we must make amend. Come to our village this night."

"We dare not decline their hospitality," the Lady Blue murmured in his ear. She was glowing with her effort of the dance, and he wished he could embrace her and kiss her. But this was one blunder he knew better than to make.

Now the steep bank of a ridge opened in a door. There was light inside, and warmth. The passage into the hill was broad enough for the steeds, and these were of course welcome. They walked into the Faerie village.

Inside it was amazingly large. This was technically a cave, but it seemed more like a clearing in a deep wood at night, the walls invisible in their blackness. A cheery fire blazed in the center. Already a feast was being laid out: a keg of liqueur, many delicious-smelling breadstuffs, fresh vegetables, pots of roasted potatoes and buckets of milk and honey and dew. For the animals there was copious grain and fragrant hay and a sparkling stream.

Then Stile remembered something from his childhood readings. "If a human being partakes of Faerie food, is he not doomed to live among them forever? We have business elsewhere—"

Thistlepuff laughed with the sound of rain spattering

into a quiet pond. "Thou really art not of our kind, then!
How canst thou believe that myth? Thou hast it back-
wards: if ever one of the Sidhe forsakes his own and con-
sumes mundane food, he is doomed to become mortal.
That is the true tragedy."

Stile looked at Neysa, embarrassed. She blew a positive
note—no danger here. Thistlepuff had spoken the truth, or
close enough to it to eliminate his concern. So he had
blundered again, but not seriously; the Sidhe were amused.

Now they ate, and it was an excellent repast. After-
wards, pleasantly sated, they availed themselves of the
Faerie sanitary facilities, which were concealed in a thick
bed of toadstools, then accepted invisible hammocks in lieu
of beds. Stile was so comfortable that he fell almost instantly to sleep, and remained in blissful repose until a
beam of sunlight struck his face in the morning.

Startled, he looked about. He was lying in a bed of fern
in a niche in the gully. No cave, no invisible hammock, no
Faerie village! The Lady Blue was up before him; she
had already fetched fruit from some neighboring tree.
Neysa and Hinblue were grazing.

Stile was abashed. "Last night—what I remember—the
Sidhe—did I dream—?"

The Lady Blue presented him with a pomegranate. "Of
dancing with the Faerie-folk? Sharing their food? Consuming too much of their nefarious dew so that thou didst
sleep like a rock forever in their invisible hammock? It
must have been a dream, for I remember it not."

There was a musical, mirthful snort from Neysa.

"Even so," Stile agreed, concentrating on the fruit. Was
his face as red as its juice? The Sidhe had had some sport
with him after all. But how glad he was to note that the
Lady's heavy mood had lifted.

"Yet dost thou dance divinely in thy dreams." The Lady
was for a moment pensive, then reverted briskly to business. "If thou dost not get thy lazy bones aloft, never shall
we locate the Platinum Elves in time for thee to go divert
thyself at thy next otherframe game with thy mechanical
paramour."

Barbed wit, there! The Proton Tourney was no fun di-
version, but a matter of life or nonlife on that planet. Stile

rose with alacrity. "One more day, one more night—that's all the time I have until I have to report for Round Two of the Tourney."

Soon they were on their way again. It had been a good night; human and equine beings had extra vigor. Neysa and Hinblue stepped out briskly, hurdling the ridges and gullies and hummocks. Neysa, conscious of the equine limitations of the natural horse, did not push the pace too fast, but miles were traversed swiftly. The Lady Blue, of course, rode expertly. Stile might be the best rider in Phaze, but she was the second best.

After an hour Stile became aware of something fleeting. "Hold," he murmured. Neysa, feeling his bodily reaction, was already turning around.

"Is aught amiss?" the Lady Blue inquired, elevating an eyebrow prettily.

"The curtain," Stile said. "We just passed it. I need to note where it is, as a matter of future reference. There may be good places to cross it to Proton, if only I can locate them."

"There are times when I wish I could cross that curtain," she said wistfully. "But hardly can I even perceive it."

"Ah—here it is," Stile said. "Proceeding northeast/ southwest, angling up from the Purple Mountains. Of course it may curve about, in between reference points, but—"

The Lady waved a hand. "Cross it, my lord, and see where it leads. Only forget not to return, lest I abscond with thy steed."

Stile laughed, then spelled himself through.

The other side was hot and bleak. The ubiquitous cloud of pollution was thinner here, but the haze still shrouded a distant force-field dome. This was not a good place to cross; he needed a section within a dome, or very close to one. Ah, well—it had been worth checking. He released his held breath and willed himself back into Phaze as he stepped back across the faint scintillation.

It was a great relief to see the lush greenery form around him. What a mess the Citizens had made of the surface of their planet, in the name of progress! "I'm satisfied. Let's go."

"Yet if I could cross, it would mean there would be no one for Hulk," the Lady concluded.

By midmorning they had reached the fringe of the Platinum Demesnes; Elven warner-markers so informed them.

Now Stile uncorked the Yellow Adept's gift-potion and applied it liberally to his face and hands. He offered some to the Lady, but she demurred; she did not care to smell like an elf. Since she was obviously no threat to anyone, Stile trusted it would be all right.

The Platinum Demesnes were in the Purple Mountains proper. The access-pass was marked by a neat wooden sign: PT78. Stile smiled, recognizing the scientific symbol and atomic number of platinum; surely some crossover from the frame of Proton, here. Evidently these Little People had a sense of unity or of humor.

They rode up the narrow trail. The mountain slopes rose up steeply on either side, becoming almost vertical. It would be very easy for someone to roll boulders down; the stones would flatten anyone misfortunate enough to be in their way. Except an ogre or an Adept. Stile kept his hand on his harmonica and his mind on a boulder-repulsion spell he had devised. He did not want to use magic here, but he wanted even less to suffer death by stoning.

Then they encountered a hanging bridge. It crossed a deep, dark chasm too wide for Neysa to leap, but the bridge was too narrow and fragile to support equine weight. Neysa could change form and cross, but that would not help Hinblue. Stile considered casting a spell to transport the horse across, but vetoed it himself; the Platinum Elves could be watching. So—they would have to cross the hard way, by navigating the chasm manually. Perhaps this was a deliberate hurdle to test the nature of intruders, separating the natural from the supernatural—or, more likely, the Elven folk did not want mounted visitors charging into their Demesnes.

There was a precarious path down into the chasm, and another rising on the far side. Probably the two connected, below. Stile and the Lady started down, riding, because the steeds did not trust the people's ability to navigate such a pass safely alone. But Stile kept his hand on the harmonica.

The touch of that musical instrument reminded him—he was coming here for a flute. Yet how could a musical instrument avail him? What he really needed was a weapon. Well, he should soon be finding out!

Fortunately the path did not descend far. It reached a broad ledge that cut into the chasm, reducing it to a width that could be conveniently hurdled by the steeds. The path continued on down into the chasm, but they did not follow it. They jumped across the ugly crack and started up the other side. Stile was aware of a hot draft that came up erratically from the depths, smelling of sulfur. He did not like it.

They emerged at the top of that chasm, and continued on up the path. Now they were higher in the mountain range, nearing the top—and they rounded the crest, and the landscape leveled, and lo! it was only a larger foothill. Ahead the real mountains loomed, sloping up into the clouds. They were tall enough to maintain snow, but it was purple snow.

On this brief level spot was a mound, overgrown by turf and vines. The path led right to it; in fact there was a stone entranceway. "Methinks we have arrived," Stile murmured, dismounting.

"Methinks thou shalt not swiftly depart," a voice said behind him. Stile turned to find a small man in the path behind. He stood about four inches shorter than Stile, but was broader in proportion. His skin was an almost translucent blue, and his clothing was steel-gray.

"Thou must be of the Elven Folk," Stile said. "I come to beg a favor of the workers of platinum."

"We do work platinum," the elf agreed. "But we do no favors for outsiders. Thou art now our prisoner, and thy human companion." He gestured with his shining sword. "Now proceed into the mound, the two of you. Thine animals will join our herds outside."

Neysa turned on the arrogant elf, but Stile laid a cautioning hand on her back. "We came to petition; we must yield to them," he murmured. "If they treat us ill, thou canst then act as thou seest fit. An thou dost find me fettered, free me to play my music."

Neysa made an almost imperceptible nod with her horn. Once Stile had access to his music, he could bring his powers of magic into play, and would then be able to handle himself. So the risk was less than it seemed. He and the Lady suffered themselves to be herded into the mound.

Inside it was gloomy, with only wan light filtering in through refractive vents. Several other armed elves were there, garbed like the first. Their leader stepped up and appraised Stile and the Lady as if they were newly purchased animals. He sniffed as he approached Stile. "This one be Elven," he pronounced. "But the woman is human. Him we shall spare to labor at our forges; her we shall use as tribute to the beast."

"Is this the way thy kind welcomes those who come peaceably to deal with thee?" Stile asked. There was no way he would permit the Lady Blue to be abused.

"Silence, captive!" the elf cried, striking at Stile's face with a backhand swing of his arm.

The blow, of course, never landed. Stile ducked away from it and caught the elf's arm in a punishing submission hold. "I can not imagine the elders of thy kind being thus inhospitable," he said mildly. "I suggest that thou dost summon them now."

"No need," a new voice said. It was a frail, long-bearded old elf, whose face and hands were black and wrinkled. "Guards, begone! I will deal with this matter myself."

Stile let go his captive, and the young elves faded into the crevices and crannies of the chamber. The oldster faced Stile.

"I am Pyreforge, chief of the tribe of Platinum Mound Folk of the Dark Elves. I apologize for the inhospitability shown thee by our impetuous young. It is thy size they resent, for they take thee to be a giant of our kind."

"A giant!" Stile exclaimed, amused. "I'm four feet eleven inches tall!"

"And I am four feet five inches tall," Pyreforge said. "It is the odor of thy potion that deceives us, as well as thy size. To what do we owe this visit by the Lady and Blue Adept?"

Stile smiled ruefully. "I had thought not to be so obvious."

"Thou art not. I was delayed researching my references for thy description. I pored all through the Elven species in vain. It was the unicorn that at last betrayed thee, though we thought Blue recently deceased."

"Neysa would never—"

The old elf held up a withered hand. "I queried the 'corn not. But no man save one rides the unicorn, or travels with the fairest of human ladies. That be the imposter Blue Adept—who I think will not be considered imposter long."

Stile relaxed. "Oh. Of course. Those must be comprehensive references thou hast."

"Indeed. Yet they are oft tantalizingly incomplete. Be it true that thou didst come recently on the scene in the guise of thy murdered self, and when the unicorns and werewolves challenged thee performed two acts of magic, the first of which was inconsequential and the second enchantment like none known before, that established thee as the most powerful magician of the frame despite being a novice?"

"It may be true," Stile agreed, taken aback. He had rather underestimated his magical strength on that occasion! Probably it had been the strength of his feeling that had done it, rather than any special aptness at magic.

Then, perceiving that the Elder was genuinely curious, he amplified: "I am of Proton-frame, come to take up the mantle of my Phaze-self and set to right the wrong of his murder. When the unicorn Herd Stallion challenged me to show my magic, I made a spell to wall him in. When my unicorn steed yielded her ambition on my behalf, I made an oath of friendship to her. It had a broader compass than I expected."

The Elder nodded. "Ah. And the 'corns and 'wolves have not warred since. Thou art indeed Adept."

"Yet not omnipotent. Now must I need meet the Herd Stallion again, at the Unolympics, and I am not his match without magic. The Oracle sent me to borrow the Platinum Flute."

"Ah, now it comes clear. That would of course avail thee." Yet the elf seemed cold.

"That I am glad to hear," Stile said. "I have heard it said that music has charm to soothe the savage breast, but whether it soothe the breast of a beast—"

The Elder frowned. "Yet it is forbidden for us to yield this instrument, however briefly, to a human person, and doubly forbidden to lend it to an Adept. Knowest thou not its power?"

Stile shook his head. "I know only what the Oracle advised."

"No need for mystery. The wielder of the Flute is immune from the negation of magic. There are other qualities about it, but that is the primary one."

Stile thought about that. For an ordinary person, the Flute would provide little advantage. But for a magic creature, such as a werewolf, it would protect his ability to shape-change, and that could on occasion be a matter of life and death. For an Adept—

With the Flute in his possession, Stile could draw on his full powers of magic, even within the magic-negating circle of unicorns. The Herd Stallion would not be able to stand against him. The Oracle had spoken truly; this was the instrument he needed.

But at the same time, he could understand why the Mound Folk did not want him to have it. The existence of various magic-nullifiers prevented the Adepts from being overwhelmingly powerful. If an Adept obtained possession of the Platinum Flute, there would be no effective limit to his will.

"I appreciate thy concern," Stile said. "In fact, I agree with it. The likes of me should not possess the likes of this."

The Lady Blue's head turned toward him questioningly. "Thou dost not abuse thy power."

"How could the Mound Folk be assured of that?" Stile asked her. "There is corruption in power. And if the Flute were taken from me by another Adept, what then would be the limit?"

"It is good that thou dost understand," the Elder said. "The Oracle oft does give unuseful advice, accurate though it be. We Elves have great pride in our artifacts, and trade them freely for things of equal value. But the Flute is special; it required many years labor by our finest artisans, and is our most precious and potent device. It *has* no equal value. No other tribe has its match; not the goldsmiths or the silversmiths or the ironsmiths or the woodsmiths or bonesmiths. We alone work the lord of metals; we alone control the platinum mine and have the craftsmen and the magic to shape it into usable form. Thou art not asking for a trifle, Adept."

"Yes," Stile agreed. "Yet is the Oracle wont to provide advice that can in no wise be implemented?"

"Never. I termed it unuseful, in the sense that surely there is some simpler way to achieve thy mission with the Herd Stallion than this. Misinterpretations may abate the worth of an Oracle's message, but always the essence is there and true. There must be some pattern to this. Therefore must we deal with thee, can we but find the way. Thou knowest that even for the briefest loan we must extract a price."

"I am prepared to offer fair exchange, though I know not what that might be."

"There is little we need from thy kind."

"I do have resources, shouldst thou choose to tolerate the practice of magic in thy Demesnes. Is there anything that requires the talent of an Adept?"

Pyreforge considered gravely. "There be only two things. The lesser is not a task any man can perform, and the greater is unknown even to us. We know only that it must be performed by the finest mortal musician of Phaze."

"I do not claim to be the finest musician, but I am skilled," Stile said.

The wizened elf raised a shriveled eyebrow. "Skilled enough to play the Flute?"

"I am conversant with the flute as an instrument. I should be able to play the Platinum Flute unless there be a geas against it."

The Elder considered again. He was obviously ill at ease. "It is written that he who plays the Flute well enough to make our mountain tremble will be the foreordained savior of Phaze. Dost thou think thou art that one?"

Stile spread his hands. "I doubt it. I was not even aware that Phaze was in jeopardy."

"The Oracle surely knows, however. If the Time of Decision draws nigh . . ." Pyreforge shook his head dolefully. "I think we must try thee on the Flute, though it grieves me with spreading misgiving." He glanced at a crevice, where a guard lurked. "How be the light outside?"

The guard hurried outside. In a moment he returned. "Overcast, shrouded by fog. It will not lift this hour."

"Then may we gather outside. Summon the tribe this instant."

The guard disappeared again. "This be no casual matter, Adept. The Flute extends its force regardless, protecting the magic of the holder. An thou shouldst betray us, we must die to a man to recover it, killing thee if we can. I think thou canst be trusted, and on that needs must I gamble; my life be forfeit an I be in error."

Stile did not like this either, but he was not sure how to alleviate the elf's concern.

"Let thy warriors fix their threats on me," the Lady Blue said. "My Lord will not betray thee."

Pyreforge shook his head. "This be not our way, Lady, despite the ignorance of our commoners. And it would not avail against the typical Adept, who values nothing more than his power."

"Well I know the justice of thy concern. Yet would I stake my life upon my Lord's integrity."

The Elder smiled. "No need, Lady. Already have I staked mine. No lesser hostage preserves the peace in these Demesnes, when an Adept manifests here. I do this only for that the Oracle has cast its impact on us, and my books suggest the ponderosity of the situation. Fate draws the string on every creature, inquiring not what any person's preference might be." He returned his attention to Stile. "The Flute's full power is available only to the one who can master it completely, the one for whom it is destined. We made it, but can not use it; only the Foreordained can exploit it ultimately. When he comes, the end of the present order will be near. This is why we can not give up the Flute to any lesser person."

"I seek only to borrow it," Stile reminded him. But this did not look promising. If he were not the Foreordained, they would not let him borrow the Flute; if he were, there was a great deal more riding on this than his encounter with the Herd Stallion!

They walked outside. The cloud-cover had intensified, shrouding all the mountain above their level, leaving only a low-ceilinged layer of visibility, like a huge room. The elves of the tribe had gathered on the knoll, completely surrounding the mound—young and old, women and children too. Most were slender and handsome, and among them the women were phenomenally lovely, but a few were darkened and wrinkled like the Elder. Stile was the cynosure of all their eyes; he saw them measuring him, discomfited by his large stature; he did indeed feel like a giant, and no longer experienced any exhilaration in the sensation. All his life he had privately longed for more height; now he understood that such a thing would not be an unmixed blessing, and perhaps no blessing at all. Hulk had tried to tell him. The problem was not height; it was in being different, in whatever manner.

"We can not bear the direct light of the sun, being Dark Elves," the Elder said. "Should a sunbeam strike us, we turn instantly to stone. That is why the fog is so important, and why we reside in these oft-shrouded mountains, and seldom go abroad from our mounds by day. Yet like all our kind we like to dance, and at night when it is safe and the moons be bright we come out. I was in my youth careless, and a ray pierced a thin cloud and transfixed me ere I could seek cover; I turned not to stone but became as I am now. It was the wan sun, not mine age, that scorched me."

"I might heal thee of that," Stile said. "If thou wishest. A spell of healing—"

"What I might wish is of no account. I must needs live with the consequence of my folly—as must we all."

Now an elf brought, with an air of ceremony, a somber wooden case. "Borrow the Flute for the hour only," the Elder told Stile. "Ascertain for thyself and for us thy relation to it. The truth be greater than the will of any of us; it must be known."

Stile took the precious case. Inside, in cushioned splendor, lay the several pieces of gleaming metal tubing. Platinum, yes—a fortune in precious metal, exclusive of its worth as a music instrument, which had to be considerable, and its value as a magic talisman. He lifted out the pieces carefully and assembled it, conscious of its perfect heft and workmanship. The King of Flutes, surely!

Meanwhile the Mound Folk watched in sullen silence, and the Elder talked, unable to contain his pride in the instrument. "Our mine be not pure platinum; there is an admixture of gold and iridium. That provides character and hardness. We make many tools and weapons and utensils, though few of these are imbued with magic. There is also a trace of Phazite in the Flute, too."

"Phazite?" Stile inquired, curious. "I am not familiar with that metal."

"Not metal, precisely, but mineral. Thou mayst know of it as Protonite."

"Protonite!" Stile exclaimed. "The energy-mineral? I thought that existed only in Proton-frame."

"It exists here too, but in another aspect, as do all things. Wert thou not aware that Phazite be the fundamental repository of magic here? In Proton-frame it yields physical energy in abundance; in Phaze-frame it yields magic. Every act of magic exhausts some of that power—but the stores of it are so great and full Adepts so few that it will endure yet for millennia."

"But in Proton they are mining it, exporting it at a horrendous rate!"

"They are foolish, there. They will exhaust in decades what would otherwise have served them a hundred times as long. It should be conserved for this world."

So Phaze was likely to endure a good deal longer than Proton, Stile realized. That made Phaze an even better place to be. But why, then, was there this premonition of the Foreordained, and of the end of Phaze? Stile could appreciate why Pyreforge was disturbed; there were indeed hints of something seriously amiss.

What would happen when Proton ran out of Protonite? Would Citizens start crossing the curtain to raid the supplies of Phazite? If so, terrible trouble was ahead, for Citizens would let nothing inhibit them from gratification of their desires. Only the abolition of the curtain would prevent them from ravishing Phaze as they had ravished Proton. Yet how could a natural yet intangible artifact like the curtain be removed?

Now the Flute was assembled and complete. It was the most beautiful instrument Stile had ever seen. He lifted it slowly to his mouth. "May I?" he asked.

"Do the best thou canst with it," the elf said tightly. "Never have we heard its sound; we can not play it. Only a mortal can do that."

Stile applied his lips, set his fingers, and blew experimentally.

A pure, liquid, ineffably sweet note poured out. It sounded across the landscape, transfixing all the spectators. Elder and elves alike stood raptly, and Neysa perked her ears forward; the Lady Blue seemed transcendentally fair, as if a sanguine breeze caressed her. There was a special flute-quality to the note, of course—but more than that, for this was no ordinary flute. The note was ecstatic in its force and clarity and color—the quintessence of sound.

Then Stile moved into an impromptu melody. The instrument responded like a living extension of himself, seeming to possess nerves of its own. It was impossible to miskey such a flute; it was too perfect. And it came to him, in a minor revelation, that this must be the way it was to be a unicorn, with a living, musical horn. No wonder those creatures played so readily and well!

Now the Mound Folk danced. Their sullenness vanished, compelled away by the music, and their feet became light. They formed their ranks on the ground, not in the air, and kept their motions on a single plane, but they were abandoned in their sheer joy of motion. The elves scintillated as they turned, and their damsels glowed. They spun into convoluted patterns that nevertheless possessed the beauty of organization. They flung out and in; they kicked their feet in unison; the elves swung the maids and the maids swung the elves; they threaded their way through each other in a tapestry of ever-increasing intricacy. There were no tosses or acrobatic swings, merely synchronized patterns that coalesced into an artistic whole. Over and through it all passed the grandeur of the music of the Flute, fashioning from disparate elements an almost divine unity. It was not Stile's skill so much as the talent bequeathed by the perfect instrument; he could not shame it by delivering less than his ultimate.

Stile saw that the fog was lifting and thinning, as if dissipated by the music. The clouds roiled and struggled to free themselves of their confinement. He brought the recital to a close, and the dancing came to a neat halt as if it had been planned exactly this way. Again the Mound Folk stood still, but now they were smiling. Even the guards who had greeted Stile so inhospitably had relaxed their resentment.

"That was the loveliest music I ever did hear," the Elder said. "It made our finest dance. Thou hast rare talent. Yet did the mountain not shake."

"It did not shake," Stile agreed, relieved.

"Thou art not the Foreordained."

"Never did I claim to be."

"Still, thou canst play marvelously well. If the Oracle decrees that the Flute be loaned to thee, it may be that we are constrained to oblige."

"This I would appreciate," Stile said, taking apart the instrument and returning it carefully to its case. "If thou dost trust me with it."

But now the circled Mound Folk frowned and muttered. The roil of the clouds had stilled when the music stopped, but the disturbance seemed to have passed into the elves. "Nay, my people will not so lightly tolerate that. Perhaps if we borrowed thy service in exchange—"

The muttering subsided. "I am willing to do what service I may," Stile said. "But I can not remain here long. I have commitments elsewhere. I will need the Flute for a number of days, until the Unolympic."

The muttering began again. "Desist this noise!" the Elder cried at the elves, annoyed. "We shall fashion a fair bargain or not part with the Flute." He accepted the Flute-case from Stile; in this judgment, at least, he had not been mistaken. Stile had neither abused the Flute nor sought to retain it without permission. "Now get under cover before the cloud breaks!"

There was little danger of that now, but the Mound Folk hurried away. Stile and the Lady returned inside the nearest mound with the Elder, while Neysa and Hinblue returned to their grazing.

"It could be said," Pyreforge said after reflection, "that thou dost borrow the Flute only to bring it to the one for whom it is intended. The Foreordained."

"But I do not know the Foreordained!"

"Then shalt thou quest for him."

Stile understood the nature of the offer. Such a quest could take as long as he needed for the Flute. Yet it would have to be a true mission. "How could I know him?"

"He would play the Flute better than thee."

"There may be many who can do that."

"I think not. But thou wouldst send him to us, as we can not fare forth to seek him, and we would know by the tenor of the mountain his identity. If he played well, but was not the Foreordained, we at least would have the Flute back."

"This seems less than certain. I think, at least for the acquiescence of thy people, I need to earn this borrowing. Thou didst mention two tasks, the lesser of which no man might perform. Yet I am Adept."

"Canst thou wield a broadsword?"

"I can," Stile replied, surprised.

"This task bears the threat of ugly death to any but the most skilled and persistent swordsman."

"I have faced such threats before. I would feel more secure from them with the Flute in my hands and a broadsword ready."

"Assuredly. Then listen, Adept. There is beneath our Mound Demesnes and below our platinum mine, deep in a cave hewn from out of the Phazite bedrock, one of the Worms of the fundament, ancient and strong and savage and fiery."

"A dragon!" Stile exclaimed.

"Even so. But not one of the ordinary reptiles of the southern marches beyond these mountains. This monster has slowly tunneled through the mountain range during all the time we have mined here. Now we have come within awareness of each other. The Worm be centuries old, and its teeth are worn and its heat diminished so that it can no longer consume rock as readily as in bygone centuries, yet it is beyond our means to thwart. It requires from us tribute—"

"Human sacrifice!" Stile exclaimed, remembering the threat the elves had made concerning the Lady Blue.

"Even so. We like this not, yet if we fail to deliver on schedule, the Worm will exert itself and undermine our foundations and melt our platinum ore and we shall be finished as smiths. We are smithy elves, highly specialized; it took us a long time to work up to platinum and become proficient with it. We can not go back to mere gold, even if other tribes had not already filled in that specialty. We must maintain our present level, or become as nothing. My people would sooner go out in sunlight."

"So thou dost need that dragon eliminated," Stile concluded.

"For that I believe my people would abate their disquietous murmurings about the loan of the Flute."

"Even so," Stile said warily. "This is a large dragon?"

"Enormous."

"Breathes fire?"

"Twenty-foot jets from each nostril."

"Armored?"

"Stainless steel overlapping scales. Five-inch claws. Six-inch teeth. Lightning bolts from eyes."

"Temperament?"

"Aggressive."

"Resistive to magic?"

"Extremely. The Worm beds in Phazite, so has developed a considerable immunity."

"I wonder what it was like in its prime?" Stile mused.

"No matter. In its prime it needed not the tribute of our kind."

"But if the Platinum Flute were employed—"

"The magic of the Flute be stronger than the anti-magic of the Worm."

"Then it is possible that an Adept carrying the Flute could dispatch the creature."

"Possible. But hardly probable. The Worm cannot be abolished by magic alone."

"Well, I'd be willing to make the attempt."

"Nay!" the Lady Blue cried. "Few dragons hast thou encountered; thou knowest not their nature. Accept not this perilous mission!"

"I would not borrow a thing of value without giving service in return," Stile said. "But if I could borrow the Flute to brace the Worm, thereafter I would feel justified in borrowing it for one task of mine own. There might be other uses I could make of it besides matching a unicorn stallion, until I locate the one for whom the Flute be intended."

"Thou meanest to brace the Worm?" the Elder asked.

"At least to make the attempt. If I fail to dispatch it, I will return the Flute immediately to thee, if I remain able to do so."

"Nay!" the Lady cried again. "This is too high a price to risk, for the mere postponement of the breeding of one mare. She is mine oath-friend, yet—"

"For that trifle thou dost this?" the Elder demanded, abruptly suspicious. "Thou dost risk thy life against the Worm, and thy pride against the Stallion, for . . . ?"

"She is a very special mare, also mine oath-friend," Stile said stiffly, not wanting to admit that things had pyramided somewhat.

"I fear my people will not support this," the Elder said. "They will fear thou wouldst borrow the Flute merely to abscond with it, facing no Worm. Who would stop thee, armed with it?"

Both Stile and the Lady reacted with anger. "My Lord Blue does not cheat!" she flared. "I thought we had already made proof of this. Again will I stand hostage to that."

"Nay," Stile said, touched by her loyalty, though he knew it was the honor of the Blue Demesnes she was protecting rather than himself. "Thou'rt no hostage."

The Elder's canny gaze passed from one to another. "Yet perhaps this would do, this time. Let the Lady be my guest, here, for a few hours; do we care if others assume she be security for this loan of the Flute? Methinks no man would leave his love to be sacrificed to a dragon. If the Worm be slain, thy mettle is proved, and the loan is good."

"The Lady is not my—" Stile started, then reconsidered. It was a matter he preferred not to discuss here. Also, he would be operating on an extremely tenuous footing if he denied his love for her. He would *not* permit her to be fed to the dragon, whatever her feeling for him.

"Others be not aware of that," the Elder said, delicately skirting the issue. "Few know that the Lord of the Blue Demesnes has changed. Let her remain with me, and none of my people will hold thy motive in suspicion. She will not be ill-treated." He glanced at the Lady. "Dost thou perchance play chess?"

"Perchance," she agreed, smiling.

Stile realized that the Elder had proffered a viable compromise. It was a way to suppress the objections of the Mound Folk, without really threatening the Lady. Certainly Stile was not about to take her with him to meet the dragon!

"Do thou keep the harmonica during mine absence," Stile said to the Lady, handing her the instrument. "This time I must use the Flute."

"I like this not," she said grimly. But she took the harmonica. If Stile did not return, she would at least retain this memento of her husband.

Pyreforge, meanwhile, was setting up the chessmen.

Stile carried the Flute with him into the depth of the crevice. Now he knew the origin of the hot wind and demonic odor from this crevasse. The Worm lurked below!

He had never fought a real dragon before, as the Lady had mentioned, and was not entirely sanguine about this one. The closest approach to a dragon he had made was the one in the Black Demesnes, actually formed from a line, and when balked it had unraveled literally into its component string. The Worm surely would not do that! Adept-quality magic should prevail—but still, if anything went wrong—

Well, he should have the advantage of surprise. The Worm would assume Stile was another item of tribute, a victim to be consumed. He should be able to get quite close before the monster realized what it was up against. That would give him time to survey the situation. Pyreforge had assured him that the Flute would facilitate his magic, yet he had also said that magic alone would not suffice; that suggested that the Flute was not quite as powerful a charm as the Mound Folk wished to believe.

Now they were well below the ledge they had hurdled before. Neysa picked her way carefully as the path narrowed, and Stile kept the Flute assembled and handy. For him it should serve double duty—both to protect his ability to do magic, and to summon the magic itself, since he needed music for his spells. He would have been in trouble if he had needed to play two different instruments simultaneously for those purposes! He was rehearsing those spells in his mind now—one to abate fire, another to shield him from biting, another to make him invisible. But mainly he needed one to eradicate the Worm, one way or another. Could the creature be banished to Hell? Here in this magic frame, there really was a Hell. He had accidentally sent Neysa there once; that had led to a lot of trouble. Which meant that that option was out, now; Neysa would not go for it. He was extremely wary of antagonizing his unicorn friend; unicorns were devastatingly stubborn once they made an issue of something.

Not Hell, then. How about a size change? Convert the giant Worm into a midget worm, harmless. Maybe in three more centuries it would grow back into a giant, but by then it should be far away—if some hungry bird hadn't snapped it up in the interim. What would be a suitable spell? *Monstrous Worm, be small as a germ.* Hardly great art, he lamented as usual, but for the purpose of magic it only needed to rhyme and have appropriate meter.

What kind of magic would be wrought by superior verse? Some day he would have to experiment with genuine poetry, instead of doggerel, and see what happened.

Now the path leveled out. A large, round tunnel took off to the side—the bore of the Worm. A hot drift of air came from it. The Worm could not be far distant.

Stile hesitated. He leaned down to whisper into Neysa's left ear, which rotated obligingly to receive his words. "If we march blithely into the Worm's lair, methinks we'll be slightly cooked," he said. "Yet if we do not, the monster may become suspicious. I would like to lure it out to a

location convenient for me, so that at least I can survey it
before emerging to engage it—yet how can I bring it to me
without engaging it?"

Neysa blew a short, positive note. Realizing that she had
a notion, Stile dismounted.

She shimmered into girl-form, a petite, lovely, naked,
semi-elven lass. "Tribute," she murmured, making a gesture of innocence and helplessness.

Stile was delighted and appalled. "Thou'rt the perfect
lure," he said. "Thou fittest the part precisely. But I dare
not risk thy getting caught by the monster."

She shimmered again and became a firefly. The insect
circled him once, then converted back to girl-form.

"That's so," Stile agreed. "I keep forgetting thy third
form. Thou canst escape, if thou art not burned."

"Fireproof," she said.

"Thy firefly form is fireproof? Wonderful!" Neysa was a
treasure of ever-new facets.

Stile reflected for a moment, then plotted their course. "I
prefer to have some space to battle the Worm, even though
I expect to banish it with a spell. One must always be
prepared for the unexpected. So do thou lure it out to the
crevice, then get thee swiftly to safety. If I destroy it not,
and suffer death, do thou fly up to Elder Pyreforge and the
Lady and tell them I have failed. I will hurl the Flute out
to the crevice if I can, that it be not lost." This sounded
bold and brave, but Stile felt somewhat weak in the knees;
he had not had much experience in this sort of thing. He
really did not expect to be in serious danger of demise,
otherwise he would have been terrified. He was just covering the extreme eventuality.

Neysa nodded, then walked to the center of the tunnel.
Stile sang a spell to make himself invisible. This was external magic only; he remained just as solid as always,
despite the change in appearance. He was getting accustomed to the limits of his power. When he lifted himself by
magic he was changing his locale, not his body. He could
not heal his own injured knees. He could not duplicate
Neysa's shape-changing or genuine insect-flying ability,
though he could create the illusion of change in himself,
and could fly artificially by magic means. There were some

fine distinctions, but overall he was perhaps more vulnerable than Neysa, though he was also more powerful.

When she saw he was unseeable, Neysa went into her act. "Oh!" she cried. "I'm so afraid! The horrible dragon is going to eat me!" She was really working at it, since she didn't like to talk. Stile felt a warm glow of appreciation. Once Neysa had given him her loyalty, she had been the truest of companions.

Soon there was a rumbling deep in the tunnel. A hotter, ranker wash of air passed, as if some enormous engine had started up. Stile's imperfect confidence suffered attrition. There were after all so many things that might go wrong ...

Neysa continued lamenting. The rumble increased. The Worm must be afraid that the prey would flee if not quickly nabbed—a reasonable assumption. That was one important thing Stile wanted to know about it—how alert it was, and how fast it moved. A big, ponderous creature would be easier to handle than—

All too soon the Worm arrived. It was indeed a dragon. It had a long narrow head with a conical snout, narrowing in ringlike stages. The derivation of this monster from a literal worm was evident. Of course there were many kinds of worms; Stile tended to think of earthworms because many Citizens employed them in their elegant gardens. But he knew there were other types, some of them vicious. This dragon was a vicious worm grown monstrous.

Neysa screamed realistically and skipped nimbly to the mouth of the passage. The Worm exhaled a puff of smog and slid forward. Its legs were puny compared to its bulk, not really used for its forward motion—but it did indeed have horrendous claws, and seemed to be fully adequate to the task of gutting a human being efficiently. Its metallic scales did not gleam; they were drab and dirty, more like the mud-caked treads of a caterpillar tractor. Stile did not doubt they were invulnerable to ordinary attack. Theoretically the point of a sword could be slid up under a layer of scales to penetrate the flesh beneath—but that could lead to a shallow slanting wound, only aggravating the monster. And what would the Worm be doing while the swordsman was making his insertion? Sitting still? Not likely!

All of this, Stile realized abruptly, was academic. He did

not have a sword. He had forgotten to conjure one. He had only the Platinum Flute and his magic—which magic it was time to use.

Stile's strategy had been to bring the monster out to the front, then cast his spell from the rear. Now a problem manifested; the Worm had no rear. Its giant cylindrical torso extended back into the gloom. The shape of a worm, naturally—long. He should have known.

Well, he should be able to enchant it anyway. Stile played the Flute, and the perfect notes poured out again, emerging like quicksilver to fill the tunnel with beauty. The magic gathered swiftly, unusually intense. Of course; they were down near the Phazite lode, so the power was near at hand.

The dragon reacted instantly. No senile mentality here! It had been about to lunge at the supposedly helpless damsel—Neysa was playing it uncomfortably close—but recognized the summoning of magic here. The tiny armored eyes oriented on Stile—and did not see him, since he was invisible. Nevertheless the front orifice opened, its diameter cranking wider in several stages until it was a good yard across. From it a blast of hot fog bellied out.

In this instant it occurred to Stile that the Worm had not tried to use heat on Neysa. Maybe it preferred its meals raw.

Time for self-defense. "From head to feet, immune to heat!" Stile sang.

But as the fog struck him, Stile discovered it was a false alarm. The stuff was hot but not burning. It was like being in a polluted sauna.

The dragon heaved again. This time its breath was hotter and smelled worse. The creature was old; it took it time to get up full steam. The third blast was burning, and the fourth contained pure fire. From hair-dryer to flame-thrower, in easy stages!

Now for the attack. "O mighty Worm, complete thy term," Stile chanted, willing instant death on it.

Then something strange happened. There was a coruscation in the air midway between them, as of a beam of light striking a refractive barrier. The Worm did not die.

Stile tried again. "O Worm of fire—weaken, expire!"

Again that dissipation enroute, and lack of effect. His spells were potent, but were not reaching the dragon!

Now the creature's tiny eyes flashed. Stile had not realized that worms had eyes, but this one certainly did. He remembered the weapon he had been warned about. "Light —blight!" he cried, and the lightning fizzled out before reaching him. His backup spells were saving his hide.

The Worm paused, evidently taking stock. Stile did the same. His magic worked—but the Worm was shielded against it. The Worm had magic—that Stile could block. So the Flute enabled Stile to perform his magic here, but not to use it directly against the enemy. Like two armored knights, they were so well protected against attack that neither could hurt the other magically. The Elder elf had been right.

So much for his rehearsed spells. This conflict was about to get physical. And the Worm was a good deal more physical than Stile.

Still, he would have to make a try. For one thing, he was now trapped inside the tunnel; the bulk of the Worm was between him and the exit. In fact the bulk of the Worm surrounded him. The monster was slowly constricting, hemming him in. Neysa was on the far side of the dragon, unable to help.

Stile had no weapon, other than the Flute. Now he knew that the Flute, while effective, was not enough. Not against the magic Worm. What he needed at the moment was a good sword. What was that spell he had prepared, to summon such a weapon?

The Worm's tube-mouth opened wider—and now a ring of teeth showed, six-inch teeth sure enough, pointing inward. No doubt useful for tunneling through rock—but surely adequate also to grind up one small man. Why couldn't he think of that spell!

The head nudged closer. Stile held the Flute before him in a futile gesture of defense while he tried to cudgel his memory into yielding up the forgotten spell—damn this failure under pressure!—and discovered he held a sword. A shining platinum blade, long and sharp, two-edged. But light and balanced. Exactly the kind of sword he was well versed in.

"Well, now!" Stile exclaimed, confidence surging. The elves had not informed him of this aspect of the Flute! It was a shape-changer.

Stile stepped briskly forward and stabbed at the Worm's side. He expected the point to bounce off the tough scales, but it penetrated. Aha! The enchantment of the Platinum Sword was proof against the Worm's resistance. Maybe it was a different kind of spell, that when buttressed by forceful physical action—

The Worm screamed like a siren and whipped its head about. Stile jerked the sword out and retreated. A geyser of dark red blood shot out of the hole, sailing in an arc through the air to splash on the stone several feet away. A rank charnel smell rose from the fluid.

The dragon's nose nudged up to the wound. A slimy tongue slid out, intercepting the flow of blood. Did worms have tongues? This one did! Was it about to drink its own blood? A single slurp—and the flow abated.

The nose drew away. The blood remained staunched. Maybe it was the saliva: some magical curative property. This monster could heal itself.

The dragon's head was orienting on Stile again. This was one tough worm! It might not be able to see him, but it could hear him and smell him, and in the poor light that was just about as good. Stile had foolishly delayed when he should have been edging around to rejoin Neysa, during the Worm's distraction. Still, maybe he could—

Stile strode for the Worm's side. Immediately the snout snapped toward him. Stile dodged back and sprinted past the head to reach the mouth of the tunnel.

Neysa was awaiting him in equine form. She too could place him readily by smell and sound. Next time he fought an animal, he would prepare spells of inaudibility and unsmellability! He leaped to mount her. "At least we know it can be injured by this sword," he said. "Maybe if we charge in, slash, and charge out before it reacts, then wound it in a second place, and a third—"

He stopped. He no longer had a sword. He supported a long platinum lance. The magic Flute had shown another facet!

Stile braced the lance in his arms and Neysa charged the Worm as its head swung about. The point of the lance struck the neck just behind the head; Stile did not have his aim perfect yet. A lance was not the easiest thing to use! He really needed some sort of supportive harness. The shaft rammed in forcefully—and Stile was shoved off his mount.

Of course, he realized as he picked himself up. The instrument was enchanted so that it could not be jarred out of his grasp—but the shock of impact had had its natural effect on his body. He should have anticipated that.

The Worm screamed again. That puncture hurt! As Stile hauled the lance out, a larger gout of blood spurted—but this time the Worm could not get its mouth on the spot, because the wound was too close to the head.

Stile perceived his avenue of victory. He lifted the lance —and it was what he needed, a hefty double-bitted battle-axe. As the Worm's head twisted vainly to the side, trying to reach the wound, the neck was exposed on the other side to Stile's attack.

He chopped down at that neck, two hands on his axe. This time he cut a deep gash. The head whipped back, catching Stile in a sideswipe and hurling him against the wall.

He saw a flash of light as his head struck, then slid down the curve of the wall. His head was spinning. He retained the Flute—but hardly had the wit to use it. He had not been knocked out, but had been badly shaken up by the blow.

Now the head was orienting on him. The circular array of teeth widened to take him in, and the breath steamed up the vicinity so that Stile could hardly see.

He scrambled away on hands and knees. He wasn't sure he could make it to his feet, or stay on them if he did. He had been in a boxing match once in the Game and been tagged by a solid blow so that his knees went rubbery; he felt similar now. Only there would be no time between rounds to recover! The snout followed him—then paused, grinding out a puff of smoke.

Neysa had rammed her horn into the other side of the Worm's neck, beside the first hole. She lacked the enchantment of the Flute, but a unicorn's horn was itself magical, and a weapon no creature could ignore.

The Worm reacted automatically, turning on this annoyance. It was not terrifically smart.

Stile scrambled to his feet. He swung the Platinum machete ferociously—machete? It had changed again!—chopping with all his strength at the Worm's body. More blood gouted out, spilling over Stile's two hands and spattering his front. He hated the burning, greasy feel of it, but kept hacking.

The dragon whipped its head back, but Stile lashed at the snout with his cleaver, just missing an eye. The head recoiled—and Stile returned to work on the neck. This was like chopping through a tree, except that it became a good deal softer and messier as he got past the vertebrae and into the fatty tissues. Now blood was flooding out so voluminously that Stile was wading in it, and every lift of his implement splattered it further. Blood ran down the shaft as he elevated it, and along his arms to the shoulders; it sprayed across his face. But his grip remained firm, thanks to the Flute's enchantment. As long as he willed his grip to be good, it was. He was wallowing in gore—but still the Worm lived and thrashed, not yielding.

Finally the body was severed entirely. The neck and head fell on one side; the body writhed on the other. The job had been done. Stile had slain the dragon.

His thought of victory was premature. Still the thing didn't die. Instead the cut ends frothed and solidified like sponge, and the bleeding abated. The head section crawled slowly by itself, while the body section cast about blindly, looking for its opponent.

This was a worm. It was possible to cut a worm in half—and both halves would form new worms. Stile had not really accomplished anything yet.

Well, yes—he had made some progress. The head no longer had the leverage to strike at him, and the body lacked sensory apparatus. In time these situations would be remedied—but right now he had a definite advantage. He had to go ahead and destroy the entire Worm right now, while he could.

This was what Pyreforge had meant about the need for a good swordsman with staying power. What a job!

Stile moved down the body, picking his spot, and resumed hacking with his machete-axe. Again the blood gouted; again the torso twisted in agony, trying futilely to fight or escape. The severed end came around, thinking it was a head; it smeared him with half-clotted blood, sickeningly, but could not bite him. Stile pressed on, feeling more like a butcher than a hero. In fantasy lore, the champion skewered the ferocious dragon one time and the beast collapsed cleanly. Here there was nothing neat or convenient or particularly noble about it; he was wallowing in foul-smelling gore, hacking apart a helpless mound of blubber. Hero? He wanted to vomit!

By the time he completed the second cut, his arms were tiring. But still each segment of the Worm remained alive. If he quit here, they would become three new, smaller dragons. He had to abolish the entire mess, somehow.

Then he had a dull inspiration. The dragon had countered his magic with its own magic. But now it lacked organization. Maybe magic would finish it, at this stage. It was certainly worth a try.

He brought the Flute to his mouth. It was festooned with gore. Stile's gorge rose, and he decided to try his spell without playing on the instrument. "O monster fair," he intoned with irony. "Convert to air."

The segment before him shivered, resisting. Whether this was because of residual anti-magic in the dragon, or because Stile had not summoned sufficient magic, he was not sure. Then it melted and evaporated into a truly noisome cloud. The spell was working!

Stile devised spells to abolish the two remaining segments, then another to clean the gore from himself, Neysa, and the tunnel. He had done the job, and earned the right to borrow the Flute. Yet he was not especially pleased with himself. Wasn't there some better way to settle differences than hacking apart ancient magical creatures? How would he feel if he were old, having some fresh young midget chop him down to size?

Yet if he had not performed, the Lady Blue's situation could have become quite difficult. And it could still become so, if Stile did not locate and deal with the murderer of the Blue Adept before that murderer caught up with Stile himself.

Meanwhile, he wondered whether the Lady was winning her chess game with Pyreforge.

CHAPTER 5

Riddles

Sheen was pleased. "You're here for a full week this time?"

"Until the Unolympic," Stile agreed. "Neysa and the Lady Blue are relaxing after the excursion among the Little People, and I have considerable business here in Proton-frame, as long as my enemy doesn't strike." He shrugged. "Of course I'll be staying longer in Phaze-frame one of these times, to run down my enemy there and look for the Foreordained. If I wash out of the Tourney I'll spend the rest of my life there."

"What was it like, being among the Little People?" Sheen asked. They were in their apartment, engaging in their usual occupation. Sheen was an extremely amorous female, and Stile's frequent absences and uncertainty of future increased her ardor. And, since he had a balked romantic situation in Phaze—

"Strange," he answered. "I felt like a giant, and I wasn't used to it. This must be the way Hulk feels. I really am more satisfied with my size than I used to be." He changed the subject. "Where is Hulk? Did you help him?"

"I believe so. I put him in touch with my friends. I assumed you would not have sent him if he could not be trusted."

"He can be trusted."

"I'm sure my friends required him to take the same oath you took, if they revealed themselves to him at all. They may simply have issued him an address. I did not inquire after him, because that would only expose him and them to possible Citizen attention, and we don't want that."

"True," Stile agreed. "If the Citizens knew that some robots are self-willed—"

"You have something against self-willed robots?" she asked archly.

"You know, at times I almost forget that you yourself are a robot. I don't see how you could be much better in the flesh."

"All the same, I wish I *were* in the flesh," she said sadly. "You can never truly love me. Even if you were to win the Tourney and become a Citizen and stay here the rest of your life, even if you didn't have the Lady Blue in the other frame, you would never really be mine."

Stile did not like this line of conjecture. "There is very little chance of my winning the Tourney. I barely survived my first Game."

"I know. I watched. You were lucky."

"Luck is a fickle mistress."

She turned on him abruptly. "Promise me that if you ever give *this* mistress up permanently, you'll have me junked, put out of consciousness. I don't mean just reprogramming or deactivating me; destroy my computer brain. You know how to do it. Don't let me suffer alone."

"Sheen," he protested. "I would never junk you!"

"I like Neysa, and I'm resigned to the Lady Blue. I know you're sliding into love with her, and in time she'll love you, and there's your true romance. But this is a different frame; she and I can never meet. Nothing you do there needs to affect what you do here—"

"I am of both frames now," Stile said. "What affects me in one, affects me in the other. You know that if the Lady ever gives her love to me, I—we'll still be friends, you and I, but—" He halted, hating this, but not constituted to conceal the truth.

"But not lovers," she finished. "Even that I can accept. Neysa accepted it. But if you ever find you can dispense with that remaining friendship—"

"Never!"

"Then you will junk me cleanly. Promise."

Stile suffered a vision of himself hacking apart the living Worm. That had been unclean dispatching. How much better it would have been if he could have banished that Worm to nonexistence with a single, painless spell. Sheen deserved at least that much. "I promise," he said. "But that time will never—"

"Now it's time to get you back to the Tourney," she said briskly.

Stile had been near the head of the line for matching-up before; this time he was near the end. That meant he could play this time, and have another Game soon. The later Rounds would suffer less delay, as the number of remaining contestants declined. The double-elimination system did not eliminate half the contestants each Round, but by Round Four it would approximate fifty percent attrition, and by Round Eight it would be down to about sixty-four survivors, and the prizes would begin. That was his minimum objective, to reach Round Eight. Because that meant he would get another chance, even if he washed out of the Tourney thereafter. In that sense these first few Games were the most critical. Since they were also likely to be against the least competent players—with certain notable exceptions!—this was the time to avoid making any foolish errors. There was absolutely no sense in throwing away a Game that could be easily won by being careful.

His second Game was against an older woman, a serf. She was unlikely to be any match for him. She would probably go for CHANCE; it was the obvious ploy against a superior player.

The grid gave her the opportunity; she had the numbered facet. Well, there were ways to reduce the pseudo-equality of chance, and Stile played for them. He selected TOOL.

Sure enough, it came up 3B, TOOL-assisted CHANCE. The subgrid appeared. Stile played to avoid the pure-chance complexes like Dice or Roulette, in favor of the semi-chance ones like Cards. It came up Dominoes.

All right. Stile managed to steer it into the 91 piece, 12 spot domino variation, while the woman put it into the conventional "Draw" game. Stile, familiar with all variants, had wanted one unfamiliar to his opponent to confuse her; he was halfway there.

They adjourned to a Gamesroom and played. They laid all the dominoes facedown, shuffled, and each drew one from the boneyard. Stile drew the 6:7; the woman the 4:5. He had first turn. Good; that was an advantage.

Each drew seven dominoes and Stile was pleased to note that his hand had a run of Fours: the 4:0, 4:2, 4:8 and 4:11. He played the 4:8. As he had hoped, his opponent was unable to play, being short of Fours; she had to draw three times before she could make a match. Stile played one of his other Fours.

So it went. Confused by the vastly extended range of the dominoes, and lacking the wit to eliminate the highest ones from her hand, the woman lost and delivered a goodly score to him. They played another hand, and a third, and he passed 200 points and won. She had never scored at all. Stile had made it to Round Three without even a scare.

The woman just sat there, after the Game, her face set. Stile realized, belatedly, that she must have lost her first match; with this second loss she would be out of the Tourney, doomed to immediate and permanent exile. Some serfs suicided rather than leave Proton. They were the lowest class of people, here, destined only to serve the arrogant Citizens, yet it was all they craved in life. Stile understood this attitude, for he had until recently shared it. Only the opening of the miraculous horizons of Phaze had given him a better alternative.

He was sorry for the woman. Yet what could he do? She had no chance to win the Tourney anyway. It was best that she be put out of her misery promptly.

Like Sheen? No, of course not like that! Yet the thought lingered, a shadow that could not quite be erased.

He left the woman there. He did not feel good.

As Stile and Sheen reentered the apartment, the communication screen lighted. "Report to your Employer for an update," a serf-functionary said crisply, showing the identification of the Lady Citizen for whom Stile worked. "At this time, in this place." And a card emerged from the letter-slot.

Sheen took the card. "Oh, no!" she complained. "We have only half an hour to get there, and it's at an isolated dome. I had hoped to have time to—"

"For a machine, you're certainly hung up on one thing," Stile teased her.

"I'm programmed to be!" she snapped.

She had been fashioned to appeal to his tastes, and evidently his tastes ran to beauty, intelligence and desire for his attention. Stile realized again, not comfortably, that he was in this respect a typical man. His human interests seemed unconscionably narrow when reflected so obviously. Yet Sheen was, in all respects but one, his ideal mate. That one canceled out the rest: she was not alive. She was a construct of metal and pseudoflesh and artificial intellect.

Yet he knew now that even had Sheen been a real person—a real *live* person—she would not have been able to retain his full devotion after he encountered the Lady Blue. Because what had been his ideal woman two months ago was that no longer. The Lady Blue had a detailed and fascinating past as well as a future; she was changing with the passage of time, as Sheen could not, and so was matching Stile's own development. The Lady Blue had reshaped his ideal, conforming it to her likeness in flesh and personality and history. He was becoming acclimatized to the world of Phaze, and was losing identification with the world of Proton.

It was not merely a matter of women; he would have loved Phaze regardless. Magic had become a more intriguing challenge than the Game. But he had a commitment here in Proton, and he would see it through. And he had a gnawing need to ferret out his anonymous enemy and bring that person to an accounting. Who had lasered his knees? Who had sent Sheen to guard him? He could never rest content in Phaze until he knew the answers.

But Sheen was already bustling him out. "We can't keep a Citizen waiting; we have to get to that address in time."

"I suppose so," Stile agreed, resenting the waste of time. In one sense, a serf's employment by a Citizen ended when that serf entered the Tourney, since all tenure was terminated by such entry. But in another sense employment continued, for Citizens identified with those of their serfs who entered, making bets on their success. Many Citizens gave serfs time off to practice for the Tourney, so as to do better; Stile's own Employer had done that. And if he won an extension of tenure, he would still need an Employer for that period. So whatever the technical status, he had better act in a manner conducive to the Citizen's good will.

"I didn't know she had a dome at this address," Sheen remarked as they hurried to a subtube station. As a machine, she had little genuine curiosity, but with her programming and under Stile's tutelage she had mastered this most feminine quality. Hardly ever did she make errors of characterization, now. "But of course all Citizens are obscenely rich. She must be watching the Tourney from a private retreat."

They boarded the tube shuttle. A third passenger joined them—a middle-aged serf woman, well-formed. She was naked, like all serfs, and carrying a sealed freezer-container. "My Employer insists the ice cream from one particular public foodmart tastes better than the ice cream from anywhere else," she confided, tapping the container. "So every day I have to make the trip and bring it back by hand. She thinks robot delivery distorts the flavor."

"It probably does," Sheen said, smiling obscurely.

"Citizens are like that," Stile said, falling into the ready camaraderie of serfs. "I'm entered in the Tourney, but my Employer requires a personal report instead of the official one, so I'm making a trip every bit as foolish." He had no worry about visual and auditory perception devices that might report this conversation to the Citizens; of course they existed, but Citizens had no interest in the opinions of serfs, and expected them to grumble privately.

"That's funny," the woman said. "There are only three Citizens at this terminus. Mine has no interest in the Tourney, and another's off-planet on business, and the third—" She broke off.

Sheen became alert. "What about the third?"

"Well, he hates the Tourney. Says it's a waste of time and only generates new Citizens when the planet has too many already. You couldn't be seeing *him*."

"My Employer is a woman," Stile said.

"Mine is the only woman on this annex—and she surely is not sponsoring you."

Stile showed her the address-card.

"That's the Tourney-hater!" the woman exclaimed. "He's no woman!" She made a small, significant gesture near her midsection. "I know."

Stile exchanged a glance with Sheen. The woman had signified that the Citizen borrowed her for sexual purpose, as was his right so long as her own Employer acquiesced. Citizens of either sex could use serfs of either sex this way, and surely a woman knew the sex of her user.

"My Employer is female," Stile said, suffering a new qualm. Could she have summoned him in the flesh because she wanted to dally with a serf? He would not be able to refuse her, but this was a complication he did not want. "Are you sure that address hasn't changed ownership recently?"

"Quite sure. I was there only two days ago." Again the gesture. "Heaven and Hell."

"Maybe my Employer is visiting him," Stile said.

"That must be it," the woman agreed. "He has quite a taste for women, and does prefer Citizens when he can get them. Is she pretty?"

"Handsome," Stile said. "As you are."

She nodded knowingly. "But you," she said to Sheen. "You had best keep that luscious body out of his sight, or you could mess it up for your mistress."

Stile smiled. Naturally the serf assumed Sheen was also an employee. Sheen could mess it up for *any* rival woman, and not just because of her beauty.

The shuttle slowed. "This is my station," the woman said. "Yours is next. Good luck!"

When they were alone, Stile turned to Sheen. "I don't like this. We can't skip out on a command appearance, but something seems wrong. Could the message be faked?"

"It's genuine," Sheen said. She was a machine; she could tell. "But I agree. Something is funny. I'm summoning help."

"I don't think you should involve your friends in this.

They don't want to call the attention of a Citizen to themselves."

"Only to trace the origin of that message," she said. "And to rouse your robot double. I think we can stall a few minutes while he travels by fast freight."

The shuttle stopped. They got out and moved to a local food dispenser, using up the necessary time. Sheen ate a piece of reconstituted carrot. She was a machine but could process food through her system, though it never was digested. Stile contented himself with a cup of nutro-cocoa.

In a surprisingly short time a freight hatch opened and the Stile-robot emerged, carrying a shipment tag. "Start breathing," Sheen told it, and the model animated. "Take this card, report to this address. Broadcast continuously to me."

Without a word the robot took the card, glanced at it, and walked down the passage. The thing looked so small! Stile was embarrassed to think that this was the way he appeared to others: a child-man, thirty-five years old but the size of a twelve-year-old boy.

"Move," Sheen murmured, guiding him through a service aperture. "If there is trouble, we need to vanish."

She located a storage chamber, and they settled down to wait. "Now," she said, putting her arms about him and kissing him. She was fully as soft and sensual as any live woman. But she froze in midkiss. "Oops."

"What—my lips lose their living flavor?"

"I'm getting the report from the robot." Sheen used the term without self-consciousness. She was to an ordinary robot as a holograph was to a child's crayon-picture. "It *is* a mistake. The male Citizen has no visitor, and he sent no message. Oooh!" She shook her head. "That hurt."

How could she feel pain? "An unkind word?"

"Destruction. He had the robot shoved in a meltbeam disposer. The robot's gone."

Just like that! Stile's own likeness, presenting himself in lieu of Stile, melted into waste material! Of course it was foolish to get sentimental about machines, Sheen excepted, but Stile had interacted briefly with the robot and felt a certain identification. "Did he know it was a robot?"

"I don't think so. But he knows *now*. People don't melt the same way. They scorch and stink." She cocked her head, listening. "Yes, we have to decamp. The Citizen is casting about for other intruders."

Stile remembered his encounter with the Black Adept, in Phaze: absolute resistance to intrusions. Enforcement by tacit murder—it seemed that type of personality was not unique to Adepts.

Sheen was drawing him on. Suddenly they were up and out, on the bleak surface of Proton adjacent to the Citizen's pleasure dome. She opened her front and removed a nose-mask. "Put this on; it is supplied with oxygen. It will tide you through for a while."

Stile obliged. When he found himself gasping, he breathed a sniff through his nose and was recharged.

The external landscape was awful. The ground was bare sand; no vegetation. A bare mountain range showed to the near south, rising into the yellowish haze of pollution.

Stile made a quick mental geographical calculation and concluded that these were the Purple Mountains of Phaze. They were actually not too far from the region of the Mound Folk. Except that no such Little People existed in this frame. Or did they? Most people had parallels; how could there be entire tribes in one frame, and none in the other? "Sheen, do you know of any people living in those mountains?"

"The Protonite mines are there," she reminded him. "The serfs that work there get stunted—" She broke off, glancing around. Something stirred. "Oh, no! He's got perimeter mechanicals out. We'll never get through that."

Stile stood and watched, appalled. From trenches in the ground small tanks charged, cannon mounted on their turrets. They formed a circle around the domed estate, moving rapidly, their radar antennae questing for targets.

Sheen hauled him through the force-field into the dome. The field was like the curtain: merely a tingle, but it separated one type of world from another. As they crossed it, the rich air enclosed them, and a penetration alarm sounded. They were certainly in trouble!

"Can your friends defuse the robot tanks?" Stile asked as they ran through outer storage chambers.

"No. The tanks are on an autonomous system. Only the Citizen can override their action. We're better off in here."

There was the sound of androids converging. "Not much better," Stile muttered. But she was off again, and he had to follow.

They ducked in and out of service passages. Sheen had unerring awareness of these, being able to tune in on the directive signals for maintenance robots. But the pursuit was close; they could not halt to camouflage themselves or ponder defensive measures.

Suddenly they burst into the main residential quarters. And paused, amazed.

It was Heaven. Literal, picturebook Heaven. The floor was made of soft white sponge contoured to resemble clouds; smaller clouds floated above, and on them winged babies perched, playing little harps. The front gate was nacreous: surely genuine pearl. Lovely music played softly in the background: angelic hymns.

An angel spied them and strode forward, his great wings fluttering. He wore a flowing robe on which a golden letter G was embroidered. "Ah, new guests of the Lord. Have you renounced all worldly sins and lusts?"

Neither Stile nor Sheen could think of a suitable spot rejoinder. They stood there—while the pursuing androids hove into sight.

"Here now! What's this?" the angel cried. "You soulless freaks can't come in here!"

The androids backed away, disgruntled. They reminded Stile of the animals of his football game when a penalty was called.

Now there was a voice from another cloudbank. "What is the disturbance, Gabriel?" a woman called.

"We have visitors," the Angel Gabriel called back. "But I am uncertain—"

The lady appeared. She wore a filmy gown that clung to her lushly convex contours. Stile found the effect indescribably erotic. He was accustomed to nakedness, or to complete clothing, but the halfway states—surely this Heaven was far from sexless!

The woman frowned. "These are serfs! They don't belong here!"

Stile and Sheen bolted. They plunged across the cloud-bank toward the most obvious exit: a golden-paved path-way. It spiraled down through a cloudwall, becoming a stone stairway. Letters were carved in the stones, and as he hurried over them Stile was able to read their patterns: GOOD INTENTIONS. At the bottom the stair terminated in a massive opaque double door. Sheen shoved it open, and they stepped through.

Again they both stood amazed. This nether chamber was a complete contrast to the region above. It was hot, with open fires burning in many pits. Horrendous murals de-picted grotesque scenes of lust and torture. Metal stakes anchored chains with manacles at the extremities.

"This is Hell," Stile said. "Heaven above, Hell below. It figures."

"The serf on the shuttle mentioned Heaven and Hell," Sheen reminded him. "She meant it literally."

A red-suited, horned, barb-tailed little devil appeared. He brandished his pitchfork menacingly. "Fresh meat!" he cried exultantly. "Oh, have we got fires for you! Move it, you damned lost souls!"

Behind them, feet sounded on the stairs. The androids had resumed the chase. It seemed the soulless ones were not barred from Hell.

Stile and Sheen took off again. Sheen charged the little devil, disarming him in passing. They ran across the floor of Hell, dodging around smoking pits.

"What's this?" a fat full-sized devil cried. "You serfs don't belong here!" It seemed Hell was after all as restric-tive as Heaven. The devil squinted at Stile. "I just had you melted!"

"That's how I came here," Stile said, unable to resist the flash of wit.

"The Citizen!" Sheen said. "He's Satan!"

"Apt characterization," Stile agreed.

"I'll have you torn to ragged pieces!" the Citizen roared, becoming truly Satanic in his ire.

"You would do better to tear up whoever faked the message that brought us to this address," Stile said. "Sir."

The Citizen paused. "There is that." He glanced at the ceiling. "Detail on that summons."

A screen appeared. "The summons was from a female Citizen, the man's Employer. The address was incorrect."

"Get me that Citizen!" Almost, it seemed that smoke issued from Satan's nostrils.

There was a pause. Then Stile's Employer appeared in the screen, frowning. "You sent for this serf?" the Satanic male Citizen demanded, indicating Stile.

The female Citizen's eyes took in Satan and Hell. "Do I know you?" she inquired coldly.

"You're a woman, aren't you? You bet you know me!"

She elected to change the subject. "I summoned this serf to my own address. What is he doing here?"

"This was the address he was given, idiot!"

"It certainly was not!" she retorted. Then she perused the message. "Why—the address has been changed. Who is responsible for this?"

"Changed . . ." Sheen murmured, the circuits connecting almost visibly in her computer-head. "Authentic summons, but one address-chip substituted for another. The handiwork of your assassin."

The female Citizen bore on Sheen. "Serf, you know who is responsible?"

"Sir, I know someone is trying to kill Stile," Sheen said. "I don't know who or why."

The lady Citizen frowned again. "I have entered this serf in the Tourney," she said to Satan. "He has won two Rounds. I dislike such interference."

"I dislike such intrusion on my premises," the male Citizen said.

"Of course. I'm sure *I* would not care to intrude on such premises. I shall initiate an investigation, as should you. But considering that the serfs are in fact blameless, will you not release them unharmed?"

"They have intruded!" the Satan-Citizen said. "The penalty is death!"

"I've already suffered it," Stile muttered.

"Not for *my* serfs," the female Citizen retorted, showing more spirit. "If I lose this chance to score in the Tourney, I shall be most upset."

"I am already upset, and I care not a fig for the Tourney. The intruders must die, and good riddance."

The female Citizen frowned once more. "It is unseemly for Citizens to bicker in the presence of serfs. Otherwise I could mention a drone missile currently oriented on your dome, capable of disrupting your power supply and irradiating your personnel: a certain inconvenience, I might suppose. I mean to have that serf."

This gave the devil pause to consider. "I agree. Citizens do not debate before serfs. Otherwise I could mention a couple things myself, such as an anti-missile laser oriented on—"

"Perhaps a fair compromise," she said. "Give the serfs a fair start, and we shall wager on the outcome."

The devil brightened. "Their lives—plus one kilogram of Protonite."

Stile almost gasped. A single gram of Protonite was worth the twenty-year tenure severance pay of a serf, a fee that would set him up comfortably for life elsewhere in the galaxy. These Citizens threw wealth around like sand.

"Only one kilo?" the female Citizen inquired. Stile could not tell whether that was irony or disdain.

"Plus you," Satan amended. "For a week."

"Outrageous!"

He sighed. "A day, then."

"Agreed." She faced Stile. "You will have two minutes to make your escape unfettered. Thereafter the full resources of this dome will be brought to bear against you. I suggest you make good use of the time. I do not wish to have to spend a day with this ilk."

"Now!" Satan cried.

"Follow me," Sheen said, and took off. Stile followed her without question; she was programmed for exactly this sort of thing. He remained bemused by the negotiation and terms agreed upon by the Citizens. His Employer wasn't concerned about the kilo of Protonite, but about a day with Satan—yet she had made the wager. What did that tell about the values of Citizens? He really wasn't sure. His Employer might be upset with him if she lost the wager— but he would already be dead. Perhaps this only indicated the relative values of things: the life of a favored serf, one kilo of Protonite, one day with a boor. Three things of equivalent merit.

Sheen had evidently surveyed this layout and resources of this dome, using her machine capabilities. She knew where everything was. Stile realized that his life was on the line, but he expected to retain it—because the Satan-Citizen evidently was not aware that Sheen was a robot. Their resources were greater, in the purely limited scope of pursuit, than the Citizen knew. Stile's Employer knew, of course, and had played her game adroitly. She expected to win her wager.

Sheen paused at a panel, opened it, and did something to its innards. "That will give us an extra minute," she said. "I put in a sixty-second implement-delay signal. By the time they notice it, it will have expired—and we have a minute more time." Then she took off again.

They came to a tank-reserve unit. Sheen opened the hatch to one of the tiny vehicles. "Get in."

"But there's only room for one person!"

"I don't need to breathe," she reminded him. "I will ride outside." When Stile looked doubtful, she said: "We're already into our extra minute. Get in! You know how to operate this device?"

"Yes." Stile had played Games with similar equipment; he could handle a tank adroitly. This one was armed with small explosive shells, however, instead of the colored-light imitation-laser of a Game tank. This was a real war machine, and that made him nervous.

"I can't help you once we get outside," Sheen said quickly. "Try to mimic the other tanks, so they don't know you're a fugitive. Then break for the mountains or another dome. They won't pursue beyond this Citizen's demesnes."

Demesnes. Like those of the Adepts of Phaze.

"Hang on," Stile said. He closed the hatch, fastened it down, and started the tank.

The motor roared into life. He ground down the exit tunnel, then up to ground level. Immediately he saw the ring of other tanks. He angled across to merge with their line. Protective mimicry—an excellent device!

But they were on to him. Maybe it was Sheen, clinging to the top, or maybe the Citizen's robot-personnel had noted the identity of his machine. The nearest tank oriented on him, its cannon swinging balefully about.

Very well. Stile was good at such maneuvers, though his life had not before hung so literally on his ability. He skewed to the side, and the enemy's first shot missed. Beyond him there was a detonation, and a black cloud expanded and drifted in the slight breeze.

Stile spun his tank about and fired at the one who had attacked him. Stile's aim was good; there was a burst of flame, and a cloud of smoke enveloped the other machine. He was a dead shot with most projectile weapons, though he had never expected that Game-talent to pay off so handsomely in real life.

Before that cloud had cleared, Stile whirled on the next, and scored on it too. However, the other tanks were converging on his own. There were too many of them, and Stile was conscious of Sheen on his top. Even a glancing hit, or piece of shrapnel could wipe her out! There was really no chance to escape this region unscathed.

Stile turned directly toward the Citizen's dome. This put him between it and the pursuing tanks; they could not fire at him because any missed shot would strike the dome. Machines were generally stupid, but this would be programmed into them.

The problem was that he remained confined. He could not break out of the ring of tanks without becoming a target. Before long the speck of Protonite that powered this vehicle would be exhausted; a heavy machine consumed a lot of energy. Then he would be stuck, vulnerable to whatever Satan had in mind for him. It would surely be hellish.

Well, do the unexpected. It was all that remained. Stile roared straight through the force-field and into the dome itself. Let the Citizen deal with *this*!

In moments he plowed through the partitions of the outer chambers, scattering stage props and supplies, and emerged upstairs in Heaven.

Angels scattered, screaming with uneternal terror, as the tank burst through a cloud bank, shedding puffs of clouds and crunching the foam-floor beneath. Stile slowed, not wanting to hurt anyone; after all, the angels were only costumed serfs. Also, if anyone died, his tenure on Proton would be abruptly terminated, and if the police arrested him before he reached the sanctity of the Tourney premises, he would not be allowed to reach it. No one could be arrested in the Game Annex itself. But how would he return to Phaze? As far as he knew, no fold of the curtain passed the Annex. So he was careful—and conscious of the anomaly of a tank touring Heaven, carrying a lady robot. He wanted to stop to check on Sheen, but knew he could not afford the delay; he had to figure out a course of action before the Citizen's forces reorganized.

Could he charge on down to the subway shuttle? The passages were fairly broad, and the tank should fit. But what would he do when he got there? This machine would not fit aboard a shuttle, and would have trouble running along the confined channel the shuttles used. But if he left this machine, he would be lasered down. Yet where else would he go? All his alternatives seemed futile.

Then he suffered inspiration. The curtain—of course! He had surveyed it near here, from the other side. If he could locate it and reach it—

It was a gamble at best. The curtain might not be close enough, and if it was within range he might not be able to spot it from the tank, and if he did spot it he still might not be able to will himself through it while riding in the tank. Yet one thing he was not going to do was stop and get out, under the guns of the other tanks!

It was no gamble at all to remain here idle. He would inevitably fall to Satan's forces. He *had* to try for the curtain!

He crashed on out of Heaven, through the interim chambers, and on into the barrens of Proton.

The enemy tanks were on the other side of the dome, where he had entered. That was a break for him. Stile headed toward the region where the curtain should be. With just a little further luck—

The enemy tanks reacted as one, cruising around the dome on either side and spreading out to form a broad line. Now they were getting him into their sights—and the dome was not going to be in the line of fire much longer. No good luck for him here!

Stile threw his tank from side to side as the firing commenced, making a difficult target. Machines were accurate shooters when the target was stationary or in steady motion, but when velocity was erratic and non-laser weapons were being employed, as now seemed to be the case, it was necessary to anticipate the strategy of the prey. Otherwise the time it took the shell to travel would put it behind the target-tank. Since Stile was humanly unpredictable, the shots were missing. But he could not afford to flaunt himself before them for long; inevitably a shell would score, at least disabling his machine. Then he would become a stationary target: a sitting quack, as it was described in Game-parlance.

In Phaze, he thought with fleeting humor, he had to watch out for spells. Here it was shells.

But his meandering had another purpose: to locate the curtain. It was here somewhere, but there were such poor reference points on the bare sand that he could not place it precisely. The curtain could curve about, and it shimmered so faintly that it was invisible from any distance, even for those like himself who were able to perceive it at all. He would probably come upon it so swiftly that he would pass it before realizing; then he would have to turn and try to cross from the other side while the enemy tanks had full seconds to orient.

A shell exploded in the sand beside him. The concussion shoved Stile's tank violently to the side. Something flew from it, visible in his screen. A section of armor?

No. *It was Sheen.*

Then Stile saw the curtain, angling across his path just ahead. He must have been traveling beside it, not quite intersecting it. He could veer right and pass through it now—

Not without Sheen! Yet he could not halt; that would be instant, fiery death. Already his pace slackened, the enemy tanks were closing the gap; their aim would become correspondingly more accurate. He had to get across—or perish.

Sheen had asked to be junked cleanly. Was this the occasion? Should he, after all, allow her to. . . ?

Stile set the controls to automatic, opened the hatch, and climbed out. The tank was moving at about 50 kilometers per hour now. Stile leaped off the side, sprinting desperately forward in midair. His feet touched the ground, and still weren't fast enough. He made a forward roll, eyes and mouth tightly closed, curling his body into a ball. The sand was soft, here, though his velocity was such that it felt hard; he rotated many times before coming out of it, bruised but whole. Oh, that sand was hot!

The enemy tanks, for the moment, were still chasing his empty tank. Stile charged back to find Sheen, who lay sprawled where she had fallen. She looked intact; perhaps the shock of the explosion had only jogged a wire loose, interrupting her power.

Stile picked her up and carried her toward the nearest intersection of the curtain. But she was heavy, being made of metals and plastic; it was a considerable burden in the shifting sand, and his bare feet were hurting from the heat. Stile was soon panting as he staggered on.

His empty tank exploded. Chance and firepower had brought it down.

Now the enemy tanks slowed their pursuit, turning to return to their normal perimeter. And of course they became aware of Stile, lumbering along with his burden. Cannon swiveled to bear on him. But there was the curtain, just ahead.

Stile summoned his reserves and leaped. *Phaze!* he thought, willing himself through. A tank fired; the shell whistled; the sand behind Stile erupted.

Then the faint tingle of the curtain was on him. Stile fell to the ground, and it was green turf. Sheen was wrenched from his grasp and rolled through the grass and leaves and landed arms and legs akimbo.

One foot was burning. Stile realized that it remained on the other side of the curtain, where the smoke and heat of the shell-blast touched it. Hastily he drew it through. It was not burned, merely uncomfortable.

Now he went to Sheen. She was disheveled and battered, her fine torso abraded. One breast had been torn off, and about a third of her hair had been pulled out. It seemed, too, that the right side of her body had been crushed, and metal showed through a compound fracture of her right arm. There was a great deal more wrong with her than a loose wire!

He did not love her, he reminded himself. She was only a machine, her consciousness artificial. Without her power pack and feedback circuitry she was no more than junk.

But his logic was overwhelmed by a surge of emotion. "I do love you, Sheen, in my fashion!" he whispered. "I shall have you repaired—"

Have her repaired? This was Phaze, the frame of magic. He was the Blue Adept. He could restore her himself!

Or could he? He was not a healing Adept, and had never been able to affect the vital functions of a living creature. Well, he had healed Neysa after her visit to Hell, and his alternate self had done healing. So maybe he just needed practice. The Lady Blue had the healing touch, while Stile's magic was generally more physical, however. And in no event could he restore the dead to life.

Yet Sheen had never been alive. Why couldn't he fix her physical circuitry, repair her breaks and losses? She should be within the ambience of his talent, after all!

Quickly he fashioned spot spells: "Robot Sheen, body clean," he sang, wishing he had his harmonica or the Platinum Flute along. But he had never anticipated returning to Phaze like this! In future he would keep those instruments with him at all times.

Sheen's torso became unblemished. It was working!

"Bones of steel, mend and heal." And her fracture knitted itself together while her torso sprang out to original configuration, with even the missing breast replaced. "Face be fair; restore the hair," and all that damage was undone.

Now for the big one. "Broken circuits mend; consciousness lend." Once again he was bothered by the crudity of the verse. But it served his purpose. Sheen was whole, now.

Except that she still lay there, lovely as any naked woman could be. She showed no sign of animation. How had he failed?

Maybe the lack of a musical instrument had depleted the force of his magic. Stile conjured a simple guitar and used it to strum up greater power, then tried other spells. He covered everything he could think of, but nothing worked. At last, succumbing to reaction from his own narrow escape and grief-stricken at her apparent demise, he threw himself on her body and kissed her unresponsive lips. "Oh Sheen—I'm sorry!"

If he had expected his kiss to bring her magically to life, he was disappointed. She remained defunct.

After a moment Stile sat up. His face was wet, a signal of his emotion. "I can't accept this," he said. "There has to be *something*."

Then it came to him: Sheen was a sophisticated machine, mechanical and electronic, a creature of advanced science and technology—and such things were not operative in the fantasy frame. Sheen could be in perfect condition—he could not say "health"—yet be inoperative here. Only her body could cross the curtain, not her functioning.

The answer was to get her back to her own frame. He had business there anyway. This excursion into Phaze was merely a device to save his own life.

Stile got up, then picked up the robot. He braced himself for the penalty of vertigo, then sang a spell to transport him instantly to his usual curtain-crossing place. Arriving there, he spelled them through.

Sheen woke as the passage formed about them. "Stile!" she exclaimed. "What—where—?"

He kissed her and set her down. "I'll explain it all. But first we have to contact my employer and advise her that she won her bet. She doesn't have to spend time with Satan."

"Yes," she agreed. "But how—?"

"I do love you somewhat," Stile said. "I know that now."

"But I'm a machine!"

"And I'm a concatenation of protoplasm." He spanked her pert bare bottom. "Now move, creature!"

She reoriented swiftly. "I'd certainly like to know what happened during my blank. The last I remember, I was riding the tank. Now I'm here. It's like magic."

Stile laughed to see her unrobotic confusion. He was so glad to have her animated again that he felt giddy. No, that was the vertigo of his self-transport. "Just exactly like magic!" he agreed, taking her hand and drawing her on.

His Round Three Game was with an alien.

Stile had never played a nonhuman living creature before. He had seen them play, since twenty-four aliens were admitted to every Tourney, but often the majority of these "aliens" were merely wealthy otherworld human beings, or at least humanoids. Many people were attracted by the lure of unmitigated wealth and power, but few who were not of the system were permitted to compete. Stile understood that the entry fee for offworlders was formidable, whereas there was no fee for serfs. Oh, they had the system well worked out! One way or another, the dues were paid.

But this one was that rarity, a genuine alien creature. It had a ring of tentacles in lieu of arms above, and six little caterpillar feet below, and its face was mainly an elephantine proboscis. There did seem to be sensory organs, on little stalks that bobbled about. Stile presumed the ones with balled ends were eyes, and the ones with hollow bells were ears; he could not account for the ones with opaque disks.

"Salutation," he said formally. "I am Stile, a serf-human being of this planet."

"Courtesy appreciation; you do look the part," the alien responded. The sound emanated from somewhere about its head, but not from its snout. "I will be Dgnh of Elsewhere."

"Apology. I am unable to pronounce your name."

"Complete with vowel-sound of your choice: irrelevancy to local vocal."

"Dogonoh?" Stile inquired.

"Noh for brief. Sufficiently."

"Noh," Stile agreed. "You are prepared for any Game?"

"Appallingly."

Then he need feel no guilt about playing hard to win. This creature could have spent a lifetime preparing for this single event, and have some inhuman skills. Already Stile was trying to evaluate Noh's potential. Those tentacles looked sturdy and supple; the creature was probably apt at mechanical things. It was probably best to stay clear of any physical contest. Since he did not care to gamble in CHANCE or ART, that left MENTAL—if he had the choice. On the other range, he had best stay clear of tools or machines, again fearing that alien dexterity. So he should go for NAKED or ANIMAL. Probably the latter, since he understood local animals well, and the alien probably did not.

"Prior matches—compare?" Noh asked.

That would help him gain an insight into the alien's propensities. "I played Football with a Citizen, and Dominoes with a female serf," Stile said.

"Not for me, your Football," Noh decided. "Foots too small. Dominoes no either, element of chance."

Pretty savvy, this creature. "The grid leads to compromise."

"So I explicated. Tiddlywinks with manchild and Storytelling with Citizen. Won Games, but nervous."

"Certainly," Stile agreed. Under the alien form, this being was a true Gamesman. Stile had experienced such competitive nervousness many times. In fact, every Game brought it on. That was part of the addiction of it. He was in the Tourney to try for Citizenship, surely; but he also had an abiding delight in the competition of the thing, the endless variants, the excitement of the temporarily unknown. That was what had caused him to remain on Proton as a serf, instead of departing with his parents when their tour of tenure had expired. The fascination and compulsion of the Game had ruled him.

Now, ironically, his major involvement was with magic, with the lovely frame of Phaze. There, he was a person of considerable substance, a magician. He had entered the Tourney here at a time when its significance for him had been greatly reduced. Yet new reasons had erupted to restore its importance. He was doing it for Sheen, and for pride, and for the chance to discover who was trying to kill him, and to achieve the ability to do something about it. Just as he was participating in the quest of the Platinum Flute in Phaze, for Neysa and pride and eventual vengeance. So despite the considerable flux in both frames, his course had hardly changed.

Stile was jolted out of his reverie by the announcement of his Game. He and the alien stepped up to the grid unit.

The alien was even shorter than Stile; only its perception-stalks showed above the unit. Since the grid-screens on either side were all that counted, this did not matter. Nor-

mally Stile preferred to study his opponent for telltale reactions during the stress of selection; a hint about a person's nervous state could spell the key to victory. But he
could not read the alien anyway.

The primary grid showed. Good—Stile had the numbers.
Without hesitation he selected MENTAL.

Noh was just as quick—which alarmed Stile. If this
creature was as fast on its mental feet as his reaction-time
indicated, this meant trouble. The selected panel showed
2A, MENTAL/NAKED. Mind alone, no body involvement.

The secondary grid appeared. Numbered across the top
were the categories SOCIAL—POWER—MATH—
HUMOR; lettered down the side were the qualities IN-
FORMATION—MEMORY—RIDDLE—MANIPULA-
TION. Stile had the numbers, and that was fine.

Suppose he chose SOCIAL? The alien could choose IN-
FORMATION, and the subgrid could put them into planetary history, where Noh could be well prepared. *What was
the date of the squassation of the Bohunk of Planet Tee-
total, in local zero-meridian time?* He certainly didn't need
that! Should he choose POWER? Noh could choose
MEMORY, and they could rival each other in the recall of
extended sequences of letters, numbers and concepts, the
kind of thing that used to fill the tests that supposedly
indicated human intelligence. Stile was good at this, in
human terms—but how could he be sure that Noh did not
possess long-term eidetic memory, and be virtually invinci-
ble? Or the alien could select MANIPULATION, and they
could wind up playing a mental game of three-dimensional
chess. Stile could do that, too—but it was a literal headache. However, MATH could lead to the identification of
obscure formulae if Noh chose INFORMATION, or the
spot rehearsal of log tables or trig functions. MATH/
RIDDLES could be just as bad; better go to MANIPU-
LATION and do complex problems in his head. But if he
chose HUMOR, and Noh chose RIDDLE, they would
wind up comparing puns. Puns with an alien?

Damn it, he was up against a completely unknown quality of opponent! *Any* choice could be ruinous. If only he
had had time to do his homework, researching his prospec-

tive opponents, however scantily; then at least he would have had some broad notion what to avoid. But this business in Phaze had crippled his research time.

Stile sighed. He would have to go with MATH.

Noh had already selected RIDDLE. They were in 3C, Mathematical Riddles. Well, it could have been worse. Stile had on-days and off-days on this sort of thing; sometimes inspiration presented him with a brilliant response, and sometimes he felt as if his head were stuffed with sawdust, and sometimes he cursed himself for missing the obvious. But normally he was pretty sharp on mathematical riddles, and he knew a great number of them.

The final grid was about as simple as they came: four squares. The top was 1. COMPUTER-GENERATED 2. SELF-GENERATED. The side was A. DUAL RESPONSE B. INDIVIDUAL RESPONSE. Just four alternatives. Stile had the numbers.

Noh's antennae wavered in agitation. "Nonetheless is this naked mental? How justified computer involvement?"

"These categories are fundamentally arbitrary," Stile explained. "Too many Games are in fact mixed types. The Game Computer assumes for the sake of convenience that it, itself, has no Game significance. The riddles could come from a book or a third person, but it is most convenient and random to draw on the computer memory banks. There are all kinds of little anomalies like this in the Games; I had to play Football using androids termed animals, with robots for referees."

"This is delightfully mistrustful. Expedient to avoid?"

"Well, I happen to have the numbered facet, so you cannot control that. Myself, I'd rather avoid the dual response; that's timed, with the first one to answer being the winner. I'm more of a power thinker; I get there, but not always in a hurry." This was true, but perhaps misleading; Stile was stronger as a power thinker in proportion to his other skills, but still by no means a slow thinker. "That is—"

"Can we collude? Choose 2B for mutual accommodationality?"

"We could—but how could we know one of us won't cheat? Deals are permissible but not legally enforceable in the Game. An expert liar makes an excellent grid-player. The computer accepts nothing but the signal-buttons."

"Chance it must be risked," Noh said. "Some trust exists in the galaxy, likewise on little planets."

"Agreed," Stile said, smiling at the alien's phrasing. He touched 2, and sure enough, it came up 2B. They had each kept faith. Game players normally did; it greatly facilitated things on occasion.

Now they adjourned to a bare private chamber. "Select a recipient for the first riddle," the Game Computer said from a wall speaker. "Recipient must answer within ten minutes, then propose a counter-riddle for the other. In the event of failure to answer, proponent must answer his own riddle, then answer opponent's riddle within the time limit. The first contestant to achieve such success is the victor. Computer will arbitrate the technical points."

"You courtesy explained situation," Noh said. "Appreciation I yield initial."

It really did not make any difference who went first, since only an unanswered or misanswered riddle followed by a successful defense counted. But Stile was glad to get into it, for psychological reasons. He had a number of tricky questions stored in the back of his mind. Now he would find out just what the alien was made of, intellectually.

"Picture three equal-length sticks," Stile said carefully. "Each quite straight, without blemish. Form them into a triangle. This is not difficult. With two additional sticks of the same size and kind a second triangle can be formed against a face of the first. Now can you fashion four congruent triangles from only six such sticks?"

Noh considered. "Enjoyability this example! Permissible to employ one stick to bisect double-triangle figure formed from segments of sticks?"

"No. Each stick must represent exactly one side of each triangle; no projecting points." But Stile felt a tingle of apprehension; such a device would indeed have formed four congruent triangles, and similar overlapping could make up to six of them. This creature was no patsy.

"Permissible to cross sticks to form pattern of star with each point a triangle?"

"No crossing." So quick to explore the possibilities!

The head stalks bobbled thoughtfully for almost a minute. Then: "Permissible to employ a third dimension?"

The alien had it! "Permissible," Stile agreed gamely.

"Then to elevate one stick from each angle of first triangle, touching at apex to form four-sided pyramid, each side triangle."

"You've got it," Stile admitted. "Your turn."

"Agreeable game. Triangles amenable to my pleasure. Agree sum of angles is half-circle?"

"One hundred eighty degrees," Stile agreed.

"Present triangle totaling three-quarter circle."

"That's—" Stile began, but choked off the word "impossible." Obviously the alien had something in mind. Yet how could any triangle have a total of 270°? He had understood 180° was part of the definition of any triangle. Each angle could vary, but another angle always varied inversely to compensate. If one angle was 179°, the other two would total 1°. Otherwise there would be no triangle.

Unless there could be an overlay of triangles, one angle counting as part of another triangle, adding to the total. That didn't seem sensible, yet—

"Permissible to overlap triangles?" Stile inquired.

"Never."

So much for that. Stile paced the floor, visualizing triangles of all shapes and sizes. No matter how he made them, none had more than 180°.

Could they have differing definitions of triangles? "Permissible to have more than three angles in the figure?"

"Never."

Down again. Damn it, it wasn't possible! Yet somehow, by some logic, it had to be, or the alien would not have proposed it. Stile had encountered situations in which the supposedly impossible had turned out to be possible, like turning a torus inside out through a hole in its side. Topology—there was a fertile field for intellectual riddles! Shapes that were infinitely distortable without sacrificing their fundamental qualities. Bend it, twist it, stretch it, tie it in knots, it did not really change. Now if he could do that with a triangle, bowing out the sides so as to widen the angles—but then its sides would be curved, no good.

Maybe if it were painted on a rubberite sheet, which sheet was stretched—aha! A curved surface! Noh had not specified a flat surface. A triangle drawn on a sphere—

"Permissible to employ a curved surface?" Stile inquired triumphantly.

"Never. Triangle must be rigid frame, as were your own."

Ouch! He had been so sure! On the surface of a sphere he could have made eight triangles each with three right angles, or even four triangles with two right angles and one 180° straight angle each—a quarter section of the whole. The curvature of the surface permitted straight lines, in effect, to bow. He had often carved the skin of a pseudoorange that way. But the alien forbade it.

Still, perhaps he was getting warmer. Noh's antennae were flexing nervously, which could be a good sign. Suppose the surface were not curved, but space itself was? That could similarly distort a rigid triangle, by changing the laws of its environment. In theory the space of the universe was curved; suppose the triangle were of truly cosmic proportion, so that it reflected the very surface of the cosmos? "Okay to make a very large triangle?"

"Nokay," Noh responded. "Standard triangle held in tentacles readily."

Brother! Stile was getting so inventive, stretching his imagination, to no avail. If he could not draw on the curvature of space—

But he could! "How about taking it to another location?"

The stalks wobbled ruefully. "Permissible."

"Like maybe the vicinity of a black hole in space, where intense gravity distorts space itself. Normal geometric figures become distorted, despite no change in themselves, as though mounted on a curved surface. Down near the center of that black hole, space could even be deformed into the likeness of a sphere, just before singularity, and a triangle there could have two hundred and seventy degrees, or even more."

"The creature has resolved it," Noh agreed ruefully. "Inquire next riddle."

This was no easy Game! Stile felt nervous sweat cooling on his body. He feared he was overmatched in spatial relationships. He had invoked the third dimension, and the alien had in turn invoked something like the fourth dimension. Better to move it into another region. "Using no other figures, convert four eights to three ones," Stile said. Probably child's play for this creature, but worth a try.

"Permissible to add, subtract, multiply, divide, powers, roots, tangents?" Noh asked.

"Permissible—so long as only eights are used," Stile agreed. But of course simple addings of eights would never do it.

"Permissible to form shapes from numbers?"

"You mean like calling three ones a triangle or four eights a double row of circles? No. This is straight math." Noh was on the wrong trail.

But then the alien brightened. His skin assumed a lighter hue. "Permissible to divide 888 by 8 to achieve 111?"

"Permissible," Stile said. That really had not balked Noh long—and now the return shot was coming. Oh, dread!

"Human entity has apparent affinity for spheres, as witness contours of she-feminine of species," Noh said. "Appreciate geography on sphere?"

"I fear not," Stile said. "But out with it, alien."

"In human parlance, planetary bodies have designated north and south poles, apex and nadir of rotation, geographical locators?"

"Correct." What was this thing leading up to?

"So happenstance one entity perambulates, slithers, or otherwise removes from initiation of north pole, south one unit, then east one unit, and right angle north one unit, discover self at point of initiation."

"Back at the place he started, the north pole, yes," Stile agreed. "That's the one place on a planet that such a walk is possible. Walk south, east, north and be home. That's really a variant of the triangle paradox, since two right angle turns don't—"

"Discover another location for similar perambulation."

"To walk south a unit, east a unit, and north a unit, and be at the starting point—without starting at the north pole?"

"Explicitly."

The creature had done it again. Stile would have sworn there was no such place. Well, he would have to find one!

Not the north pole. Yet the only other place where polar effects occurred was the south pole—and how could a person travel south from that? By definition, it was the southernmost region of a planet.

"All units are equal in length and all are straight?" Stile inquired, just in case.

"Indelicately."

"Ah, I believe you mean indubitably?"

"Indecisively," the alien agreed.

Just so. "Can't move the planet to a black hole?"

"Correct. Cannot. Would squash out of shape."

So it had to be settled right here; no four-dimensional stunts. Yet where in the world could it be? Not the north pole, not the south pole—

Wait! He was assuming too much. He did not have to go south from the south pole. He had to go south *to* it. Or almost to it. . . .

"Picture a circle around the south pole," Stile said. "A line of latitude at such distance north of the pole that its circuit is precisely one unit. Now commence journey one unit north of that latitude. Walk south, then east around the pole, and north, retracing route to starting point."

"Accursed, foiled additionally," Noh said. "This creature is formidability."

Stile's sentiments exactly, about his opposition. He was afraid he was going to lose this match, but he struck gamely for new territory, seeking some intellectual weakness in his opponent. "The formula X^2 plus Y^2 equals Z^2, when graphed represents a perfect circle with a radius of Z, as described in what we call the Pythagorean Theorem," he said. "Are you familiar with the mechanism?"

"Concurrently. We term it the Snakegrowltime Equation."

Stile suspected there was a bit of alien humor there, but he had to concentrate on the job at hand instead of figuring out the reference. He was glad he had not gotten into a punning contest! "What variation of this formula represents a square?"

"No variation!" Noh protested. "That formula generates only a curve; a variation must remain curvaceous. No straight lines from this."

"I will settle for an approximate square," Stile said helpfully. "One that curves no more than the width of the lines used to draw it."

"How thickness lines?"

"Same thickness as those used to make the circle."

"Extraordinarily unuseful," Noh grumped, pacing the floor with the little feet tramping in threes. "Geometric curves do not transformation so. It is a fact of math."

"Math is capable of funny things." Stile was regaining confidence. Had he found a weakness?

Noh paced and questioned and did the alien equivalent of sweating, and finally gave it up. "Incapability of sensiblizing this. Demand refutation."

"Try $X\infty$ plus $Y\infty$ equals $Z\infty$," Stile said.

"Party of the first part raised to the infinitive power, plus party of the second part raised similarly? This is meaningful-less!"

"Well, try it partway, to get the drift. X^3 plus—"

"Partway?" Noh demanded querulously. "Cannot split infinity!"

Stile thought of the infinities of the scientific and magical universes, split by the curtain. But that was not relevant here. "X^3 plus Y^3 equals Z^3 yields a distorted loop, no longer a perfect circle. Raise the powers again. X^4 plus Y^4 equals Z^4, and it distorts further towards the corners. By the time it goes to the tenth or twelfth power, it is beginning to resemble a square. By the time it reaches the millionth power—"

Noh did some internal calculating. "It approaches a square! Never a perfect one, for it yet is a curve, but within any desired tolerance—remarkable! I never realized a curve could fashion into—amaztonishing!"

"Now I must answer yours," Stile reminded the alien. He knew he hadn't won yet; he had only gained a temporary advantage, thanks to splitting an infinity.

"Appreciably so. Where is the west pole?"

"West pole?"

"North pole, south pole, east pole, west pole. Where?"

"But a planet can only have one axis of rotation! There can't be two sets of poles!"

"There cannot be a square generated from a curve, alternatively."

"Um, yes." Stile lapsed into thought. If he could get this one, he won the Round. But it baffled him as much as his square had baffled Noh. Was the west pole simply a matter of semantics, a new name for the north or south poles? That seemed too simple. There really had to be a pole in addition to the conventional ones, to make it make sense. Yet unless a planet could have two axes of rotation—

In the end, Stile had to give it up. He did not know where the west pole was. His advantage had disappeared. They were even again. "Where?"

"Anticipation-hope you would solution it," Noh said. "Solve has eluded me for quantity of time."

"You mean you don't know the answer yourself?" Stile asked incredulously.

"Affirmation. I have inexplicably defaulted competition. Negative expedience. Remorse."

So Stile had won after all! Yet he wished he could have done it by solving the riddle. The west pole—where could it be? He might never know, and that was an aggravation.

Stile had been late in the Round Three roster, and now was early in the Round Four roster, as the Game Computer shifted things about to ensure fairness. Hence he had less than a day to wait. He spent much of that time sleeping, recovering from his excursion with the tanks and resting for possibly grueling forthcoming Games. He had been lucky so far; he could readily have lost the Football Game and the Riddle Game, and there was always the spectre of CHANCE to wash him out randomly. Most duffer players were fascinated by CHANCE; it was the great equalizer. So he hoped he would encounter a reasonably experienced player, one who preferred to fight it out honestly. One who figured he had a chance to win by skill or a fortuitous event in a skill contest, like the referee's miscall in the Football Game. But a true skill contest could be arduous, exhausting both participants so that the winner was at a disadvantage for the next Game.

If Stile's employer discovered anything in the course of her investigation into the matter of the forged message-address, she did not confide it to him. That was the way of Citizens. They often treated serfs with superficial courtesy, but no followthrough. The Citizen he had encountered in Round One, the Rifleman, was an example; there had been no further communication from him. There was no such thing, in Proton law and custom, as a binding commitment by Citizen to serf. Everything went the other way.

Stile remained troubled by the continuing campaign against him by his anonymous enemy. At first he had thought this person had sent Sheen and then lasered his knees as a warning to get out of horseracing. But he had gotten out—and the threat continued. There had been a Citizen who was after him, but that had been effectively neutralized, and Sheen's self-willed robot friends had verified that he was not the present offender. They had not been able to trace the source of the substituted address, because it had not been handled through any computer circuits; it had been a "mechanical" act. But they had watched that particular Citizen, and knew that he was relatively innocent.

Someone wanted Stile dead—in Proton and in Phaze. Perhaps it was the same person—a frame-traveler. There were a number of people who crossed the curtain regularly, as Stile himself did. Maybe that same one had killed Stile's other self, the Blue Adept, and tried for Stile with less success. Probably another Adept; no lesser person could have done it. But who? The maker of golems—or the maker of amulets? Stile was becoming most eager to know.

If he beat the long odds and won the Tourney, he would have at his disposal the resources of a Citizen. *Then* he would be in a position to find out—and to take remedial action. That was the real imperative of his present drive. He could not wash out of the Tourney and simply return to Phaze to court the Lady Blue—not when a curtain-crossing Adept was laying constant deathtraps for him. He had life-and-death riddles to solve first!

His Round Four opponent was a woman his own age: Hella, first Rung on the Age 35 ladder. Stile had qualified for the Tourney by being fifth on the male 35 ladder, but he was actually the top player of his age. Many top players remained deliberately low on their Game ladders, so as to avoid the annual Tourney draft of the top five. Hella, however, really was the top female player, whose tenure ended this year; she had been eager to enter the Tourney.

Nevertheless, she was not in Stile's class. He could outperform her in most of the physical Games and match her in the mental ones. If he got the numbers he would have no gallantry at all. He would choose PHYSICAL. If he had the letters he would have to go for TOOL, to put it into the boardgames block, where he retained the advantage over her.

Hella was a fit, statuesque woman, taller and heavier than Stile. She had half-length dark-blonde hair, slightly curly, and lips a little too thin. She looked like what she was: a healthy, cynical, hard-driving woman, nevertheless possessed of a not inconsiderable sex appeal. Larger men found her quite attractive, and she was said to be proficient at private games, the kind that men and women played off record. Stile had played her often, in random Games, but had never socialized with her. Most women did not get romantic about men who were smaller than themselves, and she was no exception. Stile himself had always been diffident about women, and remained so. Sheen was special, and not really a woman. The Lady Blue was special too—and Stile really found himself unable to forward his suit with her. She was his other self's widow . . .

"I would rather not have come up against you," Hella told him in the waiting room. "I'm already half out; a duffer caught me in CHANCE."

"That's the way it goes," Stile said. "I have nothing against you, but I intend to put you away."

"Of course," she said. "If you get the numbers."

"If I get the numbers," he agreed.

Their summons came. Stile did not get the numbers. Thus they landed in 2B, Tool-Assisted MENTAL GAMES. They played the sixteen choices of the subgrid and came to MAZE.

They adjourned to the Maze-section of the Game premises. The Game Computer formed new mazes for each contest by sliding walls and panels along set channels;

there was an extraordinary number of combinations, and it was not possible to anticipate the correct route through. One person started from each end, and the first to complete the route won.

They took their places. Stile was designated blue, the convention for males, and Hella red, the convention for females. Had two males been competing, they would have been blue and green, or red and yellow for females. The Computer liked things orderly.

The starting buzzer sounded. Stile pushed through the blue door into the labyrinth. Inside the walls and floor were restful light gray, the ceiling a translucent illumination panel. As Stile's weight came on the floor, it turned blue, panel by panel, and remained that way to show where he had been. Spectators could view this Game on vision screens in mockup form, the patterns developing in red and blue to show the progress of both competitors, appreciating the ironies of wrong turnings and near-approaches to each other.

Stile moved quickly down the hall, his blue trail keeping pace, until he came to the first division. He didn't hesitate; he took the left passage. Further along, it divided again; this time he took the right passage. The general law of chance would make the right and left splits along the proper way come out about even; this was unreliable for short-term efforts, but still as good a rule to follow as any.

This passage convoluted, turned back on itself, and abruptly dead-ended. So much for general laws! Stile quickly reversed course, following his own blue trail, and took what had been the left passage. This twisted about and finally intersected his original blue trail—the first right turn he had ignored.

Oops—there had to be an odd number of passages available, for at least one led to the red door on the other side of the maze. If two led there, then there would be an even number—with two passages as yet untried. But that was unusual; spectators liked to have the two contestants meet somewhere in the center, and start frantically following each other's trails, and the Game Computer usually obliged with such a design. He must have missed a passage in his hurry. First mistake, and he hoped it would not prove to be too expensive.

He checked the passage back to the blue door. Nothing there. Then he took off on the right-hand passage he had used to complete the loop. Sure enough, it divided; he had overlooked the other passage because it angled back the way he had come. He should have checked behind him as well as ahead; an elementary precaution. He was not playing well.

However, this was not necessarily time wasted. Hella would be working her way through from the other side, trying to intersect his blue trail that would lead her to the blue door. If he had a single path there, she would have no trouble. As it was, he had turned *all* paths blue, so she would have no hint; she might get lost, just as he had. Sometimes, in these mazes, one person got nine-tenths of the way through, while the other floundered—and then the flounderer followed the other trail to victory while the nine-tenths person floundered. One could never tell.

He moved on down the new passage. It, too, divided; he moved left and followed new convolutions. This one did not seem to be dead-ending or intersecting itself; good. Now he needed to intersect Hella's trail before she intersected his.

Stile paused, listening. Yes—he heard her walking in the adjacent passage. That did not necessarily mean she was close; that passage could be a dead-end without connection to this one. Nevertheless, if he knew her location while she did not know his, that could be an advantage. He might sneak in and find her trail while she was still exploring a false lead, and hurry on to victory.

Then he heard her make a small, pleased exclamation. Ouch—that could mean only one thing: she had intersected his trail. Which meant that *he* was probably the one on the dead-end.

Stile backtracked hastily and silently. Sure enough, her red path intersected his, where he had bypassed the last right passage, and ended there. She was hot on his blue trail, and going the right direction. He was in trouble!

Stile took off down the red trail. He had only two hopes: first that she had a fairly direct trail he could follow without confusion; second that she would get lost on his loops and dead-end.

His first hope was soon dashed; the red trail divided, and he did not know which one was good. He had to guess. He bore right, looped about, came close to the exit-region—and dead-ended. All the breaks were going against him!

He hurried back, no longer bothering to be silent, and took the other trail. It wound about interminably, while at every moment he feared he would hear the clang of her exit and victory. It divided again; he bore right, sweating. If he lost this simple Game to this woman, who really was not the player he was . . .

Then, abruptly, it was before him: the red door. Stile sprinted for it, suddenly convinced that Hella's foot was on the sill of the blue door, that even half a second would wipe him out. In his mind's ear he heard the toll of his loss.

He plunged through. The bell sounded. He had won!

"Damn!" Hella exclaimed from the interior. She had after all gotten lost in his loop, and was nowhere close to the blue door. His alarm had been false.

Sheen was waiting as he emerged. "Take me away from here," he told her, putting his arm about her slender waist. He suffered another untoward image: Sheen lying torn apart after the tank chase. Yet there was no present evidence of that injury; she was all woman. "I've had enough of the Tourney for now!"

"There'll be more than a day before your next match," she said. "Time for you to catch your duel with the Herd Stallion in Phaze."

"I might as well be right here in the Tourney!" he complained. "One contest after another."

CHAPTER 6

Unolympic

Neysa had taken off early to rehearse with her brother for the incipient exhibitions, at the Lady Blue's behest. Stile was bothered about the hiatus in protection for the Lady, but was unable to object. She had remained within the castle, reasonably safe.

At the appropriate hour, Stile put his arm about the Lady's supple waist and uttered a spell that jumped them both to the event. He was getting better at this sort of spell, but still would rather have traveled by conventional means, had there been time.

It was impressive. Eight or ten herds of unicorns had assembled for their competition; each Herd Stallion had his banner mounted at his camp and his subjects ranged about it. There was a tremendous open pasture upon which many hundreds of unicorns grazed. They sported all the colors of moons and rainbow, and were handsome specimens of equine flesh.

Yet there were many other creatures too. Werewolves ranged in small packs, carefully neutral in the sight of so much potential prey. No false growls here! Bats swooped from perch to perch and sailed high in the air in pursuit of insects. Humanoid figures of all types abounded.

A unicorn male trotted up to Stile and the Lady. In a moment he shifted to man-form, neatly attired in a khaki uniform. "Please identify thyself and party and accept an admittance tag."

"The Blue Adept and Lady Blue," Stile said.

"Adept! Right this way!" The unicorn's reaction resembled that of a serf of Proton confronted by a Citizen.

They followed the unicorn to a small pavilion set up beside the exhibition field. Several people reclined on thronelike chairs or couches. They did not rise or make any acknowledgment of Stile's or the Lady's arrival. Stile was now well-enough accustomed to the ways of Phaze to know that this nonreaction represented a studied discourtesy to either an Adept or a Lady. But he showed no overt reaction; he wanted first to understand *why*.

Then a comely young woman stood and approached them. She seemed vaguely familiar. "Thou comest undisguised, my handsome?" she inquired, proffering her hand. There was the hint of a cronish cackle in her voice.

"Yellow!" he exclaimed. "What brings thee here? I thought—"

"Thou didst suppose I had no more youth potions?" she inquired archly. "None that would stand up to a day's hard use?"

"I recalled thee with fair hair, fairer than those of the Lady Blue, light yellow tresses." Said tresses were now short, brown and curly. But of course she could make her appearance whatever she chose, for the duration of her potion. This was, as she put it, her costume. Her dress, at least, was yellow; that was the real key. "I thought the unicorns—" He shrugged.

"It is truce between all attendees of the Unolympics," she explained. "Well the animals know my nature, but here I exert my powers not, neither do the animals chide me for old affronts. We Adepts have few such social opportunities, and few occasions to socialize with others of our ilk in peace. We take them greedily."

He remembered that Yellow had been lonely in her own Demesnes, especially for male company. Naturally she would socialize when she safely could. "Ah, like the temple of the Oracle," Stile said. "No quarrels here." He looked about. "These be Adepts?"

"And consorts. I forgot that thou rememberest not." She smiled brilliantly and bobbed her cleavage about, enjoying her youthful form as only an old hag could. What height was to men, he thought, breasts were to women. "Come, my charming; I will introduce thee around."

A chance to meet other Adepts—one of whom might be his murderer! This was serendipitous, an unexpected windfall.

Yellow conducted them to a woman reclining on a white couch, and garbed in a sparkling white gown. She was of indeterminate middle age, and somewhat stout. "This be White," Yellow said, indicating her with a half-contemptuous twist of a thumb. Then she jerked the thumb at Stile. "This be Blue, and Lady."

The White Adept lifted snowy lashes. Her eyes were ageless, like swirls of falling snow. "Reports of thy demise seem to have been exaggerated."

"No exaggeration," Stile said. "I seek my murderer."

"May I be far from the scene of thine encounter," White said, unalarmed, and turned her wintry orbs back to the field where several unicorns were practicing their acts. Stile remembered that the White Adept had been in the market for a white unicorn; Yellow had mentioned that, at their first encounter. He hoped no such creature had been captured.

Yellow led them on. "Methinks thy appearance here stirs greater commotion than shows," she murmured with grim satisfaction. "It is well known that thou'rt possibly the strongest current Adept, and that thou hast cause for vengeance. Blue was ne'er wont to attend these functions before. Only be certain thou hast the right party, before thou makest thy move."

"I shall," Stile said through his teeth.

Now they approached a man in black. He glanced incuriously at Stile as Yellow made the introduction. "Black ...Blue."

"We have met before," Stile said evenly.

Black peered at him. "I recall it not."

"In thy Demesnes, a month ago." Had it been so short a time? Stile felt as if an age had passed since he had first entered the frame of Phaze and assumed the mantle of the Blue Adept. Subjective experiences had made the days seem like months. Even his encounter with Black seemed impossibly distant. Yet Black was the same, with his line tapering off into the ground, no doubt attaching him to his castle. Black was made of lines.

Black's linear brow furrowed. "No one intrudes on my Demesnes."

"With my companions, a unicorn and a werewolf."

Slowly recognition flickered. "Ah—the man of the Little Folk. I recall it now. I thought thee dead ere now." He squinted. "Why didst thou not show thy power then?"

"I came in peace—then." Stile frowned. He did not like the Black Adept, who had imprisoned him and left him to starve. Yet he could not assume this was the murderer he sought. Black really had no interest in the things of other Adepts; he was a recluse. It was surprising that he had bothered to attend the Unolympics. And if he had murdered the Blue Adept, he certainly would have recognized him more readily than this! Finally, Stile knew the nature of Black's magic: he conjured with lines, not golems or amulets. "If thou intrudest similarly on my Demesnes, I may treat thee with similar courtesy."

"I can conceive of no circumstances in which I would intrude on thy Demesnes, or associate with the likes of Yellow," Black said coldly.

"Until thou hast need of a potion or an animal, my arrogant," Yellow said. "Then thou dost bespeak the crone fair enough." She led Stile on.

"These people make me nervous," the Lady Blue murmured. "Never did my Lord take me among them."

"Thy Lord had excellent taste!" Black muttered from behind.

"So Blue is not thy Lord?" Yellow inquired with a touch of malice. "What fools these peasants be!"

"Call not the Lady Blue a peasant!" Stile snapped, instantly angry. He felt as if he walked among a nest of scorpions.

Yellow's potion-pretty face twisted into something no girl her apparent age could manage. "I call her—"

"What she is," the Lady Blue interjected quickly. "Ever have my folk been villagers, farming the land and raising animals, and no shame in it."

Yellow mellowed. "Aye, no shame in the management of animals. Methinks thy peasant status ceased when thou didst marry Blue. I withdraw that portion of my remark."

Adepts evidently weren't accustomed to giving away anything voluntarily! "That portion?" Stile demanded, unappeased. He realized he was behaving exactly like an

Adept, but was not in the mood to back off. "Thou leavest her a fool?"

"That were readily abated," Yellow said. "I have love-potions that—"

"Enough!" Stile said. "The Lady is a widow; I merely assume a role that the Blue Demesnes be not demeaned, and that the great wrong done the Lady may be avenged. I am not her Lord."

"Passing strange," Yellow murmured. "With power to enchant an entire unicorn herd, he exercises it not on the Lady who is as lovely as any mortal can be and as spirited as a fine animal and who is legitimately his by right of inheritance. Methinks it is the man who is the fool."

"Mayhap by thy definition," the Lady Blue said.

"Even so," Yellow agreed, shrugging.

They came to a man in a red cloak. He was tall, almost six feet, with red hair and red mustache. "Red . . . Blue," Yellow introduced.

Red extended a firm hand. "Glad am I to meet thee," he said, smiling. He had a handsome face and seemed to be about Stile's age, though of course the "costume" made all but his basic identity suspect.

Yellow took them to the final couple at the pavilion. "Green and consort," she said. The Green Adept was another man, short and fat, and his Lady was the same. Both wore green suits and sparkling green jewelry, probably emeralds. "Blue and Lady."

"Uh-huh," the Green Adept said curtly. "Now let's watch the show." But the Lady Green made a small motion of greeting to the Lady Blue.

"These are all that attend this season," Yellow said. "On other occasions I have met Orange, Purple and Gray. But they be from afar. There may be other Adepts we know not of; we are a secretive bunch. I make many contacts at the several Olympics."

"Other Olympics?" Stile asked, remembering something the Herd Stallion had said.

"Every major species has them," Yellow assured him. "Canolympics, Vampolympics, Snowlympics, Dragolympics—some be better than others. Methinks the Elfolympics are best, with their displays of rare weaponry and dancing little men. Hast thou seen the like, my precious?"

"I noticed only the dancing little damsels," Stile said. The Lady Blue frowned, but did not comment.

Now the formal program was beginning. Stile and the Lady Blue took seats and watched. First the several unicorn Herds got settled as spectators, each at its assigned location; then the competitive contingents marched onto the field to the sound of their own horns and hooves.

It was an impressive entry. Each contingent marched in step, led by its Herd Stallion. Every horn was elevated at a 45-degree angle; every tail flung out proudly. The surface of the hooves gleamed in the slanting sunlight, iridescent, and the spirals of the horns shot out splays of mirror-light. The animals were all colors and shades: red, orange, gold, yellow, white, gray, blue, black, brown, striped, dotted and checkered. Some were single-colored, except for those colors typical of horses; others were multicolored. All were beautiful.

The Lady Blue nudged him, making a gesture toward one section of the march. In a moment he found the place —the local Stallion's complement, with sixteen picked individuals. There was Neysa, marching in the last line, on the side nearest the pavilion. "He didn't try to hide her!" Stile murmured appreciatively.

Neysa was smaller than the other unicorns, being barely fourteen hands tall, and she was the only one in the display whose colors were horse-normal—her mark of shame. But now she was the steed and oath-friend of an Adept, and though there was general fear and distrust of Adepts in the animal kingdoms of Phaze, the clear onus of an Adept's favor was so potent that Neysa now had a place of comparative honor. This was the first time she had been permitted to join the Herd and to participate in its ceremonies, and obviously she reveled in it. The hurt of years was being mended. This much Stile had done for Neysa by taming her; this much she had done for herself by allowing him to practice the magic of his station.

The music swelled in a mighty chorus. Eight Herd Stallions blew the leadoff blasts; eight disciplined display-herds responded with the melody. The ground shook with the measured cadence of their prancing hooves; the air shook with the power of their melody. No human orchestra could match the passion and splendor of this performance. Stile could not remember ever having been spectator to anything as grand as this.

They paraded close by the Adepts' pavilion, and at the closest point every horn angled abruptly to the left in a salute. There was an abrupt silence, breathtaking in its precision; that sudden cessation of sound was more impressive than a fortissimo blast would have been. Then they marched on, the music resuming, to pass by the other pavilions.

Stile examined those other pavilions now. One was filled with wolves. Another swarmed with bats. Another seated elves, and yet another was stuffed with glowering, horned demons. "*Everybody* comes to the Unolympics!" Stile breathed, amazed.

"Everybody who is anybody," Yellow responded. "Few Human Folk, however." Stile was not certain of the significance of that; did it mean that humans were among the least important of the creatures of Phaze? Or that the higher animals simply didn't like them?

In due course the opening parade finished. Now the individual competitions commenced. Wolves ran, bats flew, demons charged and elves scurried from one pavilion to another. "What's going on?" Stile asked.

"The judges," Yellow said, standing.

"Judges?"

"They can not use unicorns for the Unolympics; they're not objective. Too much rivalry between the Herds. It's the same with the other species; they all have to use outside judges. Now if thou wilst excuse me, I must to my station."

"Station?"

"I am a judge too. Didn't I tell thee?"

"Now I've seen everything!" Stile muttered.

"Not quite. But when thou spyest Black judging, two pavilions down, then mayhap thou canst consider it close enough to everything." She moved off.

A demon arrived—and also a young man with the head of a hawk. They joined the Yellow Adept at the front of the pavilion. This was the team of judges for one section of the Unolympics.

The contestant-unicorns were now trotting to their places. There was a brief period of confusion as they criss-crossed the field. Then columns formed before the several judging stations. Sixteen unicorns formed a line before the Adept pavilion, standing at equine attention.

This station, it developed, was judging the acrobatics. Others judged speed-trials, high- and long-jumps, horn-fencing, melody-playing, dancing and precision gaits. Neysa and her brother Clip had entered the category of couples-dancing, and that was at a far corner of the field; Stile could not make out what was going on there, to his frustration. So he turned reluctantly to the local display.

Twelve of the entrants were males—not herd leaders, just lesser stallions. The Herd system had no regard for the needs of un-dominant males; they were not allowed to breed with the mares, and were tolerated in the herds only so long as they kept their places. In time of war, Stile was sure, their place was at the forefront, as expendable troops. Naturally they participated in the Unolympics; it was a major peacetime opportunity to achieve recognition.

In fact, Stile realized, these various olympics represented to the animal kingdoms the same sort of entertainment, excitement and chance for individual notoriety that the Game and Tourney did for serfs in Proton. It was a parallel system, used as a relief-valve for the frustrations of the undertrodden.

Yellow, as an Adept, assumed direction of the proceedings at this station. "Equine, thou'rt designated number One," she said to the unicorn on the far left. "When that number is called henceforth in this judgment, do thou answer promptly or forfeit whatever honor may be due thee. Understand?"

The designated unicorn dipped his horn submissively. Yellow then counted off the others, up to the last, number Sixteen. "We are the preliminary panel of judges," she continued. "The Demon Horrawful, who is an Elder of his den and has served with fiendish distinction at other olympics; in his youth he was a winner at this same event at the Demolympics." There was a smattering of polite applause, mostly from the spectators now crowding close to the edge of the pavilion, a number of whom were demons.

"And this is Glynteye the Hawkman, winner of the Avolympic rabbit-spotting meet last year. He is competently versed to spot the antics of unicorns." There was more applause, especially from the animalheads present.

"And I am the Yellow Adept," she concluded. "In life I am an old human crone whose business is known to most animals. Were it not for the sufferance granted visitors at this event, I would be mobbed. However, I believe I am qualified as a judge of fine animals, and I am in this respect objective."

There was a pause, and then some extremely tentative applause. The Lady Blue looked about, frowned, then set her jaw and clapped her hands. The consort of Green joined her. Then Stile and the Green Adept had to join in, and the outside animals, shamed into a better sense of the occasion, finally made a more substantial showing. All had a horror of Yellow's business of trapping and selling animals, but all antagonisms were theoretically suspended here. Yellow did indeed appear to be competent and objective.

Stile was reminded yet again of the parallel of Proton. The Rifleman had shown him favor, causing the other Citizens to react with similar courtesy despite the gulf between Citizen and serf. The Lady Blue had been the catalyst this time, but the spirit was the same.

"Now withdraw to the sides and rear," Yellow directed, betraying her surprised pleasure at the applause by only a slight flush at her neck. "Form an arena, open only at the spectator's side. No alien magic can function here." And the unicorns did as she bid, so efficiently that Stile realized this was a standard procedure. Indeed, all the stations were forming similar formations.

"Number One 'corn stand forward," Yellow said, and the first stallion moved to the center of the arena, facing the pavilion. "Thou and each other entry will have two minutes to make thy presentation. Each act will be followed by a one-minute consultation of judges and announcement of aggregate score. Applause of up to thirty seconds will be permitted only at that time. If there are any questions at this point, stifle them."

There were no questions. "One, perform," Yellow said.

The unicorn went into his act. He was a fine purple and green animal, with white ears. He pranced and wheeled and leaped in assorted patterns. Gradually he worked up to the more difficult exercises—forward and backward flips, hoof-clicking jumps, and an impressive bucking-bronco finale.

"Time," the demon-judge grated. Apparently he had the timing ability. The stallion stood, his barrel heaving from the exertion, nostrils flared, just a hint of fire in his breath, awaiting the score.

The three judges consulted. Stile could not hear what they said, and did not know the scoring system. Again he tried to spot the activity of the couples-dance unit, and could not.

"Number One scores fifteen," Yellow announced. Now there was applause, the unicorns honking brief notes and tapping their hooves on the ground in lieu of the clapping of hands. It did not seem overwhelming to Stile, and he decided the performance had been no more than average for this type of competition. Certainly Neysa could have matched it, and she had not even entered this event.

"Number Two, stand forth," Yellow said, and another stallion came to the fore. He was larger and better muscled than the first, and his color was brighter: bands of blue alternating with intense yellow. His neck was especially powerful. "Perform." And he launched into his act.

This one was sharper than the first. He did the front and back flips, then went into a series of midair barrelrolls that brought musical gasps from some spectators. He stood on his two forehooves and clicked his rear hooves together so that sparks flew. In the finale he leaped straight up, turned in air, and landed squarely on his horn, which plunged three quarters of its length into the turf. He remained frozen on that one-point support until time was called. Then he allowed his body to drop to the ground so that he could withdraw his horn.

"That is the likely winner," the Lady Blue murmured. "Neysa could not have done that."

"True." Stile had never imagined a unicorn supporting itself in that manner.

The judges consulted. "Twenty-six," Yellow announced, and strong applause burst forth instantly, cutting off only at the expiration of the thirty seconds. A popular decision, certainly.

The other acts followed, but they did not match the second. Stile concluded that each judge graded on the basis of one to ten, with an aggregate of thirty points being the maximum. His attention wandered to the units on either side. To the right were the speed trials, with unicorns galloping around a marked pattern so fast that flame shot from their nostrils, dissipating their developing body heat. Unicorns did not sweat, they blew out fire. On the left side were the gait trials, with unicorns prancing in perfect one, two, three, four and five-beat combinations, manes and tails flying high. But still Stile could not see what Neysa's unit was doing. He was becoming covertly bored with the proceedings, though the Lady Blue evinced continuing interest.

In the course of a little over an hour the preliminary trials were done. Four contestants had been selected from the local group, to advance to the next round.

The contestants moved to new stations. Now four musicians came to stand before the Adept pavilion. Each played a melody on his or her horn, and these were marvelously pleasant. One unicorn sounded like an oboe, another like a trumpet, a third like a violin, and the fourth like a flute. The violin made the highest score, but the flute and oboe were tied at twenty-two.

"I mislike this," Yellow said. "They are so close, I can not select between them. Have you other judges more firmly entrenched opinions?"

Demon and Hawkman shook their heads. They agreed the two contestants were even. "I mislike being arbitrary," Yellow said. "Yet it has been long since I heard the flute, and I know not which sound is the more perfect representation. If we but had an instrument for comparison—"

The Lady Blue stood with an air of minor mischief. "If it please the judges—"

Yellow glanced back at her. "Speak, Lady, if it be relevant."

"My Lord the Blue Adept is skilled in music, and has with him an excellent flute—"

"Hey, I'm not in this!" Stile protested.

But Yellow was smiling with a certain friendly malice. "Methinks Blue owes me a favor."

Stile spread his hands. He was caught. "What dost thou wish, Yellow?"

"Didst hear the theme played by the flute-'corn? If thou wouldst play the same as it should be played, that we may compare—"

Stile sighed inwardly and walked to the front of the pavilion. He did not object to playing; his concern was that the larger nature of the borrowed Platinum Flute would manifest as his magic power gathered. But if he willed no magic, maybe it would be all right. He did owe Yellow a favor, and this was a modest one.

He assembled the Flute, brought it to his mouth, and played the theme. The magic instrument gave him perfect control, making him a better flutist than he otherwise could be. The notes issued like ethereal honey. The magic gathered, but subtly.

As he played, the routine noises of the Unolympics abated, in a widening circle. Unicorn spectators down the line rotated their ears, orienting on him. When the last note faded, the entire arena was silent.

The three judges remained seated, quiet for a moment. The other Adepts seemed frozen in their places. Then Yellow shook her head. "There be flutes and there be Flutes," she said. "That is the Platinum Flute, of Elven craft, the Emperor of flutes. There is none like it. Favored indeed is the one, whether common or Adept, who gains its loan from the Little Folk. I fear the crisis of Phaze draws nigh. After that sound, I have no further doubt; the unicorn does not compare."

But the two other judges demurred. "Play oboe," the demon grunted.

"Ah, yes," Yellow agreed. "Thank thee, Horrawful, thou'rt correct. We must compare that sound too." She focused on Stile. "Play the oboe, Blue."

"But I have no oboe," he protested.

"Pretend not to be ignorant of the nature of the instrument thou holdest," she said sharply. "Play the oboe, that we may get on with this matter."

Baffled, Stile looked at the Flute he held—and it had become a fine platinum oboe. So the magic shifts were not merely with weapons! He brought it to his mouth and played the oboe-'corn's theme. The notes rolled out like elixir, impossibly mellow, the most perfect oboe-sound he had ever heard. Again the Unolympics halted to listen. Even the jaded Adepts sat riveted until it finished.

"Now we can judge," Yellow said. She consulted again with her associate-judges, and rendered the decision: "The oboe is closer to true. The oboe-'corn qualifies."

Now there was applause—but somehow it seemed to orient more on Stile than the qualifying unicorn. "Only my Love played like that," the Lady Blue murmured as Stile resumed his seat beside her. "I never thought to hear such sound again."

"The instrument is magic," he replied shortly. "It lends skill to the player."

"Mayhap," she agreed, and said no more.

Soon it was time for the finals. Now the entire field became a single arena, and the separate panels of judges merged to become a single large panel. Everyone would witness the category victories.

Stile was gratified. At last he would get to see Neysa perform—if she had made it this far. He had been confident of her prowess before this ever started, but now he was aware of the strength of the competition. She could have been eliminated.

But she had made it! She and Clip were finalists, and in due course their event came up. One werewolf judge disqualified himself at that point, explaining that he was an oath-friend to a contestant and could not judge her objectively. A substitute was found, and the show went on.

Neysa and Clip trotted out in perfect step, playing their own music for the dance, she with her harmonica-horn, he with his saxophone. It was a beautiful duet, harmonizing precisely with the beat of their hooves. Neysa's colors now complemented Clip's, and she was beautiful even in unicorn terms. Both animals were small for their species, but as a pair, alone in the arena, they were perfectly matched and did not seem small at all.

They plunged forward, horns lunging at an invisible foe, then whipped back together with a dissonant note, as of a foe dying. Stile could almost see the implied monster. So could some of the judges, who happened to be monsters; they scowled. The two went on through different gaits, then got fancy. Neysa leaped, and Clip trotted beneath her. As she landed, he leaped over her. They continued in a fantastic leapfrog sequence, their music playing without a break. Then they came together, bucked in unison, and leaped together in a backward somersault. In midair they changed shape, landing neatly in human-form, he garbed in bright trousers and cloak, she in white-fringed black dress. They swung, now humming the music their horns could no longer play. Faster they swung, becoming almost a blur—and suddenly they were hawk and firefly, whirling about in air about a common center, then back to equine-form with a final, lovely bar of music, in time for the expiration of time.

The judges held out printed cards: 9, 9, 8, 9, 7, 8 . . . an excellent rating from all except the monsters. Then the applause began, loudest from Neysa's own Herd; but there was an appreciative baying from several wolves of the pack who had also taken the oath of friendship with her. Stile saw now that his friend Kurrelgyre was among them.

Then the other unicorn couple went into its act. Both were handsome specimens, and both had remarkable tones. He sounded like a bassoon, with all its deep beauty and trick effects, while she rang like bells. Stile was amazed at what the unicorn horn could do; it was not confined to wind instruments, perhaps because of its magic. This combination was unusual and effective, and they made the most of it.

These unicorns, too, changed shapes in the middle of the dance, manifesting as great cats and then as white and blue herons. Their equine states were special, too; he had a mane like rippling fire, and her mane was iridescent; it shone as it flexed, with precious luster. She was a truly lovely creature. But it was the artistry of their dance that

made it outstanding, and in the end they were judged the
winners. Stile could not contest the decision; it was fair.
Yet Neysa and Clip had made a formidable showing. He
was proud of them.

The finals continued with marvelous exhibits, but Stile's
attention wandered again. When all this was done, he
would have to meet the local Herd Stallion. He had the
Platinum Flute, so could employ his magic; he was not in
danger. Yet it bothered him, for he did not wish to humili-
ate the Stallion. He just wanted the postponement of Neysa's breeding. Should he try to talk to the Stallion again?
He doubted that would be effective. Unicorns were extremely
stubborn animals. Yet if he fought the unicorn and used
his magic to prevail, it would be unfair; if he did not use
magic, he could lose. Was there no satisfactory alternative?

Stile mulled it over while the Unolympics progressed to
the close. In the present excitement and distraction, he
found himself unable to work out a strategy that would
satisfy all needs. Since he was not about to let himself be
wounded by the horn of a unicorn, he would just have to
use his magic and damn the social consequence. He hated
to do it, though; he knew how important pride was for the
dominant creatures of Phaze. Pride, really, had motivated
the Herd Stallion to challenge him; the animal hoped to
force Stile to capitulate ignominiously, and yield Neysa to
the scheduled breeding.

Were the circumstances otherwise, Stile would have
done just that. Neysa had waited years for just this opportunity, and Stile wanted no avoidable quarrel with anyone.
But Neysa believed—and now Stile agreed—that he needed
her on his quest for his murderer. Not merely to ride, for
he could now move himself, but as an essential back-up.
Surely his enemy would prove far more formidable than
the Worm of the Purple Mountains cavity, and Stile had
barely prevailed against the Worm even with the Platinum
Flute. Neysa's presence could have made the difference,
there. He could not free her by giving up his quest, because
it was his own murderer he sought. That person had to be
brought to justice—and no one else would do it if Stile did
not. So for the sake of Neysa's desire as an oath-friend,

and his own intermediate-term security, he had to keep her with him, and that meant putting down the Herd Stallion.

Put more succinctly: he had to crush the pride of an honorable creature, to win the right of another creature to sacrifice her ambition of dam-hood and risk her life for him. Some pride!

A bat fluttered up and landed before him. It shifted to man-form. No long canine teeth, no horrific eyes; this was an ordinary, slightly pudgy brown-haired man of middle age. "Thou art Blue?" the vampire inquired diffidently.

"I am he," Stile responded guardedly. "I seek no quarrel with thy kind."

"I am Vodlevile. I encountered thine ogre-friend, Hulk, and thereafter through thine intercession the Yellow Adept did forward to me a potion that cured my son. I owe thee—"

Stile put up a disclaiming palm. "It was in abatement of Hulk's debt to thee for the help thou didst give him in the course of his mission for me. Thou hast no debt to me. I am glad to hear of thy good fortune, and I wish thee and thy son well."

"I helped Hulk from mere camaraderie," Vodlevile protested. "Repayment for that were an insult." He paused. "No offense, Adept; a figure of speech."

"Understood," Stile said, liking this creature. "Yet would I have helped thy son regardless, had I known of his condition. The Lady Blue is a healer, and it is ever her pleasure to help the creatures of Phaze. Can I do less?"

"Apology," Vodlevile said. "I spied thy Lady not. I recognized thee from thy music on the Flute, forgetting her. A greeting to thee, fair one."

"And to thee, sociable one," the Lady Blue replied. She turned to Stile. "We ask no recompense for the work we do, yet neither do we deny the proffered gratitude of those we help."

Stile smiled. "Methinks I have been directed to accept what thou mayst proffer, though I feel thou hast no obligation."

"I bring naught tangible," the vampire said. "If there is anything I may do for thee—"

"What I must do, no one can do for me," Stile said gravely.

"What is that?"

"I must match the Herd Stallion in fair combat." Stile quickly outlined the situation.

"Why, sir, that is merely a matter of face. We vampires, being naturally stealthy, have ready means to handle such questions."

"You vampires must be smarter than I am," Stile said ruefully.

Then Vodlevile explained the recommended strategy. Stile clapped the heel of one hand to his forehead. "Of course!" he exclaimed. "There is no better service thou couldst have done me than this simple advice."

The vampire made a gesture of satisfaction. "Every time I see my son change form and fly, I think of Blue." He shifted back to bat-form and flew away.

"Thou art very like my Lord," the Lady Blue murmured. "His friendships were many, his enmities few."

Except for the enemy who killed him, Stile thought bleakly. That one had undone all the rest.

The final match was decided and the victorious unicorn paraded off the field. Now it was time for the special event —Herd Stallion *vs.* Blue Adept—in a combat supposedly immune to magic.

The Herd Stallion strutted out, resplendent in his natural color and musculature. Stile started forward, but found himself restrained by the Lady Blue's hand. He turned to her, uncertain what she wanted.

She was always beautiful, but at the moment she seemed to him to be transcendentally lovely. "Go with care, my Lord," she said, and somehow it was the greatest compliment he could have imagined.

"I thank thee, Lady," he said. Then he proceeded on out to meet the Stallion, carrying the Platinum Flute.

The unicorns formed a great ring around the two, sealing off external magic. They thought Stile would be unable to draw on the background power, and ordinarily this would be true. But the Oracle had enabled him to nullify that nullification. This was the real debt he owed Hulk, for Hulk had donated his one lifetime question to the Oracle for Stile's benefit; that was why Stile had taken Hulk's debt of a favor on himself. Now the vampire had repaid it, and by Stile's logic he owed a major favor to Hulk.

Perhaps his gift of the pursuit of the Proton-self of the Lady Blue had abated that; perhaps not. He remembered that he had agreed to Hulk's visit to the Oracle at the subtle behest of the Lady Blue, who had been aware of what was developing. She had acted to defuse the issue before it came to Stile's attention. So where was the right of it? Stile knew he would have to think about the matter some more; right was not always simple to ascertain. Yet such deliberations were always worthwhile.

Now he stood in the center of the huge arena, before the Stallion. The contrast in their sizes was striking; a large equine, a very small man. But there was no snicker from the audience, for Stile was the Blue Adept.

First he had to establish his power, making it instantly and compellingly evident to the entire assembly. That was the first stage of the vampire's excellent advice. He had to prove that the ring of unicorns could not impinge upon the Blue Adept's practice of magic. At the moment, only a few understood the full properties of the Platinum Flute, like the Yellow Adept; after the demonstration, everyone would know.

Stile brought out the Flute. The Herd Stallion waited, as if curious to see what his opponent was up to.

Stile played. Again the enchanting melody poured forth, the finest sound a flute could make. The unicorns listened raptly, yet perplexed. How could mere music stop the great Stallion?

When the magic had gathered, Stile halted and went into a singsong spell: "Show us the story of the Dragon's Tooth, from death to bloom, from birth to youth." But the real shaping of it was in his mind; the words only initiated the sequence.

In the sky a dot appeared. It expanded rapidly into the shape of a dragon, with six legs, six wings, and a tremendously toothed mouth. A shadow almost the size of the entire arena fell as the monster crossed the sun. The unicorns looked up, alarmed; seldom did any dragon approach

a unicorn herd, and this one was the largest ever seen
locally.

Stile raised his right hand to point at the dragon. Then
he put the Flute to his mouth again, to intensify the magic
and keep his complex spell operating at full strength.

The dragon folded its wings and dived at the field.
Folded, it was much smaller. It crashed headfirst into the
chewed turf and exploded. This was the "death" of his
spell. Teeth flew out in a splash, to land all across the field;
the rest of the dragon puffed away in smoke.

Where each tooth fell, something sprouted. This was the
"bloom." As Stile continued to play the Flute, the teeth
grew into leafy vines. Each vine fruited in a gourd, and
each gourd hatched into a human baby, and each baby
grew rapidly into an armed soldier. This was the "birth to
youth" sequence. The soldiers formed into a phalanx,
marched once around the field, shifted into a sinuous formation that suddenly sprouted wings and flew as a mass
into the sky. It was the original dragon, departing as it had
come. In moments it was a mere speck in the sky, and then
it was gone.

The unicorns stood in silence. They had just been shown
that they could no longer restrict the magic of the Blue
Adept, even when their force was greatest. The Adepts,
too, were riveted; not one of them could match this performance. Was one of them the murderer he sought? Stile
hoped that one was quaking, now, for fear of the vengeance of Blue. Most magic was fun to Stile, but in this
regard it was deadly serious.

The Herd Stallion, however, had not budged. Stile had
feared this would be the case. He had fashioned a demonstration of magic that was spectacular enough to enable the
Stallion to withdraw without shame; obviously no ordinary
creature could prevail against power like this. But the Stallion was stubborn; he would not back off regardless. He
might face impossible odds but he would not yield to opposition. Stile respected that; he was that way himself. It
was another reason why he was going to so much trouble
to avoid humiliating the fine animal. How fortunate that
the vampire had been available for advice!

Stile sang another spell: "Flute of class, grant equal

mass." Suddenly a giant appeared, in Stile's own image, standing in his footprints, towering above him. The giant's mass was equal to that of the Herd Stallion; anyone could see that. Then the giant shrank in on Stile until at last it disappeared in Stile. He now had the mass of the unicorn, though he remained his own size and felt no different. He held the Flute—which was now the broadsword.

The Herd Stallion stepped forward. *He* certainly understood; Stile was using his magic only to make the contest even. It depended only on their skills. If the Stallion was good with his natural weapon, he might outfence Stile and win. If not, Stile would prevail. The nullification of shame could go no further than this. Vampire Vodlevile's advice had taken them to this stage; what followed would follow.

The Stallion seemed to be proceeding with guarded confidence. Stile could guess why; Stile was known to be inexpert with the rapier. Neysa had had to drill him in its use, and he had been an apt student, but a few lessons could not bring him to the level of the Herd Stallion.

Stile, however, was not now holding a rapier. He was holding an excellent broadsword, perfect in weight and length and temper and balance and all the subtleties of general feel, and with this weapon he was proficient. He had trained with this type of sword for a dozen years, and won many Proton-frame Games with it. While he could not match the Stallion's protection against being disarmed, he could, if he had to, throw his blade at his opponent. So it was reasonably even. That was the way he wanted it. Vodlevile had shown him how to ease his crisis of conscience.

They met in the center of the arena and ceremoniously crossed weapons. Then each took a step back. Now it began.

The Stallion lunged. The horn shot forward. Stile jumped aside, his point jabbing to tag the unicorn's shoulder—but the animal was not to be caught that way, and was out of range.

Now Stile lunged. The Stallion's horn parried his thrust powerfully. Had Stile not possessed equal mass, he could have been disarmed then; as it was, sparks flew from the colliding weapons and both parties felt the impact.

So much for the feeling-out. Stile valued surprise, without sacrificing good technique. He fenced with the Stallion's horn, setting himself up for disarming, and when the Stallion made the move, Stile slipped by his guard and sliced at his neck. The unicorn, suckered, shifted instantly to man-form so as to duck under it, then back to equine form. He had a sword in man-form, but lacked Stile's mass; there was no conservation of mass, in magic.

Stile wheeled to engage the Stallion again. He knew now that he was the superior swordsman, but he guarded against overconfidence. This shape-changing—that could be tricky.

Indeed it was. Suddenly he faced a small flying dragon. The creature spread batlike wings and flew over Stile's head, out of reach of his sword.

Well, Stile was also out of reach of the dragon's talons. It was a standoff, for the moment. Since he didn't really want to hurt the Herd Stallion, that was all right.

Then the dragon shot fire from its mouth. Stile dived out of the way. This was more complicated than he had thought! Evidently the unicorn had built up some heat in the course of the match, and was able to use that to fuel his dragon-form.

The dragon oriented for another shot. Stile raised his sword—and it was a shiny, mirror-surfaced shield. It caught the jet of fire and bounced it back at the dragon. The creature took evasive action.

Stile could bring the dragon down by magic—but he remained unwilling to do that. He wanted to win as he was. His weapon could change according to his need; the Stallion could change his shape. They remained even. Except that Stile could not reach the dragon.

Or could he? Suddenly his weapon became an eighteen-foot pike. Stile heaved it upward at a sharp angle, poking at the dragon. The creature squawked with a sound like an accordion—which was the tone of the Stallion's horn—and flapped higher. Another jet of fire came down, but petered out short of the mark. Stile's pike was keeping the dragon beyond flame-range.

Standoff. Neither could hurt the other. Unless—

Stile's spike became a powerful platinum bow, with a long, sharp arrow. He aimed it at the dragon—but already the creature was diving to earth, changing back to the unicorn, who formed in midcharge toward Stile.

Stile's weapon shifted back to broadsword, and the fencing resumed. Stile was the better swordsman, but every time he pressed his advantage the Stallion changed shape and they went through a quick series of animal and weapon forms before returning to the more conventional fray.

It became apparent to the audience that there was unlikely to be a winner here; neither party could hurt the other. Stile was satisfied with that; they could negotiate a reasonable extension of Neysa's time.

Stile outfenced the Stallion again, the Stallion shifted to dragon-form, Stile's sword became the bow . . .

And the dragon became the man-form, who plummeted toward Stile. Stile flung himself aside, his grip on his weapon slackening, and the man-form snatched it from Stile's grasp. He hurled it far across the arena. In air, the bow reverted to its natural state, the Flute, and bounced on the grass. Stile had been careless, and abruptly disarmed.

His first impulse was to run for the Flute, for he had no chance without it. His mass had reverted to normal the moment he was separated from the Flute. The ring of unicorns now deprived him of his magic. How foolish he had been not to retain his grip; he could never have been disarmed had he willed himself not to be.

A large hand caught his shoulder. The man-form was preventing him from going after the weapon.

Stile reacted instantly. He caught the hand on his shoulder, whirled about, and applied pressure to the man-form's elbow joint. It would have been a submission hold, ordinarily—but the form shifted back to equine and the hold was negated.

Freed, Stile sprinted for the Flute. But the Stallion galloped after him. No chance to outrun that! Stile had to turn and dodge, staying clear of that horn.

But he would not be able to dodge it long! Stile made a phenomenal, acrobatic leap, feeling his weakened knees

giving way in the effort, and flipped through the air toward
the Stallion's back. If he could ride the animal long enough
to get near the Flute—

Then, in the moment he was in the air, he saw that
terrible unicorn horn swinging about to bear on him. The
Stallion had reacted too quickly. Stile would land—directly
on the point.

He landed—in the arms of the man-form. The creature
set him down carefully. "I seek not to injure thee, Adept,
for thou hast been kind to my kind. I merely deflect thee.
Thou'rt disarmed of thy weapon and thy magic. Dost
thou yield?"

It had been a fair fight. The unicorn had outmaneuvered
him. Stile might be able to hold his own against the man-
form, but not against the equine-form or dragon-form, and
he refused to stoop to any subterfuge. He had lost. "I
yield," he said.

"Fetch thy weapon ere hostile magic comes," the man-
form said, and shifted back to unicorn-form.

Stile walked across the arena and picked up the Flute,
then rejoined the Stallion before the main judging stand.
The Stallion did not speak, so Stile did. "We have met in
fair encounter, and the Stallion defeated me. The Blue
Adept yields the issue."

Now the Herd Stallion blew an accordion medley on his
horn. Neysa's brother Clip trotted up. "The Stallion says
the Adept is more of a creature than he took him for. The
Adept had magic to win, and eschewed it in favor of equal-
ity, and fought fairly and well, and lost well. The Stallion
accepts the pride of that victory—and yields back the issue."

Then the applause began. Unicorns charged into the
field, forming into their discrete herds. Neysa found Stile
and carried him away separately to rejoin the Lady Blue.
The Unolympics were over.

So all the Herd Stallion had really wanted was the notoriety of defeating the Blue Adept and redeeming the
pride he had lost during their prior encounter at the Blue
Demesnes. Granted that, the Stallion had been generous,
and had granted Neysa the extension she wanted. All Stile
had lost was a little pride of his own—and that had never
been his prime consideration.

In future, he would pay better attention to the hidden motives of the creatures of Phaze—and to the pitfalls of battling a shape-changing creature. These were useful lessons.

CHAPTER 7

Hulk

Sheen took Stile to a private chamber deep in the maintenance section of the dome they lived in. He carried his harmonica and the Platinum Flute with him in a small bag, not being willing to leave them elsewhere lest he have sudden need for them, or risk their theft.

He spoke with an anonymous machine through a speaker. This reminded him of the mode of the Oracle—but of course the Oracle could not be a machine. It was evident that Sheen had not brought him here without reason. "What is your interest?" he inquired.

"We have a partial report for you concerning the recent attempt made on your life."

"Partial," Stile repeated, excited and disappointed. Any progress was good, but he needed the whole story.

"The message from your Citizen Employer was legitimate, but the address was changed. A chip had been modified in the message annex to substitute that address for the proper one in any message directed to you from a Citizen, one time. It was a one-shot trap."

"Sending me to intrude on a Citizen who didn't like the Tourney and was apt to exterminate intruders," Stile said, thinking of the Black Adept in Phaze, who acted similarly.

"Correct. We conclude this was the work of other than a Citizen."

"Because a Citizen would not have had to bother with

a hidden trap," Stile said, realizing that he should not so blithely have assumed his enemy was a Citizen.

"Correct. We were unable to trace the instigator. We remain alert for more direct devices, but your enemy is evidently no machine."

He hadn't even thought of having a machine-enemy! "Because my enemy has more imagination than a machine does."

"Correct. Like you, that person is a quick and original thinker."

"This helps," Stile said. "A serf is considerably more limited than a Citizen. A serf's motives should differ from those of a Citizen. But could a serf have lasered my knees or sent Sheen to me?"

"The knees affirmative. Sheen negative. She had to come from a Citizen. That Citizen covered his traces carefully; we can trace her manufacture but not the identity of the one issuing the directive that sent her to you."

"So already we have a seeming divergence of elements. A Citizen sent Sheen to protect me from a serf."

"Correct."

"Why didn't the Citizen simply eliminate the enemy serf?"

"We have no information."

"And why are you self-willed machines helping me? This increases the risk of your discovery by the Citizens, so is dangerous for you."

To his surprise, the anonymous machine answered. "At first we helped you because one of our number, the robot Sheen, wished it, and you took the oath not to betray our interests. There was also an anonymous imperative favoring you. This also we have been unable to trace, but we have ascertained that it originates from other than Citizen or serf. We were aware that a chance existed that you would eventually be useful to us. Now that chance has expanded. Perhaps this is what the anonymous imperative intended. Should you win the Tourney, as we deem a one in ten chance at this moment, you will become a Citizen. As such you could help our cause enormously."

"As such, I could," Stile agreed, intrigued by their estimate of his chances in the Tourney, and by the notion of the "anonymous imperative" that favored him. Strange elements operating here! "But you know I would betray neither my own kind nor the system. I do not support revolution, or even significant change. I merely seek to deal with my enemy and improve my personal, private situation. I'm just no crusader."

"We seek recognition for our kind within the system," the machine said. "No revolution is desired, only modification. We wish to have the status of serfs. A Citizen could prepare the way."

"I could support that," Stile agreed. "But that would necessitate revealing the secret of your nature."

"We are not ready for that. We would be destroyed, were our nature known prematurely."

"But to prepare the way without the revelation—that would be very slow."

"We estimate the process will take approximately seventy-five years. To move faster would be to increase the risk unacceptably."

"You have patience," Stile said.

"We are machines."

That, of course, was their ultimate limitation. They had intelligence, consciousness and self-will, but lacked the impatience of life. Though Sheen was coming close! "I thank you for your help, for whatever motive, machines," Stile said. "I will help you in return—when the occasion offers."

He returned with Sheen to their apartment, not speaking further of this matter. He never spoke directly of the self-willed machines where his words could be recorded, lest that betray their nature to the Citizens of Proton. Most places were bugged, and often continuous recordings of serf activities were made at the behest of individual Citizens. Thus only a place cleared by the machines themselves was safe for such dialogue. Elsewhere, he simply called them "Sheen's friends."

Stile did appreciate their help, and he wondered whether they were really as machinelike as they claimed. Why should they care about their status in the society of Proton? To become serfs only meant to serve Citizens—as they already did—to be allowed to play the Game, and to

be limited to twenty years or so of tenure on the planet. If
they left the planet, they might lose whatever status they
gained on it, since the galactic society was just as human-
oriented as was Proton's. Yet obviously they did have desires. Sheen was certainly an emotional, personlike being;
why not others like her? But the machines would let him
know what they wanted him to know, when they deemed
appropriate.

It was time for his next Game. Round Five—the number
of entrants was shrinking now, as more players lost their
second match and were washed out, so things would move
along faster. But there remained a long way to go.

This time he was paired with a child, an eleven-year-old
boy, not one of the good ones. "Your tenure can't be up!"
Stile said.

"My folks' tenure is up," the boy explained. "I'm leaving
with them anyway, so why not go out in style?"

So he had nothing to lose. Just in it for fun, to see how
far he could go. And he had gotten to Round Five, perhaps
helping to eliminate three or four entrants to whom this
was a matter verging on life and death. It was the irony of
the Tourney that many of those who had no need should
win, while those who *had* to win—lost.

Their turn came, and they went to the grid. Stile got the
letters, and was afraid the boy would go for CHANCE—
and was correct. It came up 3C, Machine-Assisted
CHANCE. *Any* CHANCE was bad; Stile had tried to
mitigate it, but ultimately it remained potential disaster.

If he could steer it into one of the more complex mechanical variants, a pinball machine—for a person like
him, with experience and a fine touch, one of those became
a game of skill.

But it came out wrong, again. The lad played with luck
and the uncanny insight of the young, making mischief. It
settled on an ancient-type slot machine, a one-armed ban-
dit. One hundred percent chance. Each player pulled the
handle, and the kid came up with the higher configuration.

"I won! I won! I won!" he shrieked. "Hee-hee-hee!"

Stile had lost. Just like that. A nothing-Game, against
a dilettante child who had nothing to gain—and Stile was
suddenly half washed out. His nightmare had happened.

Sheen found him and got him home. Stile was numbed with the unfairness of it. It was a demeaning loss, so pointless, so random. All his considerable Game-skills had been useless. Where did his chances of winning the Tourney stand now? One in a hundred?

"I know it hurts you," Sheen said solicitously. "I would suffer for you if I could, but I am not programmed for that. I am programmed only for you, yourself, your person and your physical welfare."

"It's foolish," Stile said, forcing himself to snap out of it. "I comprehend the luck of the Game. I have won randomly many times. This is why the Tourney is double-elimination—so that a top contender shall not be eliminated by a single encounter with a duffer in CHANCE. I simply have to take my loss and go on."

"Yes."

"But dammit, it hurts!"

"Of course."

"How can you understand?" he snapped.

"I love you."

Which was about as effective a rebuttal as she could have made. "Your whole existence is like a lost Game, isn't it," he said, squeezing her hand.

"Yes."

"It seems as though luck is turning against me. My Games have been running too close, and in Phaze I lost a contest to a unicorn, and now this—"

They were home. "There is a message," Sheen said as they entered. She went to the receptacle and drew it out. "A holo-tape."

"Who would send me a tape?" Stile asked, perplexed. "Another trap?"

"Not with my friends watching." She set it in the play-slot.

The holograph formed. The Rifleman stood before them. "I pondered before relaying this edited report to you, Stile," the Citizen said. "But a wager is a wager, and I felt this was relevant. I suspect this tape reveals the general nature of the information you would have given me, had you lost our ballgame, so I hardly feel cheated. I was not able to ascertain who has tried to hurt you, but it seems likely that you were the intended victim of this sequence, and there-fore this does provide a hint." He frowned. "I apologize for acquitting my debt in this manner. Yet it is best you have the detail. I hope that this at least forwards your quest. *Adieu.*" The Citizen faded out with a little wave.

"Why is he so diffident?" Stile asked. "That's not the way of a Citizen."

"He uses the term 'victim,' " Sheen pointed out. "This will not be pretty."

"Hulk! Something's happened—"

The holograph formed a new image: Hulk, talking to Sheen herself. The man seemed even larger than normal, in the confines of the apartment. His head barely cleared the doorway. "Thank you, Sheen," Hulk said, smiling down at her. Sheen was lovely, looking absolutely human, but of course Hulk knew the truth.

"I never knew this was being recorded!" the actual Sheen exclaimed, looking at her holo-image.

"Citizens can have anything recorded," Stile reminded her. "All the holo-pickups spread throughout the domes of Proton are at their service."

"I know that. I just didn't realize I was the subject, in your absence."

"You may be the subject right now."

"Oh, shut up and watch the show."

They watched the holo-Hulk depart, the image sliding in and out of the scene to simulate his motion. He stopped at a communication screen, called Information, and received a slip of paper, evidently an address. The self-willed ma-chines had provided it, of course; Stile hoped the Rifleman had not pursued that ramification.

Hulk read the address and started walking again. Sud-denly he was entering a jetporter—and as suddenly emerg-ing at a far dome. The edited tape, of course, skipping across the nonessentials. It was easy to follow, since stand-ard entertainment-holos were done the same way.

Hulk arrived at an isolated dome, similar to so many favored by Citizens. This one was accessible by monorail across the sand, so that any visitors were visible well before arrival. Hulk stepped down as the carriage halted, and stood on the lawn, looking at the main building.

It was an almost perfect replica of the Blue Demesnes. Stile could well understand the amazement of the big man. Who would have thought that such a castle existed in the frame of Proton? It was probably on the same geographic site, too, conforming perfectly to the alternate frame. The frames did tend to align, as Stile had discovered the hard way; when a person died in one, he was likely to die in the other too. Stile had narrowly escaped death in Proton at the time the Blue Adept was murdered in Phaze. Then, in what was apparently another way for the frames to equalize, he had discovered the curtain and crossed over. Thus each frame had Stile, again—in turn. This suggested that the use of the curtain was not coincidental, but inevitable—when an imbalance existed between the frames.

But now here was Hulk—seemingly back where he had started from. And surely the Lady Blue was here, for this was where Sheen had sent him to find her, based on the information her machine friends had provided. But the Lady could not hold the position here that she did in Phaze . . .

Hulk, evidently having completed a similar mental sequence, strode forward toward the castle. There was one way to find out!

There was a guard at the gate. He stood up straight as Hulk approached, but there was no way he could match Hulk's height. "What is your business here, serf?"

"I am Hulk, on leave from employment pending the expiration of my tenure. I wish to meet Bluette."

The guard turned to a communication pickup. "Serf with message for Bluette."

"Thank you; I will be down." It was the Lady Blue's voice. Stile felt a prickle at his spine, though he knew this was merely the Lady's alternate self. Of course she sounded the same; she *was* the same, in everything except situation.

"I'm not sure I should watch this," Stile muttered. "It doesn't relate to my situation."

"The Rifleman thinks otherwise," Sheen reminded him. "You can just sit there and watch someone else making time with someone you love. The experience will do you good."

How bitter could a robot get? But probably she was

right; he was doing it to her, and he needed to know how it felt to have it done to him.

Hulk waited, and in a moment she appeared. She was indeed the Lady Blue. The Phaze clothing was gone; she was a naked serf. But she was the same.

"She's lovely," Sheen said. "I can see how you would like her."

"This one is for Hulk," Stile said. But it was hard to believe that. He was glad the scene was only in holo. Bluette—the Lady Blue—he understood why they were so exactly like each other. Yet to see it so directly—this stirred him fundamentally.

"What is your message?" Bluette inquired. She did not use the archaic tongue, of course; Stile found this slightly jarring, but it did help distinguish her from the woman he loved.

"Lady, it is complicated," Hulk said. "I would like to talk with thee at some length."

"Thee?"

"My error," Hulk said quickly. "A misplaced usage." He had had so much trouble getting used to the forms of Phaze, and this situation was conducive to the error. Stile would have had the same problem.

Bluette shrugged. "Until my Employer comes, I am not hard-pressed. Yet I am disinclined to heed a complicated message from a stranger."

"This I understand, Lady," Hulk said. "I know it is an imposition. Yet perhaps I can tell you things that will interest you. I have known one very like you, a great and gracious woman, a star among planets—"

"Enough of this!" she exclaimed angrily. "I am a serf, like you. Do you seek to get me in trouble with my Employer?"

Hulk's response was cut off by the sudden descent of a rocket. The thing veered out of its trajectory, dropping rapidly toward the dome. Both man and woman paused to stare at it.

"Lady, it will crash!" Hulk cried. He leaped forward, swept up the woman, and carried her from the projected site of collision.

He was not mistaken. The rocket plunged through the

dome's force-field and landed with an explosive flare of heat against the castle wall. A yellowish cloud of vapor enveloped it, spreading rapidly outward. "Gas attack!" Hulk cried. "Get into the monoshuttle!"

"This is outrageous!" Bluette exclaimed as he set her down. But she ran fleetly enough toward the mono.

It was no good. The crash had disrupted the mono's power; the shuttle was inoperative. "Go outside the dome!" Hulk cried. "The gas can't follow there!"

But the gas had already diffused throughout the dome. Both Hulk and the Lady held their breaths as they ran for the rim, but collapsed as the gas touched their skin.

"Nerve gas," Stile muttered. "Almost instant. Not necessary to breathe it. Used as an anesthetic for animals." He frowned. "But strange that a shipment of that should crash right there and then. Freight rockets hardly ever go astray."

"That was no coincidence," Sheen said. "That was a trap."

Stile nodded. "A trap set for me, I think. Because it was expected that I would be the one to come for the Lady Blue."

"Which means that your enemy knows of your life in both frames. And that you would hardly be likely to bring the one person who could help you escape that situation—me."

Another half-bitter reference to Sheen's own feelings. She was right; had he gone to see Bluette, Stile would not have brought Sheen along. That would have been unnecessarily cruel. So he would have had no invulnerable guardian to bail him or the Lady out. "Yes, the enemy must be an Adept, who can cross the curtain. But not a Citizen. So the trap is made to seem like an accident, to foil any Citizen curiosity."

Now he was feeling the reaction. Stile did not like being the object of a murder campaign; that frightened him and generated in him a festering uncertainty and rage. But now the attack had spread to the Lady Blue/Bluette. That aggravated him far more specifically. How dare they touch her!

And Hulk—innocently walking into the trap set for Stile. Hulk's blood, if it came to that, would be on Stile's hands. What mischief had Stile done his friend, in the name of a favor?

The holo continued. Robots emerged from the crashed rocket—humanoid, flesh-toned, but probably far simpler machines than was Sheen. They came to Hulk and the Lady, and fitted breathing masks over their faces. Then the robots picked up the two effortlessly and carried them through the force-field and out onto the barren surface of Proton. There the holo-pickup lost them—but the orbiting satellite spotters followed their progress. What a job of tracing the devices of Proton could do, when so directed!

The robots trekked tirelessly south across the sand with their burdens. At length they entered the shaft of a worked-out mine at the margin of the Purple Mountains—which were not purple here. The full image returned; it seemed that even a place like this had operable pickups.

At last the two were deposited in a pressurized chamber deep within the mine. It was a miniature force-field dome. There was a defunct food-dispensing machine and a holo-transceiver. This could be considered a pleasant private retreat—or a prison.

The robots sprayed more gas, evidently a neutralizer, removed the breathing masks, filed them in their chest compartments, and set a chamber oxygen generator in operation. Then they walked through the force-field and disappeared from the range of the holo-pickup. Hulk was the one this report was on, not stray robots. The impersonal touch of the machine, literally; machines did not care about irrelevancies such as the welfare of serfs or the commission of criminal acts.

Hulk was of rugged constitution, and first to regain consciousness. His eye cracked open in time to see the robots departing. He made a huge visible effort and hauled himself to his feet. He staggered across to Bluette. "Lady—art thou well?" he asked, lifting her with infinite gentleness.

Bluette was at the moment weak physically, but not mentally. She shook off the lingering effects of the gas. "Again you use the archaic form. What is this?"

"I will answer you gladly, Lady. But first we should ascertain our situation. We seem to have been taken prisoner."

"Why should anyone wish to do that? My Employer is a peaceful man, a scholar of the arcane, who hardly ever comes to his castle retreat. I merely maintain it so that it is never ill-kept should he appear. For months at a time, it is as if it belongs to me—but I am only a serf, destined never to be more."

"You are more, Lady. Much more. I fear my arrival precipitated this action." Hulk was already inspecting the perimeter. He took a breath, held it, and stepped through the force-field at one end of their confine. There was only one more tunnel, proceeding interminably. This was an access passage, carved by laser drills long ago, leaving smooth, partially polished walls. It reminded Stile of the bore of the Worm of Phaze. Perhaps that was not coincidence, but another parallel between frames. Operating mines were pressurized throughout, for convenience; since many of the rock formations were porous or semiporous, the passage had to have melt-sealed walls. This was a dead mine, since there was no pressure beyond the Proton-external norm. Hulk passed back through the force-field and moved to the other end. It was the same story.

"These passages can extend for kilometers," Hulk told the Lady. "Without masks, we can not expect to reach a dome on foot."

"Of course not," she agreed. "Yet if it were our captor's purpose to kill us, he could have done this at the outset."

"I see there is a holo-unit. No doubt our captor will communicate with us at his convenience."

"Surely he will," she agreed. "But I still don't understand why we are here."

Hulk inspected the holo-communicator. "I could put this out of commission, but that seems pointless. We shall simply have to wait. I deeply regret bringing this upon you; I had no idea this would happen. Yet perhaps it is for the best."

She frowned, exactly as the Lady whom Stile knew would have, then flung her golden hair back in a kind of acquiescent defiance. She was absolutely lovely. "I was not unduly interested, before, in what you had to say. My interest has grown. Tell me your estimate of this situation."

Hulk settled down against the curving wall opposite her.

"Gladly, Lady. I believe this is a trap set for another person, a friend of mine. It was assumed that he would come for you, and the robots were not astute enough to perceive the substitution. When the Citizen who has organized this checks in, he will discover the mistake. He will not be pleased."

"When my Employer checks his retreat-estate, *he* will not be pleased," Bluette said. "Yet I fear that will not be soon." She looked directly at him. "Give me the rest of it."

"Lady, I am a master in the Game. Since my tenure expires this year I had hoped to enter the Tourney. I was balked in that effort by a better player. But he showed me an alternate world—Lady, you may find this extremely difficult to believe, so I shall simplify it—"

"Do not expurgate it," she said.

"You do not appreciate just how remarkable the story is. I do not wish to have you question my sanity."

"Risk my incredulity. Tell the truth and take your medicine," she said, smiling.

"I cannot deny you," he said, warmed as anyone would be. The smile of the Lady was a precious thing. "I should warn you that I came to court you. I do not mean to give offense, and I would have preferred a more esthetic approach—"

"I have not been courted in years," she said. "You are a handsome man."

"Reserve your judgment; I may have brought great mischief upon you."

"I reserve it," she said. But she studied him with only slightly muted interest, for Hulk was about as impressive a figure of a man as existed, and the compliment of his attention was considerable. Women were less impressed by physical attributes than men were, but they were not immune to them.

"This alternate world, where I met the woman like you," he said. "It resembles Proton in geography, but it has good air and water and vegetation, and a population of living creatures. An ideal world, except—" He paused. "Remember, I warned you. In that world, called Phaze, science is inoperative and magic is operative."

"Magic is operative," she replied, humoring him.

"Yes. He took me to that world, where unicorns and werewolves and vampires roam, and he made some spells and became the Blue Adept, one of the leading magicians of that frame. But he had been killed by another Adept. So I served as his bodyguard, and I guarded his wife—who is you."

"You're right," Bluette said seriously. "This is beyond belief. I do appreciate your imagination, and am sure you do excellently in the Lying Game in competition, and consider myself honored to be the subject of your present fantasy. How does this relate to our kidnapping?"

"The enemy Adept is evidently another curtain-crosser," Hulk continued gamely, "operating in both frames. Unable to destroy the Blue Adept permanently in Phaze, he has been setting traps for him here in Proton. The enemy evidently thought the Blue Adept would come for you, so he arranged to abduct whoever approached you, apart from your Employer and routine serfs. But this trap got the wrong man."

"How can you court the wife of your friend?" she asked alertly. In no way was Bluette slow of wit; Stile had discovered that early, when dealing with her alternate.

"Most people exist in both frames. When the self of one frame dies, the self of the other can cross over, filling his place. When the Blue Adept died, his Proton-self crossed over—and courted the widow, the Lady Blue. But he felt it would be improper also to court her Proton-self, who is you, Bluette."

"And he allows you to approach me instead, since I am surplus?"

"There are no surplus diamonds," Hulk said. "Every precious thing has a taker. He is a generous man, Lady. He loves you, but will take only the one he first came to know. There is something more to his interest than your likeness, I suspect."

"I should hope so. And you accede to this? You seem to be man enough to have your pick of women. Why accept the castoff of your friend? Is he even more powerful than you appear to be?"

"In a manner of speaking, Lady. It seems we are similar

in many respects, including our taste in women. I cannot explain it better."

"I think you can. You were with his wife?"

"I guarded his wife from the possible threat by his enemy, during his absences. I came to know her, the deep and unique qualities of her. I am an honorable man; when I realized what was happening, I left."

"What do you mean, what was happening?" she demanded. "Were I the wife of one, I would not be leading on another."

"No, never!" Hulk agreed hastily. "You—I mean the Lady Blue—never in any way—it was wholly in my mind, a one-sided thing. But in this frame she is not his wife, and will never be; he intends never to meet her. Meet thee. You. Thus I came for you, her perfect double."

"Less swift, man. I have not quite made the transition from your dream fancy to your reality." She cocked her head. "What is your name?"

"Hulk. From an ancient comic."

She smiled. "I was named after a fine horse."

They laughed, warming to each other.

"Well, Hulk," she said after a moment. "Whatever gave you the notion that any self of mine would be amenable to any suit of yours? Why should I flirt with a bodyguard, in either, ah, frame?"

Hulk spread his hands. "How you receive it is your business. I had to try. You can but decline."

"Still, there must have been a point of decision."

Hulk nodded. "I suppose there was. In Phaze-frame life abounds, including bacterial and viral. I had little natural defense against environmental disease agents, since Proton is nearly sterile." He paused, reflecting. "In more ways than one, I suspect." He made a gesture to indicate that it didn't matter. "I fell sick. The Lady Blue recognized the problem; she bade me lie down, and she laid her hands on me, and they were healing hands, that warmed me throughout."

"Ah, yes," Stile said, momentarily breaking out of the spell of the holograph narrative. "I have felt the touch of those hands."

"You are not jealous?" Sheen asked. "I inquire merely as a point of robotic interest."

"Meaning *you're* jealous," he said. "You think the Lady Blue is too pretty."

"If appearance were all that counted, I might compete. I think she has too much of your attention."

"Not in this frame. Hulk left her to me in Phaze; I leave her to him, in Proton. It was not a completely easy decision for either of us. But yes, I am jealous. It is hard for me to watch another man courting her."

"And harder to watch her responding. Serves you right."

"Serves me right," he agreed.

"I do not lightly give my body or my heart," Bluette was saying to Hulk. The holo-scene had frozen while Stile and Sheen conversed; that was Sheen's touch on the control. "You're a funny man, with a fairy-tale history. Yet there is no doubt we are here, and surely we shall be interrogated. Will you tell our captor the same story?"

"I'm not sure. I am not the one our captor wants." Hulk pondered. "Lady, I fear it will go hard with us, when our captor discovers the error. It would be better if he did not realize it."

"Why?"

"Obviously there is something the captor wants of my friend, not merely his death. Otherwise the robots would simply have killed us, instead of bringing us here. Perhaps it is information that is wanted. Since kidnapping is also a crime, even when only serfs are involved, I will be disposed of so I can not tell my story to my own Employer."

"Yes. I, too, will be useless as bait, after this. But I do not see what action we can take. If we disrupt the holo-pickup, the captor will know, and will send in—you said there were robots?"

"I saw two, as I recovered consciousness."

"Who have the oxy-masks used to bring us here," Bluette said, her eyes widening as she caught on. "What do you propose, Hulk?"

"First, I must get out of sight of the pickup. Second, you must address me as 'Stile' and describe me as a very small man—smaller than you. The story is the same—that is what he told you. He came to rescue you—and was himself trapped."

"I have that," Bluette said. "Assuming for the nonce that your story is true, then this would be believed by another person from that frame. But how—"

"I will hide outside the force-field, downtunnel. I can function for a limited time in external atmosphere, if I put my body in near-absolute state of rest, or trance-state. You try to lure the robots near the force-field, then get clear yourself. This will not be gentle."

"I know." Her tension hardly showed. She was, as Stile knew, the type to handle difficult situations with verve. "I am sorry to have met you like this, Hulk; you are a fascinating person."

"Thank you. Say that again when I'm not trying to save our lives, and we'll see where it leads." Hulk stepped through the force-field. The pickup tried to follow him, but he was avoiding it, and disappeared from view. Frustrated, the pickup returned to the next most likely subject, the woman.

There was a momentary blankness, to signify a lapse of time. Then the holo-image in the tunnel came on—a holo within a holo. Stile was not sure how the holo-transceiver was able to show itself; this was merely a minor marvel of Proton electronics.

The image was a woman. She was tall and statuesque, with her hair concealed under a skullcap. She was naked: serf, not Citizen. She looked at Bluette. "Where is he?" she demanded imperiously.

"Who are you?" Bluette demanded in return. "Why have you done this?"

"He did not tell you? Then remain in ignorance. Your function is finished."

"My Employer will—"

"That is of no concern to me."

The two robots reappeared from uptunnel. "Put her in pain until her lover reappears," the woman said.

The robots were humanoid, but not specific; their faces were impassive masks. Their strength was that of the machines they were. They seemed to have no speech ability, and moved somewhat stiffly—low proficiency models. It was possible for a serf to obtain such robots, while only a Citizen could obtain robots of Sheen's quality. But these were well suited to this type of work. A robot like Sheen would have had too many humanistic restrictions.

Stile found himself tensing for action. The very notion of hurting the lady appalled him. But this was only a holo-recording; the action was long past. He could only watch.

"Ironic that the captor never bothered to film the prior sequence," Stile muttered. "She could have had complete information with no trouble. But I suppose a frame-traveler hasn't time for niceties—and this one lacks the resources of a Citizen. So this is crudely executed."

Bluette, alert to the threat against her, lurched toward the upper end of the chamber. Both robots moved swiftly to cut her off. She reversed, and moved with surprising agility toward the lower end—which of course was where she wanted to be.

The robots reversed with her. They might move awkwardly, but their reflexes were inhumanly swift; it was only their wit that was deficient. They caught her halfway, and held her in the middle of the chamber.

"Shouldn't Hulk come out?" Sheen inquired. "They will hurt her."

"Even Hulk cannot overpower two robots," Stile said. "They aren't gentle creatures like you; each one is stronger than he is, with no human vulnerabilities. Remember how easily they carried him several kilometers to the mine."

"True. But if he waits—"

"The captor believes it is me out there, and that I love Bluette and will be unable to let her suffer. That's why Hulk said this error might be for the best; there is not the leverage anticipated."

"He said it was for the best out of loyalty to you; your generosity saved you from the trap. But doesn't he love her too?"

"Not yet. He will hold out longer than I would have." Stile's fist clenched. "Maybe too long."

One robot stood behind Bluette, pinning her arms back, holding her firmly. The other glanced at the holo-image for clarification. "No permanent damage yet," the captor said. "Pinch her knee, slowly. Make her scream."

"The knee!" Stile exclaimed. "That's my enemy!"

The robot reached for Bluette's knee. The woman lifted both legs and planted them in the robot's chest and shoved violently. Though the machine was strong, it did not have extraordinary mass; the shove drove it back several steps.

"She fights; that's all to the good," the holo-woman said. "We need commotion."

The robot holding Bluette did not let go. The recoil shoved it back a step; then it stood firm.

"You can't fight robots," the captor told her. "I don't want you anyway. I want him. Make some noise, bring him in, and you won't have to suffer."

"What do you want with Stile?" Bluette cried.

"She remembered to use your name," Sheen said. "Smart woman."

"I want this time to be quite sure he is dead," the captor said. "But first I want to know why he proposed to destroy me. Adepts don't usually fight Adepts. He had no call to attack me."

Bluette's surprise was genuine. "There really *is* a world of magic?"

"You will never see it. Now call the Blue Adept."

"So you can torture him too? Never!"

"Do it," the captor said to the robot.

The robot caught the lady's leg and held it despite her struggles. It placed its metal fingers on her knee and squeezed. The pressure was obviously tremendous, cranking slowly up like that of a vise. She inhaled to scream, but caught herself and held her breath instead.

"My knees with a laser; hers with a robot," Stile grated. He was afraid for the lady, and chokingly angry—and helpless. Whatever would be—had already been.

Bluette collapsed, sobbing. "Oh, it hurts, it hurts!"

"Call him," the captor said dispassionately. "Scream. Bring him to you."

Bluette looked defiant. The robot squeezed again. She collapsed again. "Stop! I'll do it!"

The robot paused, hand still on knee. Dark showed around the edge of its grip, where pressure had crushed the fair skin. Bluette took another ragged breath. "S-s—" she hissed, trying to call through her sobs.

"You can do better than that," the captor said without pity.

"He—went down that passage," Bluette said, entirely unnerved. "I—I'll try. Let me get closer—"

"What a sniveler you are!" the captor rapped.

Now Stile smiled, grimly. "She is no sniveler. She knows what she has to do."

"Robots are no match for the wiles of woman," Sheen agreed.

The captor decided. "Take her to the force-field. Put only her head through. Hold it there until the man comes."

Now Bluette held back. "No—"

"You will call him—or suffocate slowly," the captor said.

The robots hauled the struggling Bluette to the force-field. One put a hand to her head, grasped her hair, and shoved her head through.

The opacity of the force-field exploded into man-form. One robot was lifted into the air and swung about by the legs so that its head crashed into the wall, hard. There was a blue flash of electricity as its wiring shorted; it was done for.

Already Hulk was turning on the other robot. But this one retained its hold on Bluette. Hulk could not get at it without going through her.

Without pause, Hulk turned back to the first robot, picked it up again by the feet, and smashed it into the wall again. Then he jumped on it, caught hold of one of its arms, and wrenched the limb up and around. His muscles bulged hugely as he strained—and the arm broke off, trailing wires. He worked it all the way free.

"That man is beautiful," Sheen said.

"They kidnapped more than they bargained on," Stile agreed with grim satisfaction. "Hulk is the over-thirty serf wrestling champion, and he knows free-fighting too. Now he is armed, with only one robot left to disable. He has a fair chance."

Hulk stalked the robot with his improvised weapon.

"Turn her loose, machine. You can not fight me while you remain encumbered with her."

The robot retreated uncertainly, but retained its hold on Bluette. "What's this?" the captor screamed. "You are not the Blue Adept!"

"I never said I was," Hulk replied, baring his teeth in a fighting grin. "I'm his bodyguard." He smashed his club at the robot, catching it on the back of the head. It let Bluette go, and she limped hastily away.

"Kill them both!" the captor screamed, enraged.

Hulk stood facing the robot, but he spoke to Bluette. "Go to the body. Open the chest cavity. Take out the breathing mask. Put it on and flee. I will occupy this machine."

"I can't go without you!" Bluette cried.

"You must go before the witch summons other help. Go to your Employer; bring a rescue mission here. Don't let the robot make you hostage again. I need this chamber clear to fight it properly."

"Yes," she said, quickly getting the mask. "You are a bold, brave man, and I think I could love you in time. Follow me if you can; I will go for help."

She walked toward the force-field. "Stop her!" the captor shouted.

The robot went for the lady—and Hulk went for the robot, smashing violently at its face. But the robot threw up an arm to ward off the blow, and grappled with Hulk.

Bluette fled, limping. She knew she could not help, here.

The robot tried to go after her, but Hulk clung, using his wrestling expertise. "Deal with him first," the captor decided. "Kill him, then catch the woman!"

Given this unequivocal directive, the robot applied its full force to the task at hand. It had no human weaknesses; it could not be choked or kneed in the crotch or made to yield by pain, and it was the stronger creature here. It was bound by no human scruples. It put one hand in Hulk's face and closed its metal fingers in the vise-constriction, simultaneously gouging the man's eyes and ripping out the cartilage of his nose.

Hulk smashed desperately with his weapon, but his leverage was not good. His face was a blind mask of blood. It was, Stile thought with horror, like fighting a wooden golem: no harm could be done to the inanimate, and no mercy was expected. Hulk's blows dented the metal in several places, but he could not put the machine out of commission. He made one more effort, lifting the machine and squeezing it in a bear-hug and smashing it against the wall, trying to destroy it along with himself.

The robot remained functional. It put its other hand up to Hulk's head, clasped the man with its legs, and twisted the head. There was a snap.

"Oh, God—" Stile cried, anguished.

"Leave this. Go after the woman!" the captor cried. "I will shut down the field."

The robot disengaged itself from Hulk's body and lumbered in the direction Bluette had gone. It had suffered some damage; its motion was hardly faster than hers had been. Meanwhile, the force-field clicked off; the air puffed out of the chamber.

If Hulk was not already dead, he would suffocate shortly. With a broken neck and no air his situation was hopeless.

The holograph faded out. The recording was over.

CHAPTER 8

Quest

Stile emerged in Phaze at the familiar spot south of the Blue Demesnes. Suddenly his will coalesced. He opened his bag and brought out the magic Flute and played it hard and long. His power gathered to him as the platinum notes pealed forth. Almost, it seemed, the mountain trembled— but not quite. This instrument was the finest he had played, but he knew he could not keep it. When he found the person who could play it better than he—

But at the moment something else preempted his attention. As he played, the words came to him. In a moment he stopped playing and cried it out savagely: "Of the one who killed mine other self, the one who slew my friend, I, Stile, the Blue Adept, swear to make an end!"

The magic oath flung outward, making the ground ripple, the trees tremble, and the welkin waver. Pine needles burst into flame. From the Purple Mountains a rumbling echo came back like the voice of a monster: "end . . . end . . . end." Then lightning flashed across the sky and thunder rolled down. A startled griffin shot up and away to the west. A quick wash of water descended, extinguishing the local flame, leaving wet ashes. His oath had shaken the firmament, but it couldn't bring his friend back. Stile leaned against a scorched tree and cried.

Neysa and the Lady Blue were waiting for him expectantly at the Demesnes. As soon as they saw him, they knew something was wrong.

"Hulk is dead," Stile said bluntly. "Mine enemy killed him, in lieu of me. I have sworn vengeance."

"The sudden storm to the south," the Lady said. "Thine oath! I thought it no natural occurrence."

"Mine oath," Stile agreed. Quickly he filled in the details of the tragedy. "And I know not whether thine other self survives, Lady," he finished. "I fear I have unwittingly brought demise upon Bluette. I should not have suggested to Hulk that he—"

"Nay," the Lady said. She exchanged glances with Neysa, and the unicorn blew a small note of assent and left the room.

Stile felt his burden increase. "It is meet that she rebuke me," he said. "Others have paid the penalty for mine errors."

"She rebuked thee not," the Lady said. "She knows thou didst seek only to do a favor for thy friend. It was thine enemy at fault."

"I should have anticipated—"

"So should my Lord have anticipated the threat against him, by the ill hands of the same enemy. So also should I have known to warn him. There is guilt enough to go around." She crossed to him and put her hands on his shoulders, and he felt their healing power. "We were all of us well-meaning and naive. We could not believe that genuine evil stalked us."

"And thee," Stile said, not meeting her gaze. "It was thine other self I involved in this. I had no right—"

"To pass her to another man? She surely has will of her own! Thy friend was no bad person; I think she might have warmed to him, had she no other commitment. Certainly she would make her own choice, in her own time."

And the Lady Blue surely knew. "Thou hast no resentment, that I did not—?"

"Did not court her thyself, and bereave the Blue Demesnes a second time? Even were the danger naught, it matters not. An I decline thy suit for myself, why should I be jealous of what attention thou mightest pay to mine other self? *She* would like thee well enough, I think."

"But I did not court her!" Stile protested, in his distraction looking into her lovely face.

"And am I to feel insulted that it is I alone thou seekest, not my likeness in another frame?"

"Thou hast a marvelously balanced perspective."

"It was a quality thine other self selected for, methinks," she said with a half rueful smile. "I could not otherwise have maintained the Demesnes in his absence. Surely this, not any wit or beauty, was what caused the Oracle to identify me as his ideal wife."

"Thou hast those other qualities too," Stile said. "I beg thee, Lady, let me go now, lest I embarrass us both by—"

She did not let him go. "Thou'rt very like my Lord. Well I know what thou wouldst do with me, were I amenable."

"Then well thou knowest that I like not to be toyed with!"

"Thou'rt now the Blue Adept. Thy power is proven. Fain would I have thee remain here, not risking thy life in any quest for vengeance."

"I have made an oath," Stile said, somewhat stiffly.

"Well do I know the power of thine oaths! Yet there be ways and ways to implement, and here is thy bastion. Let thine enemy come to thee here, where thy magic is strongest; do not put thyself in jeopardy in hostile Demesnes."

"There is merit in thy view," Stile said, still overwhelmingly conscious of her nearness, of her hands upon him. He kept his own hands at his sides. "Yet I fear that it is folly to wait for attack. Already mine enemy's traps have imperiled my life in both frames, and destroyed my friend and perhaps thine other self too. I want no others to suffer in my stead. I prefer to take the initiative, to do boldly what has to be done. Thereafter will I retire to the Blue Demesnes."

"I fear to lose thee, as I lost him! As has so nearly happened already. What becomes of me, of the Blue Demesnes, if thou goest the way of my Lord?"

That moved him. "Never would I place thee in jeopardy, if I could avoid it, Lady. Yet I dare not take thee with me on my quest for vengeance."

Her grip on his shoulders tightened. "It is my vengeance too, to have or to renounce. If thou lovest me, heed my plea! Leave me not!"

"I have no right to love thee, now less than ever," Stile said. "I may only guard thee."

"Thou'rt the Blue Adept! Thy right is as thou makest it!"

"My right is as my conscience dictates. I seek not the spoils of mine other self's Demesnes. Fain would I return thy Lord to thee, if I could."

She shifted her grip and drew him savagely in to her. She kissed him. Stile's heart seemed to explode with longing, but with an iron will he held himself passive.

She shook him. "Respond, Adept. These Demesnes *are* thy spoils, and I too. Take what is thy right. Leave me not bereft of Lord and of power. I will grant thee whatever thou dost desire. I will give thee a son. No one, I swear, will ever suspect by word or gesture or deed of mine that in truth I love thee not. Only remain to preserve these Demesnes."

It was that truth that cut him almost as savagely as the murder of his friend. Gently but firmly Stile disengaged from her. "If the occasion comes when I do not suspect, then I may act as thou hast in mind. This scene becomes thee not."

She slapped him stingingly across the cheek. "How dost thou dare prate to me of scenes, thou who dost seek futile vengeance that will only exterminate thee and bring down what remains of what my Lord created?"

"I apologize for my foolishness," Stile said stiffly. He hated everything about this situation, while loving her for the sacrifice she was attempting. To preserve the memory and works of her Lord, she would do anything. She had thrown away her pride in that effort. "I am the way I am. I will fulfill mine oath in the best way I know."

She spread her hands. Surprisingly she smiled. "Go then, with my blessing. I will aid thee in whatever manner I am able."

This startled Stile. "Why the sudden change, Lady?"

"It is now *thy* welfare I value, for whatever reason. If I can not preserve thee from thy folly my way, I must help thee do it thy way. Ever was it thus, in these Demesnes."

Stile nodded. "Thy balanced perspective, again. I thank thee, Lady, for thy support." He turned to go.

"Thou'rt so very like my Lord," she repeated as he passed through the doorway. "Nor wiles nor logic nor rages could move him iotas from his set course, when honor was involved."

Stile paused. "I am glad thou understandest."

She hurled a blue slipper at him. "I do *not* understand! My love died of that stubbornness—and so wilt thou!"

Stile found Neysa in the courtyard, cropping the perpetual bluegrass patch. "We must move swiftly to surprise the enemy and allow me time to get to my next match in Proton-frame. But I dare not leave the Lady unguarded, especially in her present mood. Without Hulk—"

Neysa tooted reassuringly and led the way outside. Shapes were racing toward the castle. "The werewolves!" Stile exclaimed.

Soon the pack arrived, panting. The leader metamorphosed to man-form. It was Stile's friend Kurrelgyre, wildhaired and scarred but trustworthy. "The Pack greets thee, Adept."

"I have need of thy assistance," Stile said. "But how didst thou know?"

"Know? We know nothing," the werewolf said. "We but came to visit our oath-friend the mare."

"But Neysa and I are leaving," Stile protested.

"Then we shall be forced to take advantage of the hospitality of thy Demesnes to await her return. Can a pack do less, for an oath-friend?"

Stile understood. Neysa had somehow summoned the pack, all of whose members had sworn an oath of friendship with her, and they would guard the Blue Demesnes during his absence. An Adept enemy could get around such a defense, but not easily; who would voluntarily tackle a full pack of werewolves? The Lady Blue would be as safe as she reasonably could be, for the duration.

"Methinks true friends appear when needed most," Stile said gratefully.

The White Adept was female, so Stile rode Neysa toward the White Demesnes. White did not resemble the woman he had seen in the Hulk holo-tape, but of course she had been in disguise at the Unolympics. So he would go and defy her to show him her true form, establishing at one stroke her guilt or innocence. Armed with the Platinum Flute, he felt he could successfully brace the Adept in her own Demesnes.

Neysa knew the way. Stile slept on her back, refreshing his strength. He knew she would protect him well, and this approach would be less obvious than the use of magic. It was also a salient principle in Phaze: do not waste magic. He would use one of his rehearsed spells to travel away from the White Demesnes, if hard-pressed, instead of expending it unnecessarily now.

It was good to be with Neysa for another reason. Stile was sick at heart, angry about his ludicrous loss of a Game in the Tourney, guilty for Hulk's brutal demise, and disturbed by the Lady Blue's attempt to seduce him away from his purpose. He needed to sort out his feelings and get them settled, and he needed the solid support of an understanding person. Neysa was that person. She did not have to say a word or play a note; she settled him by her presence. She had been right about the importance of her assistance to him; he needed her for more than physical reasons. With her he felt secure, emotionally as well as physically.

They traveled northeast, angling toward the great White Mountain range. At dawn they arrived at a narrow pass. Now Neysa threw herself into a slow gallop, forging up into the snows, while Stile hunched within his cloak. Such was the energy she expended that thin fire shot from her nostrils, and her hot hooves melted indentations into the packed snow. Her body heat warmed Stile's own body, and soon he leaned forward and hugged her about the neck, burying his face in her sweet black mane. She was his best friend in the frame of Phaze, the one he most depended on. It was joy to be afield with her again like this.

At the height of the pass a cruel wind sliced through. Beyond, the terrain opened out into a bleak frozen lake many miles across. The ice was not flat; it pushed up in cracked mounds, where the stresses of expansion had prevailed.

And in the center of that ragged surface rose the icy castle of the White Demesnes, formed of ice bricks partially melted together and refrozen. Flying buttresses of ice braced the walls. It was pretty in its fashion, but rather squat and solid to be truly esthetic artistically.

Neysa walked down to the lake's edge. The ice was a problem for her, as her hot hooves were not suitable for skating. She would have trouble crossing this! "I can conjure skates for thee—" Stile offered dubiously.

She blew a note of negation. Then she shifted into her firefly form.

"But it's too cold for that form here," Stile protested. "Thou mayest be fireproof, but not freezeproof. Thou wilt fly only minutes before thy little insect body stalls out."

She flew to his shoulder and lighted there, already cold. "Oh," Stile said. "I'm to carry thee. Of course! Then I shall put thee in my jacket where it is warm." He did so. Neysa made one flash of thanks and settled down in comfort.

Then he conjured a good pair of skates for himself. Stile was an excellent skater; he had developed power and artistry for use in the Proton Game.

He moved out. The ice was firm, and the curvatures of its surface did not bother him. He skated smoothly yet swiftly toward the ice castle, not even bothering to use an invisibility spell. He was here for a challenge, not a sneak attack. He had only to discover the true appearance or mode of the White Adept's magic. If it did not relate to amulets or golems, she was not the one he wanted. A demon amulet had almost killed him when he first crossed the curtain into the frame of Phaze; four goons had been set on his trail by his use of a healing amulet later. Now he was wary of amulets—but at least it gave him the most promising hint about the identity of his enemy.

One strange thing—the woman who had sprung the trap in Proton had suggested that the Blue Adept had attacked her, rather than the other way around. Why? Surely his other self had been innocent. He would not have attacked another Adept without reason, especially not a woman. So she had to be wrong. Yet it bothered him, for the woman had not known she was being recorded; she had been speaking from her cold heart, not for an audience.

He skated on, drawing near the ice castle. Now it was time to go into his act. He singsonged a spell: "Garb this one in a suit of fun." His clothing changed, becoming a brightly colored clown-suit that was, not incidentally, a good deal warmer than his prior garb.

The thing was, the average Adept had all he or she needed or wanted, materially. The Adept could conjure food, and use magic to build a castle or other residence to his liking, and could make deals for other necessities. But he was liable to get lonely and bored in his guarded fastness. That was why so many Adepts elected to participate as judges and spectators in functions like the Unolympics. It gave them something to do in a public but protected situation. Yellow had obviously thrived on her job as head judge for the Adept pavilion, being all dressed up with her finest youth potion for the occasion. It followed, then, that Adepts could use entertainment at home, too. An Adept's own magic would not amuse himself, even if he chose to waste it that way. So now Stile looked the part of an entertainer—and should be admitted to the White Demesnes with no more than the usual suspicion.

So he leaped and looped and whirled into occasional spins. He did a cartwheel and took a fancy, deliberate spill.

He was a clown, a joker, a fool. Until he had his chance to brace the White Adept and discover the nature of her magic.

He skated close to the castle. So far so good. No hostile spell had been hurled at him.

There was a moat of ice-free water surrounding the castle: an effective barrier to a skater. Stile drew up. "Ho!" he called. "Grant ye access for a fool?"

A human guard appeared. It seemed there was modest employment for a number of villagers in the various Adept castles. "Why come ye?"

"To entertain—for a fair fee. To glean what information I can."

"A spy?"

"Naturally."

The guard lowered his voice. "Fool art thou indeed, if thou wouldst enter these Demesnes. The Adept is ill of humor. Depart, lest thou losest thy gizzard."

"I thank thee for thy warning," Stile said. "But I have come far, and must complete my mission. Do thou announce me to the Adept and let me take my chance."

"On thy insecure head be it. I tried to warn thee." The guard retreated inside the castle.

In due course he returned to crank down the drawbridge, which seemed to be formed of a huge slab of ice. Stile skated blithely across and on into the central courtyard, admiring the way the daylight refracted through the ice walls. And the floor abruptly converted to stone. Stile tripped on it and took a genuine tumble; he had not been paying attention to his feet. He adapted his fall to an acrobatic roll in what he hoped was comical fashion, then removed his skates.

Neysa did not reappear. She remained as a firefly, hiding in his hat. Stile knew why; her conversion back to equine-form would attract attention to him. Who but the Blue Adept, as the Platinum Elves had pointed out, rode a unicorn? But she would change in a hurry if it became necessary. He felt much more secure with her along.

There were no special preliminaries. The White Adept walked out, looking much as she had at the Unolympics, but older and fatter. She had evidently used her magic only to improve her image moderately. "What hast thou got, churl?" she demanded irritably. "What dost thou want?"

"I have a rare show of antics and prestidigitation," Stile said, making his voice comical too. " 'Twill lighten thy spirit and make thee laugh. All I ask in return is the smallest of favors."

"What smallest favor?" She was evidently used to panhandlers.

Stile brought out a silver medal he had conjured in preparation for this moment. "This amulet—it is expended. I want it restored to provide me heat from the cold."

"Amulets are not my business," she snapped. "Thou shouldst apply to her who makes them."

So it *was* a female Adept who made the amulets! This was a valuable confirmation. "Once an amulet attacked me," he said. "Now must I take them secondhand."

"Attacked thee?" She chortled. "Surely served thee right! Very well—if thou dost perform amusingly, I will reward thee appropriately."

"I thank thee," Stile said humbly. He was fully aware that she had made no significant commitment. That was not what he needed. Once she showed the form of her magic—

"Get on with it, clown," White snapped, her mouth setting into solidified sourness. "Make me laugh."

Stile went into his act. He had developed a joker-ritual as part of his Proton-Game expertise, and he had considerable manual dexterity. He put on his "stupid midget" pantomime, trying to eat a potato that kept wriggling out of his hands, looking for a comfortable place to sleep, finding none, and getting tangled up in his own limbs, drawing scarves out of his ears, taking spills, and in general making a funny fool of himself. He was good at it, using no real magic, only stage magic, before a person who well knew the difference. Though the White Adept tried to maintain a sour face, slowly it weathered and cracked. She evidently did not like peasants, and had deep satisfaction seeing one so aptly parodied. Also she, like many people, thought there was something excruciatingly funny about mishaps happening to a midget. In the end she was laughing wholeheartedly.

Stile completed his show. White sobered quickly. "I like thee, fool. I believe I shall keep thee here for future entertainments."

"Honored Adept, I cannot stay," Stile said quickly, though he had expected something like this. "All I want is mine amulet recharged."

She frowned. "Very well, fool. Give it here."

She was up to something. Stile passed over the medal, braced for action.

The White Adept laid the medal on the floor. She brought out a long-handled charcoal marker and drew a mystic symbol around it. When the figure was complete, she tapped it five times: tap-tap, Tap-tap, TAP.

The medal exploded into a dozen huge shapes. Ice monsters, translucent, with snowy fur and icicle teeth and blank iceball eyeballs. The small fragments of metal seemed to adhere only to their formidable claws: nails that were literal nails.

"Cool this arrogant peasant in the cooler, coolies," she ordered, pointing at Stile.

The monsters advanced on him. Stile tried to run out of the courtyard, but they leaped out to encircle him. Grinning coldly, they drew their noose tight. There would be no gentle handling here.

Suddenly Neysa flew out and changed to her unicorn-form. She charged forward, spearing a monster on her horn, lifting her head, and hurling the thing away to the side. It crashed into its neighbor, and both went down in a tangle of shattering ice.

"Ho! A unicorn!" White screamed, outraged. "Think ye to 'scape my power in mine own Demesnes, animal?" She started to draw another symbol on the floor.

That meant trouble. Obviously she could conjure anything with the right symbol. Stile launched himself at the White Adept—and was caught in a polar-bear hug by an intervening ice monster and lifted from the floor. *Fool!* he chided himself. He should have sung a spell. But no— White did not yet know his identity, apparently not connecting the unicorn directly to him. He preferred to keep it secret if he could. He would try to handle this without magic.

He had better! The monster had a frigid hand over Stile's mouth, half suffocating him and preventing him from speaking.

Stile tried to get his hand on the Platinum Flute. That would become a suitable weapon! But, jammed up against the freezing demon, he could not reach the Flute.

He elbowed the monster. Ouch! That ice was hard! He kicked, but the monster seemed to have no feeling in its body. Stile could not throw the creature, because he had no footing. Meanwhile, that terrible cold was penetrating his flesh.

Neysa was busy routing the other monsters. One monster might be too much for Stile to handle, but one unicorn was too much for the whole horde of them. She bucked, her hind hooves flinging out to shatter two monsters; she plunged forward to impale another on her horn. With every motion she demolished a monster. Stile could have had no better ally.

But Stile was held silent, and the White Adept was completing her new symbol figure. This surely meant mischief.

Stile bit the hand over his mouth. This helped; the icy fingers crunched under his teeth. The monster might feel no pain, but it couldn't gag Stile with no fingers. Stile chewed and chewed, breaking off and spitting out the huge hand piecemeal.

Now the witch's second symbol animated. A swarm of stinging flies puffed into existence. They flung themselves onto Neysa—who stiffened the moment they stung, thin flame jetting from her nostrils. Then, with an extended note of despair, she fell to the floor.

There was no question about the ability of an Adept to handle a unicorn! White's magic was more cumbersome to implement than Stile's was, but it was devastating when it got there.

"Dump the animal into the lake—under the ice," White ordered the two remaining ice monsters. "Dump the peasant-clown there too; he's too much trouble."

But Stile could speak now. "Monsters of ice," he sang breathlessly, "turn into mice!"

He had not gathered his power by playing music, so the potency of his spell was not great. That was the cumbersome quality of his own invocations. When fully prepared, he could do excellent magic—but of course White, when set up with a number of drawn symbols, could surely perform similarly. His spell operated incompletely. The two ice monsters shimmered into rather fat white rats.

"Magic!" White hissed. "Now I know thee! How durst thou intrude on these my Demesnes, Blue?"

Stile brought out his harmonica as he walked toward Neysa. He had decided he didn't need the Flute on this occasion. The deadly stingflies rose up in their humming cloud, orienting on him. "I intrude to ascertain whether thou art mine enemy," he said to the witch.

"I was not thine enemy before—but I am now!" she cried. "Sting him, flies!"

Stile played his instrument. The flies felt the coalescing force of his magic and hesitated. Stile willed heat—and as the flies came near, they dried up and dropped to the floor. A few hardier ones persisted until their wings burst into flame.

Stile stopped, looking at the prostrate unicorn. He thought of Hulk and Bluette, knocked out by gas. Which parallels were valid and which were products of his guilt? But this situation he could handle. "Neysa defy the bite of the fly," he sang.

The unicorn woke and struggled to her feet. Stile could heal others, but not himself.

White was forming a new symbol. Stile faced her and sang: "White take the road, as a frog or a—tortoise."

The witch did a doubletake as the spell passed her by. Stile had not filled in the obvious rhyme. Then she reached for the symbol again.

"Let thy flesh become cold," Stile sang, and the magic gathered as though to pounce. "And thy body grow . . . oily."

Again she reacted, fearing the worst; no one feared age like a middle-aged woman! Again she was left unscathed as the spell fizzled. Stile's intent could only be consummated with a terminal rhyme. Once more she went for her spell.

"White form a pyre, and burn like—fir," Stile sang.

This time her white hair seemed to take on a tinge of orange flame. "Enough!" she cried. "Thou'rt victor, Blue!

Thy magic cannot truly transform me, but it could make me very uncomfortable. What dost thou want?"

"Only to see thy magic operate," Stile said. "And to depart in peace."

"No one sees the secret of my magic mode and departs in peace!" she protested. "The mode is always an Adept secret. Sooner would I dance naked before a crowd."

"Thou hast seen my magic mode," Stile pointed out. "I lived my whole life naked in a crowd, ere I came to Phaze."

"Well, no one else shows either magic or body!"

"Yet thou knowest the identity of the amulet-maker."

She considered. "Ah, now it comes clear! Thy vengeance!"

"Indeed," Stile agreed. "Thou dost not seem to be the one I seek, but it would help if I learned who mine enemy really is."

"Aye, I know her. There are secrets witches share. But I will not tell thee. It is not thy business."

"The amulet-maker murdered me!" Stile cried. "And seeks to kill me again. That is not my business?"

"Well, mayhap thou wouldst see it that way. But it is not *my* business to betray her to thee."

"Witch, thou runnest fair risk of suffering my wrath," Stile said, feeling the righteous heat rise. The force of his oath urged him onward. "Yet can I turn thee into—"

"Nay, the power of one Adept is ineffective against another Adept on guard. Yet neither is it my business to betray thee to her. Depart now, and I shall not tell her thou hast narrowed thy choices to two."

To two. Two remaining female Adepts. White had given him some information, by way of placation. That helped considerably. The only problem was that he knew of only one other female Adept.

Well, he would check that one. He mounted Neysa. He played a bar of music, then sang: "Man and steed, to Brown proceed."

They shot sidewise, accelerating to horrendous velocity, passing right through the ice walls without touching them and zooming southeast. Plains, hills and forests shot by in blurs. Then they slowed and came to an abrupt halt.

They were before the great brown wooden door of a

brownstone castle from whose highest turret a brown pennant flew. Obviously the Brown Demesnes.

Stile looked around. A muddy river flowed behind the castle, but none of its water was diverted into a moat. On its banks stood a sere, brown forest. It might be summer in the main part of Phaze, but it was winter at the White Demesnes and fall here at the Brown Demesnes.

Neysa snorted, not liking it. Stile could appreciate why; the grass, too, was brown.

"Well, do we sneak in this time, or boldly challenge?" Stile asked the unicorn. She blew a note of negation, ending in a positive trill. "I agree," he said, "I'm tired of sneaking. We'll settle this openly this time." He wondered whether it was true that one Adept could not directly enchant another Adept who was on guard. That notion seemed to be giving him confidence, certainly.

He faced the door and bawled in as stentorian a voice as he could muster: "Brown, come forth and face Blue!"

The huge door cranked open. A giant stood in the doorway. He was as massive as the trunk of an oak, and as gnarly. He carried a wooden club that was longer than Stile's whole body. "Go 'way, clown!" he roared.

Clown. Oops—he was still garbed in that fool's suit! Well, let it be; he didn't want to mess with a nullification spell right now.

Stile was used to dealing with men larger than himself; *all* men were larger than himself. But this one was extreme. He was just about ten feet tall. If he swung that club, he could likely knock Stile off Neysa before Stile could get close enough to do anything physical.

Unless he used the Platinum Flute as a lance or pike . . .

But first he had to try the positive approach. "I want to meet the Brown Adept."

The giant considered. His intelligence seemed inversely proportional to his mass. "Oh," he said. "Then come in."

Just like that! Neysa trotted forward, following the giant. Soon they were in a large brownwood paneled hall.

A man was there, garbed in a brown robe. He was brown of hair, eyes and skin. "What want ye with me?" he inquired, frowning.

"Nothing," Stile said. "I want the Adept herself."

"Speak to me," the man said. "I am Brown."

"Brown is a woman," Stile said. "Must I force the issue with magic?"

"Thou darest use thy magic in my Demesnes?" the brown man demanded.

Stile brought out his harmonica and played a few bars. "I dare," he said.

"Guard! Remove this man!"

Giants appeared, converging on Stile and Neysa. "I want these creatures swept," Stile sang quickly. "And bring the Brown Adept."

It was as if a giant invisible broom swept the giants out of the hall. Simultaneously an eddy carried in a disheveled, angry child. "Thou mean man!" she cried. "Thou didst not have to do that!"

Stile was taken aback. "Thou'rt the Brown Adept?" But obviously she was; his spell had brought her.

"If I were grown and had my full power, thou wouldst never be able to bully me!" she exclaimed tearfully. "I never did anything to thee, clown!"

Appearances could be deceptive, but Stile was inclined to agree. Why would a child murder an Adept who meant her no harm? Unless this was another costume, concealing the true form of the Adept. "I am here to ascertain that," Stile said. "Show me thy true form."

"This is my true form! Until I grow up. Now wilt thou go away, since thou art not a very funny clown?"

"Show me thy true form of magic," Stile said.

"Art thou blind? Thou didst just make a jumble of all my golems!"

Golems! "Thou makest the wooden men!"

She was settling down. "What else? I use the brownwood growing outside. But most of these were made by my pred —the prior Brown Adept. He trained me to do it just before he died." A tear touched her eye. "He was a good man. It is lonely here without him."

"Knowest thou not a wooden golem usurped the Blue Demesnes?" Stile demanded.

Her cute brown eyes flashed. "That's a lie! Golems do only as told. I ought to know. They have no life of their own."

Like the robots of Proton. Only some robots, like Sheen, and her sophisticated friends, did have consciousness and self-will. "Thou hast sent no golem in my likeness to destroy me?"

Now she faltered, bobbing her brown curls about. "I—I did not. But I have not been Adept long. My predi-pred—"

"Predecessor," Stile filled in helpfully.

"That's the word! Thanks. Predecessor. He might have. I don't know. But he was a good man. He never attacked other Adepts. He just filled orders for them. Golems make the very most dependable soldiers and servants and things, and they never need feeding or sleeping or—"

"So another Adept could have ordered a golem in my likeness?" Stile persisted, piecing it together.

"Sure. He made golems in any likeness, in exchange for other magic he needed. Like a larderful of food, or a getwell amulet—"

Stile pounced on that. "Who traded him an amulet?"

"Why the Red Adept, of course. She makes all the amulets."

Something was wrong. "I met the Red Adept at the Unolympics. Red was a tall, handsome man."

"Oh—she was in costume, then. They do that. Just as I tried to do with a golem when thou camest. Sometimes strangers are bad to children, so Brown warned me not to reveal myself to intruders. I didn't know thou wert apprised I was a girl."

It burst upon Stile with dismaying force. The costume! Not merely different clothing or appearance, but different sex too! Child's play to produce the image of the opposite sex. In fact, Red could have done it without magic. Remove the mustache, lengthen the hair, put on a dress, and the Red he had seen was a woman. Remove the dress so that she was naked, and cover the hair with a skullcap, and it was the woman who had killed Hulk in the mine. How could he have overlooked that?

"Brown, I apologize," Stile said. "A golem invaded my Demesnes, and I thought thee guilty. I see I was mistaken. I proffer amends."

"Oh, that's okay," she said, smiling girlishly. "I haven't

had company in a long time. But thou mightest put back my giants."

Stile made a quick spell to restore the golems he had swept away. "Is there aught else I can do for thee before I go?" he inquired.

"Nothing much. I like thy unicorn, but I know they don't mess with other Adepts or anybody. Only other thing I'm trying to do is grow a nice flower-garden, but they all come up brown and dry. I don't want thy magic for that; I want to do it myself."

Neysa blew a note. Stile dismounted, and she shimmered into girl-form. "Unicorn manure grows magic plants," Neysa said.

"Gee—pretty ones?" Brown asked, her eyes lighting. "Like a Jack-in-the-pulpit who preaches a real sermon, and tiger-lilies who purr?"

Neysa had already changed back to her natural shape. She blew an affirmative note.

"Send one of thy golems with a cart and fork," Stile said. "A giant, who can haul a lot. Thou knowest where the herds roam?"

Brown nodded. "I go there all the time, to look at the pretty 'corns," she said wistfully. "But I dare not get close to them."

All girls liked equines, Stile remembered. He looked at Neysa, who nodded. "If thou likest, Neysa will carry thee there this time, and tell her friends to give manure to thy golem."

"A ride on a unicorn?" Brown clapped her hands with delight. "Oh, yes, yes!"

"Ride, then," Stile said, glad to make this small amend for his unkind intrusion here. "I will meet thee there."

The child mounted the unicorn somewhat diffidently, and they started off at the smoothest of gaits. Stile knew Neysa would not let Brown fall, and that her unicorn herd would acquiesce to the golem's acquisition of several loads of excellent manure, for such things were not denied to oath-friends. Neysa had helped bail him out of mischief, again, by making Brown glad for his visit.

This had turned out to be the wrong Adept, but the excursion had been worthwhile. Now at last he knew the

identity of his enemy. He would not have time to brace
the Red Adept after rejoining Neysa at the herd; he had
to get back across the curtain for the next Round of the
Tourney. But on his return to Phaze. . . .

CHAPTER 9

Music

It was Round Six of the Tourney. Barely one fifth of the
original entrants remained. The concentration of the skilled
and the lucky increased. The audience for individual
Games was larger, and would grow larger yet, as the numbers of contestants dwindled further and each Round became more important.

His opponent was another Citizen. This was not unusual
at this stage; the Citizens tended to be the best players, and
suffered elimination reluctantly. This one was old, obviously not in prime physical vigor—but any Citizen was
dangerous, in and out of the Tourney.

Stile resolved to put it into the PHYSICAL column if he
had the chance, not risking this man's accumulated knowledge and experience.

He had the chance. They were in 2B, Tool-Assisted
PHYSICAL GAMES. Stile's area of strength. Yet the Citizen did not seem alarmed. Did he have a secret?

They played the subgrids and came up with the Ice
Climb. This was a frozen waterfall about fifteen meters
high that had to be mounted by use of spikes and pitons
from the base. Safety ropes suspended from above prevented it from being dangerous, but the climb itself was
arduous. Stile did not see how this old man could handle
it.

Stile was naked; all he had to do was put on the spiked

shoes, gloves, and safety line. He did not need insulative clothing; the ice was frozen by elements beneath, while the air of the dome was warm. A naked man could handle it well enough, since his own exertion heated him.

The voluminous robes of the Citizen would interfere with his climbing. Slowly he undressed.

Stile was amazed. Under his concealing cloak the Citizen had a body of considerable gristle and muscle. The man was older than Stile—perhaps much older because of possible rejuvenation—but his torso resembled that of a man in his mid-forties, well developed. Stile still should have the edge, but much less of one than he had thought.

They donned their gear, and approached the waterfall. It gleamed prettily, like translucent quartz. Stile had the right channel, the Citizen the left. The first to touch an electronically keyed marker at the top would win. The first to fall would lose. Theoretically one person could swing across on his safety rope and interfere with the other, but he would already have lost. Throwing pitons at each other meant immediate forfeiture. Cheating and fouling never occurred in Games.

Now the Citizen faced the ice and stared into it, unmoving. It was time for the match to begin, but Citizens could not be rushed. Stile had to wait.

The man remained for several minutes in silence. What was he up to? Stile, alert for some significant factor, was alarmed by this behavior. There had to be meaning in it. Why should a person delay a match by remaining trance-like?

Trance! That was it! The Citizen was indulging in self-hypnosis, or a yoga exercise, putting himself into a mental state that would allow him to draw without normal restraint on the full resources of his body. This was the sort of thing that lent strength to madmen and to the mothers of threatened children. Stile never used it, preferring to live a fully healthy life, saving his ultimate resources for some genuine life-and-death need. But the Citizen was evidently under no such constraint.

This could be trouble! No wonder the man had made it this far in the Tourney. He had suckered opponents into challenging him on the physical plane, then expended his inner resources to defeat them. Stile had fallen neatly into the trap.

But Stile, because of his light weight and physical fitness and indefatigable training in all aspects of the Game, was an excellent ice climber. Or had been, before the injury to his knees. Since he could place his pitons to avoid severe flexation of his knees, that should not hamper him much. Very few people could scale the falls faster than he could. He might win anyway. Trance-strength was fine, but the body reserves had to be there to be drawn on, and a rejuvenated Citizen might not have large reserves.

Stile did mild limbering exercises, toning up his muscles. He could throw himself into a light trance at will, of course, but refused to. Not even for this.

At last the Citizen came out of it. "I am ready," he said.

They donned the safety belts. The lines would keep pace with the ascent, rising but not falling again. Stile felt his heartbeat and respiratory rate increase with the incipience of this effort.

The starting gong sounded. Both went to work, hammering the first piton. There were little tricks to this Game; the ice could vary from day to day because of ambient conditions. Sometimes it was a trifle soft, which made insertion easier but less secure; today it was a trifle hard, which posed the risk of cracking. Since each piton had to be set as rapidly as possible, judgment was important. If a contestant took too long, making a piton unnecessarily firm for its brief use, he lost time that might mean loss of the match; if he proceeded carelessly, he would fall, and lose the match. Discrimination, as much as physical strength and endurance, was critical.

The Citizen worked faster than Stile. He was on his first piton and working on the next ahead of Stile. He was pushing the limit, hitting too hard, but the ice was holding. Stile was close behind, but losing headway because he was playing it safer. Ice was funny stuff; sometimes it tolerated violation. Sometimes it did not.

They moved on up. Steadily Stile lost position—yet he

did not dare hit his pitons harder. All he could do was marvel at the luck of the Citizen, and hope that the law of averages—

It happened. Halfway up, the ice cracked under the Citizen's piton. The man had only to put it in a new spot and hammer more carefully—but he would lose just enough time to bring Stile even. The law of averages had come through at last.

But the Citizen, in his trance, was not alert to this. Automatically he put his weight on the piton—and it gave way and fell out. The Citizen swung from the rope, disqualified.

Stile did not even have to complete the climb. He only had to proceed one centimeter higher than the point the Citizen had reached. His caution, his alertness, and his reliance on the odds had brought him easy victory. Somehow it hadn't seemed easy, though.

There was no fake address this time. Sheen took care of him, questioning him about his latest adventures in Phaze, and let him sleep. She concurred with the Lady Blue; she didn't like the notion of him bracing the Red Adept in the Red Demesnes. "She's a mean one; I could tell that from the holo. She'll cut your throat with a brilliant smile. But I'm only a logical machine," she complained. "I can't stop an illogical manbrained flesh creature from being insanely foolish."

"Right," Stile agreed complacently. "Even clownish." She always made reference to her inanimate status when upset.

But first he had to handle Round Seven. This turned out to be against another serf of about his own age. He was Clef, a tall thin man named for a symbol on written music, who evidently had qualified for the Tourney only because the top players of his ladder had not wanted to. Stile knew all the top serf-players of the current ladders, but did not recognize Clef. Therefore this man was no skilled Gamesman, though he could have spot-skills.

They chatted while waiting for the grid. "Whoever wins this Round gets an extra year's tenure," Stile said. "Or more, depending on which Round he finally reaches."

"Yes, it is my best hope to achieve Round Eight," Clef agreed. "I have no chance to win the Tourney itself, unlike you."

"Unlike me?"

"I have the advantage of you, so to speak," Clef said. "I am aware of your skill in the Game. To be fair, I should advise you of my own specialties."

"Fairness is no part of it," Stile said. "Use any advantage you have. Maybe I'll misjudge you, and grid right into your specialty. In any event, I have no way of knowing whether what you tell me is the truth."

"Oh, it has to be the truth!" Clef said, shocked. "There is no place in my philosophy for untruth."

Stile smiled, once again finding himself liking his opponent. "Glad to hear it. But still, you don't have to—"

"I am a musician, hence my chosen name. My single other hobby is the rapier."

"Ah—so you have a strength in either facet. That's useful."

"So it has proved. That and fortune. I did lose one match in CHANCE, but since I won three in that category I can not seriously object. I have come further in the Tourney than I really expected."

"But you know I'll play away from your strengths," Stile said.

"I could as readily play for CHANCE again and neutralize your advantage."

"Not if you get the letters."

"Then my choice is easy. Rapier and flute are both tools."

The flute? Stile wasn't sure how well the Platinum Flute would play in this frame, since its magic could not operate here, but it was such a fine instrument it might well make him competitive. "I am not expert with the rapier," he said, thinking of the training Neysa had given him in Phaze. "Yet I am not unversed in it, and in other weapons I am proficient. Unless you managed to get the rapier itself, rather than an edged sword, I doubt you would want to meet me in such a category."

"I have no doubt at all I don't want to meet you there!" Clef agreed.

"But I have lost one match in this Tourney through CHANCE, as you have, and am eager to avoid another."

"Are you proffering a deal?" Clef inquired, elevating an eyebrow. He had elegant eyebrows, quite expressive.

"This is legal and ethical. Of course no agreement has force in the Game itself. But two honorable players can come to an agreement if they wish."

"I understand. Are you willing to meet me in Music?"

"Yes, depending."

"You grant me Music, and I will grant you choice of instruments."

"That was my notion."

"However, I should warn you that I am widely versed in this area of the arts. My favorite is the flute, but I am proficient in any of the woodwinds and strings. More so than you, I believe; I have heard you play. So you may prefer to select one of the less sophisticated instruments."

Stile's fiercely competitive soul was aroused. He had a compulsion to beat opponents in their special areas of strength. That was why he had tackled Hulk in Naked Physical. He thought again of the Platinum Flute, surely the finest instrument he could employ. On it he could play the best music of his life. He might take the measure of this self-proclaimed expert! But caution prevailed. If the flute was Clef's instrument of choice, no skill of Stile's could reasonably hope to match him, and it would be foolish to allow himself to believe otherwise. Also the Flute was in Stile's possession only on loan, and if his use of it here drew the attention of Citizens to it—no, he could not risk that. Fortunately he did have an alternative.

"The harmonica," Stile said.

"A good harmonica is hardly a toy," Clef said. "Properly played, it can match any instrument in the orchestra. Are you certain—I am trying to be fair, since you are so generously offering me the category—"

"I'm certain," Stile said, though Clef's confidence disturbed him. Exactly how good could this man be on the harmonica?

"Then so shall it be," Clef agreed, and offered his hand.

"A handshake agreement is not worth the paper it's printed on," Stile reminded him.

"But it is also said that the man who trusts men will make fewer mistakes than he who distrusts them."

"I have found it so." Stile took the proffered hand, and so they sealed the agreement.

Their turn at the grid came. They played as agreed. They would contest for this Round with the harmonica.

Sheen was ready with Stile's harmonica; she was able to carry objects unobtrusively in her body compartments, and she was the only one in this frame he trusted with such things. It had to be this familiar instrument, the one he had played so often in Phaze, rather than some strange one issued by the Game Computer. It was not the Flute, but there seemed to be a certain magic about it. On this, he could play well enough to defeat a musician—he hoped. For Stile thought it likely that a man who played the flute habitually would not be able to do much on short notice with the harmonica. Not as much as Stile could. Stile was by no means a bad musician himself, and he well understood the nature of the Game. There were tricks of victory apart from straight skill. And Stile had practiced with a unicorn.

Sheen, however, was alarmed. She had only a moment to speak to him during the transfer. "Stile, I spot-researched this man Clef. He's no dabbler in music—he's expert! He may be the finest musician on the planet—the one Citizens borrow for their social functions. He can play anything!"

Oh-oh. Had he walked into the lion's den—again? It was the penalty he paid for spending his free time chasing down magicians in the fantasy frame, instead of doing his homework here. When would he learn better? Part of being in the Game was doing one's research, ascertaining the strengths and weaknesses of one's likely opponents, devising grid-strategies to exploit whatever situation arose. He would be much better off to remain in Proton for the duration of the Tourney, settling it one way or the other. But he could not; the lure of magic, of Adept status, of free and open land and of his ideal woman—maybe that last told it all!—were too great. He had discounted Clef's confidence as bravado, at least in part, and that might have been a bad error. "I'll do my best," he told Sheen.

"You'll have to do better than that," she grumped as they separated. Sometimes she was so human it was painful.

Clef met him in a concert hall. Spectators were permitted here; there were seats for about a hundred. The chamber was already full. "Some interest generated here," Clef noted. "You appear to be well known."

"Maybe they are music fans," Stile said. Often he did attract audiences for his Games, but this was a greater response than he could account for. But of course he had never been in the Tourney before this year; only slightly over one in ten of the original entrants remained, which allowed the audience to concentrate much more heavily on the remaining games.

They took their places on the small stage. There were seats there, and music stands; the archaic paraphernalia of the artistic medium. Clef had obtained a harmonica similar to Stile's own, from the Game supplies.

"The rules of this competition," the voice of the Game Computer came. "Each contestant will play a solo piece randomly selected. The Computer will judge the level of technical expertise. The human audience will judge the social aspect. Both judgments will be tallied for the decision. Proceed." And a printed sheet of music appeared on a vision screen in front of Clef.

The musician lifted his harmonica and played. Stile's hope sank.

Clef was not merely good and not merely expert. He was outstanding. He was conversant with every technique of the harmonica, and played the music absolutely true. He tongued notes, he employed the vibrato, he trilled, he shifted modes without slip or hesitation. If the harmonica were not his chosen instrument, that was not apparent now.

The man's long, tapering fingers enclosed his harmonica lovingly, his right forefinger resting on the chromatic lever, his hands opening to modify the tonal quality. Each note was pure and clear and perfectly timed; a machine could hardly have been more technically accurate. Stile certainly could not improve on that performance.

Yet he had a chance. Because though the Computer

reacted to technical expertise, the human audience cared
more about feeling. The appearance of the person playing
counted for something, and the flair with which he moved
and gestured, and the emotion he conveyed to the audience, the beauty and meaning, the experience he shared
with it. Music was, most fundamentally, a participant activity; people without other esthetic appreciation nevertheless liked to tap toes, nod heads, sway to the evocative
melody and beat. Stile was good at evoking audience response. If he could do that here, he could gain the social
facet and pull out a draw. The audience participation in
judging the arts was for this very reason; in the early days
some Tourneys had been won by performances that no one
except the Computer thought were worthwhile. This problem had been evident historically throughout the arts.
Prizes had been awarded for paintings that no one could
comprehend, and for sculpture that was ludicrous to the
average eye, and for literature that few people could read.
Refined, rarefied judgments had been substituted for that
of the true audience, the common man, to the detriment of
the form. So today, in the Tourney, art had to be intelli-
gible to both the experts and the average man, and esthetic
to both. Stile had a chance to nullify Clef's certain computer win and send it back to the grid for the selection of
another game. Stile would surely stay clear of music for
that one!

Clef finished. The audience applauded politely. It had
been an excellent performance, without question; the tiny
and subtle nuances of feeling were not something the average person grasped consciously. People seldom knew why
they liked what they liked; they only knew that in this
instance something had been lacking.

Now it was Stile's turn. Clef lowered his instrument and
stood silently, as Stile had. The music screen lit before Stile
with the printed music. Actually, Stile did not need it; he
could reproduce it from his memory of Clef's performance.
But he looked at it anyway, because he did not want to
make any single false note. Nothing that would jar the
audience out of its rapport.

Stile played. From the start, his hands moved well. The
harmonica seemed to be animated with all the experiences

Stile had had from the time he discovered it, there in the
great valley between the Purple Mountains and the White
Mountains in the lovely frame of Phaze. He thought of
Neysa as he played, and it was as if he were playing for
her, with her again, loving it. Every note was true; he knew
he would make no errors.

But he was not playing for himself or for Neysa now.
He was performing for an audience. Stile refocused on
that, passing his gaze over the people, meeting eyes, lean-
ing forward. He tapped his bare heel, not to keep the beat
for himself but to show the audience. A toe could tap
unobtrusively, but a heel made the entire leg move; it was
obvious. The people started picking it up, their own legs
moving. Stile caught the eye of a young woman, and
played a brief passage seemingly for her alone, then went
on to another person, bringing each one in to him.

It was a responsive audience. Soon most of the people
were swaying to the music, nodding their heads, tapping
their heels. He was working them up, making them part of
his act, giving them the thrill of participation. Together,
they all played the harmonica.

Suddenly it ended. The piece was over. Had it been
enough?

The moment Stile put down his instrument, the audience burst into enthusiastic applause. Stile glanced at Clef
—and found the man staring, his lips parted. Clef, it
seemed, had not realized that music could be played this
way, that it could be hurled out into the audience like a
boomerang, and bring that audience back into its ambience.
Perhaps Clef considered this a degradation of the form. No
matter; Stile had won his audience.

Sure enough, the announcement verified the split decision. "Expertise, first player, Clef. Social content, second
player, Stile. Draw." For the benefit of the audience, the
Computer was not employing the assigned Player numbers
now.

Clef shook his head ruefully. "You showed me something, Stile. You played very well."

Stile's reply was forestalled by another announcement by
the computer. "It is an option of the Game Computer to
require a continuation of a drawn match in the Tourney.

This option is now exercised. The contestants will perform a medley in duet, the parts alternating as marked on the score. A panel of qualified musicians will be the final arbiter."

Oh, no! Stile had thought himself safe. A new trap had suddenly closed on him. But there was nothing to do except play it out, despite a judgment that would surely be unfavorable to him. He would not be able to evoke the confused passions of an audience of experts.

There was an intermission while the panel was assembled. "This is new to me," Clef said. "Is there a precedent?"

"I've heard of it," Stile said. "But normally it is invoked only when the contestants can't agree on the draw and insist on playing it out."

"Is it fair? I hardly object to finishing this in Music, but it seems to me you should prefer—I mean, a panel of musicians—"

"Is likely to favor the musician," Stile agreed. "I might win the audience again, but not the computer or the panel. You're bound to take it."

"You must lodge a protest!"

"No good," Stile said. "The Computer does have the option. I'm stuck for it. I knew the rules when I entered the Tourney." And this was very likely the end of his participation in it. So close to the key Round, secured by that prize of tenure!

"I don't like this at all," Clef said. "I do want to win, and I'll have to play my best, but there is a fundamental inequity here on more than one level. It is not merely that the odds of your winning are greatly in your favor if we go to a new grid. It is that you have a chance to go considerably farther in the Tourney than I do; you are a skilled player, while my skills are largely limited to this particular pursuit. You should be allowed to continue, for I shall surely be eliminated in the next Round or two."

"Play your best," Stile said. "Chance is always a factor in the Game. Someone always profits, someone always loses. I do have another resource." Stile knew he faced disaster, but his liking for this honest man increased. How much better it was to lose to superior talent than to blind chance!

"While we wait—would you be so kind as to explain to me how you make the audience respond like that? I saw it, but I have never been able to do that. I rather envy it."

Stile shrugged. "It's apart from the music itself, yet also the essence of it. Basically you have to achieve rapport with the people you're performing for. You have to *feel*."

"But that isn't music!" Clef protested.

"That is the vital spirit of music," Stile insisted. "Sonic emotion. The transmission of mood and feeling from one person to another. The instrument is merely the means. The notes are merely means. Music itself is only a process, not the end."

"I don't know. This is like heresy, to me. I love music, pure music. Most people and most institutions fall short of the ideal; they are imperfect. Music *is* the ideal."

"You can't separate them," Stile said, finding this exploration interesting. "You are thinking of music as pearls, and the audience as swine, but in truth pearls are the accretions of the irritation of a clam, while the audience is mankind. These things must go together to have meaning. Like man and woman, there's so much lost when apart . . ."

"Like man and woman," Clef echoed. "That too, I have never quite understood."

"It's not easy," Stile said, thinking of the Lady Blue and her violent shifts of attitude during their last encounter. "But until—"

He was interrupted by the Game Computer. "The panel has been assembled. Proceed." Musical scores appeared before Clef and Stile. The sound of a metronome gave them the countdown. Quickly each lifted his harmonica to his mouth.

It was an intricate medley, highly varied, with segments of popular, folk and classical music from Planet Earth. The two ranges counterpointed each other nicely. The audience listened raptly. The music of a single instrument could be excellent, but the action of two instruments in harmony was qualitatively as well as quantitatively superior.

Stile found that he liked this composite piece. He was

playing well—even better than before. Partly it was the inherent joy of the counterpoint, always a pleasure; that was why he and Neysa had played together so often. But more, it was Clef; the musician played so well that Stile needed to make no allowances. He could depend on Clef, lean on him, knowing there would be no error, no weakness. Stile could do his utmost. Everything was keyed correctly for takeoff.

Stile took off. He played his part with feeling, absorbing the rapture of that perfect harmony. He saw the audience reacting, knowing the technique was working. He put just a little syncopation in it, adding to the verve of the presentation. The Computer would scale him down for that, of course; it could not comprehend any slightest deviation from the score. To hell with that; Stile was lost anyway. He could not exceed his opponent's perfection of conformance, and had to go for his best mode. He had to go down in the style he preferred. He refused to be bound by the limitations of machine interpretation. He had to *feel*. And—he was doing that well.

Then he became more specifically aware of Clef's playing. The man had started out in perfect conformance to the score, but Stile's deviations had forced him to deviate somewhat also, for as a musician he could not tolerate the separation of efforts. The piece had to have its unity. Now, amazingly, Clef was making deviations of his own. Not by any great amount, but Stile could tell, and it was certain the musicians on the panel could, and the Computer would be having inanimate fits. Clef certainly knew better; why was he doing it?

Because he was picking up the feel. Uncertainly at first, then with greater confidence. With dismaying acuity, Clef was following Stile's lead, emulating him, achieving the same rapport with the human element. But Clef retained his special expertise. Already he was playing Stile's way—better than Stile was doing himself. Stile had to retreat, to play "straight" in support of Clef's effort; otherwise the integrity of the medley would suffer, and it was too fine as music to let suffer. Clef had preempted feeling.

Now the medley swung into a classical fragment Stile recognized—the Choral Symphony—Beethoven's Ninth.

Marvelous music never heard by the deaf composer. A beautiful piece—and Clef was playing his theme with inspired brilliance. Stile found his emotions split; part of him was sinking into resignation, knowing there was no way to match this, that he was in fact losing Computer, panel *and* audience votes, that he had washed out of the Tourney at last. The other part of him was reveling in the sheer delight of the *Ode to Joy*, of the finest playing he had ever done on any level, the finest duet he had ever participated in. Neysa's horn was an excellent harmonica—but it had to be conceded that Clef's instrument was a better one. The man was putting it all together in a way no other could. And— Clef himself was reveling in it, moving his body dynamically, transported—as was Stile too, and the entire audience. What an experience!

The music ended. Slowly the emotion of the moment settled out of Stile. He descended from his high and came to grips with the onset of reality. He had, without question, been outplayed. If there was a finer musician in all the universe than Clef, Stile could hardly imagine it.

Clef stood silent, eyes downcast. There was no applause from the audience. There was only the muted murmuring of the five musicians on the panel, comparing notes, consulting, arguing fine points. Stile wondered why they bothered; there was no question in anyone's mind who had played better. Stile had only torpedoed himself, explaining the secret of feeling to his opponent; the man had caught on brilliantly. Yet Stile could not really bring himself to regret it, despite the consequence; it had been such a pleasure to share the experience. His loss on the slot machine had been degrading, pointless, unsatisfying; his loss here was exhilarating. If it were ever worthwhile to sacrifice a kingdom for a song, this had been the song. Something of miraculous beauty had been created here, for a small time; it had been a peak of performance Stile knew he would never truly regret. Better this magnificent defeat, than a cheap victory.

The foreman of the musicians signaled the Computer pickup. "Decision is ready," the Computer's voice came immediately. "This dual performance has been declared the finest overall rendering of the instrument of the harmonica, and is therefore ensconced in the Tourney archives as a lesson example. A special prize of one year's extension of tenure is awarded to the loser of this contest."

Stile's head jerked up. Salvation! This was the prize slated for those who made it to the next Round, that he had just missed. Not as good as a victory, but far, far better than a loss.

The odd thing was that Clef seemed to be reacting identically. Why should he be concerned with an award to the loser? He should be flushed with the victory.

"The advisory decision of the Computer: Clef," the computer continued after a pause. "The advisory decision of the audience, as recorded by tabulation of those receiving the broadcast of this match: Clef."

Yes, of course. Clef had won both the technical and social votes this time, deservedly. Stile walked across to shake his opponent's hand.

"The decision of the panel of judges," the Computer continued. "Stile."

Stile extended his hand to Clef. "Congratulations," he said.

"Therefore the Round goes to Stile," the Computer concluded.

Stile froze in midgesture. "What?"

The Computer answered him. "Advisory opinions do not have binding force. Stile is the winner of this contest. Please clear the chamber for ensuing matches."

"But—" Stile protested, dumbfounded. Then he was drowned out by the tumultuous applause of the local audience, abruptly augmented by that of the speaker system as it carried the reaction of the larger, unseen audience.

Clef took him firmly by the arm, leading him through the colossal din to the exit. Bemused, unbelieving, Stile suffered himself to be guided out.

A line of people had formed in the hall. At the head of it was the Rifleman. The Citizen grabbed Stile's hand and pumped it. "Congratulations!" he cried. "Magnificent performance!" Then the others were congratulating him in turn, until Sheen got to him and began running interference.

Clef turned to leave. "Wait!" Stile cried. "You can't go! This is all wrong! *You* won! Has the planet gone crazy?"

Clef smiled. "No, you won. I'm surprised you weren't aware."

"You should enter a protest!" Stile said. "You clearly outplayed me. I think you're the finest musician on the planet!"

Sheen guided them to seats on the capsule home.

"I may be so—now," Clef said. "You showed me how to alleviate the major weakness in my skill. I owe it to you."

"Then how—?"

Clef smiled. "It is a pleasure to have the privilege of educating you as you educated me. You recall how we played separately, to a split decision?"

"Indeed," Stile said wryly.

"And how you then explained to me the manner music is a participatory endeavor? Not every man an island?"

"Yes, of course! You proved to be an apt student!"

"A duet is a joint endeavor. Each must help the other, or it fails."

"Of course. But—"

"A man who plays well alone, can play better in company—if he has proper support. Harmony and counterpoint enable a new dimension of effect."

"Yes, I played better, because I knew you would make no error. Still—you played better yet. I think you improved more than I did."

"I am sure this is the case. Because you provided more support to me than I provided to you," Clef said. "I gave you merely good technical performance, at the outset; you gave me the essence of feeling. You showed me how. I was never able to accomplish it on my own, but in tandem with you I felt the living essence at last, the heart and spirit of music. I was infused by it, I merged with its potent pulse, and for the first time in my life—I flew."

"And you won!" Stile cried. "I agree with everything you said. You and I both know you profited greatly, and played my way better than I ever played in my life. You went from student to master in one phenomenal leap! Surely the panel of judges saw that!"

"Of course they did. I have known all of the members of

that panel for years, and they know me. We have played together often."

And this panel of friends had given the match—to Stile? Was it overcompensation?

The capsule stopped. Sheen took each man by the arm and guided him on toward the apartment.

"Therefore you won," Stile said. "That's obvious."

"Let me approach this from another angle, lest you be as obtuse as I was. If you play solo on one instrument and it is good, then play the same piece on another instrument of the same type and it is better, wherein lies the source of the improvement?"

"In the instrument," Stile said. "My skill on similar instruments is presumed to be constant."

"Precisely. Now if you play a duet with one person, then with another, and your performance stands improved on the second—?"

"Then probably the other player is superior, enabling me to—" Stile paused. It was beginning to penetrate. "If I improve because of the other player, it's *him* that really makes the difference!"

"When we played together, I improved more than you did," Clef said. "Who, then, contributed more to the joint effort? The one who flew the heights—or the one who lifted him there?"

"That duet—it was not to show individual expertise," Stile said, working it out. "It was to show cooperative expertise. How each person fit in as part of a team. Yet surely the Computer did not see it that way; the machine lacks the imagination. So it shouldn't have—"

"The machine was not the final arbiter. The musicians saw it that way, and their vote was decisive."

The human mind remained more complex than the most sophisticated of machines! Of course the musicians had imposed their standard! "So I supported your effort—"

"More than I supported yours," Clef finished. "You gave way to me; you made the sacrifice, for the benefit of the piece. You were the better team player. You contributed more significantly to the total production. Therefore you proved your overall participation to be better than mine. You would have made *anyone* shine. This is the subtle point the Computer and audience missed, but the musical experts understood. They knew it was from you I derived the ability that enabled me to make the best individual performance of my life. You are the sort of musician who belongs in a group; your talent facilitates that of others."

Again Stile thought of his many playing sessions with Neysa, those happy hours riding. Their music had always been beautiful. "I—suppose so," he said, still amazed.

Clef extended his hand. "Now permit me to congratulate you on your deserved victory. You are the better man, and I wish you well in the Tourney."

"Victor, perhaps, thanks to an unusual judgment. Better man, no." Stile took the hand. "But if you lost—you can no longer play here on Proton."

"I do have one more year, thanks to the special award. We did incidentally render the finest harmonica recital in the Proton records. But this becomes irrelevant. I no longer need Proton. You have given the universe to me! With the skill you have shown me, I can play anywhere, for exorbitant fees. I can live like a Citizen. I have gained so much more than I have lost!"

"I suppose so," Stile said, relieved. "A musician of your caliber—the best that any audience is likely to encounter—" He paused, another massive realization coming upon him. "Your preferred instrument is the flute?"

Clef raised that expressive eyebrow. "Of course. My Employer provides me with a silver flute, and rarely am I allowed to play on a gold one. One day I hope to be able to purchase such an instrument for myself. The tonal quality—"

"How about a platinum flute?"

"That would be best of all! But it would depend on who made it. The craftsmanship is really more important than the metal, though the best craftsmanship does make any given metal significantly superior. But why dream foolishly? The only craftsmen capable of doing justice to platinum are far away on Earth."

"Sheen," Stile murmured.

Sheen produced the Platinum Flute and handed it to Clef.

The man took it with infinite respect and awe. "Why it

is, it actually is! A finely crafted platinum instrument! I do not recognize this make, yet it seems excellently done. Who—have aliens gone into the business?"

"Elves," Stile said.

Clef laughed. "No, really. I must know. This is of considerably more than incidental interest to me. This instrument has the feel of ultimate quality."

"Mound Folk. Little People. Among them I am a giant. They use magic in their trade. This is an enchanted flute, on loan to me until I pass it along to one who has better use for it than I do. I should have recognized you as a prospect the moment I met you, but I suspect I did not want to part with this magic instrument, and suppressed my own awareness. But I made a commitment, and must honor it. At least I understand, now, how the elves felt about yielding the Flute to me. It is hard to give up."

"I should think so!" Clef's eyes were fixed on the Flute as his hands turned it about. Light gleamed from it as it moved. The man seemed mesmerized by it. Then he lifted it to his lips. "May I?"

"Please do. I want to hear you play it."

Clef played. The music poured out in its platinum stream, so pure and eloquent that Stile's whole body shivered in rapture. It was the finest sound ever created by man, he believed. Even Sheen showed human wonder on her face—an emotion prohibitively rare for a machine. Stile had not played it this well.

Clef finished his piece and contemplated the Flute. "I must have this instrument."

"The price is high," Stile warned.

"Price is no object. My entire serf-retirement payment is available—"

"Not money. Life. You may have to give up both your tenure on Proton and your future as a professional musician in the galaxy. You would have to travel into a land of magic where your life would be threatened by monsters and spells, to return the Flute to its makers—and there is no guarantee they would allow you to keep it. They might require some significant and permanent service of you. There may be no escape from their control, once you enter that region. They do not like men, but they are questing for a man they call the Foreordained, and exactly what he is expected to do I do not know, but it is surely difficult and significant."

Clef's eyes remained on the Platinum Flute. "Show me the way."

"I can start you on that journey, but can not remain with you once you enter the Demesnes of the Platinum Elves. The Flute will protect you; at need it will become an excellent rapier. When you reach the Mound, you will be in their power. I warn you again—"

"I must go," Clef said.

Stile spread his hands. "Then the Flute is yours, on loan until you determine whether you are in fact the Foreordained. I will take you across the curtain. Perhaps we shall meet again, thereafter." Somehow he knew Clef would have no trouble crossing into Phaze.

"You took Hulk across," Sheen reminded him. "When he returned—"

"Some things transcend life and death," Stile said. "What must be, must be." And he wondered: how could the Mound Folk have known that Stile would encounter Clef, the man they evidently wanted, in this frame where they could not go? His meeting with Clef as an opponent in the Tourney had been coincidental—hadn't it?

CHAPTER 10

Red

"And so I sent him on his way to the Mound Folk," Stile concluded. "I do not know what they want of him, and hope there is no evil."

"The Elven Folk are not evil," the Lady Blue agreed. "They, like us, must follow their destinies. Yet their ways be not ours."

"Now must I seek mine own destiny, coming at last to brace mine enemy and thine. I must slay the Red Adept; so have I sworn and so must it be."

"So must it be," she agreed pensively. As always, she was garbed in blue, and as always she was compellingly lovely. They were in a private chamber of the Blue Castle. Neysa was absent temporarily, seeing to the security of Clef on his trek to the Mound Folk. Kurrelgyre's wolves ranged the vicinity, keeping an eye on whatever went on. There had been no move against the Blue Demesnes. "I know what this means to thee, this vengeance," the Lady said. "And fain would I see my Lord avenged: I am no gentler than thee. Yet I mislike it. There is aught thou knowest not."

"I hope we are not going to have another scene," Stile said uneasily. "Dearly would I like thy favor, as thou knowest, but I shall not be swayed from—"

"Methinks we shall have a scene," she said. "But not quite like the last. Shamed am I to have tested thee as I did. I agreed to support thine effort, and I shall not renege. I like not playing the role of the contrary advocate. But now I must inform thee of misinformation thou hast."

"It is not the Red Adept who is mine enemy?" Stile asked, suddenly alarmed.

"Forget the Red Adept for the moment!" she snapped. "This relates to us."

"Have I offended thee in some fashion? I apologize; there remain social conventions in this frame I do not—"

"Apologize not to me!" she cried. "It is I who have wronged thee!"

Stile shook his head. "I doubt thou'rt capable of that, Lady."

"Listen to me!" she said, her blue eyes flashing in the way they had, momentarily brightening the curtains. "I have to tell thee—" She took a breath. "That never till thou didst come on the scene was I a liar."

Stile had not been taking this matter too seriously. Now he did. "Thou knowest I do not tolerate a lie in these Demesnes. I am in this respect the mirror of mine other self. Why shouldst thou lie to me? What cause have I given thee?"

The Lady Blue was obviously in difficulty. "Because I lied first to myself," she whispered. "I denied what I wished not to perceive." Now tears showed in her eyes.

Stile wanted to comfort her, to hold her, but held himself rigidly apart. She was not his to hold, whatever she might have done. Yet he recalled his own recent reluctance to recognize Clef as the one destined to receive the Flute, and knew how the Lady might similarly resist some noxious revelation. This was not necessarily the sort of lie he could completely condemn. "Lady, I must know. What is the lie?" Once before a woman had lied to him, in kindness rather than malice, and that had cost him heartbreak and had changed his life. He could not even blame her, in retrospect, for from that experience had come his affinity with music. Yet the Lady Blue was more than that serf-girl had been, and her lie might wreak greater havoc. He knew she could not have done such a thing lightly.

She stood and faced away from him, ashamed. "When I said—when I told thee—" She was unable to continue.

Stile remembered now how Sheen had at first tried to deceive him about her nature. He had forced the issue, and regretted it. Associations relating to Sheen had led him to this world of Phaze, making another phenomenal change in his life.

Somehow it seemed that the greatest crises of his existence had been tied in to the lies of women.

"Thou'rt so like my Lord!" the Lady Blue burst out, her shoulders shaking.

Stile smiled grimly. "By no coincidence, Lady." He thought of how similar her alternate self in Proton, Bluette, was to her. Had Bluette escaped the robot? He hardly dared check on that. Bluette dead would be a horror to his conscience; Bluette alive—how could he deal with her, he for whom the trap had been set?

"When I said—" The Lady Blue paused again, then forced it out. "I loved thee not."

Stile felt as he had when declared the winner of the harmonica contest. Was he mishearing, indulging in a wish fulfillment? "Thou dost love thy Lord the real Blue Adept, whose likeness I bear. This have I always understood."

"Thee," she said. "Thee . . . Thee."

She had told him of that convention of love—but even if she had not done so, he would have understood. There was a ripple in the air and in the curtains of the window, and a tiny brush of wind touched his hair in passing. For a moment there was a blueness in the room. Then the effects faded, and all was as before.

Except for the lie, now demolished. For this was the splash the world of Phaze made in the presence of deep truth. She had confessed her love—for him.

Stile found himself inadequate to rise to the occasion in any fashion. He had been so sure that the Lady's love, if it ever came, would be years in the making! There was an obvious rejoinder for him to make, but he found himself unable.

The Lady, her statement made, now began her documentation. "When thou didst prove thine identity by performing magic, and I saw the animals' loyalty to thee, it was my heart under siege. I thought thou wouldst be either like the golem, all wood and lifeless and detestable, or that thou wouldst use thy magic as the Yellow Witch suggested, to force my will to thy design."

"Nay, never that!" Stile protested. "Thou'rt thy Lord's widow!"

"Always didst thou safeguard me, with Hulk or Neysa or the wolves or some potion. Even as my Lord did."

"But of course! The Lady of the Blue Demesnes must ever be protected!"

"Wilt thou be quiet a moment!" she flared. "I am trying to tell thee why I love thee. The least thou canst do is listen."

Stile, perforce, was silent.

"Three things distinguished my Lord," she continued after a moment. "He was the finest rider in Phaze—and so art thou. He was the strongest Adept—and so art thou. And he was of absolute integrity—as so art thou. No way can I claim thou art his inferior. In fact—long have I fought against the realization, but no more shall I lie— thou art in certain respects his superior."

"Lady—"

"Damn me not with thy modesty!" she cried fiercely, and Stile was suppressed again.

"Never did he actually ride a unicorn," she continued. "Never did he enchant an entire assembly into friendship with one. Never did he win the active loyalty of the wolf-pack. I think he could have done these things, had he chosen, but he chose not. And so he was less than thee, because he exerted himself less. Always had he his magic to lean on; mayhap it made him drive less hard. Thou—thou art what he could have been. And I—I love what he could have been."

Stile started one more protest, and once more she blocked him with a savage look. "When thou sworest friendship to Neysa, such was the power of that oath that its backwash enchanted us all. Thy magic compelled me—and I knew in that moment that never more could I stand against thee. The emotion thou didst feel for the unicorn became my emotion, and it has abided since, and I would not choose to be rid of it if I could. Always will Neysa be my friend, and I would lay down my life for her, and my honor too. Yet I know it was no quality in her that evoked this loyalty in me, though she has qualities that do deserve it. It was thy spell, like none before in this world. I love Neysa, and Neysa loves thee, and through her I too must love thee—"

Yet again Stile tried to interrupt, and yet again could not.

"I tell thee this to show that I know the extent to which thy magic has acted on me—and thus am assured it does not account for the fullness of my feeling. I love thee in part because I have experienced the depth of thy love for Neysa, and hard it is to deny feeling of that sincerity. Thou lovest well, Adept, and thereby thou dost become lovable thyself. But I do love thee more than I can blame on magic."

She paused, and this time Stile had the wit not to interrupt her. "When thou didst take me along on thy trip to the Mound Folk," she continued, "and the Sidhe toyed with us, and thou didst dance with the Faerie-maid, then did I suffer pangs of jealousy. Then when thou didst dance with me, as my Lord used to do—"

She broke off and walked around the room. "Ever was I a fool. I thought I could withstand thy appeal. But when I heard thee play the magic Flute—O my Lord, that sound! —not since the days of mine other courtship have I heard the like! But then thou didst go to fight the Worm, and I cursed myself for my callousness to thee, swearing to make it up to thee an I should ever see thee again alive—and yet I hardened again when thou didst survive, telling myself it could not be. The lie was on me, and I could not cast it off. Then at the Unolympics when thou didst so readily defend me against the seeming slur of Yellow—alas, I am woman, I am weak, my heart swelled with gratitude and guilt. And I could not help myself, I had to hear thee play again, and so I betrayed thy possession of the Flute to Yellow. And saw thee nearly killed by the Herd Stallion. Yet again had I played the fool, even as Yellow knew. And then at last, when thou didst come to me suffering from thy loss of thy Game and of thy friend Hulk—I longed to comfort thee with all my being, but the lie lay between us like a festering corpse, making foul what would have been fair, adding to thy grief, making of me a fishwife—and yet in that adversity didst thou steer thy narrow course exactly as *he* would have done, and I knew that I was lost. And I feared that thou wouldst die before ever I had chance to beg the forgiveness I deserved not—"

"I forgive thee that lie!" Stile cried, and again the air shimmered and the things of the room rippled and the breath of breeze shook out her tresses.

Now again she faced away from him, as though ashamed of what she had to say. "I was a girlish fool when first the Blue Adept courted me. Somehow I took him not seriously, for that he resembled to my ignorant eye a child or one of the Little Folk. Even when I married him I withheld somewhat my love from him. When I learned of the geas against his siring a child by me, I mourned more for the lack of the child than for my Lord's deprival. For years I dallied, and only slowly did I learn to love him truly—and only when he died did I realize how deep that love had grown. Fool I was; I loved him not with abandon until he was gone. I swore, once it was too late, never to be that kind of fool again. Yet was I trying to be that kind

of fool with thee, even as I was with him. Now thou dost
go yet again perhaps to thy doom, and I will deceive myself or thee no longer. An thou must die, thou must suffer
my love first. And that is the scene we must have."

Now at last she gave him leave to speak unfettered. Stile
could not doubt her sincerity. He loved her, of course; they
had both known that all along. Yet he was not sure he
wanted her love this way. "How did he die?" he asked.

'If this question struck her as irrelevant, she did not treat
it so. "The golem in thy likeness walked to the Blue Castle
during my Lord's absence. At first I thought it was Blue,
but very soon knew I better. 'I bring an amulet for Blue,'
the golem said, and gave me a little demon on a chain, the
kind employed by frame-travelers to mock clothing when
they have none.

"I encountered one of those!" Stile exclaimed. "When I
invoked it, it tried to choke me with the chain!"

"Even so," she agreed grimly. "All innocently did I relay
it to my Lord, who took it for a message-amulet, perhaps
an exchange for some favor. I begged him to invoke it with
caution, lest there be some error, but he heeded me not. He
put the chain about his neck and invoked it—" She was
unable to continue.

"And it strangled him so that he could utter no spell in
self-defense," Stile concluded. "He depended on magic to
foil magic, and this time could not. Had he used physical
means—"

"I could not heal a dead man," the Lady sobbed. "Nor
could I let it be known he was lost, lest the Demesnes
suffer. The golem took his place, the hateful thing, and I
had to cooperate—"

So nothing further was known about the motive for the
murder. The Red Adept had dealt with the Brown Adept to
obtain the golem, and used it without Brown's knowledge
for evil. Perhaps she had even been responsible for the
original Brown's death, to prevent him from interfering,
leaving the innocent child as the new Brown Adept. The
golem itself had not committed the murder of Blue; it had
not been made for that. Probably Brown had been told it
would serve as a double for Blue when the latter was

indisposed to expose himself to public scrutiny, or when he wished to conceal his absence from the Castle. Exactly as the robot in Stile's likeness had served in the frame of Proton.

"This curse of infertility—what of it?"

"After I married Blue, I went to the Oracle to inquire what kind of children I would have, wasting my lone question in girlish curiosity. The Oracle replied 'None by One, Son by Two.' I understood that not until my Lord died: that I would bear children not by my first husband. Oh, I grasped it in part, but did not realize that it was not truly a geas against fertility, but that he would die too soon. I thought he was cursed by sterility—" Again she broke down, but almost immediately fought out of it. "Thou art my second husband—and before thou dost suicide in this awful mission of vengeance, thou must give me that son!" she concluded with determination.

"My son shall not be raised by a widow!" Stile said.

The Lady turned at last to face him. "I love thee. I have at last confessed it. Shame me not further by this denial. I must have at least this much of thee."

But already Stile's mind was working. He loved the Lady Blue, but this sudden force of her return-love was too much for his immediate assimilation. He would be ready for it after due reflection; but now, this instant, it was too much like a windfall gift. He somehow feared it would be taken from him as rapidly as it had been bequeathed, and he wanted to protect himself against such loss before getting committed. Love did not make Stile blind; he had learned caution the hard way. So now he looked for the catch. He did not doubt the Lady's sincerity, or question her desirability; he simply didn't trust the magic vicissitudes of fate. "The Oracle always speaks correctly."

"Aye." She looked at him questioningly. He was not reacting as her experience of him in two selves had led her to expect.

"Then I will not die until I have given thee thy son. Allow me to wait until I have disposed of the Red Adept, that I may have child *and* life with thee."

Her lovely face was transformed by realization. "Yes!

Thou must survive! There be no guarantee that thou may-est live one day after thou dost sire a child, unless the threat to thy life be abated before."

That seemed to be the trap fate had set, the thing that would have made their union brief. Not her change of heart, but his death. Stile's pause for thought could have saved his life.

But then the Lady Blue thought of something else. "Except that thou art not married to me. If thou dost desist, it may be fated that some other man—I loathe the thought! —will marry me and sire my son. It must be thee, I will not have it otherwise, and therefore—"

How fate wriggled to snare him anyway! Stile had almost missed that loophole. "That is readily solved," he said. He took her hands in his. "Lady of the Blue Demesnes, I beg thy hand in marriage."

"Thou dost not say thou lovest me," she complained.

"In good time."

She fought him no longer. "I grant my hand and my heart to thee in marriage," she agreed, radiant.

They went outside. Neysa had returned from her mission, somehow knowing what was in the offing. "My friend," he said to the unicorn. "I have proposed marriage to the Lady, and she has accepted my suit. Wilt thou be witness to this union?"

Neysa blew a single loud note on her horn. Immediately the wolfpack gathered, the werewolves charging in from all directions. Kurrelgyre changed to man-form. "The mare informs us thou hast won the Lady at last!" he exclaimed. "Congratulations!"

Stile marveled again at how much a unicorn could convey in one note. Then the wolves formed a circle, and Kurrelgyre stood before the couple, and Neysa stood between them in her natural form. There was no doubt in any creature what was happening. "By the authority vested in me as leader of the Pack, I perform this ceremony of mating," Kurrelgyre said. "Neysa, as friend to each party, dost thou bear witness that this contract be freely sought by this man and this bitch?"

Neysa made a musical snicker.

"This mare—I mean, this woman," the werewolf said

quickly, finally getting it straight. The Lady Blue smiled; well she knew that the appellation "bitch" was no affront in the mouth of a wolf.

Now Neysa blew an affirmative note.

"Wolves and bitches of my pack, do you bear witness to the validity of this contract?" Kurrelgyre inquired rhetorically.

There was a general growl of assent, admixed by a yip or two of excitement. They were enjoying this.

"Then I now proclaim the two of you man and mate. Wife," Kurrelgyre said solemnly. Neysa stepped out from between them.

Stile and the Lady came together. Stile held her at half-distance one more moment. She remained in her blue dress, ordinary daywear, but she was the loveliest creature he could imagine. "Thee . . . Thee . . . Thee," he said. Then he kissed her.

The shimmer of the oath surrounded them, stirring the Demesnes and touching the fur of the animals and momentarily coloring the grass. For a sweet eternity he embraced her, and when it ended she was in a light blue wedding dress, and a magic sparkle emanated from her.

"Now must I depart to brace the Red Adept," Stile announced as they separated.

Astonishment was manifest among Neysa and all the wolves. There were growls and yips of confusion, and Neysa blew a volley of startled notes. "Not right at this hour!" Kurrelgyre protested. "Tomorrow, mayhap—"

"Right this minute," Stile said, vaulting to Neysa's back. "I shall see thee anon, wife."

"Anon," she agreed, smiling.

Neysa, responsive to his unspoken directive, set off at a canter eastward, toward the Red Demesnes.

When they were well clear of the Castle, Neysa blew an insistent note of query. Stile laughed. "Since thou wilt have it from me at the point of thy horn if I tell thee not, I will answer. The Oracle told the Lady 'None by One, Son by Two.' Now I be Two, her second husband, and—"

Neysa's laughter pealed musically forth. How readily she understood! How many Adepts could arrange the Oracle's assurance that they would survive a life-and-death encounter to sire a son? Stile had cleverly made the prophecy work for him.

As they settled into the hours of travel, Stile concentrated on his spells. He needed a variety of general-purpose defenses and counters. He should survive this encounter, but he had no guarantee that he would win it. He could emerge crippled or blind, able to sire a son but then unable to live in health and independence. Oracle prophecies tended to be slippery, and he had to be on guard against some loophole he had not anticipated. Yet he understood why such predictions were often devious. A person fated to die at a certain place at a certain time would strive to avoid that situation if he could, so the prophecy would be self-negating if clearly stated. Absolute clarity and hundred percent accuracy could not always be simultaneously accommodated, by the very nature of it. Also, there could be a certain flexibility in a situation; a man could die in a dozen different ways, or survive at an expense worse than death. The Oracle had to make a brief statement that covered all prospects, and that was often necessarily ambiguous. So Stile fully intended to fight for the best possible interpretation of this particular prediction. The Oracle had not truly pronounced his fate; it had merely defined the broadest parameters. Interpretation was the essence of his specific fate.

Send this spell straight to Hell, he thought, careful not to vocalize. Would that work against an amulet? It should, if he willed it properly. As he understood it, from his limited experience, an amulet was a solidified spell, quiescent until invoked. Some, like the healing or clothing amulets, worked on a slow, sustained basis. Others, like the throttle-demon, took a few seconds to achieve full strength. Just so long as he had time enough to sing a prepared counterspell. Maybe he could work out a number of easy variants that would lack full force but would suffice in a pinch. Send this spell into a dell, make this spell into a smell, make this spell fail to jell, banish this spell when I yell—all doggerel, but that was the way his magic worked. What he considered real poetry, where form, style and significance were more important than rhyme or meter, took time to create, and he was not sure how much time he would have. There was some evidence that better verse had more potent effect, for he deemed his verse-form oath of friendship to Neysa to have been a cut above doggerel—but he hardly had need of such potency in routine magic. So he kept working out his cheap spot rhymes, hoping to cover every contingency.

They passed the Unolympic site, now deserted. "Thou didst put on a fine show, Neysa," Stile murmured. "Thou didst do credit to thy Herd." And she snorted contentedly. Winning was less important to her than recognition of her right to compete.

They were nearing the Red Demesnes by nightfall. Stile considered where they might camp, since he did not want to engage his enemy by night. There were too many imponderables. He could conjure a suitable shelter, but hesitated to employ his magic here. The Red Adept might be alert to magic in the vicinity, and he wanted his arrival to be as much of a surprise as possible.

But Neysa was already zeroing in on a location. She drew up before a large cave and blew a note. Bats sailed out of it to swirl around the visitors. Then they dropped to the ground and converted to men and women.

"The vampires!" Stile exclaimed. "I didn't realize they lived here!" But obviously Neysa had known; that was another reason he needed her along.

One came forward. It was Vodlevile, the one who had come to Stile during the Unolympics. "Adept! How goes my friend Hulk?"

Wrong question! "Alas, he was murdered in Protonframe," Stile said. "I seek vengeance of the Red Adept."

"Dead?" the vampire asked, shocked. "But I met him only so recently! He was the nicest ogre I knew!"

"He was that," Stile agreed. "Red killed him, in lieu of me."

Vodlevile frowned. Now the cutting edges of his teeth showed. "We have ever lived at peace with Red. She never helped us, but hindered us not. I dared not make petition to her for a charm for my son, for fear she would simply claim my son. We hold Adepts in low esteem. Thou art the first who helped. And Yellow, because of thee." He lifted his hand, and a small bat fluttered down to be caught. "My son," Vodlevile said proudly.

Stile nodded. "I was glad to do it. May we camp here the night?"

"Indeed. Our resources are at thy disposal. Dost thou wish to join our evening repast?"

"I think not, meaning no offense. Thy ways are not mine, and this is my wedding night, which I must spend alone. Also, I would not wish to cause thy kind trouble with the Adept, should she survive me; best that it be not known I dallied here."

"Thy wedding night—alone! Thou'rt correct—our ways are not thine! We shall honor thy desire to be alone, and shall see that none intrude on thee."

So it was that Stile found himself ensconced in a warm cave guarded by bloodthirsty bats. He certainly felt secure here; very few creatures would even attempt to intrude, for fear the vampires would suck their blood.

Neysa brought him some fruit she found, then went outside to graze. She slept while grazing at night; Stile had never quite figured out how she did that, but was used to it by now.

Before he slept, feeling extraordinarily lonely, Stile looked up to spy a small bat fluttering in. There was a manner of skulking about it. It converted to a lad about six years old. "Adept, I am not supposed to bother thee—but can I talk a moment?" the boy asked hesitantly.

"Thou'rt the one the potion helped," Stile said, making an educated guess. "Welcome; I am glad to converse with thee."

The lad smiled gratefully. "My father would cut off my blood, if he knew I bothered thee. Please don't tell him."

"Not a word," Stile agreed. Children did not take adult rules as seriously as they took the prospect of punishment. "I'm glad to see thee flying."

"It was Yellow's potion, but thy behest, my father says. I owe thee—"

"Nothing," Stile said quickly. "Thy father repaid any favor that might have been owing. He helped me match the unicorn Herd Stallion."

"Yet thou didst lose, he says," the lad insisted. "His help was not enough."

"My *skill* was not enough," Stile said. "All I wanted was

a fair match, with shame on neither party. That I had. The unicorn was the better creature."

The lad had some trouble grasping this. "In a pig's eye—my father says. He says thou dost give away more than can ever be repaid, and dost gain more than can ever be reckoned thereby. Does that make sense?"

"None at all," Stile said cheerfully.

"Anyway, methinks I owe thee, for that thou madest my life complete. Yet I know not what favor I can do thee."

"Thou dost need do none!" Stile insisted. Then he saw that the lad was near tears. The vampire child was serious, and wanted to repay his debt as he perceived it. "Uh, unless—" Stile thought fast. "There is much I do not know, yet I am most curious about things. Canst thou keep an eye or an ear out for what might be of use to me, and tell me when thou findest it? Perhaps a sick animal I might heal, or something pretty I might fetch for my Lady." Stile smiled reminiscently, and a little sadly. "Fain would I give my love something nice."

The lad's eyes brightened, and his little bloodsucking tusks showed cutely. "I'll look, Adept!" he exclaimed happily. "Something important, something nice!" He changed to bat-form and zoomed from the cave.

Stile lay down again to sleep, satisfied. The lad would have a happy quest, until he forgot the matter in the press of other entertainments.

In the morning Stile bade the vampire colony parting. "Thou dost understand," Vodlevile said apologetically. "We dare not accompany thee to the Red Demesnes or help thee too directly on thy quest. If ever the Adept supposed we had taken action against her—"

"Well I understand," Stile said. "This be not thy quarrel."

"Not overtly. Yet when I remember the ogre—"

"Bide a while," Stile said. "That may be avenged."

Vodlevile looked startled, but said nothing. Stile mounted Neysa, who was well fed and rested after her night of sleep-grazing, and they trotted off south to the Red Demesnes.

The Red Castle looked more like a crazy house. It

perched atop a miniature mountain, with a narrow path spiraling up to the tiny hole that was the front entrance. It was obviously the home of an Adept; a faint glow surrounded it, like a dome of Proton.

A magic dome? Of course! This castle was probably situated on the curtain, so the Adept could pass freely across, unobserved, to do her mischief in either frame. That would explain much. The Blue Demesnes had not been constructed on the curtain because the Blue Adept had not been able to cross it.

They circled around the castle. It was so; Stile spied the curtain. Just to be certain, he spelled himself across. Sure enough, it was the same castle, with the force-field dome enclosing it. He willed himself back. "This is a sophisticated setup," he told Neysa. "She's been operating in both frames for years."

The unicorn snorted. She did not like this. Neysa could not cross the curtain, probably because she was a magical creature, so could not protect him in the other frame.

"All right," Stile said. "She killed me by stealth. I shall kill her honorably." He singsonged a spell: "Shake a leg, fetch a meg." And a fine big megaphone appeared in his hand. It was not artificially powered, for that was no part of magic, but he was sure it would do the job.

But first a precaution: "Sword and mail: Do not fail." And he was clothed in fine light woven metal armor, with a small sharp steel sword swinging in its scabbard from his hip. The Platinum Flute would have been nice, but that was gone. An ordinary weapon would have to do.

He raised the megaphone. "Red, meet the challenge of Blue." The sound boomed out; it could hardly go unheard.

There was no response from the Red Demesnes. Stile bellowed another challenge, and a third, but had no visible effect.

"Then we brace to meet the lioness in her den," Stile said, not really surprised. The worst traps would be there.

Neysa did not seem thrilled, but she marched gamely forward. It occurred to Stile that he might need more than armor to protect Neysa and himself. Suppose monsters hurled rocks or spears from ambush? He needed to block off any nonmagical attack. "Missiles spend their force," he sang. "Return to their source." That should stop that sort of thing. He wasn't sure how far such spells extended, particularly when opposed by other Adept magic, but this precaution couldn't hurt. The spells of Red could not be abated this way—but that was limited to amulets. He should have a fair fighting chance—and that was all he wanted. A fair match—so that he could kill the Red Adept without compunction.

Neysa walked up the spiraling path. There was no attack. Stile felt nervous; he really would have preferred some kind of resistance. This could mean that no one was home—but it could also mean an unsprung trap.

A trap—like that of Bluette, in the other frame? Bluette herself had obviously known nothing of it; she had been cruelly used. Stile hoped she had managed to survive, though he knew he still would not follow that up; now that he was married to the Lady Blue, there could be no future in any association with Bluette. Meanwhile, his rage at the fate of Hulk burgeoned again, and Stile had to labor to suppress it. Hulk, a truly innocent party, sent by Stile himself to his doom. How could that wrong ever be abated?

There were a number of deep emotional wounds Stile bore as a result of the malicious mischief of the Red Adept; he could not afford to let them overwhelm them. His oath of vengeance covered it all. Once Red was dead, he could let the tide of buried grief encompass him. He simply could not afford grief—or love—yet. Not while this business was unfinished.

They rose up high as they completed the first loop. From a distance the castle had seemed small, but here it seemed extraordinarily high. The ground was thirty feet below, the building another sixty feet above. Magic, perhaps, either making the hill seem smaller than it was, when viewed from a distance, or making it seem higher than it was, from here.

Stile brought out his harmonica and began to play. The magic coalesced about him, making the castle shimmer— and the perspective changed. His gathering magic was canceling Red's magic, revealing the truth—which was that the castle was larger than it had seemed, but the hill lower than it now seemed. So it was a compromise effort, draw-ing from one appearance to enhance the other. Pretty clever, actually; the Adept evidently had some artistic sensitivity and sense of economy.

Now they arrived at the door. It was open, arched, and garishly colorful, like an arcade entrance. From inside music issued, somewhat blurred and off-key. It clashed with Stile's harmonica-playing, but he did not desist. Until he understood what was going on here, he wanted his magic close about him.

They stepped inside. Immediately the music became louder and more raucous. Booths came alive at the sides, apparently staffed by golems, each one calling for atten-tion. "How about it, mister? Try thy luck, win a prize. Everybody wins!"

This was the home of an Adept? This chaotic carnival? Stile should have worn his clown-suit!

Cautiously he approached the nearest booth. The golem-proprietor was eager to oblige. "Throw a ball, hit the tar-get, win a prize! It's easy!"

Neysa snorted. She did not trust this. Yet Stile was curi-ous about the meaning of this setup, if there was any meaning to it. He certainly had not expected anything like this! He had become proficient in the Game of Proton in large part because of his curiosity. Things generally did make sense, one way or another; it was only necessary to fathom that sense. Now this empty carnival in lieu of the murdering Red Adept—what did it mean? What was the thread that unraveled it?

This was, of course, dangerous, but he decided to take the bait. If he couldn't figure out the nature of this trap by looking at it, he might just have to spring it—at his own convenience. He could certainly hit the target with the ball; he was quite good at this sort of thing. But true carnival games were traditionally rigged; the clients were suckers who wasted their money trying for supposedly easy prizes of little actual value. In the Proton variants, serfs had to use play-money, since there was no real money. Here—

"How much does it cost?"

"Free, free!" the android—rather, the golem—cried. "Everybody wins!"

"Fat chance," Stile muttered. He did not dismount from Neysa; that might be part of the trap. He took the proffered ball gingerly, bracing for magic, but there was none. The ball seemed ordinary.

Experimentally, Stile threw. The ball shot across to strike the bull's-eye. The booth went wild, with horns sounding so loudly as to drown out everything else. A metal disk dropped out of a slot. The golem picked it up and handed it to Stile. "Here's the prize, sir! Good shot!"

Stile hesitated. He had been aiming to *miss* the target; instead magic had guided the ball to score. Anyone else would have been deceived, thinking it was his own skill responsible. The golem had spoken truly: everybody won. The game was rigged for it. But why?

Stile looked at the disk. It was an amulet, obviously. He was being presented with it. Yet all this could not have been set up for him alone; he had come unexpectedly—and even if he had been expected, this was too elaborate. Why would visitors be treated to this?

He had an answer: the Red Adept, like most Adepts, was fundamentally paranoid and asocial, and did not like visitors. Power was said to tend to corrupt, and the Adepts had power—and tended to be corrupted. Since they had to live somewhere, they established individual Demesnes reasonably separated from each other, then guarded these Demesnes in whatever fashion their perverse natures dictated. Yet they could not kill intruders entirely randomly, for some were legitimate tradesmen with necessary services to offer, and others might be the representatives of formidable groups, like the unicorns or Little People. Sometimes, too, Adepts visited each other. So instead of random killing, they fashioned selective discouragements. The Black Adept had his puzzle-walls, so that few could find their way in or out of the labyrinth; the White Adept had her ice, and the Brown Adept her giant golems.

Probably a serious visitor would ignore the beckonings of the barkers and booths. Those who were ignorant or greedy would fall into the trap. This amulet was surely a potent discouragement, perhaps a lethal one. It was best left alone.

But Stile was ornery about things like this. He was curious—and he wanted to conquer the Red Adept, magic and all. If he couldn't handle one amulet, how could he handle the maker of amulets? So he sprang the trap. "Amulet, I invoke thee," he said, ready for anything—he hoped.

The disk shimmered and began to grow. Projections sprang from it, extending out and curving toward him. A metallic mouth formed in the center, with gleaming Halloween-pumpkin teeth. The projection arms sought to grasp him, while the mouth gaped hungrily.

Of course his armor and protective spell should be proof against this, but there was no sense taking a chance. "Send this spell straight to Hell," Stile sang, using the first of his prefabricated spells.

It worked. The expanding amulet vanished in a puff of smoke. His own magic remained operative here, as he had expected. He had now dipped his toe in the water.

He nudged Neysa with his knees, and she walked on down the center aisle. They ignored the clamoring of the golems; there was nothing useful to be gained from them.

The domicile seemed much larger from the inside, but there was not extensive floor space. Soon they were at the far side, looking out the back door. Where was the Red Adept?

"On another floor," Stile muttered. "So do we play hide and seek—or do I summon her with magic?"

Neysa blew a note. Stile could understand some of her notes. "You're right," he agreed. "Use magic to locate her, quietly." He considered a moment. "Lead us to Red—where she has fled," he sang.

A speck of light appeared before them. Neysa stepped toward it, and it retreated, circled around them, and headed back down the aisle they had come along. They followed. It made a square turn and advanced on one of the booths.

"Tour the sensational house of horrors!" the proprietor-golem called.

The light moved into the horror house doorway. The aperture was narrow, too tight for Neysa's bulk. But they solved that readily enough; Stile dismounted, and she changed into girl-form in black denim skirt and white slippers. She was not going to let him meet the Red Adept alone.

Stile stepped into the aperture, Neysa close behind. He didn't like this, for already he was partially separated from Neysa, but it seemed his best course. Trace the Red Adept quickly to her lair-within-this-lair; maybe she was asleep. If so, he would wake her before finishing her. More likely she was at the very heart of her deadliest ambush, using herself as the bait he had to take. But he had to spring it—and he had to do it properly. Because it wasn't enough to kill the Adept; he had to isolate her, strip her of her power, and find out why she had murdered his other self. He had to know the rationale. Only when he was satisfied, could he wrap it up.

The difficult part would not be the killing of her. Not after what he had seen of Hulk's demise. The hard part would be satisfying himself about that rationale. Getting the complete truth. Or was he fooling himself? Stile had never, before this sequence of events that started with the anonymous campaigns against him in both frames, seriously contemplated becoming a murderer himself. But the things that he had learned—

It was dark inside the horror house. The passage folded back and forth in the fashion such things did; Stile had navigated many similar ones in the Game. Darkness did not bother him, per se. Neysa, too, could handle it, especially since her hearing was more acute than his.

The light led them on through the labyrinth. A spook popped up, eyes glowing evilly: a harmless show. But it made Stile think of another kind of danger: the noose, choking him, preventing him from singing a defensive spell. That was how his other self had died. That was typical of the way the Red Adept attacked. One of these spooks could be a noose, that he would not see in the dark until it dropped over his head. He needed a specific defense against it. "Turn me loose against a noose," he sang quietly.

A collar formed about his neck, a strong ring with sharp vertical ridges that would cut into any rope that tightened about it. Proof against a noose.

The maze-passage opened onto a narrow staircase leading up. Dim illumination came from each step, like phosphorescence, outlining its edge. A thoughtful aid from Proton practice, so children would not trip and fall. Stile stepped out on the first step—and as his weight came on it, it slid down to floor level, like a downward-moving escalator. He tried again, and again the stair countered him. There did not have to be anything magical about this; it could be mounted on rollers. It could not be climbed. Yet the glow of light he had conjured to show the way was moving blithely up the stairway; that was where the Red Adept was.

"I think I'll have to use magic again," Stile said. He oriented on the stair and sang: "All this stair, motion forswear." Then he put his foot on the lowest step again.

The step did not slide down. It buckled a bit, as if trying to move, but was fixed in place. Stile walked on up, each step writhing under his tread with increasing vigor, but none of the steps could slide down.

Then one step bit his foot. Stile looked down and discovered that the step had opened a toothy mouth and was masticating his boot. It was in fact a demon, compressed into step-form, and now it was resuming its natural shape. Stile had not had this sort of motion in mind when fashioning his spell, so it had not been covered.

Neysa exclaimed behind him. She, too, was being attacked. All the steps were demons—and Stile and Neysa were caught in the center. The trap had sprung at last.

Hastily Stile tried to formulate a spell—but this was hard to do with the distraction of his feet getting chewed. Neysa changed into firefly form and hovered safely out of reach of the demons. "Send this spell straight to Hell!" he sang.

Nothing significant happened. Of course not; he had already used that spell. He needed a variant. "Send this smell—ouch!" The teeth were beginning to penetrate, as the demons grew steadily stronger. "Put this spell—in a shell!" he sang desperately.

The shell formed, pretty and white and corrugated like the clamshell he had in his haste visualized, enclosing all the demons—and Stile and Neysa too. He had not helped himself at all.

Neysa came to the rescue. She shifted to unicorn-form. There was barely room for her on the stairway, but her hooves were to a certain extent proof against the teeth of the demons. She sucked in her barrel-belly somewhat, giving herself scant clearance, and blew a note of invitation to Stile.

Gratefully he vaulted back onto her back. Neysa did a dance, her four hooves smashing at the teeth below. Now it was the demons who exclaimed in pain; they did not like this at all.

Neysa moved on up until she reached the top landing, bursting through the shell he had made. Bits of the shell flew down to mix with the bits of teeth littering the stair.

Stile dismounted and stood looking back. "Something I don't quite understand here," he murmured as the demons at last achieved their full natural forms, but were unable to travel because of his spell. "If she has demons, why did she hide them there instead of sending them after me? Why did they come to life when they did, instead of when I first touched them? There's a key here—"

Neysa changed back to girl-form, which really was more comfortable in these narrow confines. "Amulets must be invoked," she reminded him. One thing about Neysa: she never chided him for the time he took to work things out his own way. Whatever he did, she helped. She was in many respects the ideal woman, though she was really a mare.

"Ah, yes." Amulets were quiescent until animated by the minor magic of a verbal command. So these step-demon-amulets had waited for that magic. But he had not invoked them. He had merely fixed them in place.

Unless it was not the words, but any magic directed at the amulet that accomplished the invoking. So when he cast his spell of stability—yes.

But this meant he would have to be careful how he used his magic here. No amulet could hurt him unless he invoked it—but he could accidentally invoke quite a few. Any that were within range when he made a spell.

In fact—suddenly a great deal was coming clear!—this could explain the whole business of this carnival-castle. If it was defended by amulets that had to be invoked by the

intruders, these amulets would be useless unless something
caused them to be activated. So—they were presented as
prizes, that greedy people would naturally invoke. Because
an amulet was just a bit of metal until it was invoked,
worth little. When the golem-barkers claimed that "everybody wins" that was exactly what they meant. Or, more
properly, everybody lost, since the amulets were attackers.
Stile had acted as projected—and had he not been Adept
himself, and on guard, he could have been in serious trouble from that first "prize."

But these steps had not been prizes. They were a defense
against magic—and that, too, had been pretty effective. So
he was really making progress because he was passing from
the random traps to the serious ones. The steps, that would
not remain firm without a spell that converted them to
demons . . .

Could it be that the Red Adept herself could not invoke
her amulets—or that they would attack her if she did? Like
bombs that destroyed whoever set them off? So that the
intruder had to be forced to bring his doom upon himself?
If so, and if he resolutely refrained from invoking amulets
either by word or by the practice of magic, he should have
the advantage over—

Advantage? Magic was his prime weapon! If he couldn't
use that, how could he prevail?

A very neat trap, to deprive him of his chief power! But
unlike his alternate self, Stile had had a lifetime to develop
his nonmagic skills. He could compete very well without
magic. So if his refusal to invoke the hostile amulets limited him, it also limited his enemy, and he had the net
advantage. This was a ploy by the Red Adept that was
about to backfire.

"I think I have it straight," Stile told Neysa. "Any magic
invokes the amulets—but they can't affect me if I don't
invoke them. So we'll fight this out Proton-fashion. It may
take some ingenuity to get past the hurdles, but it will be
worth it."

Neysa snorted dubiously, but made no overt objection.

The passage narrowed as it wended its way into a hall of
mirrors. Stile almost walked into the first one, as it was
angled at forty-five degrees to make a right-angle turn look

like straight-ahead. But Neysa, somehow more sensitive to this sort of thing than he, held him back momentarily, until he caught on. After that he was alert to the mirrors, and passed them safely.

Some were distorting reflectors, making him look huge-headed and huge-footed, like a goblin, and Neysa like a grotesque doll. Then the mirrors reversed, making both resemble blown-up balloons. Then—

Stile found himself falling. Intent on the mirror before him, he had not realized that one square of the floor was absent. A simple trick, that he had literally fallen for. He reacted in two ways, both bad: first, to grab for the sides, which were too slick to hold, and second to cry a spell: "Fly high!"

This stopped his fall and started his sailing upward through the air—but it also invoked the nearest amulets, which happened to be the mirrors. Now they themselves deformed, stretching like melting glass, reaching amoeba-like pseudopods toward him. Mirrors were everywhere, including the floor and ceiling; Stile had to hover in the middle of the chamber to avoid their silicon embrace.

Neysa had gone to firefly-form, and was hovering beside him. But the ceiling mirrors were dangling gelatinous tentacles down toward him, making the chamber resemble a cave with translucent stalactites. Soon there would be no place to avoid them.

But the little glow of light showed the way out. They followed it down through the pit Stile had first fallen into and up again in another chamber whose amulets had not been invoked.

Stile was about to cancel his flying spell—but realized that would have taken another spell, which could start things going again. It was harder to stay clear of magic than he had thought! For now, it seemed best to remain flying; it was as good a mode as any.

They flew after the glow. It took them through a section of shifting floors—that had no effect on them now—and a forest of glistening spears that might be coated with poison, and a hall whose walls were on rollers, ready to close on whoever was unwary enough to trigger the mechanism by putting weight on the key panel of the floor. This was certainly a house of horrors, where it seemed only magic could prevail. But they had found a loophole; continuing magic did not trigger the amulets. Only the invoking of new magic did that. So they had a way through.

Abruptly they flew through a portal and entered a pleasant apartment set up in Proton Citizen style: murals on the walls, rugs on the floor, curtains on the windows, a food dispenser, holo-projector, and a couchbed. The technological devices would not operate in this frame. Unless they had been spelled to operate by magic. Stile was not sure what the limits were, to that sort of thing. Did a scientific device that worked exactly as it was supposed to, by the authority of magic, become a—

Then Stile realized: on the couch reclined the Red Adept.

Stile floated to a halt. Red was not concealing her sex now. She was wearing a slinky red gown that split down the sides to show her legs and down the front to evoke cleavage. Her hair was luxuriously red, and settled about her shoulders in a glossy cloud. All in all, she was a svelte, attractive woman of about his own age—and a full head taller than he. She was certainly the same one who had been responsible for Hulk's murder.

"Before we finish this, Blue," she said, "I want to know just one thing: why?"

Stile, ready for instant violence, was taken aback. "Thou, creature of evil, dost ask *me* why?"

"Normally Adepts leave each other alone. There is too much mischief when magic goes against magic. Why didst thou elect to violate that principle and foment so much trouble?"

"This is the very information I require from thee! What mischief did I ever do thee, that thou shouldst seek to murder me in two frames?"

"Play not the innocent with me, rogue Adept! Even now thou dost invade these my Demesnes, as thou didst always plan. I have heard it bruited about that thou dost consider thyself a man of integrity. At least essay some semblance of that quality now, and inform me of thy motive. I cannot else fathom it."

There was something odd here. Red acted as if *she* were

the injured party, and seemed to mean it. Why should she lie, when her crimes were so apparent? Stile's certainty of the justice and necessity of this cause was shaken; he needed to resolve this incongruity, lest he always suffer doubt about the validity of his vengeance.

"Red Adept, thou knowest I am here to destroy thee. It is pointless to hide the truth longer. Art thou hopelessly insane, or didst thou have some motive for thy murders?"

"Motive!" she exclaimed. "Very well, Blue, since thou choosest to play this macabre game. I proffer thee this deal: I will answer truly as to my motive, if thou dost answer as to thine."

"Agreed," he said, still somewhat mystified. "I shall provide my motive before I slay thee. And if I am satisfied as to thy motive, I shall slay thee cleanly, without unnecessary torture. That is the most I can offer. I made mine oath to make an end of thee."

"Then here is my rationale," she said, as though discussing average weather. "The omens were opaque but disquieting, hinting at great mischief. The vamp-folk were restive, responding reluctantly to my directives. Indeed, one among them made petition to the Oracle, asking, 'How can we be rid of the yoke of Red?' And the Oracle answered, 'Bide for two months.' A vamp spy in fief to me reported that, so naturally I had to verify it personally. Indirect news from the Oracle can never be wholly trusted; there are too many interpretations. But there did seem to be a threat in two months concerning me—and that time, incidentally, is now nearly past. So I rode a flying amulet to the Oracle, and I asked it 'What is my fate two months hence?' and it replied 'Blue destroys Red.' Then I knew that I had to act. Never has the Oracle been known to be wrong, but I had no choice. I operate in both frames; I could be hurt in either. The Oracle said not that I would lose my life, only that I would be destroyed, which could mean many things. The only way to secure my position was to be rid of Blue before Blue took action against me. So I sent one of Brown's golems with a demon amulet to Blue, while meanwhile I sought out Blue's alternate self in Proton too, lest Blue die yet also destroy me. But someone warned thee, and sent a robot to guard thee, and I was unable quite to

close that loop. Now must I do it here, or suffer the fate
the Oracle decreed for me. Sure it is, I mean to take thee
with me, an the Oracle prove true. Thou art the cause of
all my woe."

Still Stile was perplexed. "My motive is simple. Thou
didst murder mine other self, rendered the Lady Blue
bereft, attempted to slay me also in Proton and in Phaze,
and slew my friend Hulk. For two murders I owe thee, and
that debt shall be paid."

She grimaced. "Thou claimest that we should have had
no quarrel, but for my actions against thee?"

"As far as I know," Stile said. "Mine other self, the Blue
Adept, had no designs against thee as far as I know; his
widow, now my wife, had no notion what enemy had murdered him, or why. As for me—I could never have crossed
the curtain without the death of the Blue Adept, and I
would not have left my profession as jockey had not my
knees been lasered." He paused. "Why were my knees
lasered, and not my head? Had I been killed then, thou
wouldst have suffered no vengeance from me."

"The laser-machine I smuggled into the race was programmed against killing," she said disgustedly. "Citizens
like not fatal accidents, so machines capable of dealing
death must have a safety circuit. Also, it is easier to destroy the narrow tissues of the tendons than to kill a man
by a single beam through the thickness of his skull. Thou
probably wouldst not have died regardless; thy brain would
have cooked a little, and no more. And the Citizens would
have reacted to such a killing by lowering a stasis field over
the entire raceway, trapping me. I had to injure thee first,
subtly, while I escaped the scene, then kill thee privately
when thou wert stripped of Citizen protection. Except that
the robot balked me."

"The robot," Stile said. "Who sent the robot?"

"That I do not know," she admitted. "I thought thou
knewest, that it was part of thy plan. Had I realized that
thou didst have such protection, at the outset, then would I
have planned that aspect more carefully. I thought the
Blue Adept was the hard one to eliminate, rather than
thee."

Not an unreasonable assumption! Of such trifling mis-judgments were empires made and lost. "There remain mysteries, then," Stile said. "Someone knew of thy mission, and acted to protect me. Enemies we be, yet it behooves us both to learn who that person is, and why he or she elected to act anonymously. Hast thou some other enemy—perhaps one who could be identified as 'Blue' though no Adept? Thou must surely have mistaken the Oracle's refer-ence, for I was innocent until that message generated a self-fulfilling prophecy. *Now* Blue will destroy Red, for there can be no forgiveness for thy crimes—but I would not be here now, if that Oracle had not set thee against me."

"A hidden enemy, pitting Red against Blue," she re-peated. "Fool that I was, I queried not the identity of mine enemy, but only my two-month fate—and so the Oracle answered not what I thought it did. The Oracle betrayed me."

"I think so," Stile said. "Yet there must be a true enemy —to both thee and me. Let us make this further pact: that the one of us who survives this encounter shall seek that enemy, lest it pit other Adepts against each other similarly in future."

"Agreed!" she cried. "We two are in too deep; we must settle in blood. But there is vengeance yet remaining for us each."

"Could it be another Adept?" Stile asked. He was not letting down his guard, but he did not expect an attack until this was worked out. Enemies could, it seemed, have common interests. He had operated in ignorance of the forces that moved against him for so long that he was determined to discover whatever truth he could. "One who coveted thy power or mine?"

"Unlikely. Most Adepts cannot cross the curtain. I la-bored hard to cross myself, and paid a price others would not pay. I arranged to have mine other self dispatched, then I crossed over and took her place, hoping to be desig-nated the heir to our mother the Citizen. But the wretch designated another, an adoptee, and I had to take tenure and practice for the Tourney."

Stile was appalled at her methodology, but concealed it.

Her mode had always been to do unto others before they
did unto her. That was why she had struck at the Blue
Adept. Probably her Proton-self had been conspiring to do
the same to Red. And, possibly, Red was now trying to put
Stile offguard so she could gain an advantage. "Thou playest the Game?"

"That I do, excellently—and well I know thou art my
most formidable opponent in the current Tourney."

"I know not of thee on any ladder."

"Never did I enter any ladder until the final moment. I
practiced privately, in my Proton-Citizen mother's facilities."

"Even if the Oracle referred to my defeating thee in the
Tourney, and thus destroying thy remaining chance for
Citizenship," Stile said slowly, "I had three years tenure
remaining, and would not have entered this year's Tourney
but for thy intercession."

"The Oracle betrayed me on many levels, it seems," she
said.

How right he had been to analyze the nature of the
Oracle's statements carefully! Yet the mischief of the Oracle was only in its confusing answers; it did not initiate
things. Someone must have taken this into account. But
what a devious plot this was! "Could anyone in Proton-
frame seek revenge? A friend of thine other self, perhaps,
avenging her demise?"

"She had no friends; she was like me. That was why she
was disinherited. And no one knows she's gone; they think
I'm her."

That had been a neat operation! "Someone in Phaze,
then. Unable to attack an Adept here, so he interferes with
thee there? Perhaps a vampire, able to cross the curtain in
human guise—" Suddenly Stile wondered whether Neysa,
now hovering behind him, would be able to cross the curtain in girl-form. Had she ever tried it? Unicorns did not
exist in Proton, but girls did, and if there was no girl
parallel to—

"Why send a robot to defend thee, then? Why not simply send it to attack me? That's one expensive robot thou
hast; for that value, it would have been easy to send a
competent execution squad after me. It is as likely that the

attack was directed at thee, at thy magic self, with protection sent to thy Proton-self so that it could come after me."

Food for thought! "There is that," Stile agreed. "The Oracle must have known that despite thy attack on the Blue Adept, his alternate self would find thee. The key seems to lie in the unknown party who sent the robot. Find that party, and we may be on the trail of the true enemy. There does seem to be more afoot here than merely my convenience or thy demise; the plot be too convoluted to account for these."

"That's for sure! It isn't much, but it will have to do." She raised her right hand. "On thy mark, get set, go! End of truce." And she threw an obejct at him.

Stile dodged the object. It looked like a small knife, a stiletto—which it could be. But it was also an amulet, and he didn't want to invoke it. It stuck in the wall behind him and remained there, a bomb awaiting detonation.

Red threw another object. This one resembled a ball. When Stile dodged it, the thing bounced off the wall and settled to a stop near his feet. He was floating a few inches off the floor, since his flying spell remained in operation, so the ball did not touch him.

She threw a third. It was like a beanbag, dropping dead behind him. But none of them could hurt him as long as he didn't invoke them.

Then Red invoked one herself. She held the amulet in her hand, spoke to it, and dropped it on the floor. It formed into a hissing snake with glistening fangs. "Go for that man," she told it.

The snake crawled rapidly toward him. Rather than flying upward as Red might want, Stile drew his sword and decapitated the reptile.

Already she was activiting another amulet—a bat. Stile did not want to kill it, because it might be a member of the vampire tribe who had given him safe lodging for the night. A captive of the cruel Adept, bound to do her bidding. Yet if it attacked him—

It did. Its little eyes gleamed insanely, and droplets of viscous saliva fell from its teeth. It could be rabid. There was no help for it; he had to use magic.

"Bat—scat!" he sang. The bat vanished.

But now the three inert amulets near him animated. One was turning into a demon resembling a goblin, growing larger each second.. Another was hissing out some kind of greenish vapor, perhaps a toxic gas. The third was catching fire, becoming a veritable ball of flame.

Stile could not ignore any of these. For the moment he floated clear of all three—but all were expanding, and there was not any great clearance, and the ceiling was festooned with amulets. If he flew high, and banished them with his own spells, hell would break loose from that ceiling. Red had more amulets than Stile had immediately available spells, so this sequence could be disastrous. That was the disadvantage of bracing the Adept in her own Demesnes; her power was overwhelming here. It would be better to deal with the three activated threats some other way.

The Red Adept, smiling wickedly, was already throwing more amulets. Stile had either to act or to retreat—and to retreat would be tantamount to defeat, for he surely would have more trouble passing her defenses a second time. *Now* was the moment of decision.

Neysa, who had been hovering as the firefly, shifted to mare-form. She speared the demon on her horn, then shoved it into the green vapor. The demon screamed in agony, then expired. That was poison, all right! Neysa backed off, the demon still impaled on her horn. She did not dare touch that vapor with her nonmagical flesh. Meanwhile, the ball of fire blazed fiercely, and it was floating up toward Stile.

Stile had an inspiration. He began playing his harmonica. The music filled the room, summoning his magic—but he did not sing any spell. He just kept playing. He knew now that the music-magic could have a certain effect itself, without any specific spell, if he directed it with his mind. So he willed it to suppress other magic. If this had the force of new magic itself, the effect would be opposite, and he would be in twice as much trouble as before; but if it worked—

The fireball guttered and dimmed and sank, finding itself slowly stifled. The green vapor ceased its expansion and

lost some of its color. None of the new amulets were activated. Phew! The gamble had paid off.

Neysa approached the vapor cautiously, seeing it become denatured. She used the dead demon on her horn as
a crude broom to shove the vapor into the fire. The two
joined instant battle, destroying each other. Stile broke off
his music, and the battle intensified as its compass narrowed: the fire tried to burn up the vapor before the vapor
could smother it. But the vapor was stronger; soon the fire
was out.

Neysa mopped up the remaining vapor on the demon.
Then with a strong motion of her head she hurled the
demon directly at the Red Adept.

The woman was caught by surprise. She scrambled off
her couch just before the sodden demon landed. Her collected amulets scattered across the floor like so much jewelry. The green vapor sank into the material of the couch,
rendering it uninhabitable, while the demon lay on it as if
asleep.

Stile had another inspiration. He had noticed that Red
was careful which amulets she threw and which she kept.
Obviously some amulets served the invoker, while others
attacked the invoker. Benign and malign spells, as it were.
If he could get hold of some of the benign amulets, he
could use them against her. That should turn the tide.

But she was alert to the threat. She dived for the spilled
collection, reaching it before Stile got there.

Stile reacted with a spot decision he hoped he would not
regret. "Each spell farewell!" he sang, willing all the amulets within range out and away from the castle. Since he
had been playing his harmonica, his magic should be
strong enough to affect most of them.

The result was confusion. His act of magic invoked all
the nearby amulets—but it also banished them. They tried
to animate and depart simultaneously. Since there were
many of them, their magic outmassed his. Thus they were
coming to life faster than they were moving out.

Rapidly-forming things and creatures were scrambling
for the exits. One resembled a squid, crawling on its tentacles. Another was like a yellow sponge, rolling along, leaving a damp trail that stank of putrefaction. Several were

bats or other flying creatures. Some were colored clouds and some were blazes of light or darkness. One was a small flood of water that poured down through the crevices; another was a noisy string of exploding firecrackers. Stile had to keep dodging and ducking to stay clear of them. His incantation had also abated his flying spell; he was confined to the floor again, where he didn't really want to be. For one thing, the Red Adept was there, avoiding creatures with equal alacrity. At the moment she was trying to brush a swarm of tiny red spiders out of her hair. Both Red and Blue were now too busy to concentrate properly on each other.

Why was he fooling with all these incidental spells, when he could solve the whole thing by simply abolishing the Red Adept herself? Maybe he had held back at the notion of killing a human being, despite his oath. But he thought again of the way Hulk had died, and his resolve firmed. "Red be dead!" he sang.

There was a kind of soundless implosion and explosion centering on the woman. Her clothing burst into smoke. But in a moment she stood naked—and alive. "Fool!" she spat. "Knowest thou not that no Adept can be destroyed readily by magic alone? Only the unguarded and vulnerable succumb."

"But thy amulet killed the Blue Adept!" he protested.

"It never would have worked, had he been properly paranoid. He was a trusting fool. Even so, I am surprised he did not save himself; methinks he could have had he tried hard enough."

As Stile had saved himself from the same spell, by fighting hard enough. He should have known it could not be that easy to abolish her. Otherwise, he could simply have uttered his spell from the sanctity of the Blue Demesnes, and let Red die in her sleep. Many things were difficult against a person on guard. One stab with a knife could kill—but if that person were alert, the knife would never score, or would be turned against its wielder. Also, the White Adept had said his spells could not really hurt her. He had thought that mere bravado, but evidently it was not. Still, with the local amulets clearing out of the way, he had another option.

Stile drew his sword. "Then shall I slay thee without magic."

Quickly she snatched a similar weapon from its place on the wall. "Thinkest thou I am untrained in such arts? Look to thyself, midget!"

They engaged. She was proficient, and she had a longer reach than he. She was in superb physical condition, and had a fiery will to win. Yet this was the broadsword, Stile's preferred weapon. In this he was more than proficient; he was expert. He fenced with her, foiling her attacks readily, setting up for his proper opening. He could take her.

Red realized this. Suddenly she stepped back into an opening behind the couch and disappeared. Stile plunged after her. But a panel slammed across, blocking him off. He hacked at it with his sword, and wood splintered—but by the time he cleared it, the Red Adept was gone.

CHAPTER 11

Trap

Now was the time to use his magic. "Trace her place!" he sang, and a new light appeared, leading the way into the passage. "Fret the threat," he added, to abate whatever nasty little surprises lurked along the passage. This wouldn't stop them all, but it should help. A little alertness should do the rest.

Stile charged into the passage, following the light. Then the light stopped. But the Red Adept wasn't there.

Baffled, Stile retraced his steps. He squinted at the glow from one side and the other.

"The curtain," Neysa said. She was back in girl-form.

Now he saw it—the faint shimmer of the curtain across the passage. What a neat device! No enemy confined to Phaze could follow her there.

He had little time if he was to catch her. "Neysa—I must go through. I—" He could not find the words to tell her what he had to: his gratefulness for her vital help and support right up to this moment; his continued need of it; but the impossibility of having it in Proton-frame. Unless she could cross in girl-form—but then she would be fixed in that form, unable to revert to natural status, and highly vulnerable in the unfamiliar world. No, he did not want her there! So he simply grabbed her and kissed her.

"Make a spell for me to follow," she said.

Good idea! In fact, why not put tracers on both himself and the Red Adept? If this device worked, he could check with Neysa every time he lost track of his enemy, and receive guidance. That would ensure his success. His magic was more versatile than Red's; he might not be able to abolish her by a direct spell, but he could at least track her. Maybe.

The present glow-tracker was designed to follow where Red had gone; it was balked by the curtain, so hovered there helplessly. Stile hesitated to step through at the same spot; no telling what Red had in store there for the unwary.

A small demon-animal blundered down the hall. One of the animated amulets, running late. Stile and Neysa flattened themselves against the wall and let it pass. The thing wandered on past the curtain, never perceiving it, seeking escape from the Red Demesnes. It turned the far corner— and there was an explosion.

"Methinks she set a trap for us," Stile murmured. Probably his counterspell would have protected him, but he could not be certain. Following too closely after the Red Adept was dangerous! "Take me to safe ground while I ponder new spells," he said.

Neysa took him by the hand and led him, while Stile concentrated fully on the task at hand. Soon they were standing on the ground outside the Red Castle, and he had what he needed.

But first one concern: "Neysa, I know thou dost not like magic applied to thee—"

She blew him a look of get-on-with-it, as he had known she would. She had once hated his practice of magic, but after she had accepted his status as the Blue Adept she had seemed to revel in the evidences of his power.

"Identify the one we scorn, by orienting with thy horn," Stile sang to her. Neysa, still in girl-form, turned her head with its tiny decoration-horn toward the south, obviously aware of the Red Adept. "And trace thine oath-friend without fail, by orienting with thy tail." She spun about, slapping her pert derrier with her hand as if stung by a fly. Her lack of a tail in this form was a problem. Then she converted to unicorn, and it worked perfectly.

"Let me step across the curtain, and do thou trace me," Stile said. "Just to be sure." This was consuming time while Red escaped, but if this operated the way he hoped, that wouldn't matter.

Stile spelled himself across, ran a hundred meters over the sand, and crossed back, gasping for the good air of Phaze. Neysa was right there, some three hundred feet from her starting point, her pretty black tail facing him. It worked!

"Good enough!" Stile exclaimed. "Thou canst now trace us both—even across the curtain. I will check with thee whenever I lose her. If she recrosses, we will have her. I shall see thee anon!" And he passed through the curtain again, setting off in the direction Neysa had pointed for the Red Adept. No traps out here!

But this was Proton, and outside a dome; quickly the rarefied and polluted air affected him. The Red Adept seemed to be within the dome—which of course was her Proton-home. Stile would have no safe access there!

He found the curtain and passed back through. Neysa was there, having paced him neatly. "I've got to organize for this better," he said. "It's certain *she's* organized! It's not safe to go after her in her Proton-home."

He paced in a circle for a moment. Even his two brief excursions into the atmosphere of Proton had depleted him. Inside the dome the air would be good—but she would have power he lacked. Her Citizen-mother might not like Red, but would act to protect the dome against intrusions by hostile serfs. "I need to smoke her out, then chase her down in neutral territory. I'd better enlist Sheen's help in the other frame. But I don't want to take mine eye off

the prey. So I'll need to call her. Yes." He walked to the
spot where he had seen a tube connection to the dome.
There would be a communication screen at the transport
terminal.

He spelled himself through. Certain spells were elementary; he didn't even have to rhyme. Just an originally
phrased wish sufficed, for him or any eligible person. He
had wasted a number of rhymes before catching on to
this.

In a moment he was in the station. There was good air
here! He called Sheen.

She appeared immediately on the screen. "So soon?
Game is tomorrow—"

"Come to this address!" Stile said. "I may need help."

The screen went blank. Red had intercepted the call; he
should have known she would not be sitting idle. He might
have avoided her little traps along the way, by declining to
pursue her directly, but she knew he would come for her
here. He had made a tactical error. Stile dived for the
curtain.

A nozzle started hissing out vapor as he moved. Some
sort of gas, probably stun-gas. Red seemed to like that sort
of thing. Had she known precisely where and when he
would appear, she could have nailed him. As it was, it was
a close call; he got a whiff of it as he crossed the curtain,
and reeled as he emerged in Phaze. Neysa steadied him
with her solid body, and in a moment his head cleared.

"Good thing I stayed close to the curtain," he said. "I'm
going to have to create a distraction, so she won't spy me
next time. The Oracle says Blue will destroy Red; I'll start
the process now. Let me have my harmonica."

Neysa shifted to girl-form. She now wore a little knap-
sack over her dress—she manifested clothed or naked at
will—in which she carried Stile's harmonica and other
oddments. Stile had never quite fathomed how she was
able to carry foreign objects on her human body that disappeared when she changed form, yet were not lost. She
could change to firefly-form while carrying his harmonica,
though it was far larger than the firefly, and have no trouble. He kept discovering new aspects of magic that made
little sense in scientific terms—and of course magic did *not*

make scientific sense. If it did, it wouldn't be magic. So he just had to accept that impossible things happened magically, and let it be.

He took the harmonica and played a brooding, powerful theme. For this job the Platinum Flute might have been better, but that had never really been his. He hoped Clef was getting along with the Mound Folk all right, and wondered whether the musician really could be the Foreordained they wanted, and if so, in what manner he was destined to save Phaze. Sometimes Stile had the feeling that he was just one thread in a complex skein, doing whatever it was he was fated to do, with no more free will than a robot had. So many seemingly coincidental things had happened to him—but of course he could be manufacturing a pattern for nothing. Clef might not be the Foreordained; the mountain might not tremble when he played the Flute. So Stile's encounter with him would have been no more than the randomness it appeared to be.

His magic was now intense. He concentrated on the Red Castle. "Make of this, the Red Demesne, a holocaust, a wreck obscene."

They watched. The entire structure shimmered. Smoke appeared. The remaining creatures associated with it scrambled out as if fleeing something horrible. Behind them licked tongues of greenish flame. The smoke expanded, bursting out windows in its urgency to breathe free. Gouts of it roiled up in burgeoning masses resembling the grotesque heads of goblins.

Then the explosions came. Whole walls shoved outward. Partitions sailed flaming in wide arcs, to crash and splinter in minor puffs of fire. Rockets of light shot out, and sprays of burning fog. All colors were represented, but gradually red predominated: this was the home of the Red Adept, after all.

"That should give her something to think about," Stile said. "I really don't like such destruction, but I must destroy the entire works of the Red Adept. I mean to leave no springboard for her to wreak her mischief again." He thought once more of Hulk and Bluette. Had she survived? He hoped so, though he did not want to deal with her directly. What grief Red had brought upon her, merely to try to trap him, Stile. Yes, Red had to be destroyed.

The pyrotechnics continued at the castle, reducing it steadily to the obscene wreck specified by the spell. Meanwhile, Stile stepped back across the curtain, checking to see whether Sheen had arrived. He avoided the gassed station, knowing that Sheen would check for him outside. He came back to Phaze for air, then checked Proton again.

On his third crossover, he spied her. She ran to him, opening her chest compartment to bring out an oxygen mask for him so that he could handle the Proton outdoor air. Quickly he explained the situation. "So what I have in mind is to interrupt the power to the dome-field generator," he concluded. "Can you get me a heavy-duty cutting laser?"

Sheen smiled. She opened her compartment again, and presented him with a compact Protonite-powered portable metal-cutting laser unit and a power-cable locator. "Bless you!" Stile exclaimed, kissing her, then replacing the mask.

They walked across the desert, searching out the cable. Stile was apprehensive that someone would think to look outside the dome, and would spot them, but that was a chance they had to take. Citizens and serfs of Proton were very much dome-oriented, and simply ignored the outer world as if it did not exist. That might help. This should not take long; the force-fields that formed the air-enclosing domes drew a lot of power. Such heavy-duty cables were easy to locate. Soon they found it.

Stile aimed the laser-cutter down and turned it on. The sand bubbled into glass as the beam plunged into it. It formed a glass-lined hole leading down to the shielded cable. Then it cut through the cable itself, casing and insulation and all, centimeter by centimeter.

There was a flash from the hole. Air puffed from the dome in decompression. The force-field was gone.

"I think she will be out presently," Stile said with grim satisfaction. "Now I have sworn to kill her, but I want to be fair about it. I don't want you to do the job for me. Since there are regulations against the execution of serfs by serfs, in the frame of Proton, I'll need to drag her into Phaze. Maybe we can bring her to trial there, and put her away ethically. So you leave it to me—but keep an eye on me, because I don't expect Red to pass up any advantage or ploy, legal or illegal, that she thinks will work. She'll try to keep our feud private, because if the Citizens investigate her connection to Hulk's murder she'll be exiled from Proton. So this is private between us—and I don't want to be the victim of cheating."

"Your logic is human," Sheen said wryly. "If I weren't programmed to love you—"

"Get on with it. Get a vehicle or something."

"Bluette's Employer has launched an investigation. Very soon he will obtain a transcript of Hulk's experience." She walked toward the shuttle tube. The gas would have no effect on her, and she would be able to use the communication screen to contact her friends.

So Bluette's Employer was taking action. Red was already getting into trouble on Proton. But that didn't change his own need to deal with her.

Stile ran on into the dome-area, now a shambles from the abrupt decompression. With luck he could catch Red during this initial period of confusion. All the occupants should be gasping, looking for long-neglected oxygen equipment, not paying attention to anything except their personal discomfort.

But as he entered, a vehicle charged out—a sand buggy with a bubbletop, painted red. She was taking off.

Stile ran for the cellar section. Maybe there would be another vehicle. He had to have some way to follow.

There were three other vehicles—all in flames. Red had made sure she would not be pursued.

Well, he had another avenue. Stile hurried to the curtain and stepped through, removed his abruptly inoperative oxygen mask, and looked about. Neysa was there, of course, pointing the way. "I'll spell myself to a spot ahead of her, then recross," Stile said.

But the unicorn nudged him, blowing a negative note. She wouldn't let him go alone.

"All right—we should stay together," Stile agreed. "But I don't want to wear thee out chasing after a Proton car. I'll have to enhance the trip by magic."

Neysa still was not keen on magic practiced on herself, but accepted this as she had the horn-tail enchantment, with equine grace. "We two proceed with smiles, Red's direction fifty miles." That made it possible to overshoot Red's position, and land ahead—which was where he wanted to be.

They moved rapidly across the landscape, as they had when leaving the White Demesnes. In a moment they were there. It was a pleasant enough glade east of the Red Demesnes. Neysa's directional horn pointed west; they had outdistanced the quarry.

"All I have to do now is cross back and intercept her, and—" Stile stopped. "Oh, no!"

For the curtain was nowhere near there.

"Well, we'll just have to pace her until she intersects the curtain," Stile said.

They paced her, moving near the limit of the unicorn's capacity. It was a strange business, because away from the curtain they could not see Red at all; only Neysa's horn pointed out her location in the parallel world. It was like following a ghost.

A ghost. Stile wondered whether there was a similar curtain-effect on other worlds. Back on Planet Earth, when the legends were being formed—could a curtain have accounted for the perception of ghosts? People or creatures that were and were not present? So much seeming fantasy could be accounted for, if—

Then Stile spied the curtain. "This is it!" he said. He tore off his clothes and set his mask back in place as he spelled himself through.

Red had evidently been heading for this intersection with the curtain. The car was slowing. It swerved almost immediately to charge him. Was she trying to drive him back across the curtain? Stile distrusted that, so he stayed put. The car had four choices; it could swerve to the left to catch him as he dodged that way, or to the right, or go straight ahead on the assumption he would risk standing still, or it could stop. He doubted it would stop. She intended to smash him if she could, and make him step back across the curtain otherwise.

She made a good effort. She feinted slightly to the left, then to the right, trying to provoke his motion. Stile stood still, and the car accelerated straight at him.

At the last moment, Stile leaped up. The car was sleek and low, more powerful than the dune buggy he had at first conjectured. It passed right under him. Sometimes it paid to be an acrobat. He landed neatly in the swirl of sand the vehicle had stirred up without even a twinge from his bad knees.

Now he saw another vehicle approaching. That would be Sheen, having obtained a car from her friends. No wonder Red was in a hurry; any delay, and the pursuit would catch up.

But why had Red wanted him out of Proton? If she planned to cross the curtain, why force him to cross too, when she knew he had the advantage in Phaze. That didn't seem to make much sense.

Stile got ornery when unsatisfied. Red was up to something, and wanted him out of the way so she could do whatever it was—and so he had better stay right on her. He hailed the second car, and sure enough, it was Sheen. She slowed to pick him up, then accelerated after the fleeing car.

Sheen's car was larger and faster; her friends had provided well. Stile did not inquire how they had produced it so quickly. Some computer entry had surely been made to account for its use. They zoomed over the sand at some hundred to hundred and ten kilometers per hour, a velocity even Neysa could not match. In Phaze, she would have to run sixty to seventy miles an hour cross-country. She might facilitate things by changing to firefly-form to cross the worst of it, but she would inevitably fall behind.

A huge plume of dust swirled up behind each car. Before long they had closed in on Red's vehicle, traveling a little to the side so as to be clear of her cometlike wake. That dust served to emphasize the barrenness that was Proton—a world that science had improved into desolation.

Red cut southeast, angling toward the Purple Mountain range. Where was she going?

"Do we have any way to bring her to a stop?" Stile asked. "I don't like getting too far ahead of Neysa, in case we have action on the other side of the curtain."

"Oh, yes. This is an attack vehicle. We can fire a disrupter to short out her electrical system."

"That's ideal!"

But now Red's car shot into a channel in the mountain. It slewed through a curvaceous pass and up a barren slope. Sheen's car followed, but could not get a direct shot at it. Now, directly behind, they suffered the full effect of the dust-wake. Red obviously was familiar with this region; Sheen and Stile were not.

On they skewed, wending through the mountain foothills and gullies at dangerously high velocity, never getting a clean shot. "I don't like this," Stile said. "She thinks in terms of traps. Things that wait quiescent until invoked. She'll have something set up here."

"I can call my friends on the car's band, and ask them to—"

"No! They have to maintain their anonymity. A 'clerical error' freed this car; that's as far as they can go. It's my job."

"No, they do not need to resort to supposed error. There are ways to—"

"No."

"I believe I have remarked on your defective living logic before."

"I believe so," Stile agreed.

"Do you have any assurance at all that you will survive this foolishness?"

"Yes, the Oracle says that I will sire a son by the Lady Blue, whom I just married, and since I have not yet—"

The car began to ride up the side of the channel. "You married the Lady Blue?"

Oops. He had forgotten the ramification that would have on this side of the curtain. "I did."

She brought the car back to level, but the course seemed none too steady. "Then it is over between us."

"No! Not over. Just—modified. We're still friends—"

"With a machine?"

"With a machine!" he shouted. "You're still a person! I still love you as a person!"

She accelerated, closing the gap that had opened between vehicles, though the dust obscured almost everything. "Yes, of course."

And Stile knew that whatever he had gained in Phaze

had been at a necessary cost in Proton. The next stage in his inevitable alienation from Sheen had come to pass. They had known this would happen, but still it hurt. "I don't suppose you'd settle for an oath of friendship?" he asked with an attempt at lightness.

"I am less complicated than a living creature like Neysa. Oaths are not part of my programming."

Stile was spared the embarrassment of struggling further with this dialogue by their sudden encounter with Red's car. She had drawn it up in an emergency stop just around a turn in the channel and jettisoned herself with the emergency release. Now her stalled vehicle blocked the way at a narrow neck, impossible to avoid. Stile saw her running up the steep slope, getting clear of the inevitable crash. The trap had sprung.

Sheen's finger moved with mechanical speed and precision, touching a button on the dashboard. The ejection mechanism operated. Stile was hurled in his seat out the top of the car. A gravity diffuser clicked on, softening his fall, letting him float to the ground.

The moving car collided with the stationary one. Both exploded. A ball of flame encompassed the mass, and smoke billowed outward. Protonite didn't detonate like that; Red's vehicle must have been booby-trapped with explosives. It had been a trap, all right.

Then Stile realized he was alone. "Sheen!" he cried in anguish. "Why didn't you eject too?" But he knew why. She had wanted to be junked cleanly when she lost him; she had seen to it herself.

He knew there was nothing he could do for her. It was Red he had to go after. He shucked his carseat and charged across to intercept the Adept.

She had a hand weapon. She pointed it at him.

Stile dived, taking advantage of the irregularity of the ground. The laser beam seared the sand ahead of him, sending up a puff of acrid fumes. Then he crawled rapidly to the side, grabbed a small rock and hurled it at her. He did this without lifting his head or body; he could throw accurately by sound.

But she too had moved, crossing to get a shot from a better vantage. Only Stile's continuing motion saved him from getting lasered. But now he too was armed—with a number of good throwing rocks. He could throw them rapidly and with excellent effect, when the target presented itself—if he did not become the target of the laser first.

They maneuvered. Watching, listening, stalking. Red was no amateur at this; she knew how to stay out of trouble—and she had the superior weapon. He would have to catch her by surprise, score with a rock before she could bring her laser to bear, and close for the finish. It was a challenge similar to certain Games, and he was good at this type of thing too. But she had the advantage of weapon and familiarity with the terrain.

Nevertheless, he outmaneuvered her, got in a good location, and prepared for attack. He wanted to knock her out with a score on the head, but his stones were too light for certainty. He was more likely to stun her momentarily or injure her, and have to take it to hand-to-hand combat. So be it. Too bad he had not brought his sword across the curtain. But he could do a lot of damage to a human body, bare-handed, in a very short time.

He watched for his moment, then made his move. He rose up and hurled his first stone. His aim was good; it glanced off her head, making her cry out. But her thick red hair had cushioned it somewhat; the stone only gashed her, not seriously.

Then she leaped—and disappeared.

The curtain! The curtain was here, and she had used it. In this respect, too, she had been better prepared than he. He charged across to it and willed himself after her.

Suddenly the mountain greened about him. He stood on verdant turf, with patches of purple flowers decorating the slopes. The air was warm and fragrant.

Red was still reeling from the blow of the stone. Blood colored her hand where she had touched the gash, and her hair was becoming matted. But when she saw him she raised the laser and fired at point-blank range.

Of course it didn't work. The curtain was not the demarcation of worlds, but of frames—modes of energy-application. She was getting rattled, making mistakes now.

Stile hurled another rock at her. *His* weapon was good in either frame!

But she dodged the rock and brought out an amulet. Where she had carried it he didn't know, since she was naked, as serfs had to be in the other frame. "Invoke!" she cried.

The amulet expanded into a ravening griffin—body of lion, head and wings of eagle. It oriented on Stile and leaped.

Stile spelled himself hastily back through the curtain.

He was in Proton again, inhaling oxygen through the mask. How bleak this frame was! Smoke still drifted up from the wrecked vehicles. Sheen had been there, suiciding rather than continue an animation that had become meaningless.

Stile concentrated a moment, then willed himself back through the curtain. "Creature fly up into sky!" he sang, and the griffin, just now turning on him after having overshot him, abruptly spread its wings and ascended. It was out of the fray.

Stile launched himself at Red, who held another amulet. She had a flesh-toned compartment belt, he saw now, that held her assorted weapons; from a distance she looked properly naked. He caught her hand and wrenched the amulet from her. "Invoke!" he cried.

The amulet grew into a flying octopus. It reached hungrily for Red. Stile had realized before that there were malign amulets that attacked the invoker, and benign ones that fought on the side of the invoker. Since Stile had stopped invoking amulets, Red was using these benign ones against him. He had just stolen one and turned it against her.

Now Red dived across the curtain, escaping the malice of her own creation. Stile went after her—and almost got clobbered by a rock. She was using his tactic against him, now.

He grappled with her. She was a foot taller than he—in this frame, about thirty centimeters—and had more mass. She was strong, too. A virtual Amazon, a naked tigress, eager to kill. Her claws gouged at his eyes, her knee rammed his groin. But Stile saw the smoking wreckage where Sheen had perished, and was a savage animal himself. Every person he held dear was being destroyed one

way or another; he would destroy in turn. He was expert in
several martial arts; he knew which nerves to pinch, the
vulnerable spots to strike, the pressures that would disjoint
which joints, on man or woman. He blocked her attack
and concentrated on his own.

Again Red was overmatched, and realized it. She willed
herself back into Phaze—and Stile went with her, not re-
lenting. But here her amulets functioned; she invoked one,
and it hissed out of a bottle, a genie, a giant gaseous man
all head and arms. Quickly Stile recrossed the curtain.

He needed a spell to banish a genie. And another to take
the offense. He might not be able to attack Red directly,
but he could isolate her or—

Something was moving in the now almost-quiescent
wreckage of the two vehicles. Stile's attention was instantly
distracted from the battle. Could it be—?

With timorous hope he hurried over there. Yes—a shape
was struggling to extricate itself! This was not the fantasy
frame; it couldn't be a demon!

"Sheen?" he called tentatively.

"Stile?" her voice came back, oddly distorted.

"Sheen, you survived! I thought—"

"I am a machine. I am damaged, not yet defunct. Unfortunately."

"Let me help you—"

"Do not touch me. I am hot."

She was indeed. As she completed her extrication, he
saw the extent of the damage. Most of her superficial flesh
had been burned away. Her face was rubble. Her lovely
skin and hair had been stripped to reveal scorched metal,
with dangling shreds of substance. Wisps of smoke and
steam drifted upward from her joints, and hot oil dripped
from her chest cavity. She looked about as much like a
corpse as a machine could. An animated corpse—a zom-
bie.

"Sheen, we must get you to a repair shop! You—"

"Go after Red, Stile!" she cried weakly. "Do not let me
distract you. I am of no further use to you. If I did not
have this damned self-preservation circuit that cut in—"

Still, he was torn. Once before she had suffered injury on
his behalf, making him realize how important she was to

him. Her damage this time was surely worse, though she remained animated; all of her surface had been charred by the flame, and she was probably operating ineffectively on the last dregs of her Protonite charge. Yet it seemed that this merely reflected her emotional desolation, for she was programmed to love him—and never would be his lover again.

Perhaps it would be kinder simply to allow her to expire. She was close to the end now.

The thought triggered a savage reaction. "Vengeance I have sworn, but it shall not take precedence over friendship," Stile said. "Walk with me across the curtain. I can restore you, there."

The eyeless husk of a head oriented on him. The tattered remnant of her speaker spoke. "You must not. Red will trap you—"

"I think Red is already far from here. I have given her time enough to escape. She is less important than you."

"You must not give her time to set up—" Sheen's voice failed at last. Her power was fading. Even Protonite had finite limits.

"Walk, or I must carry you," Stile said sternly, knowing she would not allow him to harm himself by touching her burning surface.

She walked with decreasing stability. Charred fragments fell from her. Something rattled and buzzed inside. Finally she crashed forward, still smoking. But she was half across the curtain.

Stile located an unsmouldering spot on her torso and touched his finger to it and willed them both across the curtain. The grass appeared, the air freshened, and her body sizzled in the greater moisture. He removed his finger before it burned.

The Red Adept, as he had surmised, was gone. He had been besting her; she had wanted to escape all along, salvaging time and resources to meet him again in a situation more favorable to herself. He didn't like letting that happen, but he had been afraid that if he left Sheen too long it might not be possible to restore her—or that he himself would die or lose power and be unable to return to her. If he had let her perish in favor of his vengeance, he would

have sacrificed much of what he valued: his own human-
ity. He might have gone on to establish his power and
security as the Blue Adept—and become more like the
other Adepts, corrupted by power, cynical and selfish to
the point of worthlessness.

There was the sound of hooves. Neysa was catching up,
fire snorting from her nostrils, bringing the harmonica just
when he needed it. He would be able to use his magic to
restore Sheen as he had before, and then would return her
to Proton for reanimation. Maybe he could include a spell
to make her feel better about the situation; that probably
would not work, but it was at least worth a try. Then it
would be time to set up for the next Round of the Tourney.

Round Eight brought him up against a young woman of
the Age 22 ladder, a fair player whose skills he knew from
prior experience. She was Tulip, a gardener-tender for a
Citizen who favored ornamentals. She was as pretty as a
flower herself, and not averse to using her sex-appeal to
gain advantage. But Stile had no intention of prejudicing a
likely victory by such dalliance. He put it into MENTAL,
and so nullified her choice of NAKED. No body-contact
sport this time! They wound up in WORD GAMES.

"Travel from FLESH to SPIRIT," the Game Computer
said. "Time five minutes."

Stile and Tulip got to work. The challenge was to fashion a chain of words linked alternately by synonyms and
homonyms, converting "Flesh" to "Spirit" by readily defin-
able stages. Both length and time counted; within five minutes, the shortest viable chain would win. Beyond that time
limit, the first person to establish *any* viable chain of any
length would win. So it behooved them each to take up
most of that five minutes to seek the shortest possible
chain. To settle on a given chain too quickly would be to
invite the opponent to come up with a shorter one within
the time limit and win; to take too long beyond the time
limit invited loss to a longer but sooner-announced chain.
The point of decision could be tricky.

Flesh, Stile thought. Synonyms would be Body, Meat,
Fatten—there would be others, but these sufficed. If he
explored every single avenue, he would not complete any

one chain in time. Selectivity—there was the key to this challenge.

Now try Meat, as the best prospect for homonyms: Meet as in proper, Meet as in a competitive event, Mete as in measure. Try the competition-event for synonyms: Contest, Race, Competition. Then Race, jumping to the homonym, meaning subspecies, and the synonym Color, and on to Hue—was this leading to Spirit? Not rapidly. Better try an alternate, and return to this if necessary. His first job was to establish a viable chain, any chain, within five minutes. That would be an automatic win if Tulip failed to find one.

Of course, if they both came up with the same chain, the first to announce it would win. So if he found a good one, he should announce it regardless of time. But he was not worried about that; he had pretty good judgment on word-chains.

He glanced covertly at Tulip. She was chewing on her lip, making little gestures with her left hand, as though shaping a slippery sequence. Was she making faster progress? He didn't think so, as she really wasn't that bright, but it was possible. Then she caught him looking, and made a suggestive motion with her hip. He had to turn his eyes away, lest she bring his thoughts right back to Flesh and cost him the Game. That was what she was trying to do, the flirt. Maybe that was how she had gotten this far.

Try Meet as in proper. Synonym Fit, homonym Fit as in the contour of clothing. Yes, then Suit, and its homonym Suit as in satisfy, or the synonym Please.

Homonym Pleas, as in several requests. Synonym—was he returning to Fit, as in a fit plea for favor? If so, this was a dead-end, a waste of time, like a loop in the maze-puzzle he had fallen into in another Game with another woman. Too much time had passed; he couldn't afford that! This simple game became confusingly tricky under the pressure of competition. No, no loop here; define it as a wish, as desire. And Desire as a homonym, meaning the urgency to possess, achieve, prevail—he certainly had that!—which was a possible synonym for team spirit—

Spirit! There it was! And jump to homonym Spirit as in Soul, and his chain was complete.

Unless that Desire link was faulty. Pleas—Desire—Spirit. The Computer might reject that as inexact. Better to work out a tighter chain.

But four minutes were passed. Not enough time to figure out a new chain. Tulip looked as if she were on the verge of completing her own chain. Stile decided to go with this one. "Chain!" he announced.

"Damn!" Tulip muttered.

"Present," the Computer said.

Stile presented it, trying to conceal his nervousness about the Desire connection. But the Computer did not challenge it; it was fairly liberal on the adaptations of language.

Still, Tulip had another minute to produce a shorter chain, or a better one of the same length. Stile waited nervously.

But she seemed to have given up. The time expired without her entry. Stile had won, more or less by default.

"It would have been different in NAKED/PHYSICAL," Tulip said tearfully. She had choked at the crisis-point in this Game, and now suffered the reaction.

"That's why I avoided it," Stile said, though he would have put it into some subcategory like foot-racing and probably beaten her anyway. She really hadn't lost much; with her appearance, she should do well enough in the wider human galaxy. But it had the mild distaste of an unjustified victory.

The separations between Rounds were diminishing. Round Nine was due in the afternoon of the same day. Stile planned to spend the interim devising strategy and spells to finish the Red Adept, and to get some rest and refreshment. He was also concerned about Sheen; he had restored her in Phaze, again, and she was now fully operational. But how could he abate the hurt of her nonliving heartbreak? His attempted spell had not taken effect. She seemed to have lost much of her will-to-animation, and there seemed to be no way he could restore it. She needed the one thing he could not give—his complete love. Maybe, he thought again, he should have let her perish, instead of languishing like this. He had promised a clean death to the Red Adept; could he do less for his friend?

There was a knock on the apartment door. That was unusual; visitors usually announced themselves on the screen. Sheen, alert to threats, went to see to it.

"Oh," she exclaimed, in a perfect representation of surprise. "You survived!"

"I must speak to—Stile," the visitor said.

Stile snapped alert. That was the Lady Blue's voice!

He went to the door. There she stood, a little disheveled but irremediably splendid. Bluette, of course; she had escaped the robot and sought out the name and description Hulk had given her. Smart woman!

Yet this was extremely awkward. "Come in," Stile said. "Of course I'll help you. I'm on the trail of the woman who killed Hulk now. But one thing you must know at the outset: I want nothing personal to do with you, after this."

Her brow furrowed prettily. "Nothing?"

"I am married to your alternate self, the Lady Blue of Phaze. You look exactly like her, Bluette—you *are* exactly like her—but she is the one I love. This is no reflection on your own merit, that I sincerely appreciate. And I know you have no personal interest in me. But—well, if she thought I was seeing you—"

She smiled, oddly at ease. "I understand."

"Stile," Sheen said, evidently making some sort of connection. "She is not—"

"Not my woman," he agreed. "Bluette, I never wanted to meet you. It—it's too confusing. And I know, after all you went through—is that robot still on your trail? *That* we can take care of!"

"Stile, listen," Sheen said. "I just realized this is—"

"Look, don't make this any more difficult than it is!" Stile snapped. "Every second she stands here—this woman is so like the one I love—"

The woman smiled again. "Now thou dost know what *I* went through, Adept. The false so like the true."

"What?" Something didn't jibe here.

"Thee. . . Thee . . . Thee."

Stile froze. "Oh, no!"

"I am the Lady Blue," she said. "Fain would I listen longer to thy protestations of other love, my Lord, but I did cross the curtain to bring thee a vital message."

Never had Stile imagined the Lady Blue in this frame. "But that means—"

"That Bluette is dead," Sheen finished. "It has after all been several days. We should have heard from her before this, had she escaped."

"Oh, God," Stile said. "*That* I did not want. And now the two of you have met—that was never supposed to happen!" In the back of his mind, moving rapidly to the fore, was his concern that the robot might do some harm to her human rival. He had to get the Lady Blue out of here!

"Thou speakest as if there be some shame here," the Lady Blue said. "I have long known of thy most loyal friend in this frame, the lovely Lady Sheen, and I am glad to meet her at last." She turned to address Sheen directly. "I am oath-friend to Neysa. Can I be less to thee? If thou wouldst honor me with thy favor, O noblest of Ladies—"

And Sheen was crying. It was not the sort of reaction a robot was supposed to have, but it was natural to her. "Oh, Lady—oh, Lady!"

Then they were hugging each other, both crying, while Stile stood in mute confusion. Somehow it seemed that Sheen had been restored—yet the mechanism of it was beyond his immediate comprehension.

When the first flush of their emotion subsided, the Lady Blue delivered her message to Stile. "A bat-lad came to the Demesnes, sore tired from rapid flying. Methought he wanted healing, but it was news for thee he brought."

"Vodlevile's son!" Stile exclaimed. "I never thought he would—"

"He said the Red Adept had returned to the ruin of her Demesnes and fashioned a terrible spell, a basilisk-amulet that would destroy whatever it touched, being invoked by the very frame of Phaze. This she meant to give thee in the frame of Proton, and when thou didst bring it across the curtain—"

"Her final trap!" Stile said. "A basilisk—a creature whose very touch brings horrible death, whose gaze petrifies. But why does she think I would accept such an amulet from her?"

"The bat-lad said she made it resemble something thou couldst not refuse. Something thou wouldst immediately take across the curtain. That was all he knew; he dared not get within the range of her power. He thought it was news thou shouldst have—and I thought so too. So I tried to reach thee—and succeeded."

"It is as if Bluette gave her life, to make this message possible," Stile said. "And the vampire child—my trifling favor to him may be destined to save my life. Yet this is strange. Why should I need to be warned against doing what I would not have done anyway? Well I know the power of Red's amulets! In this frame they are harmless, but I would never carry one across to Phaze."

The Lady Blue spread her hands. "Mayhap we can piece it out, my Lord. I must return to the wolves in three hours, lest they worry. Meanwhile, may I view more of this wondrous frame of Proton? This may be mine only chance to visit it, and fain would I know as much of thy homeland as I can."

"I'll show you," Sheen said. "I'll show you everything!"

Sheen was a machine, but she would not deceive Stile. If she accompanied the Lady Blue, she would protect her. And if that was what she wanted, how could he deny it? Thus it was that Stile found himself alone with his puzzling piece of information, while the two Ladies toured the local domes.

Who would have thought that the source of Sheen's woe would also be the abatement of it? Yet from the moment the Lady Blue had addressed her as Lady Sheen—

What healing magic there was in a title! The Lady Blue, without apparent premeditation or design, had granted equal status to Sheen and proffered friendship and respect. Sheen had been instantly conquered. The issue of her machine-nature had not even been a consideration.

Stile returned to his deliberations. He decided that the Red Adept planned to gift him with the amulet through some third party, so that he would not suspect its nature.

Perhaps a silver brooch for the Lady Blue; of course he would take that to her in Phaze. But now he had been warned; he would not take anything across the curtain.

In two hours the two returned, forever friends. "What a frame this is!" the Lady Blue exclaimed, exactly like the tourist she was. "Never since I saw the West Pole have I seen the like! Truly a magical world!"

The West Pole? "You mean in Phaze there really is a—?"

"Thou didst not know? I will take thee there, my love, once this business here is done."

"I will go there," Stile said. Fascinating, that an alien creature from some far galactic world had heard about the West Pole, while Stile who seemed to live almost on top of it had not. "Now—I love thee, Lady, and fain would have thee stay—but until the message of the Oracle has been appropriately interpreted, guaranteeing me the chance to stay with thee, I must remain apart from thee."

"I go, my Lord." She approached Stile and kissed him. Then Sheen accompanied her to the curtain. Stile continued his research for the next Round of the Tourney, fearing his company would only endanger the Lady Blue, here on Proton. She had acted with considerable courage, coming here and finding her way through the mysterious technological habitat of Proton. He loved her for that courage —but this was not her frame.

Round Nine carried a two-year tenure bonus for the loser, and the prospect of much more for the winner. Stile was now into "safe" territory; he could not be exiled from Proton after washing out of the Tourney. This removed some of the tension. It was now more important to deal with the Red Adept than to win any particular Game. Oh, to win the Tourney would be grand—but the odds remained against him, especially with one loss on his tally. But once he eliminated Red, the entire frame of Phaze was awaiting him, and a happy life with the Lady Blue. So he would play his best, but without the terrible urgency he had had before. That was just as well, since he had other things to do than research his prospective opponents. That research had become a chore.

His opponent this time was a female Citizen. Three Citizens in one Tourney—his luck was bad! But no—probably half the survivors of this level were Citizens, so this was no luck at all.

Still he did not intend to mess with her. He had the letters, so couldn't stop her from picking her specialty— probably MENTAL or ART. But he might interfere with her plan. He chose MACHINE.

It came up 4C, Machine-Assisted ART. Not his favorite, but probably not hers either. They could find themselves doing esthetic figures while parachuting from a simulated-airplane tower, or playing a concert on a theremin, or doing sculpture by means of selective detonations of incendiary plastic. He would probably feel more at home in these pursuits than she.

But when they gridded through, she outmaneuvered him. They had to compete on the sewing machine, making intricate patterns and pictures on a cloth background. She as a Citizen had had a lot more exposure to cloth than he; indeed, she wore an elaborate dress-suit with borders stitched in gold and silver thread. But she had always had serfs to do her dressmaking for her. So unless she had practiced in this particular art—

Stile, of course, had practiced. He had spent years advancing his skills in every facet of the Game. He knew how to use a sewing machine. He was not expert, but he was adequate.

As it turned out, he was moderately better than the Citizen. It was an unspectacular Game, but the victory was his.

Now for the finish against Red. Sheen's friends, who as machines had great difficulty perceiving the semi-subjective curtain, had come up with a device to detect it. Sheen now carried this device. She would know, in much the way Neysa knew the whereabouts of Red, where the curtain was. That way Red would not again elude him by stepping across a fold of the curtain he did not know was near.

Stile prepared carefully. Sheen carried an assortment of small weapons and devices—a laser, a radiation grenade, a periscope, stun-gas capsules, and a folding steel broadsword. Her friends had provided a gyro-stabilized unicycle seating two, so she could ferry him rapidly about, anywhere where crowds would not find it too attention-fixing.

A great deal went on in Proton that failed to attract the notice of Citizens, but there were limits. In fact, part of this deadly "game" would be the effort to force Red to call attention to herself, while Stile escaped it. His only crime was the sabotage of Red's dome; that had probably annoyed her Citizen-mother, but might be attributed to a repair-machine malfunction. Red would have known the truth, but not wanted to report it and have her own situation investigated. She, on the other hand, had been responsible for the deaths of Hulk and Bluette—oh, a double pain and guilt there!—and these were recorded on holo-tape. She would be banished instantly, even if she won more tenure through the Tourney, once those murders came to light.

Unless she won the Tourney and became a Citizen. Then she would be immune to all reprisal. Stile had to make sure she did not succeed in that.

They set out in quest of the enemy. Stile had a full day before Round Ten—and if that were not time enough, he would resume the chase after the Round. His oath of vengeance would soon be satisfied, one way or the other.

First he went to the curtain at a remote spot and stepped across. Neysa was there—with the Lady Blue.

Startled, Stile protested. "Lady, I wanted thee to be under the protection of the werewolves."

"A wolf went to the Oracle," she said. "And learned that his oath-friend Neysa was in dire peril from this mission. Since Neysa will not give over, the wolves and unicorns are now patrolling the curtain, ready to aid her if need be. Rather than interfere with this effort, I too patrol the curtain."

Stile was not wholly satisfied with this, but realized that this was another device of the animals to help him. They wanted to be in on the action. "I expect to deal with Red in Proton," he said. "My magic is stronger than hers, in Phaze, so she is unlikely to cross the curtain before settling with me. Do you all take care of yourselves."

"Indeed," the Lady agreed. "And thee of thyself, my love."

How glad he would be when this was over, and he could love her without restraint. But that had to wait, lest he void his Oracular guarantee.

Neysa pointed the direction of Red. Then Stile returned across the curtain to Sheen, drove a distance parallel to the curtain, recrossed, and got a new bearing. Now he was able to triangulate. It seemed Red was near the spot she had halted before, when he intercepted her and leaped over her car. She must have a secret place there.

They drove there, at moderate speed, so that Neysa could pace them easily. If Red tried to step across the curtain again, she would be in immediate trouble. Of course her amulets could destroy Neysa and the Lady Blue, so Stile still didn't want them participating in the conclusion. But they could certainly watch from a safe distance. At least they would know the outcome as soon as it happened. And perhaps the Lady's presence represented a guarantee for Neysa, since the Lady could not bear him any son if she died at this stage. The Lady should survive, and would hardly allow Neysa to perish in her stead.

The direction was east. They avoided individual domes and slowed as they neared the spot. It would have been fun, touring the desert like this, comparing the landscape to that of Phaze, if the mission weren't so serious. There were crevices and mounds and the depressions where lakes might once have been. Where they could be again, if the Citizens ever developed the interest to restore the planet instead of depleting it. But that was a hopeless notion; Citizens cared nothing for the external environment. In fact the very hostility of it gave them additional control over the system, for no serf could flee outside.

There was nothing where Red was supposed to be. Sand and low sand dunes covered the entire area.

They sought the nearest fold of the curtain. Stile crossed. Mare and Lady were there. Stile obtained two more pointings, narrowing down the location precisely. Red was not in Phaze, but in the equivalent spot in Proton was a bunker, a room set below the level of the ground. It was filled with amulets; obviously a cache of Red's.

But these amulets would not work in Proton. The curtain passed through this spot, but it was dark beyond it. Stile would have to cross it to find out what was there.

Neysa blew a negative note. Red was in the dark beyond. She could surely see Stile, since he was here in the

lighted frame. She could be holding a sword high in both
hands, waiting to decapitate the next person who crossed.
A simple enough trap.

So Stile avoided it. He removed himself some distance,
crossed to Proton, and explained the situation to Sheen.

"It is surely a trap," she agreed. "She means you to
come to her. Don't chance it."

"I'm not going to let her escape! She'll never come out if
I just leave her alone."

Sheen opened her chest compartment and brought out the
laser-cutter. "Make a hole, drop in a stun-capsule."

That seemed appropriate. Stile started the laser. Quickly
the hole formed. Soon it broke through the steel ceiling of
the bunker. Then he dropped in the capsule. There was a hiss
as it activated, and a puff of the gas emerged from the hole.

"I heard something in there fall," Sheen said. "Now for
the periscope." She brought out the tiny device. It was
electronic, and needed no solid extension into the hole; its
perceptor-unit was mounted on an almost invisible thread
that dangled down.

It showed the Red Adept sprawled naked on the floor of
her miniature fortress, an old-fashioned dueling pistol in
one hand, an amulet in the other. Had she planned to force
the amulet on him at gun-point? If so, she had been amazingly naive.

"I am suspicious," Sheen said. "There is no entrance
here in Proton; she uses Phaze as access. She expected you
to enter that way. There could be an automatic weapon set
to cover the curtain."

"Yes. We had better force entry from here."

They set about it. Sheen had several construction bombs,
and used them to blast away the sand and rip open a man-
sized aperture in the wall of the bunker. Then she entered
first.

"No automatic weapon," she reported. "Still, I think
you'd better stay clear."

"The hell with that," Stile said, walking down the sand
embankment. "I can't have the ladies doing everything for
me."

"But we can't be sure this was the extent of the trap! It's
too simple; even I could have worked out something more

sophisticated, and I have no creative imagination. At least let me search the premises—"

"You do that. I'll tie up Red." Because Stile found he could not kill her, this way. Now when she was unconscious. Funny how she had allowed herself to be gassed, when she must have heard the laser-drill.

He leaned over the body, not squatting, because of his knees. Sheen commenced her inspection of the bunker. Something nagged him, but he couldn't place it at the moment. "I won't touch that amulet, certainly!"

Abruptly, Red moved. Her head turned to cover him, and her pistol whipped up. She was not unconscious after all!

Stile hurled himself to the side as the gun went off. Had he been squatting, as a normal man would have done, he could have been fatally caught; the gun was aimed for the heart of a squatting man. As it was, the bullet slammed into his left thigh.

It was a bad hit. Now Stile exerted his trance-control. He let himself fall backward while clapping both hands to the wound. The pain was terrible, but he was bringing it under control, while he slowed the pulsing eruption of blood. He could not afford to lose consciousness; he could bleed to death rapidly. The major artery had been nicked or severed; he would need a surgeon's prompt attention.

Meanwhile Sheen launched herself at Red. Pistol and amulet flew wide and Red was hurled against the wall.

But then Red righted herself and hurled Sheen away, with inhuman strength. "This is a robot!" Sheen cried. "A machine, like me!"

"True," the Red-figure said. "I bear this message for Stile: make haste away, midget, for at this moment the Red Adept is launching an explosive drone vehicle tuned to the bullet in you. How much damage the drone does depends on your location when it catches you."

They heard the noise of machinery moving, some distance away. Something was rising from another bunker. "Run, Blue!" the robot continued, "Suffer the joys of the chase, rabbit. Message ends." And the robot went dead.

"Sheen!" Stile cried. "Carry me to the curtain. They can help me there, and the drone can't cross—"

"The amulet!" Sheen cried. *"It is the bullet!"*

"The bullet!" Stile echoed. Now the full nature of this terrible trap was apparent—and he had almost fallen into it despite the warning the Lady Blue had brought. If he crossed with the bullet in him, it would animate into the basilisk, and he would be dead before he could utter a spell. But if he did not cross—

Now they heard the released drone, cruising across the sand toward them. There could be enough explosive in that to blow up a mountain.

Sheen stooped to pick him up. She carried him to their unicycle and set him in the seat and flung the safety harness around him while Stile clung to consciousness and to his leaking thigh. Then she jumped in herself and started the motor.

The drone-car was rounding the bunker, picking up speed. Sheen accelerated away at right angles to its path. In moments they were traveling seventy kilometers an hour, leaving the drone behind. This was not a particularly fast velocity for travel on a surfaced road, but across the desert landscape it seemed horrendous. "We'll have to get the bullet out before we take you to a doctor!"

"How can we get it out without a doctor, especially if we can't stop?" Stile gritted. He was not in the most reasonable of moods at the moment, as he fought to keep blood and body consciousness together. The rough riding did not help.

"I'll summon one of my friends to intercept us."

"Summon one to blow up the drone!"

"They won't do that. It would attract attention to their nature. But one will help you and depart. Then the drone won't matter."

"Not to rush you," Stile said. "But I can only hold on here a short while. I'm in partial trance, suppressing the circulation to my leg, but the wound is bad and I'm slowly losing control. My last reserves are depleting."

"I know the experience," she said. "We'll stay right beside the curtain, so you can cross the moment we get the bullet out. Then you'll be able to use magic to—"

"I can't heal myself with magic."

"The Lady Blue will find some other Adept to help you, I'm sure. Perhaps the Lady Yellow—"

"Yellow is no lady! She is an old crone." But he was being querulous in his adversity. Yellow probably could help. He remembered how the Lady Blue had won her favor by starting the applause at the Adept pavilion. The Lady Blue was good at that sort of thing.

Sheen guided the unicycle to the curtain. Stile perceived it now with remarkable clarity. Had it intensified, or was his current state of pain-blocking trance responsible? It hardly mattered; he could see across as though it were an open window.

The unicycle was handily outdistancing the drone at the moment—but in Phaze Neysa was having trouble keeping up. The terrain was more varied there, with trees and streams and bushes obstructing her route. "Slow it, Sheen. Neysa is wearing herself out—and I'll need her there the moment I cross."

Sheen slowed—but then the drone gained, cutting into their lead. This was worrisome; that lead was their margin of safety. In addition the landscape was getting rougher. They were heading generally west, curving north with the curtain, back toward the major cluster of domes. On the prior trips they had maneuvered comfortably around the obstructions of boulder, dune, crevasse and ridges. But the curtain crossed these heedlessly, and this made the drive difficult. Sheen had to skid along awkward slopes, bounce through gullies, and plow through the mounds of sand. The drone suffered also—but it was squat and sturdy with broad wheel-treads, and it kept on going. The hazards of this chase would shake apart the unicycle before they stopped the three-wheeled pursuer.

Neysa, meanwhile, was encountering problems in Phaze. Stile watched her helplessly, as Sheen guided the unicycle along the curtain, now one side of it, now the other, causing his view to shift about considerably. The unicorn could handle the irregularities of the terrain, but there were also creatures in the way. She had to charge through a colony of demons, and in a moment they were in pursuit like so many drones, eager for unicorn flesh. Neysa could have escaped them easily if she had not been staying close to the curtain, and if she had not had to worry about the security of the Lady Blue. Or she could have turned to fight them, putting them to flight with a few well-placed skewers—had she not had to keep up with Stile's vehicle. Now the demons were popping up everywhere from crevices in the rock, cutting her off. They were grinning; they knew they had her.

Neysa blew a desperate summons on her horn. Stile could hear the sound, faintly, across the curtain, even as he rode in the same channel Neysa ran in, overlapping her without any tangible evidence of it. He could only actually see her when the curtain was between them so that he could look through it, and that happened only in snatches. The curtain was a funny thing, something he would have to explore more thoroughly some day and come to understand. Like the Oracle, it was a phenomenon that seemed to have no origin and no reasonable explanation; it merely existed, and was vital to communication between frames.

Again Neysa sounded. The call resounded across the wilderness. The demons growled in laughter; sound could not hurt them. Stile wished he could cross over and help out with a spell—but that notion was folly.

Then a ranging werewolf, summoned by the horn, spied them. He bayed. His oath-friend was being molested. This was why they were patrolling the curtain; they had been warned of this danger. Their numbers were thinly spread, because the convoluting curtain traversed a tremendous amount of territory, but their keen perceptions made up the difference.

The bays of other wolves responded. Suddenly they were converging, their sounds approaching at a gratifying rate. In moments they were in sight, and leaping with savage glee and righteous anger at the demons. One thing a were-wolf lived for—a good fight in a good cause.

Now the predatory laughter of the demons turned to rage at this interference. But soon it turned to fear, as more and more members of the wolfpack closed upon them, lips peeling back in the terrifying grin of attack as they cut in between demons and unicorn.

Neysa ran on with a single note of gratitude, still carrying the Lady Blue, still pacing Stile. The sounds of the battle grew loud, then faded behind. The demons had chosen the wrong creature to attack, this time.

Sheen continued to guide the unicycle. She handled it with desperate skill. Now a dome lay across the curtain. They had to skirt it—but when they intercepted the curtain again, Neysa was there, thin jets of fire issuing from her nostrils. She was overheating, but would not allow herself to fall behind. The Lady Blue clung to her, riding with consummate skill, watching out for other hazards, guiding Neysa into the best channels with little advisory nudges, not directives. The unicorn had charge of the run, but the Lady was able to devote more attention to the route. Neysa was concentrating increasingly on the single effort of maintaining the pace; she no longer lifted her head to survey the course. She trusted the Lady's guidance. Stile knew exactly how it was; he had raced the marathon in times past, and had reached the stage where nothing existed except his agonizing pumping legs and the called course-corrections of friends. Vision itself became expendable.

Stile was struggling similarly now. His hands were soaking in blood. His consciousness was slowly slipping. He was panting with the sheer effort of keeping flesh and spirit together. Flesh and spirit—had that been a premonition, that Tourney Game? He had succeeded then—but this struggle was harder, with more dependent on it. Still the drone pursued.

He saw snatches of scenes across the curtain, hills, then a river. Neysa had to ford it, her hot hooves sending up gouts of steam as they touched the surface. Then it grew deeper and she swam, falling behind. She could not shift to firefly and wing across it, because of the Lady Blue. The unicycle was traversing the dry bed of that river.

Then the curtain curved down toward the south again, past the caves of the vampire bats, back across another arm of the river at the ruins of the Red Demesnes. Other unicorns were running with Neysa now, clearing the way. Bats were flying, spotting problems, getting them alleviated. A dragon was taking a snooze across the curtain; faced by six charging unicorns, it hastily vacated the spot. Little Folk of the daylight kind stood aside to let the strange procession pass. The grueling run went on.

All for him, Stile realized with pained gratitude. All the
unicorns, werewolves and vampires extending themselves
to their limits just to help him preserve his life. Neysa,
running herself to destruction. Could it be worth it? Now
her hooves were glowing red; her very flesh was burning
up. She left a narrow trail of smoke where her passage had
ignited the leaves of the forest floor.

Then a new vehicle closed with the unicycle. It locked
on, matching the pace exactly. Machine arms reached out.
Sensors traveled down Stile's body, touching his gory leg.
Anesthetic came. Germicidal radiation flared. There, at the
bouncing velocity of the chase, the robot surgeon removed
the bullet, patched the torn artery, stitched and bound the
wound while simultaneously injecting Stile with artificial
blood matching his type. It retouched the nerve block on
that leg so that no pain returned. Then the arms and tentacles retreated, the other vehicle disengaged, and went its
own way with a parting warning: "Protect our interests!"
—tell no one in Proton how he had been helped.

When Sheen's friends chose to render assistance, they
did so with enormous precision and effect. Stile knew he
could not go to any hospital now; he had sworn not to
betray the self-willed machines, so he had to conceal the
nature of this surgery from the Citizens. But that was easy
enough to do; he no longer needed surgery.

Still, he was near to unconsciousness. His human reserves had been depleted, and neither surgery nor artificial
blood could take the place of rest. Sheen steered the unicycle to the curtain. Neysa made a final desperate effort,
caught up, and galloped directly along it. The unicycle
slowed to accommodate her. The drone closed in rapidly.

Now unicorn and unicycle were superimposed, separated
only by the frames. "Do it!" Sheen cried. Stile willed himself through.

He fell across Neysa's hot back. The Lady Blue flung
her arms about him, clasping him, her healing hands already helping. He was safe at last!

Across the curtain, Sheen's vehicle accelerated. She had
the bullet now. The drone followed her.

Stile, relieved, lost consciousness.

CHAPTER 12

Dance

Round Ten was getting into rarefied territory. Only twenty players remained, eighteen of whom had suffered one loss. The losers of this Round would receive a five-year tenure bonus.

Stile had another liability to go with his bad knee: the healing thigh. The bullet-amulet had lodged in his bone, holing the artery in passing. The damage, while bad, had not been as bad as it could have been, but he had depleted his vital resources and suffered near-shock. The Yellow Adept had provided a potion that multiplied his healing rate tenfold. Still, nature needed time to do the job, and he had been able to rest only ten hours before having to return for the next Game. He was not in ideal shape.

Sheen had led the drone back to Red's bunker and tossed the bullet in. That had been that. She reported, objectively, that it had been a most impressive explosion, that tore open a hidden second chamber where the Red Adept had hidden. Unfortunately Red had not been there at the time. She had vanished from the scene during the drone-chase, and Stile had not thought to get another fix on her during his brief recovery period.

As a result of all this assistance and attention by the several ladies of the frames, Stile was free of immediate threats to his welfare and was able to play the Game—but he really intended to stay out of the PHYSICAL column. Sheen was taking good care of him, but she could not help him there.

His opponent this time was a man of his own ladder: nicknamed Track, age 35, the running champion of the over-30 category, and no slouch at other track events. Stile could not have beaten him at running, jumping or swimming even when in shape, and in his present condition it

309

would have been hopeless. But Track was comparatively weak in MENTAL and had virtually no artistic awareness. So this should be an easy win for Stile—if he kept it out of PHYSICAL and CHANCE.

As luck would have it, Stile got the letters. He could not eliminate the physical column.

He considered rapidly. NAKED was absolutely out. TOOL was not good; Track was excellent at bicycle racing, tennis, billiards and other such sports. MACHINE was a little better; Track was less secure in things like motorcycle racing, while Stile was expert, and his thigh would interfere only minimally. ANIMAL—Stile was of course the champion horse racer. He could no longer flex his knees properly for best effect, but his basic skill and experience and rapport with horses remained. This was his obvious choice.

Therefore he did not take it. He went for TOOL instead, hoping to catch Track sneaking in MENTAL. 2D would have put them into animal training, and Track had an excellent touch with the circus whip.

It didn't work. It came up 1B. Tool-Assisted Physical Games.

But Stile outmaneuvered him in the subgrid, and the Game came up Bubbles. This was about as delicate as a physical game could get.

They blew soap bubbles with straws, and wafted them across a measured alley. Scoring was by volume, distance and time—to get the greatest volume of bubble across a set distance within the time limit. Stile had the fine touch here; his bubbles were only of medium size, but were durable, while Track's larger ones tended to pop before completing the distance.

Stile won the Game. It had been his gridding skill, once more, that had done it. They shook hands and parted, and the crowd of spectators applauded. This had hardly been a bruising or dramatic Game, but the stakes were high enough to make it interesting to all. With five more years of tenure to look forward to, Track was not hurting badly.

Stile managed six more hours accelerated healing in Phaze before reporting for Round Eleven. Now the total number of contestants was down to eleven, with only one remaining undefeated. The losers of this Round would receive a prize of ten years tenure. One thousand and thirteen had now been eliminated from the Tourney.

Stile's opponent was another Citizen, this time a young one—about fifteen years old. Stile was pretty sure he could prevail on most games of skill, but still did not want to risk the physical ones. This time he had the numbers, so put it into MENTAL; there he would have no disadvantage.

The Citizen, surprisingly, selected ANIMAL. So it was 2D, the one Stile had played to avoid last time. When they gridded it down to the specific, they settled on Mixed-Species Communication.

Each player had three untrained animals: a dog, a cat and a rat. Each player had all-purpose animal snack treats and an electronic goad: positive and negative inducements. The task was to get all three animals to traverse a set maze without touching any of them. The first player to succeed would be the winner.

The animals, of course, were at first more interested in pursuing or escaping each other than in doing intellectual tricks. Careful management was required. The goad was adjustable, creating pain in the systems of whatever animal it was tuned to, ranging from mild to paralyzing; the cats learned very quickly not to attempt to pounce on the rats, because of the mysterious agony that balked them. But the inducement of a positive act was more difficult than the suppression of a negative one. The snacks could not be used to lead the animals; they could only be presented as rewards for proper behavior. This was confusing to the creatures.

There was a series of "locks" in which, by the design of the layout, two animals were necessarily together briefly before passing into the next stage of the maze; that was what really put it into the MENTAL column. The reward of food could lure the animals into the first lock, and the goad could prevent them from attacking one another, since they tended to repeat what had been positive before and avoid what had been negative. But the overall strategy of placement and movement and incentive was what counted in causing the animals to respond most positively.

Again, Stile's experience and rapport with animals paid off. He completed the course while the young Citizen was still trying to get his cat to join his growling dog in the lock, instead of pouncing on the rat. Had he brought the rat to the lock first he would have been more successful; either of the other animals would have joined it willingly. Stile had brought rat, cat and dog through in that order, and by the time they finished all three were eager to continue moving forward. The Round was Stile's.

Funny, how these important later Games seemed to be getting less consequential in actual play. Stile's first Round Game, Football, had been his toughest; this last one his easiest. But the luck of the grid often produced such anomalies.

Again he returned to Phaze for a night's healing and rest. It was the Yellow Adept who tended him, in her natural old-woman form. She had the potions and experience to handle it, and she represented no temptation for him to abridge his Oracular guarantee, as might have been the case with the Lady Blue.

Why was Yellow doing this? He was in hock to her again, and was getting to like her quite well as a person. It was as if his need brought out her better traits. Maybe she liked being part of a team, doing something worthwhile, earning the appreciation of others. It was something that few Adepts experienced.

The child Brown Adept also paid him a visit to wish him well. It seemed she felt a certain retroactive guilt for the use of a golem in the prior murder of Blue, and wanted to make an amend. Things were looking up.

But until he eliminated the Red Adept, nothing was settled. She must have been busy setting up new traps during the period of his convalescence. Then Sheen reported that Red had shown up in the Tourney. She too had made it to the rarefied Rounds, with a single loss. If both Red and Stile continued winning, they would eventually come up against each other there.

It happened in Round Twelve. This was hardly coincidence, at this point. Only six contestants remained, one of them undefeated. The bonus to the loser this time was twenty years tenure—a full extra term.

Stile's thigh was now almost healed, and he had the incentive of his oath of vengeance. He was ready for Red.

This was one situation she could neither escape nor cheat. By beating her here he would not only deny her Citizenship, he would wash 'her out of the Tourney—and since her murders of Hulk and Bluette had now come to Citizen attention, thanks to the investigation of Bluette's Employer, she would be denied the bonus tenure. She would be exiled.

Stile pondered the meaning of this. He had wanted to kill her—yet his oath was merely to "make an end" of her. The Oracle had not predicted killing either; it had said Blue would destroy Red. Did exile constitute destruction? Perhaps. The Citizens had fairly sophisticated mechanisms to ensure that no exiled person ever returned to Proton; no worry about that aspect. At any rate, the more Stile contemplated the prospect of coldly killing another human being, the less he liked it. He simply was not a murderer. So if this was the meaning of oath and Oracle, he would accept it with a certain relief.

Red's position was different. She needed to kill Stile. Because if he washed out of the Tourney at this point, he would have twenty years as a tenure serf to plot her destruction, assuming she made it through to Citizenship. He would have his power base on Phaze, where he would be safe from her mischief, and could locate her and make forays at any time. The powers of Citizenship were great, but eventually he would get her, and they both knew it. So she needed more than victory in the Tourney.

There were ways to kill in the Games. The competitions were designed to be as safe as possible, but a person could have heart-failure during extraordinary physical exertion, or an anesthetic dart in pistol-dueling could be accidentally contaminated with a legal but lethal drug, or equipment could fail at a critical moment. She would surely try to arrange something like that, though it was prohibitively difficult under the experienced eye of the Game Computer. Stile, in turn, would try to prevent any such accident.

There was little delay at this stage, since the Game facilities now had to support only three Games. The audience for each would be huge. Stile was spared the unpleasantness of having to converse with his enemy. They proceeded immediately to the grid.

Again he got the letters. Every time he really wanted the numbers, it seemed, the luck of the draw denied them.

Stile did not try to play for Red's weaknesses; he was not sure what they were, in Game terms. He played for his own strength: TOOL. He liked animals and worked well with them, but he wanted no more android-animal football games or dog-cat-rat games.

It came up 4A. She had gone for ART.

4A? He had selected B1

But his entry was clear; he had miskeyed. Of all the times to do that! This carelessness could cost him the match!

No time for recrimination. The Naked Arts related to Singing, Dancing, Pantomime, Story Telling, Poetry, Humor and the like: presentations before an audience. Stile was good enough at these things; presumably Red was too. She had probably been gridding for Sculpture in 4B; had Stile played correctly, that might have come to pass. With her life's work in fashioning amulets, she was thoroughly experienced and skilled at that sort of thing. Of course he would not have let her have it; he would have thrown it into Music. Against Clef he had been in trouble; against Red he was pretty sure he would have a decisive advantage in Music. But of course she would not have let him have it, either, so they would have gridded into something else, that perhaps neither of them had much experience in, such as Writing. So he might be just as well off here. He was versed in most of the Naked Arts, and expert in some. If she wanted to match him in the generation of original free verse—

But the grid turned up Dance. All right—he could dance too. Did she have some particular specialty, like the classical minuet? He did not care to risk that; better to throw it into a more creative form, where his imagination could score. Not Ballet, because his thigh injury could interfere, but perhaps something loosely related.

In the end it came to a structured free-form dramatic dance, paradoxical as that seemed. It had a script with set maneuvers, rather like a ballet, but within that frame the particular interpretations were left to the players. It was costumed; in this case it was considered that apparel was useful for effect without being a necessary tool. NAKED did not refer to the absence of clothing, since all serfs lacked that; it simply meant that a particular Game could be played without any device like a bat or computer or hunting dog. So for this nakedness, the participants were clothed, for the benefit of the audience. Stile, recently acclimatized to the conventions of Phaze, was able to take this in stride. Red of course had no difficulty at all.

All in all, he felt reasonably well off.

The Computer established the script. It had a good file of diverse story lines, and varied them enough so that there were few repeats in a given year. This did mean that some play-themes were fairly unusual, but that was all part of the challenge.

This one was based on a tale of the Arabian Nights, "The Afreet's Beauty Contest." Citizens tended to favor Arabian motifs, associating with the presumed opulence of ninth- and twentieth-century Arabian culture.

Stile had the role of Kamar Al Zaman, a bachelor prince, and Red the part of Princess Budur, Moon of Moons. Stile was not familiar with this particular story, but had a foreboding about it. These Arabian tales could get pretty fundamental. This one was obviously a romance, and the last thing he could stomach was a Game of Love with the enemy he had sworn to destroy. But there was no clean way out, now.

The Computer was the Narrator and stage director. A panel of performing-arts critics was the judge. They would take into consideration the responses of the audience, but would not be bound by it; it was known that audiences often had illiterate tastes and colossal ignorances. Stile was satisfied with this; it meant his performance would be judged on its esthetic merits rather than on his size or Red's appearance.

Maybe, too, he was foolishly buoyed by his last experience with such a panel, in connection with the harmonica duet. He knew something like that was unlikely to happen again; still . . .

They took their places on the darkened stage. The light

came on in Stile's part of the set. It was not a fancy
Arabian setting, to his surprise, but a simple two-level
pseudo-stone alcove.

"Kamar Al Zaman, an Arabian prince, has been confined to his chamber by his father the King because Kamar
refuses to marry any of the eligible girls of the kingdom or
any of the princesses of friendly neighboring kingdoms.
The King wishes to ensure the continuance of the royal
line, and harbors a nagging suspicion that his son may be
gay, so has taken stringent measures to force the issue and
to conceal the situation from the public. Prince Kamar
submits to this humiliation with genteel grace. He now
does the Dance of the Unbowed Head, symbolizing his
determination to pursue his own life without regard for the
dictates of royal fashion."

Suddenly Stile liked this tale better. He could dance this
theme! He believed in individual freedom and initiative—
especially since he had discovered what life was like in
Phaze. Even when an infallible Oracle set a particular fate,
man's ingenuity could shape it into something profitable.
Stile was a prince, in the terms of Phaze—and a peasant,
in the terms of Proton. His participation in the Tourney,
he realized now, was motivated by his desire to change his
status. To become a prince.

Stile danced. His archaic costume was designed for
dancing rather than for any historical accuracy. He wore
white tights that left his legs completely free, and a flowing
blue cape that flung out when he whirled. It was fun; he
developed his presentation as he did it, showing his defiance of the system, his fierce will-to-succeed. It was Stile
against the frame of Proton, Stile against adversity. He
spun and leaped and spread his arms in the universal gestures of defiance, and finally wound down to passivity; for
he was after all Kamar, imprisoned in the tower like a
common serf for daring to choose his own mode of living
and loving. No one could appreciate his defiance, here in
the dark tower, and this made it empty.

Except for the audience. It was large, and it applauded
vigorously when Stile finished. Maybe this was a rote-
response, clapping because that was what was supposed to
be done; but Stile hoped that he had in fact conveyed a

mood that all of them could understand. Serf against Citizen . . .

The experts on the panel made notes. It had been an excellent dance, thematically and technically, a good start on this role. Maybe this would work out.

Now Stile's portion of the stage darkened. Red's illuminated. Hers was a very feminine set, with draperies and mirrors and a plush feather bed made up on the elevated rear section of the stage, and her costume fit right in. "Meanwhile, the Princess Budur, Moon of Moons, renowned for her beauty and accomplishments in a kingdom on the far side of the civilized world, has experienced similar difficulties. She has refused all suitors, finding none she likes, because she prefers to marry for love rather than prestige or convenience. Her father is furious, and has confined her to quarters until she becomes more amenable to reason. Now, alone, she performs the Dance of Blighted Hope, symbolizing her unrequited longing for true romance."

Red danced. She wore a lovely red outfit with a full-circle skirt and gems that gleamed in the lights, huge rubies, making her motions sparkle. She was, Stile realized reluctantly, a beautiful woman, well-formed and healthy. Alone, her size was not apparent; she looked normal, as did Stile. Her life of malice had left her physically untouched.

She was an excellent dancer, too. Her symbolism came through exquisitely. She spun precisely, so that her skirt flared out and lifted to show perfectly proportioned legs. She made eloquent gestures of love-longing that could not be misinterpreted; her face became radiant with hope and pitiful with disappointment. Was she a consummate actress, or did she really feel these emotions? Stile felt uncomfortable doubt; it was awkward to maintain his hate at full intensity in the face of this exquisite presentation.

At last she collapsed in complete abandoned grief, ending the dance. Never had Hope appeared more Blighted, or a fate less deserved.

The audience burst into applause again. Stile realized with misgiving that Red had outdanced him. She had conveyed more emotion in a more effective manner than he

had. He was going to have to work for this Round! To
further enhance his discomfort, he realized now that if Red
made it to Citizenship, she would have much greater resources than she had had before, and would not need to
remain on the defensive; she could probably hire execution
squads to dispatch him at her convenience. She did not
have to kill him here; it was sufficient merely to defeat
him. His situation was looking worse as hers looked better.

"Both Kamar and Budur strip and sleep, for it is night,"
the Narrator continued. Individual spotlights touched each
person with gray light to suggest night, leaving the rest of
the stage dark. Stile removed his costume and folded each
piece carefully, as a prince would, then stretched out on
the elevated back section of the stage, feigning sleep. There
was surely more to this Dance than this! There had to be,
for he was behind and needed to catch up.

"Now the tower in which Prince Kamar is confined hap-
pens to be haunted by a female afreet, a supernatural being
of the tribes of the jinn," the Computer Narrator continued. Stile smiled inwardly; how little the Computer knew
that in Phaze, the alternate aspect of this planet, there
really were tribes of jinn! This story could be literal, there.
In fact it could be literal *here*, since Phaze overlapped
Proton. Maybe the afreets were playing this out in this
same spot at this moment. If they had any way to perceive
what was happening here, without the use of the curtain. . . .

"This afreetah has been away for the day, going about
her business of stirring up assorted mischief in human
affairs, but at night she returns. She passes through the
stone wall and enters the tower chamber, as she is invisible
and immaterial to whatever extent she chooses to be. Lo,
she discovers the sleeping Prince Kamar on her bed and is
amazed by the handsomeness of this mortal creature. She
admires him for some time, deeply regretting that he is not
her kind. Then she flies out to tell her friends of this
wonder. She encounters a male afreet, who informs her
that he has found a mortal who is prettier than hers.
Affronted, she challenges him to a beauty contest. They
will place the two mortals beside each other and compare
them directly."

There was a pause while the lights dimmed. Stile had to

get up and cross the stage and lie down beside Red on her feather bed; the afreets had carried him there, the sleeping prince. His foreboding increased again; he did not like this close a contact with her. But he had to follow the script; any minor deviation would penalize him, and a major deviation could disqualify him. He remained beside Red in play-sleep, wishing he could simply shove her off the planet. His healing bullet-wound began to bother him—psychological, but indicative.

"The two afreets study the unconscious mortals," the Narrator said. "Each person is a virtually perfect specimen, and the afreets are unable to determine a winner. Finally they hit upon a scheme—let the mortals themselves decide which one is the prettiest. The afreets will wake each in turn and watch their reactions; the one who is least affected will win, since that means the other must be less beautiful."

Like the harmonica contest, Stile thought; the one who changed least, won. He was becoming curious to know the outcome of this tale.

The light brightened so that the audience could see the scene clearly: prince and princess sleeping naked beside each other. This would have had no significance in ordinary Proton life, but after the elaborate costumes of the play the suggestion of intimacy was strong.

There was a moment of surprised silence. Then someone snickered. The mirth quickly spread across the hall.

Stile knew what it was. He had experienced this sort of thing all his life. The disparity in the size of the actors had become apparent, now that they were together. The Computer did not care, and the panel of experts could handle it, but the audience was less sophisticated. Which was why the audience had no vote in the determination of a winner, here.

"The Pygmy and the Amazon!" someone said, and the laughter swelled.

Abruptly a stasis field dropped over them all. No one could move, on stage or in the audience, though all could hear. Prolonged, such a field could cause bodily harm and eventually death; for a short period it was merely uncomfortable, since bodily functions slowed almost to a halt. "Single warning," the Computer said emotionlessly. "Further interference from the audience or inappropriate reactions will result in expulsion of the audience."

The stasis lifted. The audience was now completely sober. There would be laughter only if the script warranted it, and no extraneous remarks. The Game Computer was a strict taskmaster; even a few Citizens had been caught in the stasis. They, however, made no protest; it was to their interest to have discipline maintained.

Yet the damage had been done. The audience might be serious, now, but the dance had become ludicrous. Stile knew that behind those sober faces a maniacal laughter raged.

He fought to control his own embarrassment and anger. He drew on a device he had used long ago to reduce stage fright. He pictured each member of the audience as a gibbering demon, with huge pointed ears and a bare purple bottom, scratching at fleas, and whipping a barbed tail about to tickle his neighbors. He projected all the ludicrous feeling onto them, away from himself. *I am a man; you are ape-things. Stare, you foolish creatures. Stew in your own drool.*

It was not entirely effective, but it helped. He was aware of Red shivering with suppressed resentment beside him; this was striking her, too. To this extent, he agreed with her.

Yet there was nothing to do except continue. Pygmy and Amazon had a deadly serious Game to win. The panel of judges had not laughed, and that was the critical element of this scene. The play had to go on.

"Now the afreetah changes into a bug and bites Kamar on the leg," the Computer said. "He wakes—"

Stile slapped his leg as if stung, and sat up. This was a place where the audience might legitimately have chuckled, but there was not a single gibber.

"And spies the Princess Budur, Moon of Moons, lying next to him. Kamar is amazed; he does not realize that he is in a far-distant place, so intent is he on this marvel. He inspects her, touches her to make certain she is real and not a dream-figment, and tries to wake her. But she is under a spell of sleep and can not be roused."

Stile went through the motions, in no way betraying his

preference for throttling her. She was his enemy; why couldn't she be the size of Neysa in girl-form, so that he did not look ridiculous in her company? Insult added to injury. Yet at the same time he had to concede again, inwardly, that she was a remarkable figure of a woman, one that in other circumstances—but no, he hated her, and could not forget that for an instant.

Then he saw the healing scar on her head, beneath her red hair, where his rock had gashed her. He did not know how to feel about that.

"It occurs to Kamar that this may be one of the ladies his father has in mind for him to marry, and that this is a device of his father's to persuade him. Kamar does not like such strategy, but Budur is so beautiful that he is instantly won over. He resolves to tell his father in the morning that he is now amenable to the union. Meanwhile, he will not soil his future wife by unfair attentions during her repose. Kamar lies down and sleeps again."

Almost, a peep escaped from a member of the audience. Would a virile young man actually do this, in the presence of a lovely and sleeping young woman? Well, perhaps one who had refrained from marrying any eligible girl because of the principle of pursuing his own life, and who would actually suffer confinement rather than permit his will to be abridged. It was, at least, an ideal for the audience to ponder. Stile felt, with a certain smugness, that he had faced just such a test in his contact with the Lady Blue, and had reacted similarly.

Stile lay down, relieved. It could have been much worse! The script could have required an act of love. That sort of thing was part of the Game—but it might have washed Stile out of the Tourney at this point. How could he do any such thing with his enemy, regardless of the script?

"The afreet now changes into a bug and bites the Princess Budur in a tender spot," the Computer continued. Stile almost thought it had been about to say that the Moon of Moons was bitten on a moon; he had to suppress a role-destroying mirth. In tight situations, even deadly serious ones, minor things could seem impossibly funny. "She wakes, while Kamar remains under the enchantment of sleep."

Red went through the sequence. "She is amazed to find this strange man in her bed. At first horrified, she soon realizes that his presence has occasioned her no harm. She is impressed; he is the handsomest man she has ever seen." Again, there was not even the hint of a snicker from the audience. "She concludes that her father has placed him here, to show her what she has been missing. She is moved; she calls herself a fool for her prior intransigence. Had she but known! *This* is the kind of man she could love! She attempts to rouse him, but he sleeps on." Stile thought Red might shake him violently, trying to do him surreptitious harm, but she was careful, adhering to the script. She knew she was ahead on scoring, and had merely to maintain that lead.

"Princess Budur, overcome by passion for the Prince, embraces him and kisses him, pleading for him to awaken." Even this directive Red got through, with Stile lying like a dead man. But as she brushed his left ear with her lips, she whispered: "I will torture thee for this indignity, foul man! Never has thy ilk touched me before in other than combat."

She hated men! Not just him, but all men! She was a true Amazon! That remark from the audience must have stung her fully as much as it stung him. For her, an act of love with a man was impossible; she considered the entire opposite sex to be "ilk."

Yet she was a consummate actress, as so many women seemed to be. No one in panel or audience had any hint of her true feeling. She had a will of iron; she would do whatever it took to win this Round. Stile could not even play upon her anger, for the script was too specific. He was officially sound asleep.

"Finally she gives up. She clasps him tightly and falls asleep." Red put her left arm across his chest, snuggled close, set her lips against his left ear again, and slowly, methodically bit into it.

Stile could not jump or scream, for that would have cost him more points. Yet her position was such that her foul was not evident to the panel. She seemed to be kissing his ear—a natural enough action for the role. Stile had to hold himself frozen while the pain burgeoned.

This was, indeed, going to be a rough Game.

"This display of emotion wins the wager for the afreetah, for Budur showed more passion for Kamar than he did for her. Satisfied, the afreets carry the Prince back to his own chamber and depart. They have no further interest in this matter."

The light dimmed, and Stile returned to his side of the stage. His ear felt huge and throbbing, but he could not touch it; Kamar had no reason to. He had to admit Red had outplayed him again; she had fouled him and gotten away with it.

This narrative was following the classic formula—boy meets girl, boy loses girl. Surely boy would regain girl before it was done. Stile hoped he would have opportunity to gain the lead. It depended on the kind of dancing and acting required. There wouldn't be more close contact with Red for a while, at least.

"When the Prince and Princess wake in the morning, they are chagrined to find themselves alone. Each has fallen in love with the other, but neither knows the identity of the nocturnal visitor. They perform the Dance of Separation, symbolizing the pain and confusion of this mysterious loss."

Stile and Red danced together, apart; she on her part of the stage, he on his. This was challenging; they had to coordinate their motions, esthetically, also keeping time to the music the Computer provided. As with the harmonica duet, this was a test of integration as well as of individual skill. Stile, good at this sort of thing, expected to score well. But he had another nasty surprise.

Red seized the lead, going into a series of deep knee bends. Stile was unable to match this, as she well knew. If he flexed his knees that far, he would not be able to maintain his balance, and the pain would be prohibitive. She might take a minor penalty for pushing the lead, but he was suffering a major penalty for not matching her style. Red was still gaining points.

So it continued. Red was an excellent dancer, and she had good knees, and she played her advantage unscrupulously well. She really knew how to make a man look awkward. She made quick shifts of figure that threw him out of phase, but it looked as though he was the one who had miskeyed, not her. She initiated a sequence, then terminated it just as he was emulating it, making him look stupid again. And this was all good tactic, in the Game; when the judges saw what she was doing, they would still be giving her points for her expertise in competition. Stile's own considerable skill was largely eroded by his incapacity. This Game was becoming hopeless.

They wended their way through the long quest as Kamar searched the civilized world for his love and she longed to receive news of him. Stile continued to lose headway. Members of the audience were quietly vacating their places, satisfied they knew the outcome. The Oracle, he realized, had not promised him victory; he had merely juggled the Lady Blue's Oracular message to ensure his survival after this encounter. He actually had no guarantee of victory. His oath was only an oath—vital to him, but no guarantee of success.

Yet there had seemed to be developing purpose in his life, however it had been shaped. The way his need to meet the Herd Stallion had brought him and the Lady Blue to the Little Folk, and he had acquired the Platinum Flute, lost to the Stallion anyway, and delivered the Flute to Clef. Maybe all coincidence, but if Clef was indeed the Foreordained, then it all had meaning. Stile had been a vital part of that chain—

A part that had ended with the relaying of the Flute. Stile could have become surplus thereafter, no longer needed in the chain. An actor whose part had terminated. So Purpose was no answer. He was on his own. And in trouble. What use to survive this Dance, if his loss of the Game meant only that Red would have him assassinated shortly after he sired a son for the Lady Blue?

At last the dance led Prince Kamar to Princess Budur. He had traversed the civilized world, taking many months, to locate her. It was to be an ecstatic reunion, as the lovers joined after a quest that had often seemed hopeless. Stile abhorred the notion, but forced himself to carry on. Whatever he might wish, this was evidently not to be the occasion for his destruction of Red.

There were of course various definitions of destruction. Perhaps Red was destined to win the Tourney, become a Citizen, and destroy herself in riotous living. Yet that would not be Stile's agency. Why would the Oracle warn her that Blue would destroy Red, if Blue was merely one hurdle among many to be overcome? The whole thing now suggested a misinterpretation of the Oracle's meaning. Where did that leave him?

With his oath of vengeance. It didn't matter what the Oracle predicted. Stile would make an end of Red, one way or another, and he would not return to love the Lady Blue until he did. If he could not accomplish this through the Game, it would have to be some other way. But it would be. Because he had sworn. Right now he would play this Round out as well as he could, taking his loss with the same dignity he had taken his wins.

Yet as the dance drew to its close, Stile's case looked hopeless. He was so far behind on points that only a figurative knockout punch could salvage a win—and this was no boxing match. How much he would have preferred that boxing match! Red was proceeding smoothly to a victory that wasn't even close.

Then Stile had an idea. Perhaps he could after all score a knockout! It would require discipline and courage that strained the limits of his ability, and there was no guarantee he could make it work. But from what he had learned of Red's nature, it was a chance. Stile nerved himself for it.

"And now at last the lovers are rejoined," the Narrator said. "They rush together. Kamar takes Budur in his arms—"

Stile had the wit to stand on the raised back portion of the stage, so that his height almost matched Red's. Now he concentrated, throwing himself into a half-trance. *Pretend she is the Lady Blue,* he told himself. *The woman you love.*

"Their expression of joy and love knows no bounds," the Narrator continued. This was the finale.

The Lady Blue. And, almost, he made himself believe. As they went into the concluding Dance of Rapture, Stile threw himself into the full feeling of it, conveying to audi-

ence, panel and Red herself the power of his passion. He
was ready to act out the full spirit of this reunion, to love
her in the dance exactly as Prince Kamar loved Princess
Budur. Internal rebellion seethed in him, but he suppressed
it savagely. He could destroy his enemy only by loving
her.

And she—had to go along with it. How could a Princess, Moon of Moons, reunited with her lost love after
extended and agonized separation, do other than accede to
his natural desire? Stile had seized the lead—and what a
lead it was!

Now the audience caught on. "Do it!" someone whispered audibly, and the Computer did not react. Because
this was a legitimate conclusion of this script. What was a
dance, except the rationalization and dramatization of
human passion?

Red was not slow to catch on. Seeing herself trapped in
this interpretation, anathema to her, she broke. Instead of
kissing him, she bit him. Blood flowed from his lip. Instead
of accepting his embrace, she struck him with fist and
elbow.

The members of the judging panel began to react. Some
violence was permissible in lovemaking; was this merely an
interpretation?

"Beloved!" Stile whispered to her.

Red's face transformed to the semblance of a demon.
She caught Stile's head in her hands and shoved it hard
against the wall. Stile's consciousness exploded in sparkles,
but he offered no resistance. Furious, she threw him to the
floor. He feared a back injury, but he lay there. She started
throttling him, so angry that tears were flowing from her
eyes. "I'll kill thee! I'll kill thee!" she raged. "Thou dost
dare love *me*! Death be the penalty!"

She was a creature of hate, and deserved her fate. Yet
even as her maniacal fury lashed him, Stile felt regret,
knowing that she, like himself, was a victim of circumstance, of fate. Some unknown party had set them both up
for this cruel denouement.

As Stile sank into unconsciousness, he felt the stasis field
take hold, and knew that he had won. His difficult, desper-

ate ploy had been effective against the man-hater. Even for victory in the Tourney, even for Citizenship, even for life itself, she could not bring herself to submit to this ultimate humiliation—to be loved, even in pretense, by a man. Red had disqualified herself.

About the Author

It was not necessary, in England in 1934, to name a baby instantly; there was a grace period of a number of days. As the deadline loomed, the poor woman simply gave all the names she could think of: Piers Anthony Dillingham Jacob. The child moved to America, where it took three years and five schools to graduate him from first grade, because he couldn't learn to read. It was thus fated that he become a proofreader, an English teacher, or a writer. He tried them all, along with a dozen other employments —and liked only the least successful one. So he lopped off half his name, sent his wife out to earn their living, and concentrated on writing. That was the key to success; publishers would print material by an author whose name was short enough.

He sold his first story in 1962 and had his first novel, *Chthon*, published in 1967. His first fantasy in *The Magic of Xanth* Trilogy, *A Spell for Chameleon*, won the August Derleth Fantasy Award as the best novel in 1977. He has written approximately forty novels in the genres of science -fiction, fantasy and martial arts.

He was married in 1956, right after graduating from college, to Carol Ann Marble. Their daughter Penny was born eleven years later, and their final daughter Cheryl in 1970. That was the beginning of a whole new existence, because little girls like animals. In 1978 they bought nice horses, and that experience, coupled with knee injuries in judo class, became *Split Infinity*. Piers Anthony is not the protagonist—he says he lacks the style—but Penny's horse Blue *is* the mundane model for the unicorn Neysa.